Sheikh's
DESERT DESIRE

Sheikh's
COLLECTION

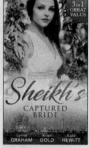

May 2017

June 2017

July 2017

August 2017

September 2017

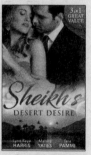

October 2017

Sheikh's
DESERT DESIRE

Lynn Raye
HARRIS

Maisey
YATES

Tara
PAMMI

& MILLS
BOON

Published in Great Britain 2017
By Mills & Boon, an imprint of HarperCollins*Publishers*
1 London Bridge Street, London, SE1 9GF

SHEIKH'S DESERT DESIRE © 2017 Harlequin Books S.A.

Carrying the Sheikh's Heir © 2014 Lynn Raye Harris
Forged in the Desert Heat © 2014 Maisey Yates
The True King of Dahaar © 2014 Tara Pammi

ISBN: 978-0-263-93114-3

09-1017

CARRYING THE
SHEIKH'S HEIR

LYNN RAYE HARRIS

*To my brainstorming partners Jean Hovey and
Stephanie Jones, who write together as Alicia
Hunter Pace. They calmly listen to my ideas,
toss out helpful suggestions, and don't get
offended when I don't use a single one. And
when I tell them there might be jackals, they
reply that you can never have too many jackals.
Thanks for having my back, ladies.*

USA TODAY bestselling author **Lynn Raye Harris**
burst onto the scene when she won a writing contest
held by Mills & Boon. The prize was an editor for a
year – but only six months later, Lynn sold her first
novel. A former finalist for the Romance Writers
of America's Golden Heart Award, Lynn lives in
Alabama with her handsome husband and two crazy
cats. Her stories have been called "exceptional and
emotional," "intense," and "sizzling." You can visit
her at www.lynnrayeharris.com

CHAPTER ONE

"A MISTAKE? HOW is this possible?"

King Rashid bin Zaid al-Hassan glared daggers at the stuttering secretary who stood in front of him. The man swallowed visibly.

"The clinic says they have made a mistake, Your Majesty. A woman…" Mostafa looked down at the note in his hand. "A woman in America was supposed to receive her brother-in-law's sperm. She received yours instead."

Rashid's blood ran hot and then cold. He felt… violated. Rage coursed through him like a flame from a blast furnace, melting the ice around his heart for only a moment before it hardened again. He knew from experience that nothing could thaw that ice for long. In five years, nothing had penetrated the darkness surrounding him.

His hands clenched into fists on his desk. This was too much. Too outrageous.

How dare they? How dare anyone take that choice away from him? He wasn't ready for a child in his life. He didn't know if he would ever be ready, though eventually he had to provide Kyr with an heir. It was his duty, but he wasn't prepared to do it quite yet.

The prospect of marrying and producing children

brought up too many memories, too much pain. He preferred the ice to the sharpness of loss and despair that would envelop him if he let the ice thaw.

He'd obeyed the law that required him to deposit sperm in two banks for the preservation of his line, but he'd never dreamed it could go so horribly wrong. A random woman had been impregnated with his sperm. He could even now be an expectant father, his seed growing into a tiny life that could break him anew.

An icy wash of terror crested inside him, left him reeling in its wake. He would be physically ill in another moment.

Rashid pushed himself up from his chair and turned away so Mostafa wouldn't see the utter desolation that he knew was on his face. This was not an auspicious beginning to his reign as Kyr's king.

Hell, as if this was the only thing that had gone wrong. His stomach churned with fresh fury.

Since his father died two months ago and his brother abdicated before he'd ever been crowned, it was now Rashid's duty to rule this nation. But nothing was the way it was supposed to be. As the eldest, he should have been the crown prince, but he'd been the despised son, a pawn in his father's game of cat and mouse. In Kyr, the king could name his successor from amongst his sons. There was no law that said it had to be the eldest, though tradition usually dictated that it was.

But not for King Zaid al-Hassan. He'd been a cruel and manipulative man, the kind who ruled his sons—and his wives—with fear and harsh punishments. He'd dangled the possibility of the throne over his sons' heads for far too long. Kadir had never wanted to rule, but it hadn't mattered to their father. It was simply a way to control his eldest son. But Rashid had refused to play, instead leaving Kyr when he was twenty-five and vowing never to come back again.

He had come back, however. And now he wore a crown he'd never expected to have. His father, the old snake, was probably spinning in his grave right this minute. King Zaid had not wanted Rashid to rule. He had only wanted to hold out the hope of it before snatching the crown away in a final act of spite. That he'd died without naming his successor didn't fill Rashid with the kind of peace that Kadir felt. Kadir wanted to believe their father had desired a reconciliation, and Rashid would not take that away from him.

But Rashid knew better. He'd had a lifetime of his father's scorn and disapproval and he just simply knew better.

Yet here he was. Rashid's gaze scanned the desert landscape, rolling over the sandstone hills in the distance, the red sand dunes, the palms and fountains that lined the ornate gardens of the palace. The sun was high and most people were inside at this hour. The horizon shimmered with heat. A primitive satisfaction rolled through him at the sight of all he loved.

He'd missed Kyr. He'd missed her perfumed night breezes, her blazing heat and her hardy people. He'd missed the call to prayer ringing from the mosque in the dawn hour, and he'd missed riding across the desert on his Arabian stallion, a hawk on his arm, hunting the small animals that were the hawk's chosen prey.

Until two months ago, he'd not set foot in Kyr in ten years. He'd thought he never would again, but then his father had called with news of his illness and demanded

Rashid's presence. Even then, Rashid had resisted. For Kadir's sake, he had finally relented.

And now he was a king when he'd given up on the idea years ago. Kadir was gone again, married to his former personal assistant and giddy with love. For Kadir, the world was a bright, happy place filled with possibilities.

Desolation swept through Rashid. It was an old and familiar companion, and his hands clenched into helpless fists. He'd been in love once and he'd been happy. But happiness was ephemeral and love didn't last. Love meant loss, and loss meant pain that never healed.

He'd been powerless to save Daria and the baby. So powerless. Who knew such a thing was possible in this day and age? A woman dying in childbirth seemed impossible, and yet it was not. It was, in fact, ridiculously easy. Rashid knew it far too well.

He stood there awhile longer, facing the windswept dunes in the distance, gathering his thoughts before he turned back to his secretary. His voice, when he spoke, was dangerously measured. He would *not* let this thing rule him.

"We chose this facility in Atlanta as the repository of the second sample for a reason. You will call them and demand to know this woman's name and where she lives. Or they will suffer the very public consequences of their mistake."

Mostafa bowed his head. "Yes, Your Majesty." He sank to his knees then and touched his forehead to the ornate carpet that graced the floor in front of Rashid's desk. "It is my fault, Your Majesty. I chose the facility. I will resign my position and leave the capital in disgrace."

Rashid gritted his teeth. Sometimes he forgot how

rigidly prideful Kyrians could be. He'd spent so many years away. But if he'd stayed, he would be a different man. A less damaged man. Or not. His mother and father had been willing to use any weapon in their protracted war against each other, and he had been the favorite. The damage had been done years before he'd ever left Kyr.

"You will do no such thing," he snapped. "I have no time to wait while you train a new secretary. The fault lies elsewhere."

Rashid stalked back to his desk and sat down again. He had many things to do and a new problem to deal with. If this American woman had truly been impregnated with his sperm, then she could very well be carrying the heir to the throne of Kyr.

His fingers tightened on the pen he'd picked up again. If he thought of the child that way, as his heir, and of the woman as a functionary performing a duty—or a vessel carrying a cargo—then he could get through these next few days. Beyond that, he did not know.

An image of Daria's pale face swam in his head, twisting the knife deep in his soul. He was not ready to do this again, to watch a woman grow big with his child and know that it could all go wrong in an instant.

And yet he had no choice. If the woman was pregnant, she was his.

"Find this woman by the end of the hour," he ordered. "Or you may yet find yourself tending camels in the Kyrian Waste."

Mostafa's color drained as he backed away. "Yes, Your Majesty."

There was a snapping sound at precisely the moment the door closed behind the secretary. Pain bloomed in Rashid's palm. He looked down to find a pen in his hand.

Or, rather, half a pen. The other half lay on the desk, dark ink spilling into a pattern on the wood like a psychologist's test blot.

A cut in his skin dripped red blood onto the black ink. He watched it drip for a long moment before there was a knock on his door and a servant entered with afternoon tea. Rashid stood and went into the nearby restroom in order to wash away the blood and tape up the cut. When he returned to his desk, the blood and ink had been wiped away. Cleaned up as if it had never happened.

He flexed his hand and felt the sting of the cut against his palm. You could sweep up messes, patch up wounds and try to forget they ever happened.

But Rashid knew the truth. The cut would heal, but there were things that never went away, no matter how deeply you buried them.

"Please stop crying, Annie." Sheridan sat at her desk with her phone to her ear and her heart in her throat. Her sister was sobbing on the other end of the line at the news from the clinic. Sheridan was still too stunned to process it. "We'll get through this. Somehow, we'll get through. I *am* having a baby for you. I promise it will happen."

Annie sobbed and wailed for twenty minutes while Sheridan tried to soothe her. Annie, the oldest by a year, was so fragile, and Sheridan felt her pain keenly. Sheridan had always been the strong one. She was still the strong one. Still the one looking out for her sister and wishing that she could give Annie some of her strength.

She felt so guilty every time Annie fell apart. It wasn't her fault, and yet she couldn't help but feel responsible. There'd only been enough money in their family for one daughter to go to college, and Sheridan had better grades. Annie had been shy and reclusive while Sheridan was outgoing. The choice had been evident to all of them, but it was yet another thing Sheridan felt guilty over. Maybe if their parents had tried harder to encourage Annie, to support her decisions, she would be stronger than she was. Instead, she let everyone else make her choices.

The one thing she wanted in this life was the one thing she couldn't have. But Sheridan could give it to her. And she was determined to do just that, in spite of this latest wrinkle in the plan.

Eventually, Annie's husband came home and took the phone away. Sheridan talked to Chris for a few minutes and then the line went dead.

She leaned back in her chair and blinked. Her eyes were gritty and swollen from the crying she'd been doing along with her sister. She snatched up a tissue from the holder on her desk and dabbed at her eyes.

How had this all gone wrong? It was supposed to be so easy. Annie couldn't carry a baby to term, but Sheridan could. So she'd offered to have a baby for her sister, knowing that it would make Annie happy and fulfill her deepest desire. It would have also made their parents happy, if they were still alive, to know they'd have a grandchild on the way. They'd had Annie and Sheridan late in life, and they'd desperately wanted grandchildren. But Annie hadn't been able to provide them, and Sheridan hadn't been ready.

Now Sheridan wished she'd had this baby earlier so her parents could have held their grandchild before they died. Though the child wouldn't be Annie's biologically, it would still share her DNA. The Sloane DNA.

Sheridan had gone in for the insemination a week

ago. They still didn't know whether it had worked or not, but now that she knew it wasn't Chris's sperm, she fervently hoped it hadn't.

She'd been given sperm from a different donor. A foreigner. The sperm bank would give them no other information beyond the physical facts. An Arab male, six-two, black hair, dark eyes, healthy.

Sheridan put her hand on her belly and drew in a deep breath. They couldn't test for another week yet. Another week of Annie crying her eyes out. Another week until Sheridan knew if she was having an anonymous man's baby or if they would try again with Chris's sperm.

But what if she was pregnant this time? Then what?

There was a knock on her door, and her partner popped her head in. Sheridan swiped her eyes again and smiled as Kelly came inside the small office at the back of the space they rented for their business.

"Hey, you okay?"

Sheridan sniffed. "Not exactly." She waved a hand. "I will be, but it's just a lot to process."

Kelly came over and took her hand, squeezed it before she sat in a chair nearby and leaned forward to look Sheridan in the eye. "Want to talk about it?"

Sheridan thought she didn't, but then she spilled the news almost as if she couldn't quite help herself. And it felt good to tell someone else. Someone who wouldn't sob and fall apart and need more reassurance than Sheridan knew how to give. If her mother was still alive, she'd know what to say to Annie. But Sheridan so often didn't.

Kelly didn't interrupt, but her eyes grew bigger as the story unfolded. Then she sat back in the chair with her jaw hanging open.

"Wow. So you might be pregnant with another man's baby. Poor Annie! She must be devastated."

Sheridan's heart throbbed. "She is. She'd pinned all her hopes on me having a baby for her and Chris. After so many disappointments, so many treatments and failed attempts of her own, she's fragile right now...." Sheridan sucked in a breath. "This was just a bad time for it to happen."

"I'm so sorry, sweetie. But maybe it won't take, and then you can try again."

"That's what I'm hoping." The doctor had said that sometimes they had to repeat the process two or three times before it was successful. And while it seemed wrong on some level to hope for failure this time, it would also be the best outcome. Sheridan stood and straightened her skirt. "Well, don't we have a party to cater? Mrs. Lands will be expecting her crab puffs and roast beef in a couple of hours."

"It's under control, Sheri. Why don't you just go home and rest? You look like hell, you know."

Sheridan laughed. "Gee, thanks." But then she shook her head. "I'll freshen up, but I'd really like to work. It'll keep my mind occupied."

Kelly looked doubtful. "All right. But if you find yourself crying in the soup, you have to go."

The party was a success. The guests loved the food, the waitstaff did a superb job and once everything was under control, Sheridan went back to the office to work on the menus for the next party they were catering in a few days' time. Kelly stayed behind to make sure there were no last-minute issues, but Sheridan knew her partner would come back to the office after it was over.

They were a great team. Had been since the first moment they'd met in school. Kelly was the cooking talent, and Sheridan was the architect behind the business. Literally the architect, Sheridan thought with a wry smile. She'd gone to the Savannah College of Art and Design for a degree in historical preservation architecture, but it was her talent at organizing parties that helped make Dixie Doin's—they'd left the *g* off *doing* on purpose, which worked well in the South but not so much when visiting Yankees called it *doynes*—into the growing business it was today.

They'd rented a building with a large commercial kitchen, hired a staff and maintained a storefront where people could come in and browse through specialty items that included table linens, dishes, gourmet oils and salts and various teas and teapots.

Sheridan settled in her office to scroll through the requirements for the next event. She had no idea how much time had passed when she heard the buzzer for the shop door. She automatically glanced up at the screen where the camera feed showed different angles of the store. Tiffany, the teenager they'd hired for the summer, was nowhere to be seen. A man stood inside the shop, looking around the room as if he had no clue what he was doing there.

Probably his wife had sent him to buy something and he had no idea what it looked like. Sheridan got up from her desk when Tiffany still hadn't appeared and went out to see if she could help him. Yes, it was annoying, and yes, she would have to speak to the girl again about not leaving the floor, but no way would she let a potential customer walk away when she could do the job herself.

The man was standing with his back to her. He was

tall, black haired and dressed in a business suit. There was something about him that seemed to dwarf the room, but then she shook that thought away. He was just a man. She'd never yet met one who impressed her all that much. Well, maybe Chris, her sister's husband. He loved Annie so much that he would do anything for her.

In Sheridan's experience, most men were far too fickle. And the better looking they were, the worse they seemed to be. On some level, she always fell for it, though. Because she was too trusting of people, and because she liked to believe the best of them. Her mother had always said she was too sunny and sweet. She was working on it, darn it, but what was the point in believing the worst of everyone you met? It was a depressing way to live—even if her last boyfriend had proved that she'd have been better off believing the worst of him from the start.

"Welcome to Dixie Doin's," she said brightly. "Can we help you today, sir?"

The man seemed to stiffen slightly. And then he turned, slowly, until Sheridan found herself holding her breath as she gazed into the most coldly handsome face she'd ever seen. There wasn't an ounce of friendliness in his dark eyes—yet, incongruously, there was an abundance of heat.

Her heart kicked up a level, pounding hard in her chest. She told herself it was the hormones from all the shots and the stress of waiting to see whether or not the fertilization had succeeded.

But it wasn't that. It wasn't even that he was breathtakingly handsome.

It was the fact he was an Arab, when she'd just been told the news of the clinic's mistake. It seemed a cruel

joke to be faced with a man like him when she didn't
know whether she was pregnant with a stranger's baby
or if she could try again for her sister.

"You are Sheridan Sloane."

He said it without even a hint of uncertainty, as if he
knew her. But she did not know him—and she didn't
like the way he stood there sizing her up as if she was
something he might step in on a sidewalk.

She was predisposed to like everyone she met. But
this man already rubbed her the wrong way.

"I am." She folded her arms beneath her breasts and
tilted her chin up. "And you are?"

She imbued those words with every last ounce of
Southern haughtiness she could manage. Sometimes
having a family who descended from the *Mayflower*
and who boasted a signer of the Declaration of Independence, as well as at least six Patriots who'd fought in the
American War of Independence was a good thing. Even
if her family had sunk into that sort of gentile poverty
that had hit generations of Southerners after Reconstruc-
tion, she had her pride and her heritage—and her mother's refined voice telling her that no one had the right
to make her feel as if she wasn't good enough for them.

He did something very odd then. He bent slightly at
the waist before touching his forehead, lips and heart.
Then he stood there so straight and tall and, well, stately,
that she got a tingle in her belly. She imagined him in
desert robes, doing that very same thing, and gooey
warmth flooded her in places that hadn't gotten warm
in a very long time.

"I am Rashid bin Zaid al-Hassan."

The door opened again and this time another man
entered. He was also in a suit, but he was wearing a

headset and she realized with a start that he must be a
bodyguard. A quick glance at the street in front of the
shop revealed a long, black limousine and another man
in a suit. And another stationed on the far side of the
street, dark sunglasses covering his eyes as he looked
up and down for any signs of trouble.

The one who'd just entered the shop stood by the door
without moving. The man before her didn't even seem
to notice his presence. Or, more likely, he was so accustomed to it that he ignored it on purpose.

"What can I help you with Mr., er, Rashid." It was
the only name she could remember from that string of
names he'd spoken.

The man at the door stiffened, but the man before
her lifted an eyebrow as if he were somehow amused.

"You have something of mine, Miss Sloane. And I
want it back."

A fine sheen of sweat broke out on her upper lip. She
hoped like hell he couldn't see it. First of all, it wasn't
ladylike. Second, she sensed that any nervousness on her
part would be an advantage for him. This was the kind
of man who pounced on weakness like a ravenous cat.

"I don't believe we've ever done business with any
Rashids, but if we accidentally packed up some of your
wife's good silver with our own, you may, of course,
have it back."

He no longer looked amused. In fact, he looked downright furious. "You do not have my silver, Miss Sloane."

He took a step toward her then, his large form as
graceful and silent as a cat. He was so close she could
smell him. He wasn't wearing heavy cologne, but he had
a scent like hot summer breezes and crisp spices. Her
fanciful imagination conjured up a desert oasis, wav-

ing palm trees, a cool spring, an Arabian stallion—and this man, dressed in desert robes like Omar Sharif or Peter O'Toole.

It was a delicious mirage. And disconcerting as hell.

Sheridan put her hand out and smoothed it over the edge of the counter as she tried to appear casual. "If you could just inform me what it is, I'll take a l-look and see if I can find it."

Damn her voice for quavering.

"I doubt you could."

His gaze dropped to her middle, lingered. It took several moments, but then her stomach began a long, slow free fall into nothingness. He couldn't possibly mean—

Oh, no. No, no, no...

But his head lifted and his eyes met hers and she knew he was not here for the family silver.

"How...?" she began. Sheridan swallowed hard. This was unbelievable. An incredible breach of confidentiality. She would sue that clinic into the next millennium. "They wouldn't tell me a thing about you. How did you get them to reveal my information?"

For one wild moment, she hoped he didn't know what she was talking about. That this was indeed some sort of misunderstanding with a tall, beautiful Arab male who meant something entirely different than she thought. He would blink, shake his head, inform her that she had accidentally packed a small family heirloom—though she'd never done such a thing before—when she'd catered his event. Then he would describe it and she would go searching for it as though her life depended on it. Anything to be rid of him and quiet this flame raging inside her as he moved even closer than before.

But she knew, deep down, that he did know what she meant. That there was no misunderstanding.

"I am a powerful man, Miss Sloane. I get what I want. Besides, imagine the scandal were it to become known that an American facility had made such a mistake." His voice dripped of self-righteousness. "Impregnating some random woman with a potential heir to the throne of Kyr? And then refusing to inform the king of the child's whereabouts?"

He shook his head while her insides turned to ice as she tried to process what he'd just said.

"It would not happen," he continued. "It did not happen. As you see."

Sheridan found herself slumping against the counter, her eyes glued to this man's face while the rest of the room began to darken and fade. "D-did you say *king?* They gave me a king's sperm?"

She pressed a shaky hand to her forehead. Her throat was dry, so dry. And her belly wanted to heave. She'd thought this couldn't possibly get worse. She'd been wrong. She swallowed the acidic bitterness and focused on the man before her.

"They did, Miss Sloane."

Oh, my God. Her brain stopped working. She'd thought he was the one whose sperm she'd gotten— he'd said she had something of his, right?—but a king would not come to her shop and tell her these things. A king would also not look so dark and dangerous.

This was someone else. An official. Perhaps even an ambassador. Or an enforcer.

It was easy to believe this man could be hired muscle. He was tall and broad, and his eyes were chips of dark ice. His voice was frosty and utterly compelling. He had come to tell her about this king and to—to…?

She couldn't imagine what he'd come here for. What he expected of her.

Sheridan worked hard to force out the words before the nausea overwhelmed her. "Please tell the king that I'm sorry. I understand how difficult this must be, but he's not the only one affected. My sister—"

She pressed her hand to her mouth as bile rose in her throat. What would she say to Annie? Her fragile sister would implode, she just knew it.

"Sorry is not enough, Miss Sloane. It is not nearly enough."

She swallowed the nausea. Her voice was thready when she spoke. "Then I don't—"

"Are you quite all right?" He was beginning to look alarmed. A much more intriguing look than the angry one he'd been giving her a moment ago.

"I'm fine." Except she didn't feel fine. She felt hot and sweaty and sick to her stomach.

"You look green."

"It's the heat. And the hormones," she added. She pushed away from the counter, her limbs shaking with the effort of holding herself upright. "I should sit down, I think."

She started to take a step, but her knees didn't want to function quite right. Mr. Rashid—or whatever his name was—lashed out and wrapped an arm around her. She found herself wedged tightly against a firm, hard, warm body. Her nerve endings started to crackle and snap with fresh heat.

It was too much, too much, and yet she couldn't get

away. Briefly, a small corner of her brain admitted that she didn't *want* to get away.

He spoke, his voice seeming farther away than before. The words were beautiful, musical, but he did not seem to be speaking them to her. And then he swept her up into his arms as if she weighed nothing and strode across her store on long legs. Her office door opened and he went and sat her down on the small couch she kept for meeting with clients.

She didn't want to let him go, but she did. Her gaze fluttered over to the entry, where saw a wide-eyed Tiffany standing there, and one of the suit-clad men, who reached in and closed the door, leaving Sheridan alone with Mr. Rashid.

He sank down on one knee beside the couch and pressed a hand to her head. She knew what he would find. She was clammy and hot and she uttered a feeble protest. The door opened again and Tiffany appeared with a glass of ice water and a folded cloth.

Sheridan took it and sipped gratefully, letting the coolness wash through her as she closed her eyes and breathed. Someone put the cool cloth on her forehead and she reached up to clutch it because it felt so nice.

She didn't know how long she sat there, holding the cloth and sipping the water, but when she finally opened her eyes and looked up, Mr. Rashid was still there, sitting across from her in one of the pretty Queen Anne chairs she'd bought from a local antiques shop. He looked ridiculous in it, far too big and masculine, but he also looked as if he didn't care.

"What happened?" His voice was not as hard as it had been. She didn't think he was capable of gentleness, and this was as close to it as he got.

"Too much stress, too many hormones, too much summer heat." She shrugged. "Take your pick, Mr. Rashid. It could be any of them."

He muttered something in Arabic and then he was looking at her, his burning gaze penetrating deep. There was frost in his voice. "Miss Sloane, I think you misunderstand something about what's going on here."

Her heart skipped. Why was he so beautiful? And why was he such a contrast? He was fire and ice in one person. Hot eyes, cold heart. It almost made her sad. But why should it? She did not know him, and what she did know so far hadn't endeared him to her. "Do I?"

"Indeed. I am not Mr. Rashid."

"Then who are you?"

He looked haughty and her stomach threatened to heave again. Because there was something familiar about that face, she realized. She'd seen it on the news a few weeks ago.

He spoke, his voice clear and firm and lightly accented. "I am King Rashid bin Zaid al-Hassan, the Great Protector of my people, the Lion of Kyr and Defender of the Throne. And you, Miss Sloane, may be carrying my heir."

CHAPTER TWO

THE WOMAN LOOKED positively frightened. Rashid did not relish making her so, but perhaps it was better if he did. Better if she agreed without question to what she must do. She could not be allowed to stay here in this...this *shop*...and work as if she did not potentially carry the next king of Kyr in her womb.

He had spent the long hours of the flight researching Sheridan Sloane. She was twenty-six, unmarried and part owner of this business that planned and catered various parties in the local area. She had one older sister, a woman named Ann Sloane Campbell, who had been trying to conceive a child for six years now.

Sheridan was supposed to carry the baby her sister could not conceive. It was an admirable enough thing to do, he supposed, but since he'd now been dragged into it, he had his own legacy to protect. If her sister was upset about it, then he could not help that.

Sheridan Sloane was a pretty woman, though not especially striking in any way. She was of average height and small boned, with golden-blond hair of indeterminate length since it was wrapped in a coil on her head. Her eyes, wide as she gazed at him, were a blue so dark they were almost violet. There were bruises under them, marring her pale skin.

She was tired and overwhelmed and no match for him. She was the sort of woman who did what she was told, in spite of her small rebellion earlier. She was a pleaser, and he was not. He would order her to come with him, and she would do it.

But, as he watched her, her body seemed to grow stiff. He could see the shutters closing, the walls rising. It was an unpleasant surprise to find she had a backbone after all. Still, he'd broken stronger people—men, usually—than her.

She shifted until she was sitting fully upright, her feet swinging onto the floor now. She faced him across a small tea table, her eyes snapping with fresh sparks. He was intrigued in spite of himself.

"*You* are the king? You could have said that right away, you know, and saved us a few steps."

He arched an eyebrow. "Yes, but what would you have done then? You nearly fainted when I informed you that you had been inseminated with a king's sperm."

Her lips pursed. "I nearly fainted because it's been a long, stressful day. Do you have any idea how my sister took the news, Mr.—oh, hell, I have no idea what to call you."

"*Your Majesty* will work."

Her face flooded with color. And there went that little chin again, thrusting into the air. Who was she trying to convince that she was a tigress? Him, or herself? Before he could ask, she imbued her voice with steel.

"I realize we find ourselves in an untenable situation, but someone inserted your sperm into my body a few days ago. I think that warrants a first-name basis, don't you? At least until this is resolved."

Rashid would have coughed if he'd been drinking anything. As it was, he could only glare at her. She shocked him. Oddly, she also amused him. It was this last that should alarm him, but in fact it was the first normal thing that had happened to him since he'd taken the throne two months ago.

He shouldn't allow any familiarity between them. But she might be carrying his child—*his child!*—and it seemed wrong to treat her as a complete stranger. He thought of Daria, of her soft brown eyes and swollen belly, and he wanted to stand up and flee this room. But of course he could not do so. He was a king now, and he had a responsibility to his nation. To his people.

And to his child.

Daria would want him to be kind to this woman. So he would try, though it went against his nature to be kind to anyone. He was not cruel; he was indifferent. He'd learned to be so over the hellish years of his childhood. If you did not care, people couldn't hurt you.

When you did… Well, he knew what happened when you cared. He had the scars on his soul to prove it. The only person he cared about these days was Kadir, and that was as much as he was capable of.

He inclined his head briefly. "You may call me Rashid." And then he added, "I suggest, however, you do not do it in front of my staff. They will not understand the informality."

She wrapped her arms around herself and rubbed her upper arms almost absently. "You can call me Sheridan, then. And I don't see why you need worry about your staff. We won't know for another week if there's a baby.

I can call you with the information, if you'd like. Then we can decide what to do if it's necessary."

He blinked at her. She truly did not understand. Or she was being stubbornly obtuse on purpose. His temper rose anew.

"You will not call me."

She frowned at his tone. "Fine. You can call me. Either way, we'll work it out."

He clenched his fingers into fists in his lap. Stubborn woman!

"There is nothing to work out. You have been artificially inseminated with my sperm. You might be carrying the next king of Kyr. There is no possible choice other than the one I offer you now."

"I honestly don't think—"

"Silence, Miss Sloane," he snapped, coming to the end of his tether. "You are not here to think. You will accompany me to the airport, where you will board the royal jet. We will be in Kyr by morning, and you will be shown every courtesy while we await the results. Should you fail to conceive my child, you will be escorted home again."

Her jaw had dropped as he talked. He tried not to focus on the pink curve of her lower lip. It glistened with moisture and he found himself wanting to lean forward and touch his tongue just there to see if she tasted as sweet and delicate as she looked.

The thought shocked him. And angered him. He did not want this woman.

She was shaking her head almost violently now. A lock of hair dropped from her twist and curved in front of her cheekbone. She impatiently tucked it behind an ear.

"I can't drop everything and go away with you! I have a business to run. And my bank account, unlike yours, I'm sure, isn't bursting with money. No way. No way in hell."

Her response stunned him. He shot to his feet then, his temper beginning to boil. He had a country to run and one crisis after another to solve these days. He had a council waiting for him, a stack of dossiers on potential brides to scour through and an upcoming meeting with kings from surrounding nations to discuss oil production, mineral rights and reciprocity agreements.

And yet he was being thwarted by one small, irritating woman who refused to give an inch of ground in this battle. A people pleaser? She didn't look as if she cared one bit about pleasing him at the moment.

Rashid gave her the look that made the palace staff tremble. "I wasn't giving you a choice, Miss Sloane."

She sucked in a breath, and he knew he had her.

But then her face reddened and her eyes flashed purple fire and Rashid stood there in shock.

"You think you have the right to make decisions for me? This is America and I don't have to go anywhere with you. Not only that, but I *won't* go. If I'm pregnant, we'll figure it out. But as of this moment, we do not know that. I can't just leave because you wish it. Nor do I intend to."

His entire body vibrated with fury. He was not accustomed to being told no. Not by his employees at Hassan Oil—a company he'd built on his own and still owned to this day, even if he'd had to turn over the day-to-day operations to a CEO—not by his staff in the palace, not by anyone anywhere in the past several years. He was an al-Hassan, with money and influence, and people did not tell him no.

And now he was a king, and they *really* did not tell him no.

But Sheridan Sloane had. She sat there on her couch, looking pale and delicate and too small to safely carry a baby for nine months, and spoke to him like he was her gardener. It infuriated him. And stunned him, too, if he was willing to admit it.

No matter how much he admired her fighting spirit, he would not be merciful. He'd left mercy behind a long time ago.

"Miss Sloane," he said, very coolly and clearly. "It would be unwise to anger me. This business you run?" He snapped his fingers. "I could destroy it in a moment. I could destroy *you* in a moment. Continue to defy me, and I shall."

Sheridan's pulse skipped and slid like it was tumbling down a hill and couldn't find purchase. He'd just threatened her. Threatened Dixie Doin's. At first she wanted to laugh him off. But then she looked at him standing there, at his tall, dark form and the dark glitter of his eyes, and knew he was not only perfectly serious, but that he was also probably capable of accomplishing it.

He was a king. *A king!*

Of an incredibly rich, oil-producing nation in the Arabian Desert. She knew where Kyr was. Hadn't they just had a crisis that was plastered all over the news? The king had been very ill and no one had known who his successor was going to be.

She'd found it fascinating that a monarch could choose his successor from among his sons, and puzzling that he had not done so by that point. They were grown after all, and he must surely know which of them was best suited to the job.

The fact he had not done so surely spoke volumes about him—or about his children. She wasn't sure which.

But the crisis had passed and Kyr had a king. This man. Rashid bin Zaid al-Hassan. Oh, yes, his name was imprinted on her memory now. She would never forget it again as long as she lived.

Still, she had not been raised to blindly follow orders and she would not start now. Even though he terrified her on some level. He was so cold and angry, and he was a king. But he was not *her* king. Hadn't her ancestors fought to divest themselves of kings?

Sheridan cleared her throat. "It's only seven more days until the test. You could stay in Savannah. Or maybe you could come back when the results are due. It seems far simpler than what you're proposing."

He did not look in the least bit appeased. "Does it, now? Because your business, which has another owner and employees to help, needs your presence far more than a nation needs her king, yes? How extraordinary, Miss Sloane."

Sheridan pushed the stray lock of hair behind her ear again. How did he manage to make her feel petty when all she wanted was to continue to live her life as normally as possible until the moment when she found out if everything was going to change or not? She didn't even want to contemplate what it would mean if she *were* carrying this man's child.

A royal baby. Madness.

She twisted the cloth that she'd earlier pressed to her

forehead. "I didn't mean to suggest any such thing. But yes, my business is important to me, and I can't leave Kelly to do everything by herself. I have menus to plan, and supplies to buy—"

"And I have a peace agreement to broker and a nation to run." He'd already dismissed her, she realized. He slipped a phone from his pocket and put it to his ear. And then he was speaking in mellifluous Arabic to someone on the other end. When he finished, cool dark eyes raked over her again. "You will come, Miss Sloane, and you will do it now. My lawyer has instructions to purchase your loan from the bank. I assure you he will accomplish this, as I am willing to offer far more than this business is worth."

Sheridan's jaw dropped even as a fine sheen of sweat broke out between her breasts. He was quite easily the most obnoxious man she'd ever met. And the most attractive.

No. The most evil man. Yes, definitely that. Evil.

Because she knew he was not bluffing. A man who had the power to obtain her information from the fertility clinic—information protected by law—as if it was freely available to anyone who asked, was not a man to make bluffs.

He had the power to buy Dixie Doin's and do whatever he wanted with it. Close the doors. Put people out of work. Ruin hers and Kelly's dream. She didn't care so much for herself right now, but Kelly? Kelly had been so kind when Sheridan told her she wanted to have a baby for Chris and Annie, even though it would impact the business for her to be pregnant.

Not to mention the impact while Sheridan went through the insemination process. You just didn't show up at the clinic one day and ask for sperm after all, and Kelly had stoically accepted it all without even a hint of disapproval or fear.

So how could she allow this overbearing, rude tyrant of a man to ruin Kelly's dream just because Sheridan wanted so very desperately to defy him?

She couldn't.

She rose on shaky feet and faced him. He was so very tall, so overwhelming, but she faced him head on with her chin up and her back straight. She pulled in a breath that shook with anger.

"Am I to be allowed to collect any clothing? Surely I need my passport."

She thought he would look satisfied or triumphant at her capitulation, but he in fact looked bored. As if he'd never doubted she would agree. She hated him in that moment, and Sheridan had never hated anyone in her life.

"You do not need a passport if you are traveling with me. But we will make a brief stop at your home. You will get what you need for the next week."

Fear skirted the edges of her anger. Was she truly proposing to board a plane to a far-off nation where she didn't speak the language and didn't understand the customs? But how could she refuse? If she did, he would ruin Dixie Doin's and put them out of business. All the money she and Kelly had invested would be gone.

But what happened in a week? Would he force her to stay in Kyr forever if she were carrying his child?

Sheridan put a hand to her mouth to press back the sudden cry welling up in her throat. In reality, she was being kidnapped by a desert king, forced into a harem for all she knew, and there was nothing she could do about it.

Not if she wanted to protect her friend and her employees. Not to mention Annie and Chris. What would this man do to them if she didn't comply? Could he get Chris fired? He could certainly buy the loan on their house—they'd mortgaged it to the hilt to pay for one failed fertility treatment after another—and then what?

Ice formed in her veins. He would throw them out of their home with no sympathy or shame. She could see it in his eyes, in the hard set to his jaw. This man was ruthless and incapable of empathy.

"How do I know I'll be safe?" Sheridan asked, her voice smaller than she would have liked.

His brows drew down swiftly as his anger flared. "Safe? Do you think me a barbarian, Miss Sloane? A terrorist? I am a king and you are my honored guest. You will have every luxury for the duration of your stay in Kyr."

She swallowed at the vehemence in his tone. "And what if I'm pregnant? What then?"

Because she had to know. For herself, for the child. She had to know what this man would do, what he would expect.

His icy gaze sharpened in a way that sent a shiver rippling through her. "You were planning to give the child away. Why would this change?"

An unexpected arrow of pain dived into her belly, hollowing out a space there. Yes, she'd been planning to give the baby up. But to her sister. Carrying a child for Annie and Chris was one thing. She would not be the baby's mother, even if she was the biological mother, but she would still be part of his or her life. An aunt who would spoil the child of her body rotten, kiss and hug him, buy him presents, shower him with love.

But to give her baby to a stranger, even if the stranger was the other half of the child's DNA?

It went against everything she felt inside.

"I won't give up my baby." Her voice was hoarse. But what choice did she have? He would destroy everyone she loved.

His eyes glittered like ice and she trembled inside. "Yes, I see," he murmured after a long moment. "I am a king, and my son will be a king. Why would you willingly relinquish a child so valuable?"

Sheridan had never wanted to harm another human being in her life, but if she could slap this one and get away with it, she would. He was evil, hateful. Her face flooded with heat and her stomach flipped, but this time it wasn't a sickening flip so much as an angry one.

"You're disgusting," she spat. "I don't care how amazing and fabulous you think you are, but until today I'd never heard of you." *A small lie.* "My feelings about this baby have nothing to do with who you are and everything to do with the fact he *or* she is half mine."

She lifted a shaking finger and pointed at the door. He didn't own her, and until they knew whether or not she was pregnant, she wasn't going anywhere with him. It was a risk, but she needed time to figure out what to do, time to consult an attorney and talk to her family. If she left the country with him, it was over. He would own her and any baby within her.

"You should leave."

He stared at her for a long moment, that handsome

countenance wreathed in dark anger. And then he burst
out laughing. It shocked her. The sound was so rich, so
beautiful. And chilling in a way.

"I don't see what's so funny," she said, her heart fluttering like a hummingbird's wings. "I am perfectly serious. I'll see you in court, *Your Majesty*."

The door opened behind her. She turned, hoping it
was Kelly or even Tiffany coming to save her, but it was
merely one of the bodyguards.

"The car is ready, Your Majesty."

"Excellent."

Sheridan turned toward the king, but he'd moved
when she'd been looking at his bodyguard. Before she
knew what he was about, he swept an arm behind her
knees and jerked her into his arms. Once more, she was
pressed against his hard, taut body, his scent in her nostrils, conjuring images of heat and sand and cool water.
A hot, tight feeling flared beneath her skin, burning
through her and stopping the breath in her chest until
he was halfway across the storefront.

There were customers, she noted vaguely. And Tiffany, who looked up as Rashid al-Hassan walked by with
Sheridan in his arms. Tiffany didn't even look surprised,
the silly girl. She just looked bored, like always.

Sheridan knew she needed to scream. She needed to
get these people's attention and get this man to put her
down immediately. She felt her lungs working again—
of course they'd never stopped, but she hadn't felt them,
hadn't felt anything but heat and unbearable want when
he'd picked her up—and she sucked in air, preparing to
release it in the most eardrum-shattering cry she could
manage.

But she never got the chance because Rashid al-

Hassan—the Great Protector of his people, the Lion of Kyr and Defender of the Throne—dropped his mouth over hers and silenced her.

CHAPTER THREE

RASHID HADN'T MEANT to kiss her. But the damned woman was going to scream and he could not allow it. So he'd silenced her in the only way he could.

Her mouth was soft and pliant and sweet. He took advantage of the fact her lips were open to slip his tongue inside and stroke across the velvety softness of her mouth. She didn't move for a long moment and he began to wonder if she would bite him.

She was certainly capable of it. He'd not encountered a woman such as this one in…well, ever. Usually, women softened around him. Their eyes got big and wide and their mouths fell open invitingly. They sighed. They purred. They pouted.

They did not act as if he were poison. They did not glare daggers at him and spit fire and tell him to get out in prim little voices that belonged to the starchy librarians he'd encountered when he'd gone to university.

Sheridan's breath hitched in and he knew he had her. Knew she was his, for the moment.

He deepened the kiss, demanding more of a response from her. He had to keep her mouth busy and her thoughts focused on him until he could get her out of the store and into the car. It was a mercenary act on his part and he had no trouble pushing it as far as he needed in order to keep the fool woman silenced.

Her mouth opened a little wider, her tongue stroking tentatively against his.

Rashid's body turned to stone in a heartbeat. He had not expected that. But then he reminded himself there was a reason for his reaction. It had been a while since he'd had a woman. Being king had taken all his time these past couple of months. He was no longer a private citizen. No longer a man who could walk into a club, spot a gorgeous woman and take her home for a night of hot sex and no recriminations.

He was a king, and kings did not go anywhere without an entourage. They also did not pick up women and take them back to the palace for sex.

Certainly, he could have sent for a woman. But what kind of man would he be if he sent others to pick out women for him for the express purpose of having sex?

He was no prude, and he figured what people did with their bodies was their own business, but he'd never paid for sex in his life and he wasn't going to start now. Because that was what it would be if he ordered a woman for the evening as if she were an item on a room service menu.

Oh, she would not be a common prostitute. She wouldn't be a prostitute at all. But that didn't make it any better in his mind.

Another reason why he was going to have to choose a wife soon from the handful of princesses and heiresses his council had recommended. And yet he couldn't imagine having sex with any of the women whose dossiers he'd been sent thus far, much less facing one of them across a breakfast table for the rest of his life.

Damn Kadir for forcing him to take the throne. Yes, Rashid had always wanted to be king, but he hadn't quite realized how very confined he would feel. He was a ruler, a man with the power of life and death over his subjects, a man with absolute authority—and he had no private life to speak of. No one with whom he could share the simple pleasures.

He had not thought that would bother him so much, but it did. He missed Daria. Missed having someone in his life who loved him because of his flaws, not in spite of them. But Daria was gone, and there was no one.

Sheridan shifted in his arms and he felt her confusion, her hesitation. She was fighting herself, fighting her nature, and if he'd learned anything about her in these last few minutes, he knew she would conquer her baser instincts and fight against him soon enough.

A people pleaser? Perhaps she was, but she was not a Rashid pleaser. He knew that well enough now.

Because he was angry, because he was frustrated, he took the kiss to another level, ravaged her mouth like a man starved. He wanted to confuse her, wanted to keep her quiet and, hell, yes, he wanted to disconcert her. How dare she disobey him?

She gripped his lapels, twisted her fists in them. And then she met him as savagely as he met her. His body responded with a surge of heat he'd not felt in a long time. Her breath grew shallower and she made a sound in her throat.

He broke the kiss then, uncertain if he was pushing her too far too fast. Alarmed at his body's reaction to her, he tucked her head against his chest before she could speak.

"Quiet, *habibti*. Let me get you home." He smiled

at the women in the shop who threw them astonished looks and then strode outside and down the front steps before Sheridan could regain her ability to think clearly.

The car door swung smoothly open and Rashid bent to place Sheridan on the seat. She was so small and light that it was like handling a piece of china. He didn't want to break her, but he also knew she was stronger than she looked.

He got in beside her, the door sealed shut, and the car slid smoothly away from the curb and down the sun-dappled streets. The partition was up between them and the driver, and silence hung heavy in the car.

"You kidnapped me." Her voice was small and frightened and Rashid swung to look at her. Her golden hair gleamed in the sunlight that filtered into the car and her eyes were wide with fear. He did not enjoy that, but he told himself it was necessary. Whatever it took to force her to obey.

Rashid sat back and tugged a sleeve into place. He was not precisely pleased with himself, and yet he'd done what had to be done. A man like him claimed his child. And the woman carrying it.

"I did warn you."

"You said you weren't a barbarian." Her hands clenched into fists in her lap. She wore a pink dress and smelled like cotton candy and Rashid wanted to lean into her and press his nose to her hair.

"Indeed."

"Then I must be confused, because I thought barbarians did precisely what you just did. Or did you perhaps say you weren't a *barber* and I simply misunderstood?"

And there was the attitude. Clearly, she was not

damaged in any way. It gave his temper permission to emerge.

"I am a desert king. Of course I'm a barbarian. Isn't that what you believe? Because I speak Arabic and come from a nation where the men wear robes and the women are veiled, that I must surely be less civilized than you?"

Her lips pressed into a tight, white line. "Even if I didn't believe it, don't you think you just proved it? What kind of man kidnaps a woman he's never met just because there's been a mix-up in the clinic?"

Her eyes were flashing purple fire again. For some reason, that intrigued him almost as much as it angered him.

"A man who has no time for arguments. A man who holds the lives of an entire nation in his hands and who needs to get back to his duties. A man who has no reason whatsoever to trust that the woman carrying his heir will turn over the child when it is time."

Her eyes darkened with anger. "I won't give up my baby just because you wish it."

"You were willing to do so for your sister."

"That's different and you know it. I would still be part of the child's life. A beloved aunt." She shook her head suddenly. "Why are we arguing about this? There's no guarantee I'm pregnant. It doesn't always work the first time."

"Perhaps not, but I will take no chances. My child will be a king one day, Sheridan Sloane. He will not be raised in an apartment in America by a woman who works sixteen-hour days and ignores him in favor of her own interests."

Her skin flushed bright red. "How dare you?" she growled. "How dare you act as if you know me when you don't have the faintest clue? I would never ignore my child. Never!"

He infuriated her. No, she'd not planned for a child in her life—the baby was supposed to be Annie's—but the fact he would sit there and smugly inform her that he believed she would neglect her baby in favor of her business made her defensive and angry. Of course she would still have to work, but she would figure it out.

Except there would be no figuring it out. This man was a king, and if she was pregnant, he wasn't going to abandon her to raise the child alone. He would be a part of her life from now on.

Sheridan shivered at the thought. How did one work out custody with a king?

"This baby is supposed to be Annie's," she said, working hard to keep the panic from her voice. "I hadn't planned on a baby of my own, but that doesn't mean I would be a bad or neglectful mother. And I won't let you steamroll right over me just because you're a king. I have rights, too."

His eyes were hooded as he studied her. Did he have to be so damned beautiful? She'd never seen hair so black or eyes so fathomless. If he was an actor, she'd wonder if his cheekbones were the work of a plastic surgeon. His face was a study in perfection, angles and planes and smooth, bronzed skin. He was golden, as if he spent long hours under the sun, and there were fine lines at the corners of his eyes where they crinkled as he studied her.

Her gaze focused on his mouth, those firm, beautiful lips that had pressed against hers. She felt a fresh wave of heat creeping up her throat. He'd only kissed her to shut her up, but she'd forgotten for long minutes why that was a bad thing. His mouth had ravaged hers and she'd only wanted more. Even now, her lips tingled with the memory of his assault on them. She was bruised and swollen, but in a good way. In the kind of way that said a woman had been well kissed and had enjoyed every moment of it.

Sheridan dropped her gaze from his, suddenly self-conscious. It had been a long time since she'd kissed anyone. A long time since she'd lain in bed with a man and felt the heat and wonder of joining her body with another. She hadn't thought she was deprived. Rather, she'd thought she was busy and that she just didn't have time to invest in a relationship.

But now that he'd kissed her, she felt as if she'd been starving for affection. As if the drought in her sex life was suddenly much larger than she'd thought it was. How could he make her feel this way when he was not a nice man?

After her last relationship, a short-lived romance with a womanizing accountant who'd made her feel like the only woman in his life until the moment she'd caught him with his tongue down someone else's throat, she'd vowed to only date nice, trustworthy men.

Rashid al-Hassan was definitely not a nice man. Or trustworthy. But he made things hum and spark inside her, damn him. She'd only kissed him once, but already she wanted to lean forward, tunnel her fingers through that thick mane of hair and claim his lips for another round.

Insanity, Sheridan.

"Surely there is something you want more than this child," he said smoothly, cutting into her thoughts, and her heart began to beat a crazy rhythm.

"No."

He lifted an eyebrow in that superior arch she despised. "Money? I can give you quite a lot of it, you know. Once our divorce is final, you could be a wealthy woman."

Divorce? Her stomach fell to the floor at the thought of being married to this man for even an hour.

"I don't want your money. And I'm definitely not going to marry you." There was only one thing she wanted. It also wasn't something he could give. Unless he had the power of miracles.

She was certain he did not. If a dozen doctors couldn't fix Annie's fertility issues, then neither could a king, no matter how arrogant and entitled.

"Everyone has a price, Sheridan. And if you are pregnant, you most certainly *will* be my wife. In name only, of course. My child will not be born illegitimate."

Her name on his lips was too exotic, too sensual. It stroked over her senses, set up a drumbeat in her veins. And embarrassed her because he clearly wasn't suffering from an unwanted attraction, too. *In name only.*

"All I want is a baby for my sister. And I intend to give her one."

"After you give me my heir, of course."

Her lips tightened. "You make it sound so cold and clinical. As if you're selecting a prized broodmare to give you a champion foal."

The car glided through the streets. Outside the windows, people behaved as usual. Tourists chattered excitedly and pointed from their seats in the horse-drawn carriages that traveled through Savannah's historic district. Part of Sheridan wanted to open the door and run when the car came to a standstill in traffic.

But there was no escape. Not like this anyway. The only way to fight a man like him was with lawyers, and even that was no guarantee because he could afford far better representation than she could.

"It is a clinical thing, is it not?" His voice was rich and smooth and crusted in ice. "We have never been intimate, and yet you may be pregnant with my child. Put there with a syringe in a doctor's office. How is this not clinical?"

Sheridan swallowed the lump in her throat. "I was supposed to be having a baby for my sister. With my brother-in-law's sperm. What would you propose we do differently?"

Of course, it would have been cheaper and easier for her and Chris to just sleep together until she was pregnant, but what a horrifying thought that was. He was her sister's husband and her friend, and there was no way in hell. Lying on a table with her feet in stirrups might be clinical, but it was the only solution.

He ignored the question. "Nevertheless, it is my sperm you received. How do you think this makes me feel?"

She swung around to look at him. Up to this point, she hadn't thought of how it must have affected him. She was almost ashamed of herself for the lapse. Almost.

That ended when she met his gaze. He was looking at her as coldly as ever. King Rashid al-Hassan was a block of ice. A block of ice that had burned strangely hot when he'd pressed his mouth to hers.

Sheridan nervously smoothed the fabric of her dress. "I admit I hadn't thought of it. I imagine you're angry."

"That is one way of putting it." His dark eyes flashed. "I am a king and my country has laws I must obey. You may think us barbarians, but there is a certain logic to the king depositing sperm in a bank outside his nation. It was never meant to be used. Or not under normal circumstances."

She didn't want to think about what kind of circumstances would precipitate using the sperm, but she imagined it would involve his untimely death and no heir to follow him to the throne. She might not like him, but she wouldn't wish him dead.

Yet.

"No, I can see how it might be useful. It's forward thinking to do such a thing."

"Apparently not, when mistakes such as this are allowed to occur."

Sheridan put her hand over her middle instinctively. Fresh anger swirled in her belly. "Calling this baby a mistake is unlikely to inspire my confidence, don't you think? You want me to give him or her up, but you speak as if you don't care about him other than as your heir."

"He will be my heir. Until there is another child, at least."

Her heart thumped. "Because you can choose your successor in Kyr. Of course." Her fingers tightened over her flat belly. She didn't even know if there was a baby in there yet, but already she felt protective and angry.

"It is the way of our people."

Maybe so, but it seemed a horrible way for children to grow up. Talk about an unhealthy sense of competition. "You weren't chosen until right before your father died. How did that make you feel?"

His eyes glittered hot and she had the feeling she'd tweaked the lion's tail. He looked at her as if he would snap her in two with one fierce bite. Yet his voice was still as icy as ever.

"You push me too far, Sheridan Sloane. You should be more cautious."

Maybe she should, but she couldn't seem to do so. "Why? Because you might kidnap me or something?"

His dark eyes raked over her. "Or something."

CHAPTER FOUR

KYR WAS HOT. Savannah was hot, too, but it was also muggy because they were so near the ocean. Kyr was not muggy, though the Persian Gulf was nearby. It was just hot, with the kind of heat that sucked all the moisture right out of you and left you gasping for breath. It was also beautiful, which Sheridan had not expected.

The desert sands were almost red and the dunes rose high in the distance, undulating like waves on the ocean. As they'd approached the city from the airport, she'd viewed tall date palms that grew in ordered rows. Sheridan had been in the same car with Rashid, but once they'd arrived at the palace she'd been taken to what appeared to be a lonely wing with no one else in it. If he had a harem, this was not it.

She still couldn't believe she was here. She paced around the cavernous room of the suite she'd been shown to and marveled at the architecture. There were soaring arches, mosaics of delicate and colorful tile and painted walls and ceilings. There was a sunken area in the middle of the room, lined with colorful cushions, and above her the ceiling soared into a dome shape that was punctuated with small windows, which let light filter down to the floor and spread in warm puddles across its gleaming tiles.

It was a beautiful and lonely space. Sheridan sank onto the cushions and sat by herself in that big room, listening to nothing. There was no television, no radio, no telephone that she could find. She had her cell phone, but no signal.

She leaned back against the cushions and swore she wouldn't cry. For someone like her, a person who craved light and sound and activity, this silent cavern was torture. Just yesterday—had it really been only yesterday?—she'd been surrounded by people at Mrs. Lands's party. And then she'd been in her office, with her beautiful store outside her door, listening to the sounds of people on the street and the low hum of her radio as it played the latest top-forty hits.

She hadn't exactly been happy, not after the news from the clinic and Annie's reaction, but she'd been far more content than she'd given herself credit for. Tears pushed against her eyes at the thought of all she'd left behind, but she didn't let them fall.

Rashid al-Hassan was a tyrant. He'd swept into her life, swept her up against her will and deposited her here alone. And all because the stupid sperm bank had used the wrong sperm. She'd wanted to give her sister a precious gift, but she was here, a veritable prisoner to a rude, arrogant, sinfully attractive man who had all the warmth and friendliness of an iceberg.

He hadn't let her call anyone until they were on his plane. She was still astounded at the opulence of the royal jet. It was one of the most amazing things she'd ever seen, with leather and gold and fine carpets. The bath had even been made of marble. Marble on a jet!

It had also been bigger than her bathroom in her apartment. There were uniformed flight attendants who performed their duties with bright smiles and soft words—and deep bows to their king. She could hardly forget that sight. Any time anyone on that plane had come close to Rashid al-Hassan, they'd dipped almost to the floor. He hadn't even deigned to notice half the time.

It stunned her and unnerved her. She kept telling herself he was just a man, but there hadn't been a single person on that plane who'd acted like he was. When she'd finally been allowed to phone Kelly and Chris—not Annie, goodness, no—she'd held the phone tightly in her hand and explained as best she could that she would be gone for the next week.

They'd taken the news of Rashid much better than she had. Kelly, always a hopeless romantic, had wanted to know if he was handsome and if she would have to marry him. Sheridan had clutched the phone tight and hadn't told her friend that even though Rashid expected her to marry him, she'd rather marry a shark. She'd just said they were taking this one day at a time and would deal with a pregnancy when and if it happened. As if Rashid was reasonable and kind instead of an unfeeling block of stone.

Chris had told her to be strong, and not to worry about Annie. It would all be fine, he'd said. She'd had to bite her lip to keep from crying at the thought of Chris telling her sister the news, but she'd thanked him and told him she'd be in touch.

She spread her fingers over her abdomen. What would become of her if there were a baby inside here?

She stared up at the beam of sunlight filtering into her prison and pressed her fist to her mouth to contain her sob. Nine months as his wife in name only, his prisoner, shut away from the world—and then he would coldly divorce her and send her on her way with empty arms.

Despair filled her until she thought she would choke with it. Soon there was a noise at the entrance to her prison. A woman in a dress and wearing a scarf over her head came in and sat a tray down on a table nearby. Sheridan shot to her feet and went over to where the woman was removing covers from dishes.

"That smells lovely." She was surprised when her stomach growled, especially considering how queasy she'd been feeling since Rashid had come to the store yesterday.

The woman gave her a polite smile. "His Majesty says you must eat, miss."

Must. Of course he did. And as much as she would love to defy him, she wasn't so stupid as to starve herself just to prove a point.

"Can you please tell me where His Majesty is? I would like to speak with him."

Because she was going to go quietly insane if she had to remain in this room alone with no stimulation. The books—and there were plenty of them—were written in Arabic.

The woman shook her head and kept smiling. "Eat, miss."

She gave Sheridan a half bow and glided gracefully toward the door. Sheridan thought about it for two seconds and then followed her. But the woman was through the door and the door shut before Sheridan could reach it.

She jerked it open only to be confronted with the same thing she'd been confronted with earlier: a man in desert robes standing in the corridor, arms crossed, sword strapped to his side. He looked at her no less coolly than his boss had.

"I want to speak to King Rashid," she said.

The man didn't move or speak.

Anger welled up inside her, pressing hard against the confines of her skin until she thought she might burst with it. She started toward the guard. He was big and broad, but she was determined that she would walk past him and keep going until she found people.

The man stepped into her path and she had to stop abruptly or collide nose first with his chest.

"Get out of my way." She glared up at him, but he didn't seem in the least bit concerned. She gathered her courage and ducked the other way. But he was there, in front of her, his big body blocking her progress.

Fury howled deep in her gut. She was in a strange place, being guarded by a huge man who wouldn't speak to her, and she was lonely and furious and scared all at once.

So she did something she had never done in her life. She stomped on his foot.

And gasped. Whatever he was wearing, it was a lot harder than her delicate little sandal. She resisted the urge to clutch her foot and hop around in circles. Barely. The mountain of a man didn't even make a noise. He just took her firmly by the arm and steered her back into the suite. And then he shut the door on her so that she stood there staring at the carved wood with her jaw hanging open. Her foot and her pride stung. She thought about yanking open the door and trying again, like an annoying fly, but she knew she'd only get more of the same from him.

She stood with her hands on her hips, her gaze moving around the room, her brain churning. And then she halted on the tray of food. The tray was big, solid, possibly made of silver. It would be heavy.

Sheridan closed her eyes and pulled in a deep breath. She wasn't really thinking of sneaking into the hall and braining the poor guard, was she? That wasn't nice. He was only doing what he'd been ordered to do. It wasn't polite to smack him with the tray when she really wanted to smack Rashid al-Hassan instead.

She opened her eyes again, continued her circuit of the room. There were windows. All that glass would make a hell of a noise if she busted it. Part of her protested that it was an extreme idea, that a lady didn't go around breaking other people's property. Worse, an architect who specialized in historical preservation didn't go around breaking windows in old palaces, even if the glass was a modern addition to the structure. Which she could tell by the tint and finish.

But this could hardly be termed a normal circumstance. King Rashid al-Hassan had already made the first move, and it hadn't been polite or considerate. So why should she be polite in return?

Game on....

Rashid had just settled in for lunch after a long morning spent in meetings with his council when Mostafa hurried into his office, a wide-eyed look on his face. The man dropped into a deep bow before rising again.

"Speak," Rashid said, knowing Mostafa would not do so until told.

"Majesty, it's the woman."

Rashid went still, his hand hovering over a dish of rice and chicken. He set the spoon down. *The woman* was such an inadequate description for Sheridan Sloane, but if he tried to point that out to Mostafa, the man would think him cracked in the head.

"What about her, Mostafa?"

"She has, er, broken a window. And she is asking to see you."

A prickle of alarm slid through him. "Is she hurt?"

"A few small cuts."

Rashid was on his feet in a second. Steely anger hardened in his veins as he strode out the door and down the corridors of the palace toward the women's quarters. He'd placed her there because it was supposed to be safe—and also because he didn't quite know what to do with her now that he had her here. He'd sent his father's remaining two wives to homes of their own, ostensibly in preparation for taking his own wife—or wives—but in truth he'd wanted to rid the palace of their presence.

They were women his father had married later in life, and so they were much younger than King Zaid had been. Rashid had no idea what kind of relationship his father had had with either of them, but they made him think too often of his father's tempestuous relationship with his own mother. Rashid would not live with women who reminded him of those dark days.

Palace workers dropped to their knees as he passed, a giant wave of obeisance that he hardly noticed. He kept going until he reached the women's suite and the mountainous form of Daoud, the guard he'd placed here.

Daoud fell to his knees and pressed his forehead to the floor. "Forgive me, Your Majesty."

"What happened?"

Daoud looked up from the floor and Rashid made an impatient motion. The man had been with him for years now, long before Rashid became king. Daoud stood. "The woman tried to leave. I prevented her."

"Did you harm her?" His voice was a whip and Daoud paled.

"No, Your Majesty. I took her by the arm, placed her inside the room and closed the door. A few minutes later, I heard the crash."

Rashid brushed past him and went into the room. One tall window was open to the outside. Hot air and fine grains of sand rushed inside along with the sounds of activity on the palace grounds below. Two men worked to clean up the glass that had blown across the floor.

Sheridan sat on cushions in the middle of the room, looking small and dejected. There were a couple of small red lines on her arms and his heart clenched tight. But the ice he lived with on a daily basis didn't fail him. It rushed in, filled all the dark corners of his soul and hardened any sympathetic feelings he may have had for her.

Sheridan looked up then. "And the mighty king has come to call."

"Out," Rashid said to the room in general. The servants who were busy picking up the glass rose and hurried out the door. A woman appeared from the direction of the bath. She dropped a small bowl and cloth on the side table and then she left, as well.

The door behind him sealed shut. Rashid stalked toward the small woman on the cushions. Her golden-blond hair was down today. It hit him with a jolt that it was long and silky and perfectly straight. She was wearing flat white sandals with little jewels set on the bands and a light blue dress with tiny flowers on it. She did not look like a woman who might be carrying a royal baby.

She looked like a misbehaving girl, fresh and pretty and filled with mischief.

And sporting small cuts to her flesh. Cuts she'd caused, he reminded himself. She picked up the cloth and dabbed at her hand. The white fabric came away pink.

"What did you do, Miss Sloane?"

As if he couldn't tell. The window was open to the heat and a silver tray lay discarded to one side. Such violence in such a small package. It astonished him.

She wouldn't look at him. "I admit it was childish of me, but I was angry." Then her violet eyes lifted to his. "I don't ordinarily act this way, I assure you. But you put me here with nothing to do and no one to talk to."

"And this is how you behave when you don't get your way?"

Her gaze didn't waver. In fact, he thought it flickered with anger. Or maybe it was fear. That gave him pause. She had no reason to fear him. Daria would be ashamed of him for scaring this woman.

He tried to look unperturbed. He didn't think it was working based on the way her throat moved as he stared back at her.

"In fact, I realize that we can't always have our way," she said primly. "But this is my first time as a prisoner, and I thought perhaps the rules were different. So I decided to do something about it."

Rashid blinked. "Prisoner?" He spread his hands to encompass the room. It was plush and comfortable and feminine. He remembered it from when he was a child, but he'd not entered these quarters in many years. They hadn't changed much, he decided. "I've been in exclusive hotels that lacked accommodations this fine. You think this is a prison?"

A small shard of guilt pricked him even as he spoke. His rooms with Kadir had been opulent, too, and he'd always thought of them as a cage from which he couldn't wait to escape. Beautiful surroundings did not make a person happy. He knew that better than most.

And she looked decidedly unhappy. "Even the cheapest hotels tend to have televisions. And computers, radios, telephones. There are plenty of books here, I'll grant you that—but I can't read them because they aren't in English."

Rashid's brows drew down. He turned and looked around the room. And realized that she was correct. There was no television, no computer, nothing but furniture and fabric and walls. When the women left, they'd taken their belongings with them. Clearly, they'd considered the electronics to be theirs, too.

"I will have that corrected."

"Which part, Rashid?"

He nearly startled at the sound of his name on her lips. He hadn't forgotten that he'd told her she could call him by name, but he somehow hadn't expected it here and now. Her voice was soft, her accent buttery and sweet.

He suddenly wanted her to speak again, to say his name so he could marvel at how it sounded when she did. Deliciously foreign. Soft.

He shoved away such ridiculous thoughts. "I will have a television installed. And a computer. Whatever you need for your comfort."

"But I am still a prisoner."

He clenched his jaw. "You are not a prisoner. You are my guest. Your every comfort is assured."

"And what if I want to talk to people? Have things to do besides watch television all day? I'm a businesswoman, Rashid. I don't sit around my home and do nothing all day."

"I will find a companion for you."

She sighed heavily. And then she went back to dabbing the cuts on the back of her hand. His anger flared hot again.

"You could have hurt yourself far worse than you did," he growled. "Did you even consider the baby when you behaved so foolishly?"

Her head snapped up, guilt flashing in her gaze. "I've already admitted it was a mistake. And yes, I considered what I was doing before I acted. But I didn't expect the glass to shatter everywhere like that. I threw the tray from a distance, but I guess I threw it harder than I thought."

She'd thrown the tray. At the window. She could have been seriously hurt, the foolish woman. But she sat there looking contrite and dejected—and yes, defiant, too— and he wanted to shake her. And tell her he was sorry.

Now where had that come from? He had nothing to apologize for.

Don't I?

He had brought her to Kyr against her will, but what choice did he have? She could be pregnant with his child. Until he knew for certain, he was not about to let her stay in America, living alone and working. What if something happened? What if her store was robbed or someone broke into her apartment?

He'd seen how flimsy her door locks were. Oh, she thought they were state-of-the-art, no doubt, but he'd hired some of the best lock pickers in existence when he'd been building his business from scratch. He'd wanted to test his security, and he knew how easily locks could be breached.

If someone wanted to get to her, they could. And if it became known that she might carry an heir to the throne of Kyr? He shuddered to think of it.

"You will not do anything so foolish again, Miss Sloane."

"I don't intend to—but I also don't want a companion. I want my freedom to come and go from this room, to talk to whomever I want to. And I want to talk to you from time to time. If there's a baby, then I want to know its father as something more than an arrogant stranger. And if there isn't, then I'll go home and forget I ever met you."

Rashid stood stiffly and stared down at her sitting there like some sort of tiny potentate. She had nerve, this woman. But it was absolutely out of the question. He wanted nothing to do with her. If she was pregnant, he'd deal with it when the time came—he could hardly think the word *wife*—but for now she was safely stowed away and he could go about business and forget she existed.

"You may come and go if that is what you wish. But you will have a servant to guide you, and you will do what you are told. You will not wear that clothing, Miss Sloane. You will dress as a Kyrian woman and you will be respectful."

Her chin lifted again. "I am always respectful of those who are respectful of me. But I refuse to be swathed head to toe in black robes—"

His anger was swift as he cut her off. "Once more, you make dangerous assumptions about us. I will send a seamstress to you and you may choose your own colors. This is nonnegotiable."

Her mouth flattened for the barest moment. And then her lips were lush and pink again as she nibbled the bottom one. "And am I to see you, too? Have conversations with you that aren't about what I'm wearing or where I plan to live?"

He almost said yes. The word hovered on his tongue and he bit it back. Shock coursed through him at that near slip. Why would he want to spend any time with her? Why would he ever do such a thing? It was not in him. It was not what he did, regardless that he'd thought of that kiss for half the night during the flight home. He'd told himself it had simply been too long since he'd been with a woman and that was why he kept thinking about it.

But this woman was not the one he was going to break his fast with. That road was fraught with too many dangers. Too many complications.

"I think that is unnecessary," he said curtly. "I have a kingdom to run and very little time."

"I think it *is* necessary." Her voice was soft and filled with a hurt he didn't understand.

He refused to let her get to him. She was a stranger, a vessel who might be carrying his child. He did not care for her. He would not care for her.

"Yet this, too, is nonnegotiable," he told her before turning and striding from the room.

CHAPTER FIVE

SHERIDAN DIDN'T KNOW why it hurt so much to watch him walk out, but it did. She didn't care about him at all—she actively disliked him, in fact—but his rejection stung. She might be carrying his child and he didn't even care about who she was as a person. He didn't want to know her, and he didn't seem to want her to know him.

She didn't move when the workmen came back inside to continue cleaning the glass, or when Fatima—the woman who'd brought her food and had returned after Sheridan broke the window—came over and took the cloth from her to wipe the remaining cuts. They were small, but they stung.

Oh, she'd been so stupid. So emotional. She'd behaved crazily—but it had worked because he'd come. And he'd promised her a small measure of freedom. That had to be a triumph. Fatima dabbed some ointment on her cuts, and then disappeared into the bathroom to put everything away.

How had it come to this? Sheridan was a nice person. She was friendly to everyone, she loved talking to people and she'd never met anyone she didn't like. Until yesterday when Rashid al-Hassan had shown up, she hadn't even thought it was possible to dislike someone.

There were people she got mad at, certainly. She got mad at Annie for not being stronger, but that only made her feel guilty. Annie hadn't had all the advantages that Sheridan had—she wasn't as outgoing, she hadn't been popular, she didn't know how to talk to people and make friends and now she couldn't even have a baby—so it was wrong of Sheridan to get angry with her. Sheridan could hear her mother's answer when she'd been a teen complaining that it wasn't fair she had to stay home from the party because her friends hadn't invited Annie, too.

Annie's not like you, Sheri. We have to be gentle with her. We have to watch out for her.

Not for the first time, Sheridan wondered if maybe Annie would be tougher if everyone in her life hadn't coddled her. If she'd had to stand up for herself, make her own friends, fight her own battles.

Sheridan clenched her hand into a fist and sat there as still as a statue for what seemed the longest time. Even now, she felt like she should be calling Annie to ask how she was instead of worrying about her own situation.

She looked up to see yet more men arriving in her room. They chattered in fast, musical Arabic, dragging out measuring tapes and writing things down on paper. Then they disappeared.

Everything transpired quickly and efficiently over the next couple of hours. Sheridan didn't see the new glass going in because by that time she was in her bedchamber— seriously, it was a chamber, not a bedroom—with three seamstresses, several bolts of fabric and ready-made samples hanging from a portable rack. A young woman who spoke English had come along to translate.

"This one, miss?"

Sheridan looked at the satiny peach fabric and felt a rush of pleasure. "Definitely."

The clothing the women wore was beautiful. Sheridan felt another wash of heat roll through her as she thought about her preconceived notions. She'd expected they would wear black burkas covering them from head to foot, but that was not at all the case.

The garments these women wore were colorful, lightweight and beautiful. They were long, modestly fitted dresses with embroidery and beading on the necks and bodices. The hijab, or head covering, was optional. Two of the women wore them and two did not.

But the possibilities there were beautiful, as well. The fabric was gossamer, colorful and draped in such a way that it created a sense of mystery and beauty.

The women worked quickly, draping bolts of fabric over her body, slipping pins inside and pulling the fabric away only to replace it with a new bolt. Sheridan tried on two dresses they had on the rack—one a gorgeous coral and the other a pretty shade of lavender that brought out the color of her eyes. The seamstress in charge promised they could have those two ready in a matter of hours once they returned to their shop and got to work. The others would take a full day.

Sheridan didn't want to imagine that she needed many dresses for her stay, but how could she know for certain?

The women packed everything up and left just as two men came in with Fatima. They were carrying a box with a flat-screen television in it and they proceeded to set it up on one of the credenzas nearest the bed.

Sheridan wandered into the living area of the suite and found a new television there, too, as well as a state-of-the-art computer and a newly installed telephone. The new glass was set into the casement and the men were sweeping up.

Her throat grew tight. Rashid had done what he'd promised. Thus far. He'd seemed surprised she'd had no television or computer, and he'd worked fast to correct it. But, as nice as this was, she'd wanted more from him. She'd wanted *his* time, wanted to understand more about this man who might just be the father of her baby. He could not be wholly unlikable, could he?

But he seemed determined not to give it to her.

She picked up the remote and flipped on the television. The one in the living area was mounted to the wall, and it was huge—it was almost like having a movie screen when all the colors suddenly came to life and filled the surface. It didn't take too long to figure out how the satellite worked—and her throat tightened again as she landed on CNN International and English conversation filled her ears.

It was nice to hear, but it only brought home how alone she was here. How would she get through a week of this? Nine months of this?

Rashid had said she could come and go, but only with an escort and only when she had the proper clothing. Since she still didn't, she wouldn't attempt to leave her quarters yet. She'd already behaved abominably.

She could still see him standing there, looking at her with the most furious expression on his face. He'd also, for a moment, seemed not fearful...but, well, something besides angry. Maybe *wary* was the word. Like he didn't want to be in the same room with her, but knew he had to be.

It hit her then that not only was he not attracted to her, but she also revolted him. He was tall and handsome and kingly, and she was a short blond woman who organized parties for people. She was pale and slight compared to him. He was the Lion of Kyr, or some such thing like that, and she was an ordinary house cat.

Who might just be pregnant with the next king of the jungle.

She would have laughed if it wasn't so serious. Sheridan went over to where Fatima had set a fresh pot of tea and some pastries and poured a cup. Despite the nausea, which came and went, she decided to try a pastry and see if it stayed down. After she'd made an impulsive decision to throw the tray at the window, she'd not eaten any of the food that she'd carefully set aside to get to the tray. Things had happened so quickly after that and she hadn't had time.

Sheridan frowned as she nibbled on a pastry. Rashid was repulsed by her. It made sense, in a way, and it certainly explained the way he acted.

But then she thought of their kiss again, of the way it had slid down into her skin and made her want things she'd almost forgotten existed. Even now, the memory of it made her tremble. He'd slid his tongue into her mouth and she'd practically devoured him.

How embarrassing.

But she'd thought, dammit, at least for a minute anyway, that he'd been equally affected. He'd kissed her with such hunger, such passion, that she'd been swept up in the moment.

Yes, swept up enough so that he could carry her to the car before she managed to make a peep. Sheridan set the pastry down with disgust. He'd certainly known what he was doing. And she'd been just sensation deprived enough to let him.

"Miss?"

Sheridan looked up to find Fatima standing over her. The two men were leaving, carting the remnants of television and computer boxes with them.

"Yes?"

"Do you require anything else?"

That was a loaded question if ever she heard one. "Your English is good, Fatima."

"Thank you, miss. I studied in school."

"Have you worked in the palace long?"

"A few months."

"Do you know the king well?"

She shook her head. "No, miss. King Rashid, may Allah bless him, has come home again after many years away. We will prosper under his benevolent reign."

Sheridan wasn't going to laugh over that *benevolent reign* remark, though she wanted to. But she also felt a spark of curiosity. "Many years away?"

Fatima looked a little worried then. "I have heard this in the palace. I do not know for certain. If you will excuse me, miss. Unless you need something?" she added, her eyes wide and almost pleading with Sheridan not to ask anything more about Rashid.

"Thank you, but I'm fine," she replied, offering the woman a smile to reassure her.

Fatima curtsied and then hurried out of the room, closing the door behind her with one last fearful glance at Sheridan.

After a long day sorting through national problems, including one between two desert tribes arguing over who owned a water well, Rashid was glad to retire to his quarters. These rooms had once been his father's, but he'd gotten the decorators to work immediately so that they no longer bore any resemblance to the man who'd lived in them for thirty-seven years.

Gone were the ornate furnishings and narcissistic portraits, the statuary, the huge bed on a platform complete with heavy damask draperies. In their place, Rashid had asked for clean lines, comfortable furniture, paintings that didn't overwhelm with color or subject matter and breezy fabrics more in fitting with the desert. Certainly the desert was bitterly cold at night, but he didn't need damask draperies for that.

The palace had been modernized years ago and had working air and heat for those rare occasions when it was needed. Rashid slipped his headdress off and dropped it on a couch. Then he raked his hand through his hair and pulled out his phone. He stared at it for a long moment before he punched the button that would call up his favorites.

Kadir answered on the third ring. "Rashid, it's good to hear from you."

"*Salaam,* brother." He chewed the inside of his lip and stared off toward the dunes and the setting sun. It blazed bright orange as it sank like a stone. He'd debated for hours on whether or not to call Kadir. They weren't as close as they'd once been, and he found it hard to admit he needed people. "How are you?"

Kadir laughed. "Wonderful. Happy. Ecstatic."

"Marriage agrees with you." He tried not to let any bitterness slip into his voice, but he feared it did anyway. Still, Kadir took it like a blissfully happy man would: as the uninformed judgment of a bachelor.

"Apparently so. Emily keeps me on my toes. But she

forces me to eat kale, Rashid. Because it has micronutrients or some such thing, she says it's good for me."

"That doesn't sound so bad." It sounded horrible.

"She makes a healthy drink for breakfast. It's green. Looks disgusting, but thankfully doesn't taste as bad as it looks." He sighed. "I miss pancakes and bacon."

Rashid was familiar with pancakes, though he'd never developed a taste for them during the brief time he'd spent in America. He almost laughed, but then he thought of Daria cooking meals for him and swallowed. She used to make these wonderful savory pies from her native Ural Mountains. He'd loved them. He'd loved her.

Rashid swallowed. "I want you to build a skyscraper for me, Kadir."

He could practically hear Kadir's brain kick into gear. "You do? Is this a Kyrian project, or a personal one?"

"I need a building for Hassan Oil in Kyr. I want you to build it."

"Then I am happy to do so. Let me check the schedule and I'll see when we can come for a meeting."

"That would be good."

Kadir sighed, as if sensing there was more to the call. "I will come anyway, Rashid, if you wish it."

He did wish it. For the first time in a long time, he wanted a friend. And Kadir was the closest thing he had. But a lifetime of shutting people out was hard to overcome. He'd let in Daria, but look how that had turned out.

"Whenever you can make it is good. I'm busy with many things since you left."

"I'm sorry we didn't make the coronation. It was my intention, and then—"

"It's fine." He pulled in a breath. "Kadir, there is something I want to talk about."

"Then I will come immediately."

That Kadir would still do that, after everything that had passed between them, made an uncomfortable rush of feeling fill Rashid's chest. "No, that is not necessary. But there's a woman. A situation."

"A situation?" He could hear the confusion in his brother's voice.

Rashid sighed. And then he told Kadir what had happened—the sperm mix-up, the trip to America, the way he'd given Sheridan no choice but to return with him. Kadir was silent for a long moment. Rashid knew his brother was trying to grasp the ramifications of the situation. At any rate, he couldn't know half of why this unnerved Rashid so much. Rashid hadn't hidden his marriage to Daria, but he'd been living in Russia then and the information hadn't precisely filtered out.

And the baby? He did not talk of that to anyone.

"So she might be pregnant?"

The ice in his chest was brittle. "Yes."

"What will you do? Marry her?"

Rashid hated the way that single word ground into his brain. *Marry.* "I will have to, won't I? But once the child is born, she can leave him here and return to America."

Kadir blew out a breath. Rashid wondered for a moment if he might be laughing. But his voice, when he spoke, was even. "I don't know, Rashid. The American I married would put my balls in a vise before she agreed to such a thing. In fact, I think most women would."

"Not if you pay them enough to disappear."

Kadir might have groaned. Rashid wasn't certain, because his blood was rushing in his ears. "You could try. It would certainly make it easier with the council if she would agree to disappear afterward. If she's pregnant, they will have to accept her. But they won't like it."

Rashid growled. "I don't give a damn what the council likes."

And it was true. The council was old and traditional, but there were lines he would not allow them to cross. He was the king. They had power because he allowed it, not in spite of it. They wanted him to marry a Kyrian. But if he wanted to marry a dancing bear, he would. And if he wanted to marry an American girl, he would do that, too.

"At least be nice to the woman, Rashid. You *are* being nice to her, yes?"

"Of course I am." But a current of guilt sizzled through him. He could still see her eyes, so wide and wounded, looking up at him today when he'd told her there was no reason for them to spend time together. No reason to know each other.

And perhaps there wasn't. But the days were ticking down and they would soon know if she were pregnant. And then he would have to take her as his wife.

It made him want to howl.

"We will come for a visit soon," Kadir said. "Perhaps it would be good to have Emily there. The poor woman is probably confused and scared."

He didn't think Sheridan was all that scared. He could still see her standing up to him, spitting like a wet cat when he'd told her he would take the child and raise him in Kyr.

"I am nice to her," he said defensively. "She is my guest."

Kadir laughed softly. "Somehow, I don't think she sees it quite the same way."

They spoke for a few more minutes about other things, and then Rashid ended the call. He sighed and went out onto one of the many terraces that opened off his rooms. There was a soft breeze tonight, hot and scented with jasmine from the gardens. In another few hours, it would turn chilly, but for now it was still warm.

The minarets glowed ocher in the last rays of the setting sun. The sounds of vendors shouting in the streets filtered to him on the wind, along with the fresh scent of spicy meat and hot bread.

Rashid breathed it all in. This was home. Unbidden, an image of Sheridan Sloane came to mind. She had a home, too, and he'd forced her out of it. For her own protection, yes, but nevertheless she was here in a strange place and nothing was familiar.

Guilt pricked him. He should not care about her feelings at all, but if she was truly carrying his child, did he want her upset and stressed? Wasn't it better to make her welcome?

He sighed again, knowing what he had to do. Tomorrow, he would take lunch with her. They would talk, she would be happy and he would leave again, content in the knowledge he'd done his part.

It was only an hour—and he could be nice to anyone for an hour.

Sheridan awoke in the middle of the night. It was dark and still and she was cold. She sat up, intending to pull the blanket up from the bottom of the bed, but she wasn't all that tired now. Her sleep was erratic because of the time difference. She checked her phone for the time—

still no signal—and calculated that it was midafternoon at home. She never napped during the day, so it was no wonder she was messed up.

She got up and pulled on her silky robe over her night-gown before going into the bathroom. Hair combed, teeth brushed, she wandered into the living area. And then, because she was curious, she went and opened the door to her suite. The guard was not there. She stood there for a moment in shock, and then she crept into the corridor.

She didn't know where she was going or what she expected, but she kept moving along, thinking someone would stop her at any moment. But no one did. The corridors were quiet, as if everyone was asleep. She didn't know how it usually worked in palaces, but it made sense they were all in bed.

When she reached the end of a corridor and came up against a firmly locked door, she turned and went back the way she'd come. There were doors off the corridor, and she tentatively opened one. It was a space with seating, but it wasn't quite as ornate as hers. It was, not plain precisely, but modern. Personally, she preferred some antiques, but this space was intended for someone who liked little fuss.

She thought perhaps she'd stumbled into a meeting area since it was so sterile. A breeze came in through doors that were open to the night air and she headed toward them. She hadn't been outside since she'd arrived, and she wondered what it would be like in the desert at night.

She stepped onto a wide terrace. The city lights spread out around her and, in the distance, the darkness of the desert was like a crouching tiger waiting for an excuse to pounce. She moved to the railing and stood, gripping it and sucking in the clean night air. It was chilly now, which amazed her considering how hot it had been when she'd arrived.

A frisson of excitement dripped down her spine. It surprised her, but in some ways it didn't. She'd never been to the desert before. Never been to an Arab country with dunes and palaces and camels and men who wore headdresses and robes. It was foreign, exotic and, yes, exciting in a way. She wanted to explore. She wanted to ride a horse into that desert and see what was out there.

She heard a noise behind her, footsteps across tile, and she whirled with her heart in her throat. How would she explain her presence here to her guard? To anyone?

But it wasn't just anyone standing there. It was a man she recognized on a level that stunned her. Rashid al-Hassan stood in a shaft of light, his chest and legs bare. He looked like an underwear model, she thought crazily, all lean muscle and golden flesh. He was not soft—not that she'd expected he would be after he'd pressed her against him—but the corrugated muscle over his abdomen was a bit of a sensual shock. Real men weren't supposed to look like that.

"What are you doing here, Miss Sloane?" he demanded, his voice hard and cold and so very dangerous.

The warmth that had been undulating through her like a gentle wave abruptly shut off.

Run! That was the single word that echoed in her brain.

But she couldn't move. Her limbs were frozen. Not only that, but Rashid al-Hassan also stood between her and escape....

CHAPTER SIX

SHERIDAN SUCKED IN a deep breath and pulled her robe tighter, even though it couldn't protect her from the fury in his dark eyes. She thought of Fatima's fearful look earlier today and wondered if perhaps this man was more frightening than she'd thought. Her blood ran cold.

"The door was open. I—I wanted to see outside."

"You are in my quarters, Miss Sloane."

Oh, dear. "I'm sorry. I didn't know."

He still hadn't moved. He stood in the door, his broad frame imposing. She told herself not to look below the level of his chin. She failed.

"So you decided to wander in the middle of the night and open random doors?"

She twisted the tie of her robe. "Something like that. I'm on a different schedule than you, I'm afraid. Wide-awake and nothing to do."

"Nothing to do." His voice was somehow full of meaning. Or perhaps she imagined it.

"I didn't mean to disturb you."

He still looked imposing and impossible. And then he shoved his hand through his hair and moved out of the doorway and onto the terrace. Sheridan stood frozen.

"You didn't disturb me. I was awake."

"You should try hot milk. It helps with insomnia." Oh, no, she was babbling. Sheridan bit her lip and told herself to shut up. This man was dangerous, for heaven's sake. Not at all the sort to put up with babbling in the middle of the night.

"I don't need much sleep," he said. "And I don't like hot milk."

"I don't either, actually. But I understand it works for some."

He went and leaned on the railing, near her. She thought she should take this opportunity to escape, and yet she was curious enough to want to stay. He made her nerves pop and sing. It was an interesting sensation.

"When it's light, you can see all the way to the gulf from here," he said. He lifted his hand. "In that direction, you can see the dunes of the Kyrian Desert. The Waste is out there, too."

"The Waste?" She moved closer, reached for the railing and wound her fingers around the iron.

He turned his head toward her. "A very harsh, very hot part of the desert. There is no water for one hundred miles. The sands are baked during the day, and at night they give up their heat and turn cool. You can freeze out there, if you don't die of heatstroke during the day."

It was hard to imagine such a place in this day and age. "Surely there are ways to bring water into it."

"There are. But there is no reason to do so. It would be cost prohibitive, for one thing. And who would live there? There are nomads, but the people who are accustomed to the cities would never go."

"Have you been there?"

He didn't speak for a long moment. "I have. There is an oasis midway. It was once part of a trade route across the desert. I went as a boy. It was part of my training as an al-Hassan."

She could imagine this harsh, dark man out there now. But as a child? It seemed so dangerous and uncertain. "I've never been to a desert before. I've never been anywhere but the Caribbean. Until now, I mean."

He looked at her. "Are you more comfortable now that you have a television and internet access?"

"It helps. But I'm still used to doing more than I have the last day. I like to be busy."

"Consider it a vacation."

"That would be easier if it actually were."

"Miss Sloane—"

"Sheridan. Please." Because she felt so out of place when he called her Miss Sloane. She needed him to acknowledge her as more than a random stranger. Because, regardless of whether or not there was a baby, they'd shared something incredibly intimate. Even if it had been clinical.

"Sheridan."

She shivered at the sound of her name on his lips. Why? Because it sounded like a silken caress. "Thank you," she said.

"I was going to say that I realize this is not easy for you. It is not easy for me, either."

"I know."

He turned to look out at the city lights and she watched the play of the wind in his hair and the soft glow of moonlight on his profile. He was a very beautiful man. And a lonely one. She didn't know why she thought he was lonely, but she did.

"I have decided to give you what you've requested," he said, and her heart thrummed. "I want your stay to be pleasant. If it pleases you to talk to me, then I will grant it."

She was surprised and pleased at once. "I appreciate that very much."

They stood there in silence for a long moment. "It is an extraordinary length to go to, to have a baby for someone else."

She felt a touch defensive. "It's not just for anyone. Annie is my sister."

"I am aware of this."

Sheridan sighed. The night breeze whipped up then, just for a moment, and she shivered. "She and Chris have tried and tried. They've seen doctors and been through one treatment after another. Nothing seems to work." She gripped the railing tightly, staring off toward the flickering lights of the city. "There was one doctor who mentioned an experimental treatment in Europe. Annie wanted to do it, and Chris would do anything for her. But the cost… Well, it's a lot. And there are no guarantees. They would have to sell everything and then hope…" She swallowed the lump in her throat. "I offered to step in before they went deeper into debt."

"So you would put your own life on hold to have this child for your sister. And then you would hand him or her over as if the previous nine months had happened to her instead of you."

The lump in her throat wouldn't go away. She hugged her arms around herself to keep from shivering. The air seemed colder now. "I didn't say it would be easy, but it's what you do when you love someone. You make sacrifices."

He seemed very quiet and still as he watched her. She'd expected him to make some sort of remark, but he said nothing at all. It began to worry her, though she didn't quite know why. She cleared her throat softly and told him the truth.

"I don't quite know what to say to you," she admitted. "I never know if you're angry or if you're just the kind of man who doesn't speak much."

He was looking at her with renewed interest. "I'm not angry. I'm frustrated."

"We're both frustrated."

"Are we?"

"I…" She sensed that this conversation had moved out of her control somehow. His eyes glittered in the night. He seemed suddenly very intense. And very— dear heaven—*naked*. "Yes, uh, of course. Why wouldn't we be? This is a frustrating circumstance."

"I find it very interesting that you could be carrying my child, and yet we've never been intimate. I've never undressed you, never tasted your skin."

She was growing hot now. So very hot. "Well, er…"

"Have you thought of it, Sheridan? After that kiss, have you wondered?"

Her heart hammered hard. Another moment and she would be dizzy. Yes she'd thought of that kiss. And she'd thought of her flesh pressed against his, nothing between them but skin and heat. She'd wondered what it would be like to be this man's lover. This dynamic, incredible man.

"Of course I have," she said, shocking herself with the admission. And him, too, if the way his muscles seemed to coil tight beneath his skin was any indication. He was like a great cat ready to pounce. The Lion of Kyr, indeed. "But that doesn't mean I want to do anything about it."

Liar.

"Then I think perhaps you should be more careful which rooms you wander into in the middle of the night."

His voice was icy again, yet it was somehow hot, too. Not menacing, but promising in a way that had her limbs quivering.

"I didn't know this was your room. And I didn't come here for…for…"

She couldn't finish the sentence. Her ears were hot, which was ridiculous because she wasn't a naive virgin. She hadn't had many lovers—well, only two, in fact—but that didn't mean she didn't know what happened when a man and a woman got naked together.

But it was the imagining that was killing her here. Rashid was beautiful, dark and dangerous and mysterious, and the idea of him completely focused on her body was more arousing than she could have imagined possible. She reminded herself that she didn't like him, but her body didn't seem to care. *So what?* That was the message throbbing in her sex, her veins, her belly. A relentless throb of tension and yearning that would only be broken if this man took her to his bed.

"Perhaps you did not," he said smoothly, "but you want it nevertheless. I can see it in your eyes, Sheridan."

She tried to stiffen in outrage. She was fully aware her nipples had beaded tight against the silk of the robe. Instead of trying to hide them, she wrapped her arms beneath her breasts and hugged herself against the chill air. Not that she was all that cold with Rashid al-Hassan looking at her like he might devour her. Which was a bit of a shock since she'd convinced herself that he wasn't really attracted to her.

Apparently she was wrong.…

"You're being too polite, Rashid. You mean to say you can see it in my nipples, but the truth is it's cold out here," she said brazenly. "It has nothing to do with you."

"I'm not the kind of man one issues challenges to, *habibti*. I have a pathological need to prove the issuer wrong."

She took a step backward. "We don't know each other well enough. Touch me and I'll scream."

He laughed. It was completely unexpected. She didn't like the warmth dripping into her limbs at the sound. "You forget this is the royal palace of Kyr and I am the king. If I wish to tie you to my bed and have my way with you on a nightly basis, there is no one who will stop me."

Her heart hammered. She wasn't supposed to be titillated by the idea of being tied to Rashid's bed. And yet she was.

He moved then, toward her, and she didn't even try to get away. She was frozen like a gazelle, waiting for the big cat to strike. And strike he did. He tugged her against him, her body in the thin silk robe flush to his naked flesh, and spread his hands over her backside.

Yet he didn't hold her tight. She could escape if she wished. She knew it and he knew it—and she didn't even try.

He laughed again, softly, triumphantly. "Such a liar, Sheridan," he said thickly. And then his mouth came down on hers.

If the kiss in her store had been surprising in its intensity, this one was downright earth-shattering. Rashid's tongue traced the seam of her lips and she opened to him, tangling her tongue with his almost eagerly.

The sensations rioting through her were more intense than she ever recalled experiencing before. It was the hormones from the shots, she told herself—but it was also the man. He was more exciting than anyone she'd ever known. Which didn't make any sense because he was also the least likable person she'd ever known.

Not to mention she didn't even really know him at all. He was a king, a desert sheikh, an autocratic ruler accustomed to ordering people around and getting his way.

And she was giving him precisely what he expected.

But it felt so good. Their tongues fought a blistering duel, her skin grew moist and impossibly hot and wetness flooded her sex. Her limbs were weakened by the kiss and she lifted her arms to put them around his neck. The shock of his hot skin beneath hers made her whimper.

Rashid turned her until her back was against the railing—and then he untied her robe and slipped it off her shoulders. The next thing she knew, his hot mouth was tracing a path down the column of her throat while she threaded her fingers into his dark hair and clutched him to her.

His teeth bit down on her nipple through the silken fabric of her nightgown and she gasped. It wasn't a hard bite, but it had the effect of sending pleasure shooting straight to her core. Her body clenched hard with desire as she gripped his shoulders and thrust her breasts toward his mouth.

She wanted him to remove the thin tissue of silk between his mouth and her body, but he didn't. He licked her through the fabric, nibbled and sucked until she was wild with need. Her nipples were more sensitive than ever since she'd had the hormone shots. If he did nothing but this all night, she knew she would come from the stimulation.

But he had no intention of doing only that. He reached down and gathered the hem of her nightie, lifting it up her legs, exposing her. Sheridan thought she needed to protest, but some needy, wicked part of her really didn't want to.

Rashid's hands glided beneath her gown, up the flesh of her abdomen, until he was cupping her breasts beneath the fabric, his hot hands spanning her skin, making it burn.

His mouth claimed hers again. It wasn't a tender kiss, or even a teasing kiss. It was a full-out assault on her senses. He stepped in closer, pinning her body to the railing with his much bigger, much harder one.

And that was when she felt him. That insistently hard part of him that pressed into her, letting her know that he was every bit as affected by the tension and heat between them as she was.

Sheridan acted instinctively. She reached for him, cupped her hands over that hard part of him she shouldn't crave but did. It had been so long since she'd been with anyone and she was suddenly ravenous. Rashid made a noise, a growl of satisfaction or encouragement in his throat. A thrill shot through her.

She'd thought he'd be disgusted by her, but that clearly wasn't the case. He wanted her. And, right now, she wanted him. It was insane, but nothing about this situation was normal. If she slept with him, what would change? Not a damn thing.

She pushed her hands beneath his briefs, cupped him in her hands. He was big and full and so very ready that it almost scared her. She didn't know this man at all, and what she did know hadn't been very pleasant up until this point.

He'd threatened her, taken her against her will and brought her here and treated her as if she was someone he'd hired to do a job instead of a woman caught up in a mistake not of her own making. He'd been angry with her, and he'd started this to prove a point, to punish her.

Now he was in her hands, his body hard and taut and ready. He broke the kiss and stared down at her, his eyes dark and deep and so fathomless she was almost frightened. But he was just a man, she reminded herself, and he'd not harmed her. He'd never given a single indication that he would force her to do anything she didn't want to do.

"Sheridan," he growled, his voice as tight as she'd yet heard it. "If you don't mean to give yourself to me, you need to leave. Now. Because if you continue to touch me like that, I'm not stopping until I've tasted you as thoroughly as I desire."

Sheridan bit her lip as her heart skittered recklessly in her chest. A sane woman would leave right this instant. A sane woman would not give her body to a man she barely knew simply because he made her feel more excited than she'd ever felt before.

She was not precisely sane at this moment. Maybe it was the heat of the desert, or the sand, or the opulent palace. She had no idea, but she wanted things she shouldn't want.

"I don't want to leave. I don't want to stop touching you."

With a groan, he swept her up into his arms and carried her through the door.

CHAPTER SEVEN

SOMEWHERE ON THE trip to his bed, panic began to flood her system. But before she could react, he set her on the bed and stripped her nightgown from her body. And then he was hovering over her, kissing her until her fear melted and her body caught on fire again.

Oh, this was so wrong—and so right. Sheridan put her arms around him, ran her hands over his broad back, the thick muscles and tendons, down his biceps and over his pecs. He was magnificent, and he no doubt knew it.

He left her mouth to lick his way to her breasts again. He took his time, sliding his tongue around and around before he sucked one aching nipple into his mouth. Sheridan cried out with the intensity of the pleasure spiking through her.

"You are sensitive," he murmured, his breath hot against her skin and yet cold where it drifted over her wet nipple. "So sensitive."

Sheridan couldn't speak. Her stomach churned with anticipation and, yes, even fear. Because what was she doing? Part of her brain kept wondering, but the rest refused to entertain any alternatives to what was currently happening.

And then Rashid moved down her body, his hands

spanning her hips and peeling her panties down until he pulled them free and dropped them somewhere on the floor. She could see his beautiful face illuminated by moonlight, see the vaulted ceilings of the chamber, hear the exotic sounds of the Kyrian night drifting inside—and it made her feel as if she wasn't herself. As if this was a fantasy. A thousand and one Arabian nights with her own desert king.

Sheridan bowed up off the bed as he touched his mouth to the wet seam of her body. The pleasure was so intense, so spellbinding, that she practically sobbed his name. He gave her no relief from the feelings rocketing through her. He held her legs open and licked her until she was a shuddering mass of nerve endings.

Sheridan's world exploded in a white-hot blaze of light, her body tightening almost painfully before soaring over the edge. But before she could manage to come back to herself, Rashid was there, his mouth capturing hers, demanding her full attention. She melted into his kiss.

And then she felt him, big and hard and poised at her body's entrance. He put a hand under her bottom, lifted her toward him. She wrapped her legs around him, her heart pounding as she waited for what happened next.

He seemed to hesitate for a long moment. And then he said something in Arabic, some muttered phrase, before he pushed into her body. He didn't move fast, didn't jam himself inside her. He took his time. And then he was deep within her, the two of them joined in the most intimate of ways, and fresh panic began to unwind inside her belly.

What was she doing? What was wrong with her? Sex with a stranger wasn't like her at all!

Rashid's head dropped slowly toward hers and she closed her eyes, tilting her mouth up until he captured it. She sighed—or maybe that was him. But then he started to move and she no longer cared about anything except what he was doing to her.

He was gentle at first. But as she arched her body into his, he took her harder and harder, until they were moving into each other in an almost punishing rhythm. She ran her hands over his skin until he gripped her wrists and shoved her hands over her head, binding her.

It was erotic, sensual and utterly exhilarating. Their skin grew hot and moist as they tangled together and the tension inside her coiled tighter than the lid on a pressure cooker.

And then she couldn't hold on a moment longer. He was too good at this, too compelling, and she came in a rush of blinding intensity that left her gasping for air and crying his name at the same time.

She felt his body tighten inside hers, and then he flew over the edge with her, his breath a harsh groan in her ear. They lay together for a few moments, hearts pounding, skin slicked with perspiration, breaths razoring in and out. Sheridan's legs trembled from gripping his hips so tightly with her thighs. She eased them down and lay still beneath him, her eyes closed and her brain finally began to whir into consciousness again.

What did one say after sex like that? Especially with a man you hardly knew and definitely didn't like?

She didn't get a chance to find out.

He pushed off her and stood, and cool air wafted over her skin, chilling her. She wanted to grab the covers and pull them up, and yet she couldn't seem to move. Because he was staring down at her, his face stark in the darkness, his chest rising and falling with more than exertion.

He was angry. Or tormented. She wasn't sure which, and it alarmed her. She sat up and wrapped her arms around her knees, trying to hide herself.

"Thank you, Sheridan," he said, his voice so courteous and calm. And cold. Sheridan shivered at the frost in his tone. He bent down a moment and then straightened, laying her nightgown and underwear on the bed at her feet. "Get dressed and I will escort you back to your room."

Rashid was up at dawn. He'd tossed and turned for the past couple of hours in a bed that still smelled like the woman he'd shared it with. The corners of his mouth turned down in a frown as his stomach twisted with guilt.

But why should that be? He enjoyed sex as well as the next man. He'd only ever loved one woman with his heart, but he'd loved many women in the physical way. He was not a monk and he hadn't been celibate for the past five years. It had taken him over a year to take a woman to his bed again, but he'd done so.

Sex with Sheridan Sloane was nothing out of the ordinary for him. And yet it was. Because she might be carrying his child, and though he'd been so focused and intent on her body, on tasting her and enjoying her, he hadn't expected the gravity of that fact to hit him with such a jolt after he'd found his pleasure in her body.

He'd bedded the woman who could be pregnant with his heir. A woman he didn't love, but who he would have to take as his wife if she was.

Still, he should be happy he'd finally released some

of this pent-up tension. He was not. He was strangely restless. Keyed up.

Ready to explore Sheridan's creamy skin and secret recesses again and again.

That was the part that unnerved him. The sex had been pretty spectacular, hot and exciting and intense, and he'd been utterly focused on it, lost in it.

But then it was over and they'd lain there together, breathing hard, her heart throbbing against his own—and he'd wanted to escape. He didn't understand how he could be so cold and unemotional one minute and so gutted the next.

She'd gutted him. Sex with her had gotten into his head in a way that sex with other women did not—and he didn't like it one bit. So he'd risen and gone to get her robe from the terrace while she dressed. When he'd come back, he'd handed it to her silently. It had been cold from being outdoors, but she'd put it on anyway and belted it tight.

Then he'd escorted her back to her quarters because he hadn't been certain she could find her way alone. She hadn't spoken on the walk back down the corridors. He'd stopped in front of the door to the women's quarters, vowing to himself to station a guard there at night in the future instead of outside the entrance to the private wing.

There was another way to her rooms, through his own, but he'd refused to use it. It would be too easy to go through that entry again if he started now, so he simply didn't.

She'd hesitated at the door as if she wanted to say something to him, but he'd put his hands in her hair and held her face up for his kiss. To silence her. To end any awkwardness.

When she'd been rubbery and clinging to him, when his body was beginning to respond with fresh heat that he knew would ignite into a fire at any moment, he'd let her go, striding away without another word.

Her reaction had been a very resounding door slam. But it was for the best, really. He had too much to do, too many things to worry about, and no time to navigate the mire of repeatedly bedding a woman who might be carrying his heir. A woman who might soon be his wife.

If she was angry with him, so much the better. He'd intended to be nice to her, but he'd gone way overboard. And now he would have to stay away from her, as he'd intended in the first place.

Sheridan didn't believe that Rashid would come to see her that day. After the confusing—and paradigm changing—previous night, she didn't really think his decision to talk to her would stand.

And of course she was right. As the day wore into night, there was no sign of Rashid. She was allowed to wander the palace, as he'd promised, but she did not bump into him anywhere. She wore one of the dresses from the dressmaker, along with a hijab that covered her hair, and then she spent fascinating hours walking through the palace and studying the architecture.

But in spite of her enjoyment of everything the palace had to offer, she remained preoccupied with Rashid. With last night. She couldn't think of it without blushing. She'd had sex with him—hot, wild, crazy, passionate sex—after knowing him for two days.

Worse, she wanted more. She knew it wasn't going to

happen—that it *shouldn't* happen—but she couldn't help but imagine Rashid coming to her room in the night. He would peel her clothing away, and then use that magical mouth of his to drive her insane with wild need.

Sheridan fanned herself absently with her hand. The guard who strode silently along wherever she went didn't bat an eyelash. She'd tried to talk to him about mundane things, but he remained silent.

When she ventured out to the stables after dinner, he followed. But when she tried to touch one of the horses, just to pet its velvety nose, he stopped her.

"His Majesty would not want you to get bitten, miss."

"I've been around horses before," she said, more than a little surprised that he spoke English. She'd started to think he was ignoring her because he didn't speak her language. "I think I can tell when they're going to bite."

Still, she strolled along until they came to a room at the end of the stable. She looked over the top of the door and practically melted.

"Puppies!" She turned to her guard. "What kind of dogs are they?"

He seemed to hesitate, as if he didn't want to engage in conversation, but then he relented. "They are Canaan dogs, miss. A hardy and ancient breed."

The puppies were small and squat, and had curled tails. They almost looked like huskies, except they weren't gray and didn't have thick fur. The mother dog was nowhere to be seen at the moment.

"They're precious."

Sheridan stood and watched the puppies wiggling happily, playing and yipping, and wished she could go in and sit down and let them climb all over her. But she knew her guard wouldn't approve of that. Eventually, the sound of approaching hoofbeats made her turn her head. A man in desert robes sat astride a beautiful bay horse as it trotted toward the stable. When they reached the building, he swung down and handed the reins to a groom, who had appeared out of nowhere.

And then the man turned his head until dark glittering eyes met hers, boring into her with that combination of heat and anger that seemed unique to Rashid. Her belly clenched at the primal recognition that stirred to life inside her.

Beside her, her guard had dropped into a low bow. Sheridan, not quite knowing what to do, decided to curtsy. Oh, she was plenty angry with Rashid, but she would not create trouble by refusing to acknowledge his power over his subjects. She wasn't stupid and she knew it was important to have her guard's respect.

Rashid's eyes narrowed—and then he came toward her. His gaze raked over her, taking in the hijab and dress—which she'd realized weren't strictly necessary since she'd seen women in his palace dressed in Western business attire—before landing on her face again.

"Miss Sloane, isn't it a bit late to be touring the stables?"

Miss Sloane. As if he hadn't been inside her just a few hours ago. She lifted her chin. "I believe I already established that I'm still on a different sleep schedule than Kyr. Though it isn't quite eight o'clock here yet, which I would consider early even were I acclimated to your time zone."

Her heart thundered relentlessly in her breast as she stared at him. He was no longer quite the stranger he'd been before last night's passionate encounter, and it disconcerted her.

He turned his attention to the guard. "Leave us."

The guard rose and melted into the night. Sheridan felt a hot wash of anger move through her.

"I realize you're a king, but do you have to talk to people like that?"

His brows drew down. "Like what? I told him what he needed to know. Do you prefer I ask him politely to go?"

"It might be nice, but no, I don't really expect that out of you."

"You sound like my brother."

She blinked. "Do I? Is he a nice, sensible man?"

"Nicer than I am."

"So you admit you aren't very nice."

"I'm not trying to be." He shrugged. "I am who I am. I don't have to explain myself to anyone."

She dropped her gaze. It was an odd conversation in some respects. Odd because of what they'd done the night before, and odd because she could feel that fire beneath the surface. It was only waiting for ignition.

"After last night, I really didn't expect an explanation."

Oh, wow, had she really said that? She wanted to bite her tongue.

He searched her features. "You are upset because I did not allow you to stay in my bed."

"Allow?" She resisted the urge to poke him in the chest, but only barely. "What makes you think I wanted to stay? We were finished and it would have been awkward to stay. You don't strike me as the type for small talk, and I'd rather not have to attempt it. It was better that I left."

His dark eyes flashed with some unidentifiable emotion. "You continually surprise me. I thought you would be upset. Regretful. Wringing your hands and wishing you could undo the things we did together."

She shrugged as if casual sex was her thing when it really wasn't. "Why would I want to undo it? It was nice."

"Nice?" His voice was a growl and she suddenly wanted to laugh. Even superior kings had fragile egos when it came to their performance in bed. Hint that you were less than satisfied and you found yourself faced with a dangerously tense male animal with a point to prove.

"Unlike *you,* yes, it was nice. Very nice, if you insist."

He stiffened. And then he laughed softly. Once more, the sound of his laughter had a way of surprising her. It was as if he didn't laugh often enough and wasn't quite sure how. "You are baiting me. I see it now. If I said the moon was golden tonight, you'd say it was yellow."

That pesky warmth was flowing in her limbs again. Her body ached with his nearness, and though she had another, more immediate ache between her thighs to remind her of his possession, that didn't stop her from wanting it again.

"And what am I supposed to be baiting you into?" Her voice was huskier than she would have liked it. But he already knew how he affected her. One corner of his mouth lifted in a superior grin.

"Perhaps you want another demonstration of my niceness."

Heat flooded her cheeks. "Hardly. Once was enough, thank you."

Once was not enough. And that really worried her. Why did she want him? It wasn't like her to crave a man the way she craved him after only one night. Plus, this was too complicated. They weren't dating. This wasn't a man she'd met in Savannah, a man with the freedom and ability to pursue a relationship with her.

This was a king. A man who ruled a desert nation. A man who was so unlike any man she'd ever known that he confused her. He was arrogant, bossy and he already acted as if he owned her.

And she *let* him. She'd always thought she was a feminist, but the way he made her behave was decidedly not liberated. It was needy, physical and completely focused on sexual pleasure. If he threw her into a stall right now and had his way with her on the hay, she'd only urge him on.

He moved away from her and she tried not to let her disappointment show.

"Come, I will take you back to your quarters."

She threw another glance at the puppies before joining him. They walked side by side, but not touching, toward the palace.

"You like puppies?" he said.

"I love puppies. I've never had a dog, but I plan to get one some day."

"You've never had a dog?"

She shook her head as they walked across the courtyard. "My sister was bitten by a neighbor's dog when she was four. So we never got one because she was too scared."

"That hardly seems fair," he said.

Sheridan felt that old familiar prick of resentment flaring deep inside. It was followed, as always, by guilt. It wasn't Annie's fault.

"Maybe not, but she cried whenever my parents

talked about getting a dog for the family, so they gave up. We didn't even have a cat."

"Did a cat bite her, too?"

Sheridan stopped abruptly. Rashid was a few steps ahead when he turned toward her, waiting. "She had allergies," Sheridan said. "And it's not her fault."

He moved toward her again. She had to tilt her head back to look up at him. He bristled with a coiled energy that she was certain contained a hint of anger. At her? At Annie?

"Perhaps not, but it seems to me as if your sister's problems have done nothing but impact your life. Did you always give up everything you wanted for her sake?"

Sheridan's chest grew tight. The lump in her throat was huge. "Don't talk to me that way. You don't know my sister and you have no right to judge her. Annie's fragile. She needs me."

His gaze raked her face. "Yes, she needs you. She needs you to acquiesce to her demands, to give her what she wants, to provide the thing she believes she's been cheated out of."

Sheridan gasped. And then she reacted. She moved to slap him, but he caught her wrist and held it tight. His dark eyes were hard. And filled with a sympathy she'd not seen there before.

She was shaking deep inside. "How dare you? Annie didn't ask me to have this baby for her. I offered! And I'm going to do it, even if it takes another year to start again."

He ran his fingers down her cheek tenderly, and she trembled. "Of course you offered, *habibti*. Because you love her and because you were afraid for her. I don't fault you for this. I fault her for refusing to see what it might cost you."

She shook her head softly. "They are paying for the procedure and the birth. It's not costing me anything."

He let her go and stepped back. His mouth was a white line now. "It costs nine months of your life, it places a burden on your body and then there is the emotional impact of giving up the child at the end. That is not *nothing*."

He was confusing her. Just a couple of days ago he'd suggested she turn over any child to him and now he was talking about the emotional impact of that kind of decision. Who was this man?

"I knew that when I offered."

His expression was black. "Yes, but did you also know that you were offering to risk your life? Did you consider that? Did she?"

Sheridan's heart pounded. "Childbirth is safe. This isn't the eighteenth century."

He stood stone-still but she sensed his muscles had coiled tight. As if he was a nuclear reaction waiting to happen. But then he pulled in a deep breath and huffed it out again and she knew he'd found the switch to turn it off.

"Of course it's not. You are correct."

Sheridan had a strong urge to reach for him, but she didn't. Something was bothering him. Some dark emotion reflected in his gaze, but she wasn't quite sure what it was.

"What's this about, Rashid?"

"It's not about anything," he finally said.

Her voice was little more than a whisper. "I don't believe you."

He stood there for a long moment, as if he was fighting an internal battle. And then he turned and strode away without another word, disappearing into the long gallery running along the back of the palace.

CHAPTER EIGHT

THE DAYS PASSED too slowly. Sheridan kept hoping to see Rashid, but he seemed to be avoiding her. She emailed with Kelly, planned the menus for two upcoming parties and felt guilty for not being there to help with the physical preparations. But there was really no need. Dixie Doin's operated like the efficient party machine it was meant to be.

Sheridan had spent a lot of time making sure that was so when she'd decided to have a baby for her sister. Though she'd intended to work until the birth, there were never any guarantees and she'd wanted to be prepared for anything.

Kelly hardly missed her, though she assured Sheridan that she missed her personally. Emails from Annie were another story. Sheridan dreaded to open them. She knew Annie was upset, but the lack of understanding about the situation made her stomach hurt. Her sister actively hoped that the IUI had failed. Sheridan understood that wish, understood it would be the easiest thing for them all. She'd thought the same thing when she'd first been told, but now that she was here with Rashid and he was real to her, not just a random sperm donor, the situation was much more complicated.

She thought of the man who had touched her so sensually, the man who heated her blood and chilled her bones and confused her to no end. No, this situation was no longer random and impersonal. It had ceased to be so the instant he'd walked into her life.

If Rashid hadn't come looking for her in Savannah, what would Annie have wanted her to do? Sheridan didn't want to know, and yet she couldn't help thinking about it. Would Annie have wanted this baby, too? Or would she have wanted Sheridan to terminate the pregnancy so she could start fresh with Chris's sperm?

She didn't even know if she was pregnant yet, but already she was emotional over the idea of losing this baby. Would it have been simpler if she'd never met Rashid, never slept with him?

Probably, but it was too late for that.

Sheridan took her usual route through the palace, stopping in the kitchen to see the staff and find out what they were preparing. She was fascinated with the food here, the fresh olive oil and breads, the fruits and nuts, and the flavorful dishes made with chicken and goat. The staff seemed wary at first, but as her visits increased—and Daoud, her formerly silent guard, or Fatima translated for her—they began to look forward to her arrival.

She tasted food, oohed and aahed appropriately and discussed ingredients. She even made note of some things to try for Dixie Doin's. Not everything was Kyrian, however. There was plenty of French cuisine as well, which surprised her at first but not when she considered that the French had once sent colonists to Kyr.

If anyone found it odd that an American woman roamed the palace, they did not say so. In spite of the women she saw in business attire, she kept to the rules

Rashid had set and wore Kyrian clothing. She even wore the hijab, because when her blond hair was hidden people seemed less likely to see her as an outsider.

Not that all Kyrians had black hair—there were some brown and tawny gold heads she'd seen—but her hair was so pale as to be noticeable when uncovered.

She'd gone to see the puppies again. When there was no sign of the mother dog, she asked Daoud why. That was when she learned that the puppies were orphans. They were being bottle-fed and taken care of by the grooms. She'd had Daoud ask if she could feed them, though he'd seemed reluctant to let her.

But she'd done it, and then she'd found herself surrounded by yipping dogs while she giggled and petted them and watched them suck down the milk. They were so sweet and she loved spending time with them. It was the highlight of each day, especially as she never saw Rashid.

She thought about him. She lay in her bed at night with her hand over her belly and thought about the man she'd made love to only once. The man whose baby might be in her womb right now.

She wondered where he was, if he was in his own bed and thinking of her, or if that single night had been an aberration and he now gave her no more consideration than what he'd had for breakfast. Probably the latter, considering she hadn't seen him since that night when he'd left her standing in the darkened courtyard.

She'd considered walking down the corridor in the middle of the night again, opening his door and making him talk to her. But when she'd gotten brave enough to act on it, a guard had been stationed outside her own door. He'd looked up from his tablet computer, his eyes meeting hers steadily until she'd shut the door.

Clearly, Rashid had thought she might come looking for him and had taken steps to prevent it. She was somehow both embarrassed and furious at once at the notion.

Still, Sheridan went through the days and did not ask where Rashid was. If he thought she was pining for him, then she was going to prove she wasn't. How could she when he was still such a stranger?

An enigmatic, compelling stranger that she wanted to know better.

Soon it was the night before her pregnancy test and Sheridan couldn't seem to settle down. Her stomach was twisted in knots and nothing Fatima brought seemed appealing. She finally tried a little bread and some sparkling water and settled onto the couch to read for a bit when the door to her suite opened and Rashid walked in without preamble.

Emotion flooded her in an instant: happiness, anger, fear, sorrow. So many things it was hard to sort them all out, and all caused by this dark man who stood there in a smartly tailored gray suit and Kyrian headdress. Not for the first time, he made her heart skip a beat.

"Fatima says you aren't eating," he said, his voice tight and diamond edged. Just the way she expected it.

Of course he was getting reports about her. "I'm not hungry."

He came over and glared down at her. If he would put his hands on his hips, it would be the perfect admonishing parent pose.

"You have to eat. It's not good for you or the baby not to eat."

She put her hand over her belly automatically. "We don't know if there is a baby."

"We will know soon enough. Besides, it's better to assume there is a baby and do everything to take care of it properly."

She wanted to yell at him. "I didn't refuse, Rashid. I can't keep anything down right now. My stomach is upset." She set the book aside and matched his glare. "You promised we would spend some time together so we could know each other better, and yet I've not seen you in five days now."

His expression didn't ease. "I've been busy. This is what happens when one is a king."

"Yet you found time to come here tonight and chastise me for not eating."

He stripped off the *kaffiyeh* and tossed it aside. Then he raked a hand through his hair. "I came straight here from a meeting." He walked over to the table where Fatima had left food in chafing dishes and examined the contents. Then he picked up a plate and dished some things onto it.

Sheridan bristled. "If you think you're going to force me to eat—"

"Not at all," he said, picking up a fork and heading over to sit in a nearby chair. "I haven't eaten yet and I'm starving."

Sheridan blinked. After days of silence, he was planning to eat with her? He'd taken her to bed, made her feel things that excited and confused her and then when she'd been certain he was planning to do it again, he'd left her standing alone in the courtyard.

To say she didn't understand him was an understatement.

"Wow, I'm being graced with your majestic presence for dinner? I'm honored."

He looked up at her, his eyes gleaming. But not with anger. "You said you wanted to talk to me. Here I am. Talk. Bore me silly if you must."

She folded her arms. "Perhaps I'm a sparkling conversationalist. Did you ever consider that?"

"It has not been my experience with most women, but perhaps you will be different."

She told herself it would be unwise to throw a pillow at him. She chose instead to focus on one aspect of what he'd said. "Most women? Who has managed to please you conversationally?"

He took a bite of food, chewed and swallowed. She didn't think he would answer her, but then he looked up again and speared her with his hot gaze. "My wife did," he said. "Not always, it's true. But often enough. She died five years ago, in case you were wondering."

Her belly had tightened into a hot ball of nerves. Of all the things he could have said, she hadn't seen that one coming. Her heart ached for him. "I'm sorry, Rashid."

She didn't know what else to say. To lose someone you loved had to be such a tragedy. And someone so young, too. No wonder he sometimes seemed cold and lonely. It made sense now.

He set the plate aside. "This is not something I speak of, but if we are to marry, I thought you should know it."

Her throat was tight and her heart hammered in her stomach, her chest, her ears. "I appreciate you telling me. But I'm not certain marriage is the answer to our dilemma. Assuming there is one."

He frowned. "This child has to be born legitimate, Sheridan. It is the only way."

Panic bloomed inside her. She didn't want to take away a child's heritage, but she also didn't want to have to marry a man she hardly knew. They had sexual chemistry, but what if that was all they had? How could she live a lifetime with a man who'd only married her to claim a child?

"I assume I have no say in this?"

"You would prefer options? Marry me and be this child's mother, or go home after you give birth. Those are your options."

She figured it was a good thing there were no weapons nearby. "Those aren't options."

His eyes flashed. "They are the ones you have."

"I won't leave my child."

"No, I didn't think you would. I might have thought so once, but no longer."

Her head was beginning to ache. "And what brought about this blinding revelation?"

"Daoud tells me you've been playing with the puppies. Feeding them, taking care of them. And then there is my kitchen staff, Fatima and even the stable hands. They like you, and you like them. They all say how kind you are, how caring. Yet even without these things, there is this deed you set out to do for your sister. You are a giving person, Sheridan, but I don't believe you are so giving as to leave your child in Kyr. You will stay."

His words wrapped around her heart and squeezed. She liked Daoud, Fatima and the kitchen staff. To know they liked her, too, was touching. "There is every possibility I will go home tomorrow."

"Yes, there is."

Pain sliced into her at the thought. It confused her. She wanted to go home, wanted to go back to her life in Savannah, her business, her friends. She wanted her life the way it was before Rashid al-Hassan had walked into it.

And yet that thought filled her with despair. Never to see him again? Never to make love to him? He didn't seem much bothered either way, and that hurt, too.

"All this talk of marriage is premature," she said tightly.

"Is it? We will know tomorrow. If you are pregnant, things must be done quickly."

"And you've already decided everything. Without asking me what I might want."

It was just like him, of course. King Rashid acted. He did not consult a soul. He simply did what he deemed best. Just like when he'd scooped her up and brought her to Kyr against her will.

"I have told you your options." His voice was smooth and even, as if he was explaining things to a child.

Anger wrapped long fingers around her throat and squeezed. "I still have Annie to consider. What about her?"

His expression grew hard. Hard and cold and unapproachable. "What about her?"

That was the moment when the bile in Sheridan's stomach started swirling hard, pushing upward, demanding release. She got to her feet and staggered toward the bathroom. She barely made it in time, and then she was bending over the sink, retching.

There was a hand in her hair, holding it back. He put another hand on her back and rubbed gently while tears sprang to her eyes and she felt utterly miserable. She wanted to tell him to stop touching her, but in fact it felt nice to have him soothe her. She was a traitor even to herself.

"I'm not trying to be harsh," he said, his voice gentle for once. "But your sister cannot figure into my dynastic responsibilities. There are other solutions to her problem. You told me yourself about an experimental treatment."

Sheridan put her hands on the counter, bracing herself, her eyes squeezed shut as she prayed there was nothing else left to come up.

"They can't afford it," she said miserably when she could speak.

"I can."

Sheridan turned on the water and gulped some down before she straightened shakily and turned to face him. His beauty always hit her with a punch and now was no exception. A king had just held her hair while she'd thrown up the little bit of food she'd managed to eat.

If anyone had ever told her such a thing could happen, she'd have never believed them.

"You would do that for them?" Her heart was still pounding, but for a different reason now. It was everything she could have wanted for Annie. There were no guarantees the treatment would work, but it was a chance.

"I would not do it for them," Rashid said very softly. "I would do it for you."

Rashid watched her mouth fall open on a soft "oh" and was seized with a desire to claim her lips and take everything he desired. But she wasn't feeling well, and he hadn't come here for that anyway.

No, he'd come because Fatima had said she wasn't eating. And because he'd been getting endless reports about her roaming the palace, commenting on the architecture, talking with endless people, playing with orphaned puppies and spending time in the kitchen discussing recipes and food service.

At a recent lunch he'd attended with some visiting dignitaries, the napkins were folded in shapes. They had been lotus flowers, he'd realized, and he'd been so fascinated that he'd missed the first half of what one of the dignitaries had been saying to him about water rights and oil production.

When he'd asked about it afterward, someone had told him that Miss Sloane had taught the staff how to do it. Lotus napkins. Puppies. Even Daoud spoke her name with a quiet reverence that set Rashid's teeth on edge.

Everyone liked Miss Sloane, and that had made him think about her more than he wished. He liked her, too, but in a different way. He liked the way her body moved beneath his, the sounds she made when she came and the way her mouth tasted his so greedily. He'd thought about it for days now.

He'd deliberately stayed away because he didn't trust himself not to act upon the hot feelings she ignited in him.

He'd been right, considering that he was staring at her mouth and thinking about it drifting over his skin.

Her eyes filled with tears. It was almost a shock, considering that she'd been so strong from the moment he'd first seen her until now. One spilled down her cheek and she quickly dashed it away.

"I don't know what to say." She pulled in a breath and rubbed her hand over her mouth.

His throat was tight and he didn't know why. He cleared it. "You need to rest, *habibti*."

She pushed a lock of golden hair behind her ear. Her fingers were trembling. "Yes, I probably should. I am quite tired."

She was sagging against the counter and he reached over and swept her into his arms.

"What are you doing?" she gasped.

She was so light, so small. She weighed nothing and it made something move deep in his chest as he thought of her huge with child. "Taking you to bed."

Her cheeks reddened. "I don't feel up to, to…"

He carried her into the bedroom and set her on the bed. "And that is not what I'm suggesting."

He picked up her gown from where it lay neatly folded on her pillow and handed it to her. She clutched it to her chest. On impulse, he ran his fingers over her cheek.

"Change. I'm going to finish eating. Then I will come back. If you still wish to talk, we will talk."

Her eyes were red rimmed. "All right."

He turned away and went back into the living area to finish eating while she changed. He didn't like the way she'd seemed so shattered just now. So stunned and confused. He preferred the Sheridan who stood up to him. The Sheridan who got spitting mad and told him there was no way she would give up her baby.

That Sheridan was strong and would survive anything he threw at her. Anything the world threw at her. But would she survive a baby? She was so small, so delicate.

Rashid couldn't help the memories crowding his head. They made him shiver, made him ache. He would not go through that again. His heart had to remain hard, no matter that Sheridan threatened to soften it.

When he figured she'd had enough time to change, he strode back toward her room, expecting her to pelt him with questions or rebuke him for making decisions for her. Perhaps he'd let her say whatever she wished, since her fire aroused him, and then maybe he'd undress and climb in bed with her. If one thing led to another, who was he to complain?

But when he got there, she was sound asleep in the middle of the bed.

CHAPTER NINE

"THE TEST IS POSITIVE."

The doctor, a lean, short man with glasses, was looking at the results on a printout. No peeing on a stick for Sheridan. It had been far more involved, with urine and blood samples and an excruciating wait while the lab processed the results. "Your hCG levels are doubling nicely and all looks normal at this stage."

Sheridan sat in her chair in Rashid's office and felt as if her heart had stopped. Across from her, Rashid sat at his desk, his lips compressed into a tight line. The doctor seemed oblivious to the undercurrents in the room as he stood and bowed low.

"Congratulations, Your Majesty."

Rashid waved the man out and then they were alone. But Rashid didn't speak. He simply sat there with that bloodless look on his face until her belly was a tight ball of nerves.

"I'm not sure I really believed it would happen the first time." Her voice shook but Rashid didn't seem to notice.

He looked up at her as if just realizing she was there. "What?"

But he didn't wait for an answer. He sprang to his

feet and began pacing like a caged beast. He was wearing his desert robes today, complete with the headdress held in place by a golden *igal*. He was regal and magnificent and breathtaking. She watched him pacing, her hand over her stomach, and tried to come to grips with the fact she was having his baby.

"We'll marry immediately. The council will have to be informed and then we can sign the documents. We can have a wedding ceremony for the public, but that can be done in a few weeks. You won't be showing by then and—"

"Stop." Sheridan was on her feet, her blood pounding in her throat and temples. She didn't know why she'd spoken, but she felt as if her entire life was altering right before her eyes and there was nothing she could do to stop the tidal wave of change.

Rashid was looking at her now, his dark gaze dangerous and compelling. She reminded herself that he was capable of tenderness. He had touched her tenderly only last night when holding her hair and rubbing her back. And then there was the night he'd made love to her, so hot and intense and, yes, tender in his own way.

"You're making all these plans without asking me how I feel about any of them."

His brows drew down. "This is the way things are done in Kyr. How would you know what the arrangements should be?"

She dug her fingernails into her palms. She was sweating, but not from illness. From shock. And fear.

"I wasn't talking about how things are done in Kyr. I'm talking about this marriage."

As if she could refuse it. She was here, in his palace, and he was a king. This child had to be born legitimate.

And he'd said he would pay for Annie's treatment. What more could she want?

Love. Yes, she could want love. She could want to marry a man because she loved him, not because she had to.

His gaze narrowed. "You are pregnant—this marriage will take place."

She held her arms stiffly at her sides. "Maybe I want to be asked. Did you ever consider that? Maybe I wanted to get married in an old church somewhere, with my family surrounding me, and maybe I wanted to be in love with the man I marry."

Oh, why say that out loud? Why let him know what a hopeless romantic you are?

His expression grew hard. "Life does not always give us what we want. We have to take what's offered and do the best we can with it."

Her heart fell. He was infuriating. Cold and calculating and arrogant. She wanted him to care, at least a little bit, about what this meant for her. To him, she was a woman who carried a potential king. He wanted to order her about the way he ordered Daoud or Fatima or Mostafa.

And she knew, if she knew nothing else, that she couldn't allow him to do that without protest.

"I didn't say yes yet. You're making plans and I didn't say yes."

There was a huge lump in her throat now. Huge. It was like she'd swallowed all the pain she'd ever felt and was about to choke on it.

He picked up a pen on his desk and flipped it in his fingers as if he needed something to do. As if he was irritated. "You are carrying my child and we are going to marry. There's nothing to say yes to." He fixed her with a hard stare. "But if you could say no, would you? Knowing what's at stake for everyone involved, would you say no and deny your child the opportunity to be my heir? Or your sister the chance to have her own child?"

Sheridan's throat hurt. "I didn't say that."

He threw the pen down and sank into his chair again. "Then I fail to see the problem. You will be a princess consort, *habibti*. You will have a life of privilege. And you will be the mother of our child, which is what you've assured me you want. Or am I mistaken? Would you rather leave the child with me and return to America once he is born?"

Sheridan clenched her fists in her lap. Once more, it was a good thing there were no weapons handy. "This baby might be a girl, you know. And no, I don't want to leave her with you."

"Then we will marry immediately and be done with this matter."

This matter. As if marriage and children were the equivalent of deciding where to go on vacation or which carpet to order for the new house.

"Thank you for settling that." Sheridan got to her feet. She was shaking with rage and fear, and sick with the helplessness she felt. "I guess I'll return to my rooms now and await your next command. How I got through life for twenty-six years without you to tell me what to do is quite the mystery. I'm pleased I don't have to think for myself a moment longer."

"Careful, Sheridan," he growled.

A sensual shiver traveled down her spine at the sound. Oh, what was it about him growling at her that turned her on? She'd just told him off for being autocratic, so why did part of her thrill at the edge in his voice?

"Why? If I make a mistake, you'll just tell me what to do to correct it." She sank into the deepest curtsy she'd yet done and then turned and strode toward the door. He was there before her, his arm shooting out and wrapping around her before she could escape.

Her breath caught as he spun her around. "You dare to walk out on a king?"

"You aren't *my* king," she said hotly. But her body was melting where it touched his and that inconvenient fire was beginning to sizzle through her.

"Maybe I am," he said, his voice heavy and angry at once. "Maybe I am utterly *your* king."

Her reply was lost as he ripped the hijab from her hair. "You're mine now, Sheridan," he said hotly, backing her against the wall and pressing his body to hers. "And I keep what's mine."

And then he brought his mouth down on hers. Sheridan stiffened. She was determined to fight him, to keep her mouth closed to his invasion, to push him away.

But she did none of those things. Of course she didn't. Rashid al-Hassan was an unstoppable sensual force and he had a power over her that she couldn't deny. His tongue slid between her lips, demanding her response— and then they were kissing each other frantically, hotly, with all the pent-up passion of the past few days of deprivation. She'd never had such a physical connection to a man before. A connection that went against sense and reason and just *was*.

His hands spanned her rib cage, his thumbs grazing her nipples as he pinned her body to the wall with his own. Her pulse raced as her nipples tightened painfully. Her breasts were so sensitive now and they both knew why.

He found the closures to her dress and opened them deftly. Then he was pushing the garment off her shoulders, letting it fall to the floor. She wrapped her arms around his neck and arched into him until he growled again and stepped back to rip her panties down her legs. She stepped out of them as she fumbled with the soft trousers he wore beneath his *dishdasha,* trying to free him.

He helped her and soon she had her hands on his hot erection. But he didn't give her a chance to play. His broad hands went to her bottom, lifted her high against the wall—and then he plunged into her as they both gasped.

"Sheridan." His voice was a hot whisper in her ear and her heart twisted tight. "I need you."

"Kiss me, Rashid," she begged. Her skin was too tight, her belly too hollow, her body too hot. She needed the things he gave her, needed the connection and release. She didn't understand it, but she craved it. Craved him.

He fused his mouth to hers—and then he began to drive up into her, harder and faster and deeper than before, until her body was alive with sensation, until she had to wrench her mouth from his and sob his name as she splintered apart in his arms.

He didn't release her, though. He took her again and again, until she was a quivering mass of nerve endings, until her body couldn't take another moment's pleasure, until he finally let go of his rigid control and came, his seed filling her in warm jets.

He laid his forehead against the wall behind her, his

breath coming in gusts. His skin was hot and moist and so was hers. She turned her head into him, tasted the salt on his skin on impulse.

And found herself released. He stepped away from her and fixed his trousers, then reached down and picked up her gown for her. She snatched it out of his hand and he met her gaze evenly.

They stared at each other for a long moment, her clutching the dress in front of her like a shield, him clenching his fingers into tight fists at his side. As if he wanted to touch her again but had to force himself not to.

Her legs were weak and anger bubbled hot in her veins, but if he reached for her, if he kissed her again, she'd open to him like a flower.

And she really despised that about herself. There was such a thing as being delightfully impulsive, as being friendly and open, but this was too much.

"I don't understand you," she said. "If you don't like being with me, why do you touch me in the first place?"

She thought they had a chemistry that was unusual, but maybe she was fooling herself. Maybe he just saw her as an option for quick sex. He found his pleasure in her body and he was done. And she was just stupid enough to make the same mistake twice.

He shoved a hand through his hair. "I like being with you. But it's over and I have work to do."

She shook out her dress angrily and slipped into it. Then she turned her back on him. "I can't do this without your help."

He came over and stood behind her, his fingers brushing her skin as he zipped her up and fastened the hooks. When he finished, she turned around and glared at him.

"This can't happen again," she told him tightly. "I

have feelings, Rashid, and I won't let you stomp all over them just to get your way. And another thing," she added, pointing at him. "There are women in this palace in dresses and business suits and slacks. I've seen them, and while I played along with your commands to dress as a Kyrian woman, I won't blindly do it anymore. Kyrian women seem to represent a range of styles, which you purposely did not tell me. If I want to wear my jeans, I'm wearing them."

His expression was tightly controlled. "When you appear before the council, you will wear traditional clothing. Aside from that, I don't care."

She lifted her chin as she met his dark stare. "Oh, I already gathered that, Rashid. You don't care at all."

Rashid met with the council and informed them he would be marrying, and why. The council wasn't pleased that Sheridan wasn't Kyrian, but they could hardly argue with the fact she was carrying his child.

"And would you consider a Kyrian woman for a second wife, Your Majesty?" one of the men asked.

Rashid let his hard stare glide over the gathering. They were good men, wise men, men whose families had spent generations on the council. And while they had gotten far more progressive over the years, they still clung to some traditions. A pure Kyrian dynasty was one of those, though they all knew that past sheikhs had sometimes married foreigners and had children with them. Still, it cost him nothing to appease them. They would not accept Sheridan as queen, but as a princess consort. And with a future queen of Kyrian descent to be named, they would be happy.

"I will," he said coolly. "But not immediately."

That seemed to satisfy them and the council was dismissed. Rashid returned to his office to work, but he couldn't seem to stop picturing Sheridan up against the wall, her lovely legs wrapped around him, her sweet voice panting in his ear as he took her over the edge.

He pushed back from his desk and sat there staring at the place where they'd been. He'd taken her like a savage. Like a man for whom control was impossible to attain, when nothing could be further from the truth.

She wound him into knots and he didn't like it. She'd said he didn't care, but he very much feared he might. Not a lot, certainly, but more than he was comfortable with. Because he couldn't stop thinking about her, or about how it felt to lose himself in her body.

He was not the sort of man to become obsessed with a woman, yet she intrigued him. Had from the first moment he'd seen her standing in her shop, all small and blond and seemingly sweet.

But then he'd kissed her and his world had gone sideways. He'd wanted her every moment since.

And he hated that he did.

She was pregnant. Thinking the words sent that same cold chill through him, as always—but there was something else, too. Pride, possession, ownership. She was carrying his child and he was going to marry her. For Kyr.

Rashid got to his feet and left the office, striding through the palace until he came to his rooms. It wasn't quite dark yet, but the hour was growing late. He changed into jeans—not without thinking of her informing him that she would be wearing her jeans whenever she wanted, that defiant tilt to her chin—and a button-down shirt, and then went through his suite of rooms to the hidden door that connected to the women's quarters.

He stood there for a long moment, staring at the lock. And then he released it and stepped inside. She wasn't in bed so he moved through the rooms until he saw her at the computer. She was hunched over it, her head in her hands, and his heart squeezed.

Then she reached for a tissue and he knew she was crying. Damn it. His fault, no doubt. Because he'd pushed her away. But how could he explain to her that being in her arms after they had sex felt like a betrayal? Not because of the sex, but because of the way he wanted to linger, the way he wanted to know everything about her.

"Sheridan."

She startled, shooting up out of her chair and whirling to face him. Her nose was red. "My God, you scared me to death."

"I'm sorry."

She was wearing her jeans and a silky shirt and she looked so small and alone as she stood there with her shoulders bent. "How did you get in here?"

"There's a hidden door in the bedroom. It leads to my rooms."

"Oh," she said softly, and he knew she must be wondering why he hadn't used it to bring her back the other night. But there were more immediate things to think about.

"What is wrong?"

She gave a half shrug. "I was just reading email from my business partner. I think we're both realizing our dream is over now."

"I know you blame me for these things, but I am not

the one who caused this." And yet he did feel guilty for his part in changing her life.

"Believe it or not, I do know that. But it seems so odd that a single oversight could impact so many lives."

"This is quite often the case."

"For a king, I'm sure it is. For a girl from Savannah who just wanted to give her sister a gift, this is all a bit of a shock."

She walked over and put her hands on the back of a chair, gripping it so tightly that her knuckles whitened. He watched her, torn between going to her and holding her and staying where he was. In the end, he decided to stay. She would not welcome him at the moment.

She swiped the tissue over her nose again and stuffed it in her pocket. "So what did you come here to tell me to do now?"

Rashid's brows drew down. Why had he come? *Because you can't stay away. Because she has a brightness to her that draws you like a moth. Because you want to feel that brightness wrapped around you again.*

"I didn't come to tell you to do anything."

She waved a hand as if she were sweeping aside a bothersome fly. "Well, isn't that a relief? What can I help you with, then?"

For once in his life, he was left with nothing to say. He dug down into the recesses of his brain. "My brother is going to build a skyscraper for me. I understand you have architecture experience. Perhaps you could consult?"

She blinked at him. Several times. "I…well, I did train as an architect, but I worked on historical preservation. Old buildings. Skyscrapers aren't quite my thing. Not to mention I left the profession to start Dixie Doin's with Kelly."

"Why did you do that?" He truly wanted to know. She'd gone to school for one thing and ended up doing another.

She shrugged. "I enjoyed architecture, but it wasn't as fun as party planning. I like organizing things, making people happy. Preserving old buildings takes time, but making people happy with food and fun is instant gratification."

"Which explains why you spend so much time in the kitchen. I enjoyed the lotus-shaped napkins, by the way."

She smiled at him, a genuine smile for once, and his heart did that little hitch thing again. "I'm glad. I'll show them ferns next. Then maybe some swans."

"No swans at the state dinner, I beg you."

She laughed. "Fine, no swans." But then her smile faded and she slumped against the back of the chair. "Will I get to attend these functions, or am I to be kept shut away like that cousin you can't trust not to drink too much and dance on the tables?"

The way she said things amused him. "Do you drink too much or dance on tables?"

"Not since college." He must have looked surprised because she laughed again. "I'm kidding. I danced on the tables *without* drinking. Because it was fun sometimes to let loose."

He tried to imagine her on top of a table, dancing and having fun. "Do you let loose often?"

She hesitated a moment. "Too often where you're concerned."

The words hung in the air between them. He could feel his body hardening, and she hadn't said anything provocative. Or done anything provocative. But he knew how she tasted, how she felt, and he wanted to unwrap her and taste and feel her again.

And again.

"We've only been together twice," he pointed out.

"And if you hadn't avoided me for so long, I imagine it would have been far more often than that. Though I suppose it's a very good thing you did."

Okay, he was seriously hard now. Ready to walk over there and take her in his arms. "You say the most unexpected things."

"I'm too honest for my own good sometimes. I've always been this way, but I like it because it beats keeping things inside."

"But you do keep some things inside." He was thinking of her sister and the way she defended the other woman's weaknesses even when they affected her life. He wondered why she did that, but he supposed he didn't really have to ask. When he'd been a kid, he'd done everything he could to keep Kadir insulated from their father's wrath. It hadn't always worked, but he'd tried.

She bowed her head. "I suppose I do. But everyone needs a few secrets, right?"

Who was he to contradict her? He had secrets of his own. "I don't know if *needs* is the right word. But yes, I know what you mean."

Her blue eyes gleamed. "I'm still angry with you. But if you walked over here and took me in your arms, you could make me forget it all for a few hours."

He was poised to do just that when she continued.

"But I'm asking you not to." She shook her head. "I need time to process this, Rashid. I need time to figure out how to fit my life into this box you've handed me. I can't do that if you confuse me with sex."

CHAPTER TEN

SHERIDAN'S HEART POUNDED as she gazed at the handsome sheikh standing across the room. Just a word from her and he would cross the distance separating them and make her feel as if she were the most important, wonderful thing in his life for a few hours.

But she couldn't let it happen again. Not after the way she'd felt this afternoon when they'd made love so urgently against a wall. After, when she'd felt shattered by the emotions he stirred inside her, when she'd needed tenderness and closeness, he'd pushed her away. Every effort she made to be close to him, he rebuffed. So why did she keep doing it?

And now she had to marry him. She didn't know how she was going to survive if she had to keep navigating a sexual minefield with him. They'd done everything backward. Baby, sex and now marriage, and she couldn't keep going down the same path without knowing who he was. Really knowing.

"The sex doesn't mean anything to you," she said. He did not contradict her, and her belly squeezed a little tighter. "And it doesn't mean anything to me either, but it could start to mean more than it should just because I feel so out of place here."

That was what truly frightened her. She was a stranger in a strange land, wholly dependent on this man, bound to him by ties greater than any devised by law. She had to keep her feelings grounded in reality. To do that, she couldn't fall into bed with him every time he came near her.

He shoved his hands into his pockets—God, he was delicious in faded jeans—and adopted a casual pose that belied the tension in the set of his shoulders. He was a man poised on the edge of action. Always. That he would attempt to hide that from her was encouraging.

Because they both knew who had the true power. That he would allow her to have her own both stunned and warmed her. It was progress.

"I am not trying to place you in a box. You seem not to realize how very privileged your life is about to become."

"A gilded box is still a box."

He rubbed a temple and came around to sink down on the cushions of a settee. "I do in fact know this." He leaned back and gazed up at the domed ceiling above them. "I hated living in this palace as a child. It was hell in many ways."

She came around the chair and perched on the edge of it, her heart in her throat and a dull pain stinging her eyes.

He shrugged. "My father was a harsh man, *habibti*. He did not believe in sparing the rod, so to speak."

She swallowed. Was he actually sharing things with her? Or was this an anomaly? "I heard that you only recently returned to Kyr. Is that why?"

His eyes glittered. "The palace is full of information, it would seem."

"The person I heard it from seemed rather terrified to impart it. As if you would be angry. As if you are a tyrant who punishes people for slights."

He looked rather stunned at that revelation. "I am a king, and I must be harsh at times. But I am not a tyrant. The only people who feel my wrath are the council and my immediate staff. I have no need to terrify maids or cooks, I assure you."

"Honestly, I didn't think you did." Because the people she'd met seemed happy to have him as their king, though they were also more than a little awestruck by him. He didn't speak much, they said. He kept to himself. He was serious and responsible and he didn't smile.

But he was fair. No one had yet claimed he wasn't.

One dark eyebrow arched as if he didn't quite believe her. "Really? I would imagine you were my greatest critic. Did I not kidnap you and force you to come to Kyr? Am I not forcing you to marry me against your will?"

She clasped her hands together in her lap. "Well, those things are pretty bad and you should feel quite ashamed of yourself. But you haven't been cruel. Exasperating and arrogant, but never cruel."

He held her gaze steadily. "I am intimately acquainted with cruelty, and therefore I have striven never to be the kind of man who resorts to it in order to achieve his aims."

Again, her heart twisted for the child he'd been. "I believe you."

He blew out a breath. "Well, we have progress, then." He stood suddenly. "Good night, Sheridan. Sleep well."

"Rashid, wait."

He turned back to her, a question in his expression.

Why had she stopped him? What did she want to say? Her heart beat hard and her throat ached and she didn't understand this urge to go to him and wrap her arms around him. Not for the sexual chemistry, but for the boy he'd once been. The boy who'd had a cruel father and hadn't known much love.

She wanted to know more. So much more. But he was finished and she didn't know how to make him start again.

"Sleep well," she said, her voice little more than a whisper.

He tilted his head in acknowledgment. And then he was gone.

Kadir al-Hassan arrived the next day with his wife, Emily. Sheridan had just returned from playing with the puppies when she found the palace staff in an uproar. Or the domestic staff anyway. She swallowed hard and hurried to her room to change out of her jeans and T-shirt. It was quite a relief to be able to dress in something she wasn't worried about getting dirty, though she'd chosen to wear the hijab, too. She liked the fabric covering her head when she went out into the hot Kyrian sunshine. It helped keep her cool.

Now she hesitated as she stood in her closet. She had her clothes from home and the Kyrian clothing. In the end, she chose to wear a blouse and trousers with the hijab. Then she checked her email and waited nervously for someone to decide she should be sent for.

Finally, there was a knock at her door and Emily al-Hassan was on the other side. She was a pretty girl, tall and slender and elegantly dressed in a designer suit and low heels. And she was smiling.

"You must be Sheridan," she said after she introduced herself. "I'm so pleased to meet you."

Sheridan was happy to meet her, too. Emily was American, and it was like having a visitor from home even though they'd never met before.

Emily took a seat and talked easily while Fatima arrived with tea. Once Fatima was gone, Emily's expression changed to something more sympathetic and concerned.

"How are you holding up?" she asked. "Is Rashid behaving himself?"

Sheridan felt a little odd talking about her life with a stranger, but then Emily was the only other person she knew who shared the novel experience of marrying a Kyrian royal.

"I'm not sure he knows how," Sheridan said, and Emily laughed.

"Truthfully, when I first met him, Rashid scared me half to death. He's so quiet. So intense." She frowned then. "I probably shouldn't say anything, but you are marrying him now and so I feel you should be armed with as much information as possible. Rashid and Kadir didn't have a good relationship with their father. He was very harsh."

"Rashid mentioned it."

Emily's eyes widened a bit. "Did he? How interesting. Did he also mention that their father refused to choose an heir? It should have always been Rashid, but King Zaid wanted to punish him. So he left the succession undecided."

"But he decided in the end."

Emily sipped her tea. "No. Kadir did. Rashid did not come when their father died, and so Kadir had to take the throne. But Rashid finally showed up before the formal declaration. And Kadir abdicated."

Sheridan blinked. "Why would he do that?"

Emily's cheeks reddened a bit then. "It's a long story, but he did it for me. I was too scandalous for Kyr, you see. And Kadir never wanted to be a king. He only married me to get out of it."

"But you're still married."

Emily laughed. "Oh, yes. Marrying Kadir for all the wrong reasons is still the best thing I ever did. Because it turns out the reasons were right in the end."

Sheridan's throat ached. It was clear that Emily al-Hassan loved her husband very much. And he must love her equally as much to have given up a throne. It was incredibly romantic. And it made her sad when she thought of her and Rashid and their impending marriage.

She shook her head as hot feelings welled up inside her. "I don't want to marry Rashid. I don't love him, and he doesn't love me. But there's the baby to consider. A baby born to an unmarried mother can't inherit a throne, apparently, even when the king of Kyr is most definitely the father. And forget shared custody." She waved a hand. "Not happening here."

"No, that is definitely Kyr for you." Emily leaned forward and squeezed her hand. Sheridan liked how sympathetic and friendly the other woman was. "Kyr has its charms, and the al-Hassan brothers have even more. I promise you they are worth it in the end. Even grouchy Rashid."

Sheridan laughed. She'd been on the edge of tears, but laughing helped to banish them. At least temporarily. God, she'd needed this. Someone who didn't think the sun rose and set on Rashid, who knew he was flawed and who didn't mind saying it.

"He is grouchy," she said. "And bossy."

Emily laughed. "Bossiness is an al-Hassan trait. But you have to admit they are devilishly handsome."

"I haven't seen your husband yet, but if he looks anything like Rashid, I'd say you're a very lucky woman."

Emily's eyebrows waggled. "I am a *very* lucky woman. And you will be, too, once you tame Rashid."

Sheridan sighed. The other woman was so certain everything would work out in the end. Sheridan didn't feel that way at all. She thought of Rashid pushing her away after sex and her heart wanted to break. "I don't know that he's tamable. Or that I want to. In truth, I wish I could just go home."

But that wasn't as true as she claimed, and she felt a blush stain her cheeks. Emily very politely didn't comment.

"Would you like more tea?" Emily asked instead, reaching for the pot.

"Please."

After they settled down with fresh cups, Emily looked at her very thoughtfully. "Kadir tells me that Rashid has always been intense, but he has not always been the sort of emotionally closed-off man he is now. Kadir does not know what happened, but he thinks something did. There were a few years when they only had the barest of contact. Kadir was building his business and Rashid was in Russia." Emily sipped her tea. "I've only known grouchy Rashid, so I can't say for certain. But Kadir loves his brother very much, and he would not do that if Rashid was not good."

Sheridan's heart thumped. She wouldn't have guessed

that Kadir didn't know about his brother's marriage and his wife's subsequent death, but clearly he did not. It wasn't her place to say anything, so she sipped her tea and kept silent. But she hurt for Rashid as she thought of him losing the woman he loved and having no one to turn to.

They sat there for another hour, chatting about many different things. Emily explained the Kyrian wedding procedure to Sheridan, who found it comfortingly sterile. Oh, she'd always wanted the big emotional wedding, but signing her name on a document and then watching Rashid do the same would be quite enough for her. It was like signing loan papers at the bank. She could handle that.

But when the time came to do just that later the same day, Sheridan found herself more emotional than she'd thought she would be. The signing took place in Rashid's office with Kadir and Emily for witnesses, along with the lawyers who presided over the entire thing. It lasted all of a few minutes as they sat on one side of a conference table with the lawyers on the other and Kadir and Emily at either end.

There was a translator who read the documents to Sheridan, and then she was directed to sign her name on a line. She could feel Rashid beside her, his gaze intent on her as if he expected her to refuse. She almost did. She almost stood and ran from the room, but in the end she knew it would merely be a stalling tactic.

She signed and put the pen down, then stared at her fingers clenched in her lap. Rashid scratched his signature across the document in a hasty scrawl, and then shoved the whole thing across the table.

He was angry, she realized, but she didn't know why.

She glanced over at Emily, who gave her a smile of encouragement and a firm nod, as if to say, "You can do this."

Another few moments and the men on the other side of the table were filing the documents into briefcases and rising. They left the room, and then Emily went to Kadir, who took her hand in his and gave her a look that could only be called hot. He was very handsome, of course. The al-Hassan brothers had been designed by God to make female hearts beat a little harder when they walked into a room.

"Congratulations, Rashid," Kadir said, shaking his brother's hand. "And Sheridan, welcome to the family."

He kissed her on both cheeks. Emily did the same while Kadir took his brother aside for a quick conversation at the other end of the room. Sheridan's heart was beating hard and her stomach fluttered.

"It'll be fine," Emily said. "He's a good man. He's just a little lost, I think. Kadir was, too, but we found our way." She squeezed Sheridan's shoulders. "You will, too. I'm certain of it."

Sheridan wished she shared Emily's confidence, but all she could do was smile wanly and thank the other woman for being there.

Kadir joined his wife then, his arm going around her shoulders. He couldn't seem to be near her without touching her. It made Sheridan wistful. Rashid touched her, but only to initiate sex. After he'd found his release, he was finished with the touching.

"We should leave them alone now, *habibti*," Kadir said.

And then Kadir and Emily were gone and Sheridan was left standing in Rashid's private office—where they'd had mad sex against the wall—with the beautiful view of the sandstone cliffs in the distance on one side and the ocean on another. The room was quiet. Too quiet.

She turned to look at Rashid and found him watching her. He did not look pleased. She thought of him shoving the papers across the table and her belly tightened. He wanted to be married even less than she did, it would seem.

She thought of him last night, telling her about his wife. He'd said it plainly, unfeelingly, but she knew he must have been deeply affected by the death of the woman he'd loved.

And he must have loved her, since he'd married her willingly and not because she was pregnant with an heir to the throne.

Now he was married to her, and no matter how much he'd said it had to be done and there was no choice, he clearly wasn't happy about it now that it had taken place.

His frown deepened. "Kadir says you are frightened of me."

Sheridan shook her head. "I'm not."

"I didn't think you were. You've been giving me hell since the first moment I saw you. If you weren't frightened then, you could hardly be so now that I've made you a royal princess."

Her belly rolled with nerves. A princess, but not a queen. In order for there to be a queen, the king had to make a proclamation. That much she'd learned from Emily. And while it was silly to even think about the difference, it was quite obvious that Rashid did not intend to issue a proclamation. His father had never done so, either.

"I don't feel like a princess."

"You will soon enough. You'll have to go before the council, and then there are state functions to preside over, meetings to attend. You'll have a secretary and a staff. You will have to choose a cause to support, and then you will need to make appearances for it—"

"Rashid, please." He stopped speaking. There was no moisture in her throat at all. She thought of everything he'd just said and wanted to run and hide. She wasn't shy, but it was too much to process so soon. "Can I please get used to the idea of being married before you start throwing duties at me?"

He looked stiff. Formal. He was so incredibly handsome in his dark desert robes today. They were trimmed in fine gold embroidery that sparkled and shimmered as he moved. Her own dress—a deep purple silk gown with a cream hijab—was not as beautiful.

"Since you informed me you did not wish to be married, and that you did not like having nothing to do, I assumed you would be happy to do things that would take you away from me."

This conversation was like navigating a minefield. How did one respond? Did she ignore the jab about marriage and focus on the part about being busy? Or did she address them both?

"You know what my objections to this marriage are, so I'm not repeating them. And I *would* like to be busy, but the things you've mentioned are not like running a party-planning and catering business."

His mouth flattened. "Some of the skills are the same. You said you liked to make people happy. You will be doing the same as a royal princess. And there will be functions to plan, if you wish to be involved in that."

"I think you know I would."

"Then you will inform your secretary. She will arrange everything for you." He went over to his desk and shuffled through some papers while she stood there and felt like a kid who'd been called into the principal's office for misbehaving.

"Are you angry with me?" she finally asked, deciding that the only way to get anywhere with him was to speak her mind.

He looked up then, his dark gaze spearing her in place. Her blood thumped slowly in her veins at the heat she saw there.

"Angry? No."

He went back to what he was doing and she huffed a sigh. "Rashid, you don't act like someone who's not angry."

He dropped the papers he'd been going through and came around the desk. Then he leaned back on it and crossed his arms. "You looked like a lamb being dragged to the slaughter at that table just now."

Her blood was beginning to hum with irritation. It was a welcome feeling compared to the ones she'd been having. "You didn't seem all that happy, either. I don't think there was a person in this room who believed either of us wanted to get married, so don't you go blaming me for your mood."

"I do blame you, Sheridan. My mood is one of frustration. Because I could smell you beside me and I couldn't touch you. You've told me not to touch you and I won't. But it frustrates me greatly. A man should be able to touch his wife."

Her heart skipped. Of all the things she'd thought were bothering him...

The blood rushed wildly through her veins. He was

sexually frustrated, not angry. He wanted her. In spite of everything, little bubbles of excitement popped and fizzed in her tummy.

"I thought you said we would have a marriage in name only." Because he had said so in the car in Savannah, and though they'd already had sex twice, she wanted him to admit he'd changed his mind. Because she wasn't going to keep having wild encounters with him and then be sent away as if she'd somehow misbehaved.

His eyebrows shot up. "Do you honestly think after this past week that's going to happen?"

She shrugged. "You tell me. Both times we've been together, you couldn't wait to get away."

He put his forehead in one palm for a moment, his fingers spanning his temples. And then he was looking at her again.

"It's not you."

There was a pinch in her chest. "That's a cliché, Rashid. It's not you, it's me. It's also what people usually say right before they say something awful, like 'I think we need to take a break' or 'I just can't love you the way you deserve.'"

As soon as she said the word *love* she wished she could call it back. It had no place here, and judging by the way he was looking at her now, it never would.

"We are clearly not taking a break. We've only just started. And as for love…" His expression grew stony. "I'm not capable of it, Sheridan."

Sheridan swallowed hard. Why did it hurt to hear him say it? Did she really expect love to enter the equation?

Yes. Yes, she did. Maybe not now, but someday. How could you live with someone, have such undeniable sexual chemistry with them, and not fall in love at some

point? It didn't seem possible. There was more heat between her and Rashid than there'd ever been in both of
her other relationships combined.

But maybe that was just her. Maybe Rashid took that
kind of response for granted.

Sheridan turned toward the door. "I think I should
go now. You clearly have work to do."

"I'm not trying to hurt you, *habibti*." She thought of
the way Kadir had said that word to his wife and tears
welled behind her eyes.

"Why would I be hurt?" She lifted her chin. "We are
nothing to each other, Rashid. Apparently, we're going
to remain that way."

CHAPTER ELEVEN

THEY ATE DINNER in Rashid's private dining room with Kadir and Emily. That was an exercise in torture for Sheridan since those two were so clearly in love that it hurt to watch. Not because she expected Rashid to love her or because she wanted to love him, but when you found yourself pregnant and married without a mention of love, you felt rather cheated over the whole thing.

Why had she used that word earlier? Because she'd been hurt, that was why, and she'd tried to cover it up. She'd blundered, and then she'd found herself stumbling down a path where her new husband had informed her that he wasn't capable of love. It was not an auspicious beginning to a marriage.

She'd half expected Rashid to stop her when she'd walked out on him earlier, but he'd not done so. When she'd walked out of his office, Daoud was there. And for the first time ever, he dropped to his knees and bowed his head.

"Your Royal Highness."

Sheridan had started to shake then. "Daoud, please. Get up."

He'd done so, his dark eyes searching her face in a way that warmed her. As if he'd been looking for sadness and willing to pummel whomever had made her so. But then he'd dropped his head again and she'd realized that Rashid was in the hall behind her.

"Take Her Highness to her room, Daoud. She needs to rest."

"Yes, Your Majesty."

So she'd rested. And when she'd finished resting, she'd gone to the stables to check on the puppies again. They were getting bigger by the day. Soon, Daoud informed her, they would be given to new homes and she wouldn't get to see them anymore. She'd picked one up and held its soft furry body against her cheek before handing it back to the groom and returning to the palace.

And now they were at dinner and Sheridan was trying to follow the conversation, though not doing a good job. They were speaking English, because Emily didn't speak Arabic either, but the laughter and sound of voices just droned over her head while she wallowed in her own misery over her situation.

She'd spoken to Annie earlier, and Chris. Annie was over the moon with excitement about seeing the specialist. Chris was more subdued, as if he knew what this opportunity was costing Sheridan. But he was grateful nevertheless. He expressed it adequately enough for them both, though Sheridan might have liked her sister to realize how huge a change was occurring in her life.

For Annie, the prize was a baby of her own. Nothing and no one got in the way of that fact.

Kelly had been shocked, but she'd taken it all in and started making plans for the future of Dixie Doin's without Sheridan. That had hurt, but it was also necessary.

"Sheridan. Sheridan?"

She stirred after her name was repeated and looked up to find three sets of eyes looking back at her.

"Are you ill?" Rashid asked. "Do you need to lie down?"

She shook her head. "No, I'm fine. I was just thinking." She smiled as she picked up her water glass. "Please don't stop talking on my account."

Kadir shot his wife a look. "Actually, we were going to turn in. It's been a long day."

"Yes," Emily said. "I'm pretty tired. It's been a lovely day, though."

Everyone agreed it had been a lovely day. And then they took their leave of each other with hugs and kisses on the cheek. The room was quiet when Kadir and Emily were gone. Oppressively so, just like before.

"We keep finding ourselves alone together in spite of our best efforts," Sheridan said cheerfully as she turned toward Rashid.

"This is not necessarily a bad thing." Rashid's gaze was bright. Hot. And her stomach flipped even as her body began to melt at the promise in those eyes.

"I think I should go."

"And what if I said your place tonight is here? In my bed?"

She felt light-headed, dizzy. It was anticipation, fear and, yes, even a certain kind of joy she found astonishing.

"I don't think that's wise," she said, even though the voice in her head said something else entirely.

He moved toward her, took her hand and slowly pulled her into his arms. She went reluctantly, but she went. Her palms rested on his broad chest as his heat slid into her bones, her blood. Why did being held by

Rashid feel so right? And why did she want to wrap her arms around him and comfort him? She wanted to know why he had that haunted look in his eyes, and she wanted to know why he pushed her away in the most tender of moments.

"I think it's very wise," he told her. "The wisest thing possible."

His head dipped toward hers and her eyes drifted closed. But then she pictured how it would go. The delicious silkiness of his kiss, the inflammatory response of her own, the frantic revealing of bodies and the cataclysmic joining that would strip all her defenses and leave her heart bare.

And then the ice at the end. She couldn't take the ice.

"I'd rather talk," she blurted out.

He stopped, his lips a whisper away from hers. "Sheridan, you torture me."

Her fingers curled into his shirt. "We can't keep having wild sex like this, Rashid. We have to talk sometime."

He straightened, looking perfectly dejected. Like a kid who'd just had a treat taken away. "I don't see why we can't have sex first and then talk."

"Because you won't talk then. You'll run, or you'll take me back to my rooms, and nothing will ever get said."

He studied her very solemnly. And then he stepped back and drew her into the living area. She sank onto one of the couches and curled her feet beneath her. Rashid went to the opposite end of the couch.

"What do you wish to talk about?"

Sheridan bit her lip as she watched him. What did she wish to talk about? Anything. Everything. Only she'd never really expected he would do as she asked, so here she was with no leading question. No carefully thought-out phrase to begin prying into his life.

So she launched into it like a cannonball off a diving board.

"Why are you incapable of love?"

His eyes widened. And then his mouth flattened and she was certain he would brush her off. He did not, however, but she found herself almost wishing he had.

"Because it hurts. Because people die and you're left figuring out how to live your life without them. It's easier not to love."

"But choosing not to love and being incapable of it are two different things, right?"

He rubbed a hand over his face and looked away from her. "Maybe so. But I've chosen what works best for me."

"You will love this child, though." She wanted to understand him. He'd lost a wife and that had affected him greatly. But surely he would love their baby. She needed to know he was capable of that much at least.

"Sheridan." He didn't say anything else for a long moment. And then he closed his eyes and swallowed. "My wife was pregnant. She had a rare congenital defect that caused her to hemorrhage."

He swallowed and his skin paled visibly. Sheridan wished she could stop him, wished she could go over and pull his head to her chest and just hold him. But how could she do such a thing when he was talking about the death of a wife and child he'd loved?

"There was nothing the doctors could do. And the baby, who until that time had seemed healthy, was still-born."

"Oh, Rashid." Her eyes filled with tears. What could

she say? What could she do? His anger over her having
a baby for Annie made so much more sense now. He'd
talked about risking her life that night. And when she'd
asked him what was wrong, he'd told her it was nothing.
She'd known it was not nothing.

She hadn't known it was anything so tragic, however.

"Yes, I will love this child. But I'm terrified to do so.
Perhaps now you can understand why."

She clasped her hands tight in her lap. "I do."

"Kadir doesn't know about this. No one does. I was
in Russia then, running my business, and had very little contact with anyone outside of the microcosm of my
life."

It humbled her that he would share something with
her that he hadn't even shared with his family. She
thought of Emily telling her earlier that Kadir knew
something had happened to his brother, but not what.
"Maybe you should tell him. Maybe he has words of
wisdom that I can't seem to find."

"There are no words of wisdom, Sheridan. You simply get through each day until the pain isn't as great.
You never forget, but you learn how to live anyway."

She couldn't sit here any longer and not reach out to
him. So she got up and moved closer, taking his hand
and squeezing it in hers. That was all. Just a touch. He
squeezed back and then they were looking at each other,
their gazes tangling, searching, locking together for what
seemed forever, but was probably only a few minutes.

"I'm sorry I pried. It wasn't my intention to make you
share painful memories."

He lifted her hand to his mouth and kissed her knuckles. "You're very sweet. When you aren't telling me to
go to hell, that is."

She smiled. It shook at the corners, but she held it together anyway. "If I didn't tell you, who would? You have far too many people bowing and scraping and bending over backward to serve you. You need someone to remind you that you aren't perfect."

"No, I am definitely not perfect. In this, you are very like Daria."

"That's very sweet of you to say."

"But also mercenary."

"Mercenary?" Her blood beat in her temples, her throat.

His eyes glittered hot. "Life is for the living. And I want you, Sheridan. Now, tonight. I want to take you to my bed and keep you there until you can't move a muscle. Until your body is liquid with pleasure, weak with desire and sated beyond your wildest imaginings."

Her breath caught. "That sounds quite amazing, Your Majesty. But I'm still not certain it's a good idea."

Because he made her heart thrum and her body melt and her eyes sting with tears. She was drawn to him physically, but it was also more than that. And that was what frightened her. How could she spend time with him and not be drawn deeper into that spell? He was so much more than an arrogant and entitled king.

He was a man who'd lived an imperfect life, who'd experienced pain and loss and incredible sadness. He was also lonely, and that loneliness called to her because it was so familiar. He took care of everyone else first—his nation, his duties—and whatever was left over he gave to himself. But it wasn't much.

For a man who was rich in material things, he was sorely lacking in emotional fulfillment.

"We have to start somewhere," he said softly.

Oh, how she wanted to accept, to let him know he didn't need to be alone. But the risk...

"I can't go to bed with you now only to have you freeze me out later."

"I don't want to freeze you out."

"But you do. You have."

"I know."

But he tugged her hand until she had to move right up against him. And then he speared his other hand into her hair and lowered his mouth to hers. She didn't stop him. She closed her eyes, and then his lips met hers and she sighed. He kissed her sweetly, so sweetly, and yet the heat swelled inside her, rolled through her, intensified with each gentle stroke of his tongue against hers.

"I won't get up and go back to my room in the middle of the night," she said between kisses. "I won't, Rashid."

"I understand." And then he kissed her deeper, harder, until the passion unfurled between them, until he pushed her back on the couch and shaped her body with his hands, exploring her curves endlessly.

She thought he would undress her there, but he soon lifted her up and pulled her outside onto the terrace. It was a beautiful night, not too cool yet, with stars winking over the dunes. He took her to the railing and stood there gazing out over the darkened desert. Behind them, the city lights tinted the sky, but it wasn't enough to drown out the vast darkness before them.

"I left Kyr for many years," he said, standing behind her at the railing and putting his arms around her, caging her in. "I gave up the expectation I would become king when I was a young man. I wandered the world, and I started my own business, which I built into the powerful oil company it is today. I became who I am because of my life here in Kyr. And one thing I vowed many years ago was that no child of mine would ever believe I did not love or approve of him. Or her."

He turned her in his arms then and she gazed up at him with eyes blurred with tears. "I believed you the first time you said it," she said softly.

"Yes, but I wanted you to know that I was certain. This child will not lack for love."

Sheridan swallowed the lump in her throat. She wanted to ask him if there could ever be love between them, but she knew it was not a question he wanted to hear. He'd told her he chose not to love, not that he was incapable of it, and so that gave her hope.

She put a hand to his cheek and watched his eyes darken. "You're a good man, Rashid. And I know you'll be a good father."

He turned his head and pressed a kiss into her palm. "You will want for nothing here, *habibti*. I know this is not the life you would have chosen, but I believe you will come to love Kyr as I do."

"I hope I do," she said, her heart pounding at the realization she could love so much more than Kyr if he would let her.

He kissed her suddenly. And this time he did not stop. This time, he kissed her until she was melting and pliant, and then he swept her into his arms—how many times had he done this now, and why did it thrill her every time he did?—and carried her into his bedroom, where he undressed her slowly, kissing and caressing each bit of skin he revealed, until she was quivering with anticipation, until she was ready to beg him for release.

He made love to her first with his mouth, and then, when she was sated and shattered, he settled between her thighs and entered her on a breath-stealing plunge. Sheridan wrapped her legs around him as he rode her, arched her body into his and let him take her over the edge of passion and into the depths of a pleasure so intense it made her cry his name again and again.

When she was shattered and spent again, when she couldn't lift a muscle, Rashid found his release in her body. He rolled away from her and she lay there with the cool air wafting over her heated skin and her brain racing, wondering if he would get up and hand her the clothing he'd dropped onto the floor.

She didn't dare reach out to him. Long minutes passed in which she worried and wondered and thought of what she would say if he withdrew again. And then she thought maybe she should just get up and go. Take the decision away from him. Show him she didn't care about his rejection.

Sheridan pushed herself upright and swung her legs off the bed. She fumbled for her clothes in the dark, her eyes stinging, as Rashid didn't say a word. He didn't care if she left. After everything he'd said, he didn't even care.

But then he was there, his hand smoothing over the curve of her back, her buttock, and she stopped what she was doing as her skin reacted with the same predictable flare of heat as always. Oh, it wasn't fair. It just wasn't fair.

"Don't go," he said. And then he pulled her down, into his arms, and she was lost all over again.

CHAPTER TWELVE

HE'D BEEN RIGHT about her, Rashid thought. She *was* a people pleaser. Sheridan was the kind of bright, sunny sort of person that he was not and never had been. She was light to his dark, sweet to his sour, sunshine to his ice. She made people happy. She spoke with everyone she met as if she was genuinely interested in them. She had to have a translator, but she was beginning to learn a few words and when she tried them out, no matter how badly she mangled them, even the council smiled indulgently.

He did not fool himself that would last, however. The council would eventually begin to demand he take a second wife. He'd told them he would, but he was in no hurry to do so.

Besides, when would he have time for another woman? He was busy enough with Sheridan. Not that she demanded his time, but he often found himself giving it. He went looking for her during the day, found her with her secretary or in the kitchen. Occasionally, he found her in the stables with the puppies.

He looked down at the basket that Mostafa had placed silently beside his desk and took a moment to wonder at himself. Was he going soft?

Soon there was a knock on his door, and Sheridan breezed into the room. She was wearing cream trousers and a red shirt today, and her hair tumbled in blond curls over her shoulders. She was fresh and pretty and glowing.

He glanced at her belly worriedly, but then he told himself it was silly. She wasn't even showing yet. There was nothing to worry about.

"You wanted to see me?" she said.

He stood and went to her side. "I did." He leaned in and kissed her cheek. And then he had to tell himself it was the middle of the day and he had appointments in a few minutes. But he was already hard. It surprised him how quickly she got to him.

As if she knew what kind of internal battle he was having, she slid her arms around him and brought her body against his.

"You smell good, Rashid."

"Stop flirting with me." He tried to sound stern but she only laughed. And then she stood on tiptoe and pulled his head down. He thought she was going to kiss him on the mouth, but she turned her head at the last moment and landed a kiss on his jaw. Then she laughed and pulled out of his arms.

He snatched her back and kissed her properly until she clung to him, until her body went soft and her tongue glided against his and she sighed.

He considered taking her on the desk when there was a noise. A whimper. Sheridan pushed him away and stood with her eyes wide. "What was that?"

"What was what?"

"That...that sound. Like a puppy—" And then her breath caught and her eyes brightened and Rashid reached for the basket. He opened the lid and a pale golden puppy sat there, blinking and yawning.

When it saw Sheridan, the little tail thumped. Sheridan squealed as she reached into the basket and took the puppy out. "Oh, sweet baby, what are you doing in the big, bad king's office? Are you hiding?"

She looked up at him, her eyes shining, and he couldn't remember why he wasn't supposed to feel a flood of warmth at that look. Why it was dangerous to do so.

"The puppies are old enough to go to permanent homes now. I thought you might like one of your own. Daoud said this one was your favorite."

"Oh, Rashid." She bent her head and put her face in the dog's fur. "Yes," she said softly. "He's a precious little guy."

Rashid was beginning to feel uncomfortable. Not in a bad way, but in a "what the hell do I do now" way. Why hadn't he just sent Daoud to her room with the puppy? Except that she wasn't staying in her room lately, was she?

No, she'd been in his every night for the past two weeks. He liked having her there. He thought back to that very first night when he'd found her on his terrace and made love to her. And then he'd jumped out of bed like he'd been singed and escorted her back to her room. He'd followed it up by doing the same thing the next time he'd lost control with her, and she'd thought that meant he didn't want to be touched.

Nothing was further from the truth. He loved when she touched him, loved the tenderness in her fingers, the sweetness in her tongue, the wickedness in her mouth when she took him between her lips. He was beginning to crave her touch.

She beamed at him, her sweet face lighting up with joy. His heart, that organ that was supposed to be encased in ice, kicked. He reached down deep, searching for the ice, jerked it back into place like a blanket.

He could smile, he could be warm and make love, but he could not let his heart be touched. That was the last battleground and the one he would not allow to be breached.

Rashid reached out and stroked the dog's head. "It will be good for the baby to grow up with a dog."

Her smile didn't waver. "It will be good for me, too. Thank you."

She stood on tiptoe to kiss him and then she wandered over to the seating area and set the dog on the floor. The little guy scampered around happily, and Rashid hoped he didn't pee on the rug.

"Are you prepared for the trip?" he asked. They were traveling out into the desert so that he could fulfill his duties to meet with some of the nomadic tribes that still ranged the vast Kyrian Desert. It was mostly ceremonial, but necessary. And while he could leave Sheridan behind for the week or so he would be gone, he wanted her to see the desert as he saw it. The beauty, the majesty, the overwhelming might of all that sand and sun. He wanted his child to feel it inside the womb, to become one with the land, the same as he was.

"I think so. My secretary has been telling me what to expect and what to take."

"How is Layla working out for you?"

He'd sent her a woman who'd trained in European universities and who had a fresh, open manner. Not that he supposed Sheridan would have had any trouble if Layla had been dour, considering how she'd wound Daoud around her finger. If Daoud didn't have a fiancée he adored, Rashid might be jealous.

"I like her. She never makes me feel stupid for not knowing what I'm supposed to do."

Layla had been teaching her protocol and schooling her on Kyrian history in preparation for their upcoming public wedding. Rashid had pushed that out as far as he could, simply because he hadn't wanted to deal with a long day of ceremony and pomp, but the day would arrive soon enough and they'd have to give the Kyrian people something to celebrate.

"I'm glad to hear it."

She frowned a little then. "I asked Annie and Chris if they would come for the formal wedding, but I don't think Annie wants to come."

"I'm sorry, Sheridan." He was predisposed to dislike her sister simply because the other woman seemed not to care how her actions hurt Sheridan, but he knew that it wasn't quite as simple as that. Annie was shy and frightened of new situations. He understood that now, but it didn't mean he liked the way it affected Sheridan.

"I knew it was a long shot. All the pomp and noise, the dignitaries, the heat and strangeness of a place she's never been. It would be too much for her."

He didn't point out that apparently the strangeness of Switzerland, where Annie would have her experimental treatment to try to give her a chance to conceive, didn't seem to bother her.

"We will bring them here another time, then. I will make it happen, I assure you."

She laughed. "Please tell me you're not going to kidnap my sister and her husband, Rashid. If you keep snatching people from the States, eventually you'll be caught, and then there'll be an international incident."

He came and sat down beside her while the puppy yipped and tried to chase his tail. "I won't kidnap them."

"Well, that's a relief."

He tugged her onto his lap because he couldn't quite control himself.

"But I'm not sorry I kidnapped you," he told her, pushing her blond hair back behind her ears and watching the way her eyes darkened with passion as he ghosted a thumb over one budding nipple.

Her voice was a purr. "I thought you had appointments?"

"I'm the king. I can reschedule if I want to." He reached for his phone and punched a button. Mostafa answered. "Reschedule everything for the next two hours."

Sheridan laughed as he tossed the phone aside again. "Such a bossy man. And so certain of yourself. What if I have appointments?"

He pulled her head down to his. "None are more important than this one."

Her mouth brushed his softly, sweetly, and his groin tightened.

"No," she agreed. "None are."

The car that would take Sheridan to her doctor's appointment was waiting for her the next morning. Daoud escorted her down the steps and out the door, but before he could help her into the car Rashid strode outside, looking regal and magnificent in his desert robes.

"I thought you had a meeting," Sheridan said.

Rashid grinned at her. "Did I not explain to you how this works? I am the king. I can reschedule meetings."

Sheridan settled onto the seat and Rashid climbed in beside her. Then the door sealed shut and the car started toward the city.

"It's not necessary for you to be there the first time."

He took her hand in his and butterflies soared in her belly. "I know you're trying to spare me any pain, but I feel as if I should be there for you."

Sheridan's heart squeezed tight as she gazed up at his handsome face. She'd spent every night for the past two weeks in his bed, and she still felt the same butterflies whenever he touched her. Butterflies, heat, need and a melting, aching, wonderful tension that suffused her whole being as he worshipped her body with his own.

And now he'd given her a dog. She'd named the little guy Leo because it just seemed to fit. He was the same tawny gold as a lion, plus he'd been given to her by the Lion of Kyr. Her husband. She dropped her gaze to their linked hands and felt a bittersweet happiness flood her.

Because she was falling for this man. So very hard. Sometimes she thought he cared about her, too, but then she'd catch him standing on the terrace in the middle of the night, leaning against the railing, caught up in thought. She didn't disturb him. She just watched and waited and when she couldn't stay awake any longer, she fell asleep in his bed alone. He never left her right after they made love anymore, but he did leave. Often.

And it hurt. She could admit that to herself. It hurt that he still felt the need to get away from her. She could never understand the depth of the loss he'd experienced, but he couldn't live his life mired in the past. That wasn't good for him. Or for their child.

Or for her, but then she felt as if that was a selfish thought to have. She knew she was not a replacement for his lost wife, a woman he'd loved very much, according to Daoud.

Daoud didn't talk about his king often, and never about anything private, but he had once let it slip to Sheridan that he'd been with Rashid in Russia and that he'd watched him change after the tragedy. Rashid had never been a bubbly person, but he'd closed down completely in the aftermath of his wife and child's death.

Sheridan squeezed Rashid's hand and hoped he didn't regret coming with her today.

They soon arrived at the Royal Kyrian Hospital and were ushered into a spotless examining room. There was no such thing as waiting to be seen when you were the king of Kyr, because the doctor and her staff were already there and waiting for Sheridan to arrive.

After being directed to change and then ushered onto the table, Sheridan lay there while the doctor used the ultrasound wand to search for a heartbeat. Rashid stood beside her, holding her hand, his eyes on the screen as the doctor found the tiny bean that was their baby.

And then the heartbeat filled the speaker and Sheridan couldn't contain a sob. She bit her lip, trembling from head to toe, while the doctor took photos. Rashid's grip tightened. She looked up at him, at the whiteness of his skin, and her heart skipped.

He was reliving an earlier moment just like this, she imagined, and she wished she could tell him it was okay, that it would all be okay. But she couldn't really guarantee such a thing, could she?

The doctor said something in Arabic that suddenly

had Rashid's fingers tightening even more. The wand stopped moving and the doctor stared at the screen.

"Twins," she said after a long moment. She turned to look at Sheridan. "You are having twins, Your Highness."

Rashid stood looking at the screen, his body as rigid as a board. "Twins? You are certain?"

The doctor smiled. "Yes, Your Majesty. There are two heartbeats." She turned the sound on again. And Sheridan could hear it, the faint beat of another heart beneath the pounding of the first.

"They're so fast," Sheridan said, worried at the quick tempo.

"This is perfectly normal," the doctor replied.

She finished up the exam and then they discussed things like vitamins, exercise and birthing classes. It all seemed so surreal to Sheridan. When it was finally over, the staff made another appointment for her and then she and Rashid were back in the car and returning to the palace.

The silence between them was uncomfortably thick. Sheridan searched for things to say, but discarded most of them. What did you say to a man who was staring out the window and ignoring you after hearing the heartbeats of his children? If he was any other man, she might ask him what was wrong.

But she knew, didn't she? It was the ones who didn't make it, the ones he'd loved and lost that were on his mind.

"Are you all right?" she finally asked when the silence stretched too thin. Outside the car, life went on as usual, but inside it was quiet and strained.

He turned to look at her. His eyes were bleak. "I'm fine."

"You shouldn't have come."

He was polite and distant at once. "You shouldn't have to go through this alone. I wanted to be there."

"But it causes you pain."

"I've been through this before, Sheridan. I knew what to expect when I went with you."

"You haven't said anything since we heard the heartbeats."

His jaw flexed. "It was a shock. I didn't expect two babies. I don't think you did, either."

"No. But twins run in my family, though in my aunts and cousins, not my mother. I didn't even consider it would happen to me."

His gaze raked her. "You are so slight. Are the other women in your family as small?"

"My Aunt Liz is, yes, and she had twins. No problems other than a bit of preeclampsia at the end." She sighed. "It will be fine, Rashid. What happened to your wife—well, it was uncommon. Tragic and terrible, but uncommon."

He seemed so detached and cold. "I am aware of this."

They reached the palace then and the doors swung open. Rashid helped her out of the car and led her inside while the palace guards saluted and other servants bowed as they passed. Her heart pounded as they walked through the ornate and beautiful corridors. She wanted to rewind the clock, to go back to the way things were before they'd gone to the hospital, but that was impossible now. She simply had to deal with the aloof man at her side and wait for him to thaw again.

When they reached the private wing, he stopped before the door. He looked as if he'd like nothing better than to escape. "The doctor said you should rest."

"Yes, but it's not even lunchtime yet and I just got up a couple of hours ago."

"Still. Two babies will sap your strength if you aren't careful."

"They are the size of beans, Rashid. I think I can handle some activity. Besides, I still have things to do before we go into the desert. Layla has promised to give me some more lessons this morning on protocol. I think it would be wise to learn as much as I can if I'm not to embarrass you out there."

He grew very still then and a tiny thread of unease uncoiled within her. She knew what he would say before he said it. "Perhaps you should not go with me, *habibti*. We'll be moving around a lot. Besides, it's dreadfully hot, and you might get ill. You should stay here and think about the public wedding. There is much to be done yet."

Sheridan put her hand on his arm. He stiffened beneath her touch and she dropped her hand, hurt by his rejection. Frustration pounded into her. She would not be silent.

"Why are you behaving like this? I'm not any *more* pregnant than when we left here this morning. Why is it suddenly too hot for me to go with you?"

He swallowed. "It's not suddenly too hot. It's always been too hot. I failed to consider it before."

Of course she knew what was wrong with him. She'd been worried about it since he'd insisted on going with her to the hospital. How could he contain his anxiety at what might happen to his children when his previous experience had been so tragic?

"So now that you've seen the babies and heard their

heartbeats, it's too hot? What else, Rashid? Is it too dangerous to have sex now, too? Too dark at night, too light during the day, too many steps between the bedroom and the kitchen? Is Leo too energetic for me? Should I lie down in bed and not get out for the next few months?"

She was on the edge of hysteria. She knew it, but she was just so furious. It was like she'd had him for a little while, had the beginnings of such a perfect life going with him, and now he was slipping away. Slipping into the past and the tragedy that had happened to him.

Slipping away from her.

Because he was afraid of caring and afraid of being hurt. Her heart ached so much for him. She wanted to slap him silly and she wanted to hold him close and tell him that he had to learn to feel again. For their family. Because he deserved to know love again.

She wanted him to know that *she* loved him. She couldn't help it. She'd tried not to fall, but how could she not?

The way he touched her, held her, the way he said her name when they were in bed together, and the way he reached out to her when she knew it was a difficult thing for him to do. He had feelings that went deep, and he was terrified of them.

But how could she love a man who didn't love her? How could she watch him with her children and know he would always keep part of himself separate from them?

At this moment, he'd retreated behind his barriers. He was aloof and cool and she wanted to scream.

"Don't be melodramatic, Sheridan," he snapped. "I'm thinking of your health and the babies. There is nothing wrong with this. You should be thankful I give a damn at all."

And that was it, the blow that had her reeling. The metaphorical slap to the face that reminded her of her place and jolted right down to her soul. She knew she wasn't a replacement wife, but she'd hoped—no, she'd begun to believe—that she might mean something to him in her own right.

But this sarcasm, this utter arrogance? She couldn't stomach it, no matter how she ached for him.

"I see," she said, quietly shaking inside. He was stiff and formal now, all trace of the thoughtful lover gone. It hurt so much. She'd be damned if she'd let him see it, though. "Thank you for letting me know. I am so fortunate that you care."

His nostrils flared, a single concession to emotion. She hoped he might break then, hoped he might tell her he was sorry, that he hadn't meant that the way it sounded.

He almost did.

"Sheridan, I—" He stopped, clenched his jaw, shook his head. And then he looked at her again with eyes that were cold and empty. Icy. "Go rest. I'll see you when I return in a week."

CHAPTER THIRTEEN

RASHID HAD BEEN gone for three days when the rumor reached her. Sheridan stared at Fatima and blinked. Hard. Her belly twisted into knots as she asked Fatima to repeat what she'd said.

Fatima didn't seem to hear the note of anxiety in Sheridan's voice.

"There is talk His Majesty will choose a second wife from one of the tribes, Your Highness."

"A second wife." How had she been in Kyr for over a month now and not considered that Rashid could have another wife?

"A Kyrian wife."

"I see." But she didn't. Fatima clearly thought this was not a problem because she went about her work as if she hadn't just upended the foundation of Sheridan's entire being. A second wife. A Kyrian wife. Why hadn't she seen this coming? And why hadn't Rashid told her it was possible?

After they'd returned from the hospital, she'd been angry and hurt by Rashid's sudden distance. But she'd known it would do no good to push him. She had to give him space, had to let him come around to it in his own time. He was an intelligent man and he would eventually realize he couldn't hide from life. He would miss her in his bed and he would want to continue the relationship they'd had. She'd had every faith they would grow together as a couple.

They might not have married for love, but that didn't mean love wouldn't grow.

But what if she was only fooling herself? He'd spent two weeks taking her to his bed every night and making love to her. He'd given her a puppy because he knew she'd never had one. But what else did he do that indicated his feelings for her might evolve?

He'd gone to the hospital with her so he could show his support, but he'd come away more distant than ever.

And now he'd gone into the desert without her. Could he possibly be looking for another wife? It didn't seem plausible, since he'd planned to take her with him up until the last possible moment. Would he really have gone wife shopping with her along?

His mood had changed so drastically after the revelation they were going to have twins that she couldn't be certain what was on his mind anymore. They weren't from the same world, and it certainly wasn't unusual in his to contemplate such a thing.

She grew chilled as she considered what it would mean for Rashid to have another wife. He would take another woman to his bed. Sheridan would have to wait her *turn* to be with him. She would grow big with his children and she would be shunned while he chose to spend his evenings with another.

In spite of the churning of her brain, Sheridan tried to go about the business of helping Layla to plan the wedding ceremony. It was to be a day of celebration in Kyr, a holiday for the people, and no expense was to be spared.

But she kept asking herself if she'd be helping to plan another of these events for Rashid and a second wife. And that was something she could not do. Not ever. Her stomach twisted in on itself until she couldn't even stand the thought of food. She grew shaky and hot and had to go lie down.

But she couldn't really rest. She kept thinking about how much her life had changed, how Rashid had come and snatched her out of Savannah with little thought to what she wanted, and then how he'd managed to woo her with hot kisses and silky caresses. She'd fallen deep under his spell.

But she had to be brutally honest with herself: it wasn't mutual. She wasn't sure it ever would be. And she couldn't live like that. She just couldn't. She was patient and she'd been willing to give him time—but if he brought home another wife? Hot tears fell down her cheeks and she swiped them away angrily.

No. Just *no*.

Sheridan got up and went to wash her face. She changed into a Kyrian dress and covered her hair with a hijab. She wasn't going to sit here and wait for Rashid to return with another woman on his arm. She'd been the good girl for so long. All her life, she'd given up things she wanted so that Annie would be happy.

It was the ultimate irony that she was here with Rashid *because* she'd been trying to make Annie happy. No other reason. And she'd been doing what she always did with loved ones, which was to be supportive and understanding and hope that they could come to happiness on their own. She'd tried to give Annie a baby, and she'd tried to give Rashid time and space.

Nothing she'd done worked. It was time she admitted that. And it was time she stood up for herself. *Past* time. Sheridan was done putting everyone but herself first. It was time she took action.

Time she demanded that Rashid make a choice.

Rashid sat through yet another meeting in yet another desert enclave, listening to his people's concerns and making plans for how to best help them. The nomads weren't quite the same as when he'd been a boy. Now they had generators, televisions, cell phones and satellite dishes. These things brought concerns of their own, so of course he promised to look into them.

And then there were the daughters. At every stop, he was presented with daughters who would, it was hinted, make fine wives. All of Kyr knew of his marriage to Sheridan, and of the upcoming national holiday in celebration. Soon they would announce the impending arrival of the royal twins, but not until Sheridan was safely into the second trimester.

Rashid's teeth ground together at that thought. Was there truly anything quite so ironic as safety during a pregnancy? So many things could go wrong. Babies were fine up until birth, and then they were stillborn. Mothers hemorrhaged to death. Things went wrong.

It made him break out into a cold sweat.

Not because he was in love with Sheridan, but he did like her. Against all his plans otherwise, he liked the woman he'd had to marry. She was so open and giving, so thoughtful. She'd been worried about his reaction at the hospital before anything had happened—and he'd proved her correct, had he not, when he'd been unable to handle the news she was pregnant with twins?

He'd hurt her by being so cold after, but he'd had to

escape. He'd had a sensation very like panic that had wanted to crawl up his throat and wrap its fingers around his neck. He hadn't known what would happen if that was allowed to occur. And so he'd planned his escape. He'd left her there and embarked on his trip without her.

And now he missed her. Missed her sweet scent, her sensual body, her soft hands and wicked tongue. He sat through meetings and pictured her naked, and then he shook his head and forced those thoughts away before he embarrassed himself in front of the tribal chieftains.

At dusk, Rashid returned to the tent they'd set up for him—an opulent tent adorned with the usual beautiful carpets, but also with most of the modern conveniences one would expect in the city, thanks to the generators that hummed efficiently nearby.

Rashid peeled off his head covering and shrugged out of the long robe, leaving only the light trousers beneath. Maybe he should call Sheridan, see how she was faring. He'd had reports from Mostafa that all was well with her, and the tight knot around his heart had slowly begun to ease.

He would go back to the palace in four days, and he would no doubt take her to his bed again. But he wouldn't let himself forget there were consequences to allowing a woman to get too close. Not ever again.

Yet part of him chafed at that restriction. Finally, he reached for his phone, determined to call her and see how she was doing.

But it rang right as he was about to dial. He answered to find a very breathless Mostafa on the other end. "Your Majesty," he said, and Rashid could hear the panic in his voice. The thread of utter chaos running through that familiar baritone.

Ice water ran in his veins then, flooding him with that familiar calm before the storm. "What is it, Mostafa?"

"Her Highness," he began, and Rashid's gut twisted. "She is gone."

Rashid was tempted to take the phone from his head and stare at it, but instead he forced himself to be cool. "What do you mean gone, Mostafa? Has she left the palace to go shopping? Gone to the airport in order to run away? Or is she hiding in the stables, perhaps?"

"She took a horse, Your Majesty."

Rashid blinked. "A horse?" Had Mostafa lost his mind? Had Sheridan? "Where is Daoud?"

"He is gone, too. When we discovered Her Highness had left on horseback, he went after her."

Daoud and Sheridan were on horseback. In the Kyrian Desert. But for what purpose? Why had Sheridan done such a thing? To get his attention? To bring him back to her side? The fear he'd tried to keep at bay broke through his barriers and flooded his system like a swirling tornado of sand. It scoured through him, raked him bare and filled him with utter dread.

And fury.

She'd taken a horse. She was pregnant and she'd taken a horse. Climbed on top of its back and rode it into the desert. Why? Why?

And then realization hit him. Hard. What if she wanted to harm herself? The desert was dangerous and she'd gone into it alone. Had he pushed her to the edge? Was she trying to get his attention—or trying to end her life?

That thought made the ice in his veins harder than ever—but for a different reason. He couldn't imagine Sheridan gone from his life. Couldn't imagine waking up without her in this world, without her smile or her touch or the look in her eyes when he entered her body and then took her with him to paradise.

She wasn't Daria but she was…she was *Sheridan*. And Sheridan meant something to him. She really meant something….

He was still reeling from the realization that he cared, that he'd not insulated himself from a damn thing by running away from her, that he couldn't control his emotions as if they had an on/off switch the way he'd always believed, when Mostafa said something that made his gut turn to stone.

Mostafa was talking about a search party and the coming night—and a thunderstorm.

A thunderstorm. Sandstorms in the desert were bad enough, but rain was the true danger. It was such a rare occurrence that when it happened, the rain created floods in the wadis—and the sand turned to sludge. Sludge that could trap anything in its path and annihilate it.

Rain was the true enemy of the desert, and a woman alone on a horse in unfamiliar territory—even if she did survive the brutality of a night exposed to the cold and sand, the jackals and scorpions and lions—was no match for a thunderstorm.

Rashid dressed quickly and then strode from the tent, calling orders as he went. Someone saddled a horse at the same time the Bedouin men emerged from their tents where they'd been preparing for dinner. Rashid and two dozen other men swung into saddles simultaneously. Arabian horses pranced and pawed and snorted, but ultimately they were ready for a ride into the night.

Sheridan could be anywhere out there, but Rashid

knew the direction of the city and he knew the most traveled routes. All who were raised in the desert did. Rashid spurred his horse into a gallop and twenty-four men did the same. It was still light, though only barely, the sky a pink stain across the horizon. The moon was full tonight and they would have it for a couple of hours once it rose, until the predicted storm swept in off the gulf and wreaked its havoc.

Rashid only prayed they would find Sheridan before that happened. Because if they did not, if she had to endure a storm in the desert alone... His breath caught painfully in his lungs as the truth hit him full force: if they did not find her soon, there was no way she would survive.

It had seemed like such a good idea at the time, Sheridan thought. She'd been going to the stables so often that no one had thought anything of it when she went again. Even Daoud had relaxed his guard because he was accustomed to her visiting the stables. There were still a couple of the puppies who were waiting for their forever homes, and she wouldn't stop playing with them just because Rashid had given her Leo.

It had been ridiculously easy to saddle a horse and ride out of the barn. She hadn't been thinking too much at the time, but she'd known from listening in the palace that the Bedouin were only a few hours away by horseback. Had she really thought she could ride out to the oasis and find Rashid?

Fatima had told her he was in a place called the King's Oasis, and she'd described it in great detail. Sheridan wasn't an idiot. She had a map and a compass—handy devices, those, and still quite necessary. She'd located one in the palace after a bit of inquiry. All smartphones had them these days, but of course there were battery and satellite issues to contend with.

So now she was riding along a ridge on a delicate Arabian mare, with the desert a sea of sand in front of her and the city a speck behind her, and beginning to come to her senses. Not only that, but darkness was also falling fast and she had no idea how she was supposed to keep riding in the night. To her left, there was a dark wall of clouds in the distance, and she didn't know if they were headed her way or not. They looked ominous, though, like thunderheads off the coast in Savannah.

The occasional brightening of those clouds told her that was exactly what they were as lightning sizzled through them and painted parts of the bank white and pink. She'd never realized there were thunderstorms in this area of the world, but why wouldn't there be? Her only comfort was that this was a desert and therefore they would lose their destructive power long before they arrived. Or so she thought, since a desert by definition was dry.

She was tempted to turn around, but the compass told her she had gone past the point of no return. If she stayed on track, she would reach the oasis in two more hours.

And Rashid would blow a gasket. Sheridan sank into the saddle as she imagined his face when he saw her. At first, she'd thought she would ride in like a general at the head of the army, triumphant and oozing righteousness. Now she imagined she would limp in like a worn-out puppy, her tail between her legs and her body aching from the punishment of a long ride.

In another hour, it was completely dark, except for the silver light of the moon painting the dunes. It was gorgeous and wild out here and Sheridan was at least partly enchanted by the beauty. But she was also worried, because the clouds were drawing ever closer. The moon would be blotted out before long, and while the flashing in the clouds would give light, it was a lot more worrisome the closer they got.

Not to mention the sand was beginning to blow in gusts, stinging her exposed skin. The horse trudged along sure footedly, but Sheridan wasn't certain how much longer that could last. She'd been so stupid. She'd behaved impulsively, rashly, and Rashid was going to be ashamed of her.

She could hear thunder in the clouds now—and something else. Something that set the hair on the back of her neck prickling. There was a howl somewhere to her right. And then another howl behind her. The horse snorted and kicked up her heels, and Sheridan snatched at the reins, desperate to keep the mare from bolting.

And then something snarled nearby and there was the sound of many animals moving at once. The mare tossed her head and reared onto her hind legs—and then she bolted forward while Sheridan cried out and tried to wrap her hands into the mare's mane.

But she'd been caught by surprise and she couldn't hold on. She fell to the sand with a scream.

CHAPTER FOURTEEN

THE ANIMALS BORE down on her quickly, snarling and thumping and snorting, and Sheridan rolled into a ball and tried to protect her head. She would die out here in the Kyrian Desert, her babies with her, and all because she'd been so tormented over a man that she'd lost her head.

There was another howl, and a shriek that was quickly cut off. And then the thumping grew louder and Sheridan realized there was shouting. Men shouting. She was afraid to uncoil her body, just in case the beasts were still there, but then she felt rough hands on her. She didn't even scream as a man jerked her up and against his body. He called out in rough Arabic and then she was flung onto a horse and the man climbed up behind her.

The hijab had fallen around her eyes and she couldn't see anything at all, but there was a man and a horse and she hung on to his waist for dear life as the horse bolted forward into the night. Around them, she thought she heard more hooves, more horses, but the sound became a dull throbbing as thunder split the night.

And then she felt the first cold drops of rain on her back and head. She was stunned as the rain began to fall harder. She would have never guessed. But the wind howled and the horses ran and the rain fell, and Sheridan had no idea where she was or who she was with.

But since the man was infinitely preferable to the beasts, whatever they were, she was grateful for the moment just to be where she was.

They rode for what seemed forever, the rain pounding down, the wind whipping, the horses straining forward, until finally they came to an abrupt halt and Sheridan knocked her head on the man's chest.

There was more Arabic ringing through the night, and then another man put hands around her waist and helped her down. The man on the horse followed, and then he swept her into his arms as if she was a rag doll and strode into a tent. Sheridan struggled to push the fabric from her face. Her teeth were chattering and her skin prickled with goose bumps.

The man dumped her unceremoniously onto her feet and began to remove her clothing. That was when Sheridan came to her senses. She batted at his hands and tried to scramble away. He said something, but the blood rushing in her ears prevented her from understanding. She just knew she had to get away from him. She had to find Rashid.

She drew in breath to scream—

And the man jerked her into his arms, his mouth coming roughly down on top of hers, silencing her.

Sheridan struggled for only a moment before she realized whose mouth was ravaging hers, whose arms wrapped around her, whose hands speared into her hair and tilted her head back for greater access.

She clung to him, her body softening, hands clutching his wet robes. When he realized she knew, he set her away from him, though she whimpered and wanted to stay in his arms.

"We have to get you out of that wet clothing, *habibti*," he said, his voice rough and beautiful.

Her teeth were chattering again and this time when he began to strip her, she didn't stop him. Her hands were too cold to help and so she simply stood there while he stripped the clothing from her body and then wrapped her in a warm blanket. He chafed her arms and then he picked her up and carried her to the bed, where he set her down and pulled a soft fur on top of her.

"Rashid," she said when he started to walk away, but he only turned and shot her a look that she couldn't read.

He was wet, too, his hair sticking to his head, his face streaked with moisture. He did not seem to be as cold as she was, however.

"I'm going to send for something hot to drink. I'm not leaving."

When he walked out, she huddled under the blankets, her brain whirling. She'd made a grave mistake coming here like this. He would be furious, and he would think her unbalanced for even attempting such a crazy thing. Why wouldn't he want another wife? A more sensible one who didn't act on her emotions without fully considering her actions first?

He returned soon with a brass pot and two cups. He poured tea for her, laced it with sugar and handed her a cup.

"I'm afraid the Bedouin don't drink decaffeinated tea, but this is weak. It shouldn't hurt the babies."

She dropped her eyes as she studied the cup, blowing on the steam curling over the top of the liquid. Shame rolled through her.

She could hear him pouring tea for himself, stirring the tiny spoon against the glass, and her nerves tightened as she waited for the explosion.

When it didn't come, she looked up and met a hot, dark gaze staring back at her. Her heart turned over.

"I'm sorry," she said. "I shouldn't have left the palace."

"No, you shouldn't have." He lifted his cup and she thought his hands were shaking, but then she decided it was just her who was shaking. "You could have died out there, Sheridan. The desert is very unforgiving."

"I know."

Strong fingers suddenly gripped her chin and lifted her face until she had to look directly at him again. His gaze was searching.

"Is that what you wanted to do?"

She blinked. "Wh-what?" It took her a moment to process it, but when she did, she sucked in a hard breath. "God, no! I wasn't trying to kill myself!"

"Then what were you doing?" He sounded angry now. Harsh. "Because you almost did just that, *habibti!* You and the babies were moments away from being mauled by jackals. If we had not come along when we did—"

The color drained from his face and he closed his eyes, his jaw tight.

At that look on his face, there was nothing she could do but tell him the truth. The reason she'd set out on a journey toward this oasis in the first place. Besides, she was too weary to dance around the subject any longer.

"I heard you were going to bring home another wife."

His head snapped up then, his black gaze boring into her. "Where did you hear this?"

"In the palace. The rumor is that you will marry one

of the chieftains' daughters." She lifted her chin. "I know that's not unusual in Kyr, but it's unusual for me."

"And so you decided to risk your life, and the lives of our children, to make your opinion known? Did it not occur to you to ask me about this when I returned?"

She snorted. "With a new wife on your arm? No, it didn't occur to me to wait."

"Sheridan." He shook his head. Said something in Arabic. And then he was looking at her again, his eyes filled with fury. "This stubbornness of yours could have cost you your life!"

"I realize that now!" she shouted back. "I behaved stupidly, I know it, and you're embarrassed and furious and no doubt the new wife is signing documents as we speak. Well, I won't live like that! I can't."

She put a fist to her heart, felt hot tears begin to roll down her cheeks and cursed herself for being so damned emotional. *Hormones,* she reminded herself.

"I won't do it, Rashid."

He looked stunned. "You do realize I am the king? That it's not your place to advise me on this?"

The trembling in her limbs was no longer only due to the cold. "Just tell me if it's true. Are you planning to take another wife?"

His jaw was marble. "Kyrian politics are complicated, Sheridan."

"That's not an answer." Her voice was a painful whisper over the lump in her throat.

He closed his eyes and put his forehead in his palm. "The council wishes me to take a Kyrian wife. But I did not come out here to do that."

"And yet it's only a matter of time."

"It would seem so."

She sipped the tea as if they were having a polite conversation rather than one that broke her heart and ripped out her guts.

"Well, thank you for being honest. If you could perhaps wait until the babies are born, I'll be busy enough then that I won't mind so much."

He growled. "You won't *mind* so much?"

She looked at him evenly, though her face was still hot with tears. "As you've taken pains to inform me from the beginning, I have no choice. And no say in the matter, either. If you take another wife, I'll endeavor not to disembowel you both with Daoud's sword."

If Rashid was amused or alarmed, he didn't show it. "He followed you, you know."

She didn't, but her heart skipped a beat at the thought of Daoud out there alone, too. Guilt filled her then. And fear. "Is he all right? The jackals didn't get him, did they?"

"He is fine. His horse went lame, which is why he didn't catch you. I sent men after him once we found you. They returned a few moments ago, and Daoud is well. For the moment."

She heard the dangerous note in his voice. "Rashid, it's not his fault. He trusted me and I gave him the slip."

"He should not have trusted you at all."

"Maybe not." She bowed her head. "Probably not."

"Apparently I should not, either. Or at least not with any swords."

She glared at him. "Are you making fun of me?"

"I'd rather do something else with you."

She sat there in shock for a moment. And then she shook her head violently. "No. I can't. Not ever again, Rashid. Not if you're going to marry another woman."

He reached for her, gripped her chin and forced her to look at him again. His eyes were bright. "Why not, *habibti?* Why would this bother you? Is it because you are American? Or is there another reason?"

Her heart thrummed and her throat ached and she wanted to sink beneath the covers and hide. He was holding her, demanding an answer, and all she could think was that she wanted him to kiss her. And then she wanted to strangle him.

"I've grown fond of you," she said as primly as she could manage under the circumstances. It was such a bald-faced lie, but she'd die before she'd admit that she loved him now.

She did not expect him to grin. "Fond? I like the sound of that."

She swatted at his hand. "I meant to say I *was* fond of you. I've changed my mind now. Who could be fond of a dictator?"

He took her teacup and set it aside. Then he moved closer, threaded his hand through her still-damp hair. "Who indeed?"

His head descended and she closed her eyes, aching for his kiss. But a hot feeling swelled inside her, bubbling up until she put her hand over his mouth and stopped him from kissing her. If he kissed her, she would sob her heart out and confess all her tragic feelings for him.

And she couldn't do that and keep her dignity.

"No, Rashid. You kiss me and charm me and make me forget myself, but this is where it has to stop. I can't do this anymore. I can't be with a man who runs away from his feelings, a man who can't even be with me without wanting to escape. I can't give you everything I have and only get part of you in return. I've spent too much of my life making other people happy and I'm not going to keep doing it with you when you can't even give me something so basic as a normal marriage between two people. I deserve better than that. I *demand* better than that."

She took her hand away slowly, expecting him to explode in arrogant pronouncements about being a king and her having a place, but he caught her hand and held it in his. His skin burned into her. She wanted to pull her hand away and she wanted to curl into his heat at once.

Why did she have to love a man who was so wrong for her on so many levels?

His brows drew together as he studied her. And then he lifted a finger and traced her mouth lightly, so lightly. She refused to whimper.

"When Mostafa called to say you were missing, I thought I was about to relive that moment when I lost Daria and our son. And I was terrified, but not because of what happened in the past and how much it hurt."

He pulled in a deep breath, his nostrils flaring. "I was terrified because it could happen again, and it would hurt just as much this time as the last. It would hurt because of you, Sheridan."

Tears filled her eyes then, but she shook her head and wished she could plug her ears. Because the beautiful words didn't mean what she so desperately wished they meant. They couldn't. Could they?

"Don't say that, Rashid. Don't say things like that to me when you intend to marry someone else someday."

He held her hard against him and she could feel his heart beating strong and fast. "I don't intend to marry anyone else, *habibti*. I said the council wishes it. I even agreed to it because it made political sense, but I am the king and I can change my mind. And I have changed my mind, Sheridan. I don't want any woman but you. I won't have any woman in my bed but you. You're all I need. You and our children."

Sheridan's fingers curled into his damp clothes as she squeezed her eyes tight shut and held on. It was as if she'd suddenly gotten onto a crazy merry-go-round and she couldn't get off. She was dizzy with the feelings ricocheting through her and confused about what was happening.

She pushed away from him until she could see his eyes. "What does this mean, Rashid? I need you to say it plainly. I need to understand."

He pushed the damp hair off her face. He looked so serious. So worried. "It means that I tried to harden my heart against you, but I failed. It means that I'm terrified about you carrying two babies, and that as much as I might like to spank you right now for what you did tonight, I'd much rather fall to my knees and worship your body and thank Allah that you are mine. It means that I love you, Sheridan, though I tried not to. I'm finished with running from this thing between us."

The lump in her throat was huge. "This thing between us?"

He laughed softly. "Have you not noticed? It's incendiary. I touch you, you touch me, and the room goes up in flame. But it's not just sex, Sheridan. I've had sex before, and it doesn't feel quite like that. With you, I can't get enough. Not just of sex, but of you. When I'm not with you, I want to be. And when I am with you, I want to be closer. I know you feel these things, too. You would have to in order to put up with me these past few weeks."

She smoothed her hand over his chest. "Oh, Rashid,

just when I think you can't say anything else that surprises me, you say this. I thought it was just me who couldn't get enough. I thought I was weak where you were concerned and I kept telling myself I needed to be stronger, that I should tell you no. But I couldn't."

"You haven't said you love me, *habibti*." He ran his fingers over her cheek. "And you don't have to. I already know. And if I had any doubts before, the fact you risked your life to come out here because of a rumor would have erased them all. I'm still angry with you for this, by the way. You should have called me."

"I wasn't sure you wouldn't run away from the question. I had to see your eyes."

He sighed. "Yes, I understand. But never do this again. If you had perished out there—" He swallowed hard. "I would have perished with you, Sheridan. Do you understand that? I would have perished, too."

Tears slid down her cheeks again, only this time she felt free enough to lean forward and kiss him. He was hers, really hers, and she wasn't hiding her feelings another moment. He caught her to him again and kissed her until she was on fire. She was no longer cold, but burning up from the inside out, her entire being filled with flame.

Somehow they got him out of his damp clothing and then he was under the furs with her, their hot limbs tangling together as they rolled together beneath the covers. She ended up on top, straddling him, sinking down on top of him until they both groaned with the rightness of it.

"Sheridan," he gasped, gazing up at her, his expression filled with so much more than simply heat.

She lowered her mouth to his, kissed him tenderly,

teasing it out until neither of them could stand it a moment longer. He gripped her hips and drove up into her while she rode him faster and faster.

They came together, gasping and crying out as the flame rolled through them. And then they collapsed into each other's arms with soft caresses and even softer kisses.

"I love you, Rashid," she said shyly, and he squeezed her tight. She could feel his smile against her hair.

"I love you, too, Sheridan. You keep me grounded."

"You mean I keep your ego in check," she said, laughing.

"That, too." He stroked his fingers up and down her arm. "I didn't know how lost I was until you entered my life."

"And I didn't know I would find home with a man who lived in such a different world than my own. But I did."

"Do you like it here?" he asked, and she thought he seemed a little hesitant. As if it worried him.

"I love it more every day. But the truth is I would love any place in this world so long as you were there. *You* are my home. You."

He squeezed her to him and they said nothing for a long while. But then they began to talk and they spent the evening speaking softly about so many things, and then they made love again, tenderly, before falling asleep curled tightly together.

They would return to the city in a few days and Rashid would issue the proclamation, at their public wedding ceremony, that Sheridan was to be his queen and not just a princess consort. He would deal with the council and they would learn to be happy. In time, they would come to love Queen Sheri, as they called her, as fiercely as if she had been born one of their own.

But tonight was precisely how the royal couple would spend every night for the rest of their lives. Curled together, complete in each other. First, last and always.

EPILOGUE

TWINS. RASHID STILL couldn't believe it, though he'd known for months they were coming. Sheridan had gotten huge and he'd worried himself silly, but his babies were born—a boy and a girl named Tarek and Amira—and his wife was safe. He watched her sleeping now, her hand held lightly in his as she rested after the long ordeal of giving birth.

Eventually her eyes fluttered open and found his. And then she smiled and his whole world lit up from within.

"Habibti," he said, his voice choked with emotion. Such incredible emotion. He'd never thought he could love so deeply more than once in a lifetime. But he did. He'd experienced it numerous times now, he realized. His wife. His children.

He was a lucky, lucky man.

"Have you been here long?" she asked.

He pressed his lips to her hand, her palm to his cheek, and reached forward to slide his fingers over her jaw. "Every moment."

Her eyes widened then. "Rashid! You have to get some rest. Go to the adjoining room and sleep. That's why they prepared this suite for us after all. So the king could rest with his wife in the hospital."

"I couldn't leave you."

Her smile was tender. "It's okay, Rashid. I'm not going anywhere. I plan to hang around and give you hell for the rest of your life. And I plan to give you more babies, too. Though maybe we'd better get used to two for right now."

His throat was tight. She understood his fears and knew just what to say to him. "I love you, Sheridan."

Her eyes were soft and filled with love. For him. It continually astounded him. "I love you, too, arrogant man. Now go and sleep for a while."

"I napped here in the chair. I'm fine. I also have some news for you."

Her gaze sparkled with interest. "What kind of news?"

"Your brother-in-law called."

Her eyes lit up with hope. "And?"

"The twenty-week scan shows a girl. A healthy girl."

Her eyes squeezed tightly shut. "Oh, thank God."

"He says your sister is very happy and she looks forward to talking to you when you feel up to it."

She pushed herself upright, wincing only a little. "I feel up to it now. What time is it?"

He almost laughed. "It's the middle of the night in Georgia. I think you need to wait a few more hours."

She sank back down again. "If I must."

"Kadir and Emily arrived a few hours ago. They're resting in the palace, but they will come by and visit soon."

Sheridan smiled. "I can't wait to see them."

"I believe they have some news to share, as well."

Her eyes widened. "Is Emily pregnant? Oh, that's so wonderful!"

He laughed at the way she didn't even let him answer the question before she exclaimed it was wonderful. "I did not confirm this to you, but yes. Kadir told me that Emily wanted to tell you herself, so you will act surprised."

"I promise I will."

There was a knock on the door and a nurse came in. "Your Majesty, are you ready for the babies? They're awake and hungry."

Sheridan's face lit up. "Yes, please, bring them here."

Two nurses came in and gently placed little Tarek and Amira on Sheridan's lap. Rashid watched his wife settle down with their children and his heart filled with emotion. He'd never thought he would experience this kind of utter happiness in his life, but he was so grateful he'd been given the chance. It continually astounded him that he had been.

When the twins were content and starting to sleep, Sheridan looked up at him, her eyes filled with love. "Would you like to hold one of them?"

Fear crowded him then, but he sucked in a breath, determined to be brave for his family. "Yes, I will do this."

She laughed. "You'll be a natural, Rashid. And you have to start some time."

He reached down and picked up a baby—he didn't know which one—and held it close to his chest, making sure to support the head the way he'd been told. The little face was pinched tight, the eyes closed, but the tiny creature's chest rose and fell regularly and the little lips moved.

"I don't know which one this is," he said softly, gazing with wonder at the baby and not wanting to wake it.

Sheridan laughed again. "That's Tarek. See the blue band on his little wrist?"

"Tarek." Rashid could only stare at the sweet little face. And then he lifted the baby higher and pressed a kiss to his cheek. "My son."

* * * * *

FORGED IN THE
DESERT HEAT

MAISEY YATES

*To daughter. Never be afraid to stand up
for yourself, or to stand for what's right.
You're the hero of your story.*

Maisey Yates is a *USA TODAY* bestselling author
of more than thirty romance novels. She has a
coffee habit she has no interest in kicking, and
a slight Pinterest addiction. She lives with her
husband and children in the Pacific Northwest.
When Maisey isn't writing she can be found
singing in the grocery store, shopping for shoes
online and probably not doing dishes.

Check out her website: www.maiseyyates.com.

CHAPTER ONE

SHEIKH ZAFAR NEJEM scanned the encampment, the sun burning what little of his skin was revealed. He was as covered as he could possibly be, both to avoid the harsh elements of the desert, and to avoid being recognized.

Though, for most, the odds of that would be low out here, hundreds of miles from any city. But this was his home. Where he'd been raised. The place where he'd made his name as the most fearsome man in Al Sabah.

And considering his competition for the position, there was weight to the title.

Nothing seemed out of the ordinary here. Cooking fires were smoldering, and he could hear voices in the tents. He stopped for a moment. This was no family encampment, but that of a band of highway men. Thieves. Outlaws, not unlike himself. He knew these men, and they knew him. He had a tentative truce with them, but that didn't mean he was ready to show himself.

It didn't mean he trusted them. He trusted no one.

Especially not now.

Not now that there was certain to be unrest. Anger, backlash over his installation in the palace. On the throne.

Back to his rightful position.

The Gypsy Sheikh's return had not been met with delight, at least not in the more "civilized" corners of the country. His uncle had done far too efficient a job in destroying his reputation for anyone to be pleased at his coronation.

If only he could dispel the rumors surrounding his exile. But he could not.

Because they were true.

But here, among the people who felt like his own—among the people who had suffered most at his uncle's hand—there was happiness here at least. They knew that whatever his sins, he had been working to atone.

Zafar looked out toward the horizon, all flat and barren from this point to Bihar. There was one more place to stop and seek shelter, but it was another five hours' ride, and he didn't relish the idea of more time spent in the saddle today.

He dismounted his horse and patted the animal, dust rising from his black coat. "I think we'll take our chances here," he said, leading him to a makeshift corral, where other horses were hemmed in, and opened the gate.

He closed it, making sure it was secure before walking back toward the main tent.

One of the men was already coming out to greet him.

"Sheikh," he said, inclining his head. "A surprise."

"Is it? You had to know I was heading back to Bihar." A growing suspicion. The desert was vast and it seemed strange to intersect with Jamal's band of thugs at this particular moment.

"I may have heard something about it. But there is more than one road to the capital city."

"So you had no desire for a meeting with me?"

The other man smiled, dark eyes glinting in the golden light. "I didn't say that. We were hoping to run into you. Or, at least, someone of your means."

"My means are still limited. I haven't yet been back to Bihar."

"And yet, you do find ways to acquire what you need."

Zafar looked the man over. "As do you. Will you invite me in?"

"Not yet."

Zafar knew something wasn't right. His truce with Jamal and his men was tentative. It was probably why they wanted to see him. He was in a position to put a stop to what they did out here in the desert, and he knew the places they liked to hit.

They weren't dangerous men; at least, they weren't entirely without conscience. And so they were on the bottom of a long list of concerns, but, as was human nature, they clearly believed themselves more important in his world than they were.

"Then have you gifts to offer me in place of hospitality?" Zafar asked dryly, a reference to common custom out in the desert.

"Hospitality will come," Jamal said. "And while we don't have gifts, we do have some items you might take an interest in."

"The horses in the corral?"

"Most are for sale."

"Camels?"

"Them, as well."

"What use have I for camels? I imagine there is an entire menagerie of them waiting for me in Bihar. Cars, as well." It had been a long time since he'd ridden in a car. Utterly impractical for his lifestyle. They were a near-foreign thought now, as were most other modern conveniences.

The other man smiled, his teeth brilliantly white against his dark beard. "I have something better. An offer we hope might appease you."

"Not a gift, though."

"Items this rare and precious cannot be given away, your highness."

"Perhaps you should allow me to be the judge of that."

Jamal turned and shouted toward the tent and Zafar watched as two men emerged, holding a small, blonde woman between them. She looked up at him, pale eyes wide, red rimmed. She wasn't dirty, neither did she look like she'd been handled too roughly. She wasn't attempting an escape, either, but given their location...there would be no point. She would have nowhere to go.

"You have brought me a woman?"

"A potential bride, perhaps? Or just a plaything."

"When have I ever given the indication that I'm the sort of man who buys women?"

"You seem like the sort of man who would not leave a woman in the middle of the desert."

"And you would?" he asked.

"In no uncertain terms, Your Highness."

"Why should I care about one Western woman? I have a country to consider."

"You will buy her, I think. And for our asking price."

Zafar shrugged and turned away. "Ransom her. I'm sure her loved ones will pay much more than I am willing or able to."

"I would ransom her, but it is not my intention to start a war."

Zafar stopped and turned, his muscles locked tight, his heart pounding hard. "What?"

"A war, Sheikh. It is not in my best interest to start one. I don't want those Shakari bastards all over my desert."

Shakar was the closest neighboring country to Al Sabah and relations between the two nations were at a breaking point, thanks to Zafar's uncle. "What does Shakar have to do with this woman? She's Western, clearly."

"Yes. Clearly. She is also, if we believe her ranting from when we first took her, American heiress Analise Christensen. I imagine you have heard the name. She is betrothed to the Sheikh of Shakar."

Yes, he had heard the name. He was largely cut off from matters of State but he still heard things. He made sure he did. And clearly, Jamal made certain he heard things, as well. "And how is it I play into this? What is it you want with her?" he spat.

"We can start a war here, or end one, the choice is yours. Also, with the wrong words in the right ear, even if you take her, but threaten us? We can put you in a very bad position. How is it you ended up with her? The future bride of a man rumored to be the enemy of Al Sabah? Your hands are bound, Zafar."

In truth, he would never have considered leaving the woman here with them, but what they were suggesting was blackmail, and one problem he didn't need. One problem too many.

So, buy her and drop her off at the nearest airport.

Yes. He could do. He didn't have very much money on him, but he didn't think their aim was to get the highest price off the beauty's head so much as to seek protection. Zafar was, after all, ready to assume the throne, and he knew all of their secrets.

He looked down at the woman who claimed to be an heiress, betrothed to a sheikh. Anger blazed from those eyes, he could see it clearly now. She was not defeated, but she was also smart enough to save her energy. To not waste time fighting here and now.

"You have not harmed her?" he asked, his throat getting tight with disgust at the thought.

"We have not laid a finger on her, beyond binding her to keep her from escaping. Where would her value be, where would our protection be, if she were damaged?"

They were offering him a chance to see her returned as if nothing had happened, he understood. If she were assaulted, it would be clear, and Al Sabah, and by extension the new and much-maligned sheikh, would be blamed.

And war would be imminent.

Either from Shakar or from his own people, were they to learn of what had happened under his "watch."

He made an offer. Every bit of money he had. "I'm not dealing," he said. "That is my only offer."

Jamal looked at him, his expression hard. "Done." He extended his hand, and Zafar didn't for one moment mistake it as an offer for a handshake. He reached into his robes and produced a drawstring coin purse, old-fashioned, not used widely in the culture of the day.

But he'd been disconnected from the culture of the day for fifteen years so that was no surprise.

He poured the coins into his hand. "The woman," he said, extending his arm, fist closed. "The woman first."

One of the men walked her forward, and Zafar took hold of her arm, drawing her tight into his body. She was still, stiff, her eyes straight ahead, not once resting on him.

He then passed the coins to Jamal. "I think I will not be stopping for the night."

"Eager to try her out, Sheikh?"

"Hardly," he said, his lip curling. "As you said, there is no surer way to start a war."

He tightened his hold on her and walked her to the corral. She was quiet, unnaturally so and he wondered if she was in shock. He looked down at her face, expecting to see her eyes looking glassy or confused. Instead, she was looking around, calculating.

"No point, princess," he said in English. "There is nowhere to go out here, but unlike those men, I mean you no harm."

"And I'm supposed to believe you?" she asked.

"For now." He opened the gate and his horse approached. He led him from the enclosure. "Can you get on the horse? Are you hurt?"

"I don't want to get on the horse," she said, her voice monotone.

He let out a long breath and hauled her up into his arms, pulling her, and himself, up onto the horse in one fluid motion, bringing her to rest in front of his body. "Too bad. I paid too much for you to leave you behind."

He tapped his horse and the animal moved to a trot, taking them away from the camp.

"You…you bought me?"

"All things considered I got a very good deal."

"A good…a good deal!"

"I didn't even look at your teeth. For all I know I was taken advantage of." He wasn't in the mood to deal with a hysterical woman. Or a woman in general, no matter her mental state. But he was stuck with one now.

He supposed he should be…sympathetic, or something like that. He no longer knew how.

"You were not," she said, her voice clipped. "Who are you?"

"You do not speak Arabic?"

"Not the particular dialect you were speaking, no. I recognized some but not all."

"The Bedouins out here have their own form of the language. Sometimes larger families have their own variation, though that is less common."

"Thank you for the history lesson. I shall make a note. Who are you?"

"I am Sheikh Zafar Nejem, and I daresay I am your salvation."

"I think I would have been better off if I were left to burn."

Ana clung to the horse as it galloped over the sand, the night air starting to cool, no longer burning her face. This must be what shock felt like. Numb and aware of nothing, except for the heat at her back from the man behind her, and the sound of the horse's hooves on the sand.

He'd stopped talking to her now, the man who claimed to be the Sheikh of Al Sabah, a man whose entire face was obscured by a headdress, save for his obsidian eyes. But before she'd been kidnapped…and it surely had only been a couple of days…Farooq Nejem had been the ruler of the country. A large and looming problem for Shakar, and one that Tariq had been very concerned with.

"Zafar," she said. "Zafar Nejem. I don't know your name. I can't…remember. I thought Farooq…"

"Not anymore," he said, his voice hard, deep, rumbling through him as he spoke.

The horse's gait slowed, and Ana looked around the barren landscape, trying to figure out any reason at all for them to be stopping. There was nothing. Nothing but more sand and more…nothing. It was why she hadn't made an escape attempt before. Going out alone and unprepared in the desert of Al Sabah was as good as signing your own death certificate.

They'd been warned of that so many times by their guide, and after traveling over the desert in the tour group on camelback for a day, she believed him.

So much for a fun, secret jaunt into the desert with her friends before her engagement to Tariq was announced. This was not really fun anymore. And it confirmed what she'd always suspected: that stepping out of line was a recipe for disaster.

She was so fair, too much exposure to the midday sun and she'd go up in a puff of smoke and leave nothing but a little pile of ash behind.

So bolting was out of the question, but the fact that they were stopping made her very, very uneasy. She'd been lucky, so lucky that the men that had kidnapped her had seen value in leaving her untouched. She wasn't totally sure about her new captor.

She took a deep breath and tried to ignore the burn in her lungs, compliments of the arid, late-afternoon air. It was so thin. So dry. Just existing here was an effort. More confirmation on why running was a bad idea.

But she had to be calm. She had to keep control, and if she couldn't have control over the situation, she would have it over herself.

Her captor got down off the horse, quickly, gracefully, and offered his hand. She accepted. Because with the way she was feeling at the moment, she might just slide off the horse and crumble into a heap in the sand. That would be one humiliation too many. She had been purchased today, after all.

"Where are we?" she asked.

"At a stopping point."

"Why? Where? How is it a stopping point?" She looked around for a sign of civilization. A sign of something. Someone.

"It is a stopping point, because I am ready to stop. I have been riding for eight hours."

"Why don't you have a car if you're a sheikh?" she asked, feeling irritated over everything.

"Completely impractical. I live in the middle of the desert. Fuel would become a major issue."

Oh yes. Fuel. Oil. Oil was always the issue. It was something she knew well, having grown up the daughter of the richest oil baron in the United States. Her father had a knack for finding *black gold*. But he was a businessman, and that meant that the search was never done. It was all about getting more. Getting better.

And that was how she'd met Sheikh Tariq. It was how she'd ended up in Shakar, and then, in Al Sabah.

Oil was the grandaddy of this entire mess.

But it would be okay. It would be. She thought of Tariq, his warm dark eyes, his smile. The thought of him always made her stomach flip. Not so much at the moment, but given she was hot, tired, dusty, and currently leaning into the embrace of a stranger, thanks to her klutzy dismount, it seemed understandable.

She straightened and pushed away from him, heart pounding. He was nothing like Tariq. For a start, his eyes were flat black, no laughter. No warmth. But so very compelling…

"Where are we?" she asked, looking away from him, and at their surroundings.

"In the middle of the desert. I would give you coordinates, but I imagine they would mean nothing to you."

"Less than nothing." She squinted, trying to see through the haze of purple, the sun gone completely behind the distant mountains now. "How long until we reach civilization? Until I can contact my father? Or Tariq?"

"Who says I'll allow you to contact them? Perhaps I have purchased you for my harem."

"What happened to you being my salvation?"

"Have you ever lived in a harem?" He lifted a brow. "Perhaps you would like it."

"Do you even have a harem?"

"Sadly," he said, his tone as dry as the sand, "I do not. But I am only just getting started in the position as sheikh, so there is time to amass one."

She nearly choked, fear clutching at her. "I am…stranded in the middle of a foreign desert…."

"It's not foreign."

"Not to you!" she said.

"Continue."

"I am stranded in the desert with a stranger who claims he's a sheikh, a sheikh who bought me, and you are joking about my future! I have no patience for it."

She had no patience left in her entire body. At this moment, she had two options: get angry, or sink to the ground and cry. And crying was never the preferred option. No, the schools she'd attended, the ones she'd been sent to after her mother left, had been exclusive, private and very strict. She'd been taught that strength and composure were everything. She'd been taught never to run when she could walk. Never to shout when a composed, even statement would do. And she'd learned that tears never helped anything in life. They didn't change things. They hadn't brought her mother back home, certainly.

So she was going with anger.

His manner changed, dark brows locking together. His black eyes glittering with dark fire. He tugged at the bottom portion of the scarf, which had kept most of his face hidden until that moment, and revealed his lips, which were currently curled into a snarl.

"And you think I have the patience for this? These men are playing at starting a war between two nations simply to keep their petty ring of thieves intact. They are trying to buy my loyalty with blackmail. Because they know that if your precious Tariq finds out you were taken by citizens of Al Sabah, or God forbid, they find out the Sheikh of Al Sabah possessed you for any length of time against your will, that the tenuous truce we have between the countries will shatter entirely. How do you suppose my patience is?"

She blinked, feeling dizzy. "I…I'm going to start a war?"

"Not if I play it right."

"I imagine putting me in your harem wouldn't defuse things."

"True enough. But then…perhaps I want the war."

"What?"

"I am undecided on the matter."

"How can you be undecided on the matter?"

"Easily," he said. "I have yet to have a look at any of the papers left behind by my uncle. I have had limited contact with the palace since finding out I was to be installed as ruler."

"Why?"

"Could have something to do with the fact that my first, albeit distant, act was to fire every single person who worked for my uncle. Regime changes are rough."

"Is this a…hostile takeover?"

"No. I am the rightful heir. My uncle is dead."

"I'm sorry." Her manners were apparently bred into her strongly enough that they came out even in the middle of a crisis of this magnitude.

"I'm not. My uncle was the worst thing to happen to Al Sabah in its history. He brought nothing but poverty and violence to my country. And stress between us and neighboring countries." His dark gaze swept over her. "You are unfortunate enough to have become a pawn in the paradigm shift. And I have yet to decide how I will move you."

CHAPTER TWO

FOR ONE MOMENT, Zafar almost felt something akin to sympathy for the pale woman standing in front of him. Almost.

He had no time for emotions like that. More than that, he was nearly certain he had lost the ability to feel them in any deep, meaningful way.

He'd spent nearly half of his life away from society, away from family. He'd had no emotional connections at all in the past fifteen years. He'd had purpose. A drive that transcended feeling, that transcended comfort, hunger, pain. A need to keep watch over Al Sabah, to protect the weakest of his people. To see justice served.

Even at the expense of this woman's happiness.

Fortunately for her, while he imagined she would be delayed longer than she would like, he had a feeling their ultimate goals would be much the same. Seeing her back to Tariq would be the simplest way to keep peace, he was certain. But he had to figure out how to finesse it.

And finesse was something he generally lacked.

Brute force was more his strength.

"I don't like the idea of that at all," she said. "I'm not really inclined to hang around and be moved by you. I want to go home." She choked on the last word, a crack showing in her icy façade. Or maybe the shock was wearing off. It was very likely she'd been in shock for the past few days.

He remembered being in that state. A blissful cushion

against the harsh reality of life. Oh yes, he remembered that well. It had driven him out into the desert and the searing heat had hardly mattered at all.

He hadn't felt it.

He was numb. Bloody memories blunted because there was no way he could process them fully. Deep crimson stains washed pink by the bone-white sun.

If she was lucky, she was being insulated in that way. If not…if not he might have a woman dissolving in front of him soon. And he really didn't have the patience for that.

"I'm afraid that's impossible."

"Right. War. Et cetera."

"You were listening. Now, hold that thought while I go and set up a tent. Can you do that? And can you also not wander off?"

"I don't have a death wish," she said. "I'm not about to wander off into the desert at night. Or during the day. Why do you think I haven't escaped?"

"That begs the question how you were taken in the first place." He took the tent, rolled up and strapped to the back of his horse, and walked over the outcrop of rock. He would hide them from view as best as he could.

Jamal and his men were hardly the only thieves, or the only danger, they could face out in the desert.

"I was on a desert tour. Of the Bedouin camps in Shakar. On the border."

"So my people went into Shakar to take you?"

She nodded. "Yes."

"You are damned lucky they knew who you were." He didn't like to think of the fate she might have met otherwise.

"My ring," she said. "It gave me away. It was part of the Shakari crown jewels." She flexed her fingers, bare now. "They kept that. But then, they would be pretty bad thieves if they didn't."

"Fortunate you had it," he said. "Odd they did not produce it as proof."

Pale eyes widened, panic flaring in their depths. "But you must know about me," she said. "You must know that Tariq planned to marry soon. I would imagine even base intelligence would have brought you that bit of information."

"An alliance that pertains to the political, I believe," he said.

"Yes. And he loves me."

"I'm sure he does," Zafar said dryly.

"He does. I'm not fool enough to think that my connections have nothing to do with it, but we've been...we've been engaged for years. Distantly, but we have spent time together."

"And you love him?"

"Yes," she said, tilting her chin up, blue eyes defiant. "I do. With all my heart. I was looking forward to the marriage."

"When was the marriage to take place?"

"A few months yet. I was to be introduced to his people, our courtship to be played out before the media."

"But your courtship has already taken place."

"Yes. But you know...appearances. I mean, that's the whole point of not taking me straight back to Shakar, isn't it? Appearances. You don't want Tariq to know your people, or by extension, you were involved in this. And you don't want to appear weak. You don't want people to know it happened on your watch." She nodded once, as if agreeing with herself. "That's a big part of it, isn't it?"

"I haven't had a single day in the palace yet. I don't want to be at the center of a scandal involving a kidnapped future sheikha of a neighboring country, so yes, you're right."

"I see."

"What is it you see, *habibti*?" he asked, the endearment flowing off his tongue. It had become a habit to call women that. Because it was easier than remembering names. Safer, in many ways. It kept them at a distance and that was how he preferred it.

Life in the desert, on the move, made it difficult to find lovers, but he had them in a few of his routine stops. A couple of widows in particular Bedouin camps, and a woman in the capital city who was very good at supplying him with necessary information.

She squinted, pale eyes assessing him. "That this is a threat to you personally."

"I am not the most well-liked man in Al Sabah. Let's just say that. This is an issue when one means to rule a country."

It was the understatement of the century. If he had been recognized anywhere in the city while his uncle was in command, his life would have been forfeit. His exile had been under the darkest of circumstances, and since then, he'd hardly done anything to improve his standing, particularly with those loyal to his uncle.

His loyalty was to the Bedouins. To ensure they never suffered because of his uncle's rule, and without him, they would have. No medical, no emergency services of any kind. His uncle had put them at the mercy of foreign aid while taxing them with particular brutality.

They had become Zafar's people.

And now…now somehow he had to assume the throne and unite Al Sabah again, redeem himself in the eyes of the people in the cities while not losing the people in the desert.

And without incurring the wrath of the Sheikh of Shakar.

Not a tall order at all.

"It doesn't really make me feel all that good about being out here with you."

"I'm certain it does not. I'm also certain that's not my problem. Now, I have a tent to pitch so that we don't have to sleep in the open."

"You expect me to sleep in a tent with you?"

"I do. The alternative is for one of us to sleep without any sort of protection and I'm not going to do that. I assume you won't, either. You should see all the bugs that come out at night."

Ana shuddered. The idea of sleeping in the vast openness of the desert with no walls around her at all was completely freaky, and she didn't want any part of it. But the thought of sleeping next to this man…this stranger…was hardly any better.

Her one and constant comfort was the fact that he didn't want to start a war.

Maybe she should tell him she was a virgin. And that Tariq knew it. So if he tried anything he shouldn't there would be no getting out of it. War would be upon him.

A war over her hymen. Yuck. But potentially true.

And if it would help protect her, well, she wasn't above using it as an excuse. But she would save it. Because… yuck.

"How long do you intend to keep me with you?" she asked, watching as he began to work at setting up what looked to be a far-too-small tent.

"Until I no longer need to." He was wearing so many layers, robes to keep him protected from the sun, that it was hard to tell just how his body was shaped, and yet, because of the ease of his movements and the grace in them, she got a sense that he was a man in superior physical condition.

Not that she should notice or care.

"That's not very informative."

"Because I have no more information to give. I will

have to evaluate the situation upon arrival at the palace, and until then, we are stuck with each other."

He continued to work, his movements quick and agile, practiced.

"So...you do this a lot?"

"Nearly every night."

"You buy kidnapped women and then carry them off on your horse every night?"

"I was just referring to the tent."

"I know," she said, looking up at the sky, vast and dotted with stars. "Just trying to lighten the mood." Otherwise she really would cry. She didn't have enough energy for anger anymore. Lame jokes were her last line of defense.

And she couldn't fall apart. Not now. Her father would need her to keep it together, to make sure she made it back to him. Back to Tariq. She'd done everything right, had spent so many years doing her best to be helpful. To not be a burden.

Falling down in the home stretch like this was devastating.

"Technically," he said, tying a knot in a rope at the top of the tent. "I didn't buy you. I ransomed you."

"That does sound nicer."

"Think of it that way then. If it helps."

"A small comfort, all things considered, but I'll take it."

"There, it is done. Are you ready to sleep?"

No and yes. She didn't want to get into the tent with him and sleep on the ground. It was demoralizing. More than that, it was scary. The idea of being so close to him made her heart pound, made her feel dizzy. But she was also ready to collapse with exhaustion. No matter that Zafar was a stranger, he wasn't her kidnapper. He wasn't the same as the men who'd been holding her these past few days.

No matter how austere and frightening he was, he had saved her from her kidnappers.

"Oh…thank you," she said, a tear sliding down her cheek. "Thank you so much."

And something in her broke that she hadn't even realize had been there. The dam on her emotions that had been keeping her strong, keeping her from falling apart since she'd been taken from the camp all those days ago. Or maybe the same dam that had been in place for years, holding back tears for ages, and unable to withstand this new onslaught of life's little horrors.

And control was suddenly no longer an option.

A sob shook her body, emotion tightening her throat. And then she broke down completely. Great gasps of breath escaping, tears rolling down her face.

He didn't move to comfort her; he didn't move at all. He simply let her cry, her sobs echoing in the still night. She didn't need his touch. She just needed this. This release after days of trying to be strong. Of trying not to show how scared and alone she felt.

And when she was done she felt weak, embarrassed and then angry again.

"Done?"

She looked up and saw him regarding her with an expression of total impassivity. Her outburst hadn't moved him. Not at all. Not that she really wanted comfort from this big…beast man. But even so. A little reaction would have been nice. Sympathy. Offer of a cold compress or smelling salts or…something.

"Yes," she said, her throat still tight, her voice croaky. "I am done. Thank you."

"Ready to sleep?"

"Yes." The word escaped on a gust of breath. She was completely ready to collapse where she was standing. She didn't know how that had happened. How exhaustion had taken over so completely.

And then she realized she was shaking. Shivering. She couldn't do this. She had to be strong and keep control. She had to hold it together.

"I don't know why," she said through chattering teeth.

He swore, at least she assumed it was a swearword, based on the tone, and took two long strides toward her, gripping her by the arms and drawing her into the warmth of his body. It wasn't a hug. She knew that right away. This was no show of affection; it was just him trying to keep her from rattling apart.

She trembled violently, his strong arms, his chest, a wall of support. It was amazing that he smelled as good as he did. Yes, it was a weird thought, but it was simple, basic and one she could process.

All those layers in the heat and she would have imagined he might smell like body odor. Instead he smelled spicy, like fine dust and cloves. And he did smell of sweat, but it wasn't offensive in any way. He smelled like a man who had been working, a man who had earned every drop of that sweat through honest effort.

That, somehow, made it seem different than other sweat.

Not that she could really claim to be an expert in the quality of sweat, male or otherwise, but for some reason, that was just how it seemed to her.

This current train of thought was probably a sign of a complete mental breakdown. Highly likely, in fact. Yes, very likely, because she was still shaking.

And adding to the signs of a breakdown, was the fact that part of her wanted to curl her fingers around his robe and hold him tightly to her. Cling to him. Beg him not to let her go.

"The nearest mobile medical unit is...not very near,"

he said, his voice rough. "So please don't do anything stupid like dying."

"If I were dead, how much help would a mobile medical unit be anyway?" she asked, resting her head on his chest, something about the sound of his heartbeat making her feel more connected to the world. To living. She was so completely drained; it felt like it was the reminder of his life that kept her connected with hers. "Besides I don't think I'm dying."

"Does anyone ever think they're dying?"

"I'm not hurt."

"How long has it been since you had a drink?"

She thought back. "A while. I'm not even really sure how many days it's been since I was kidnapped."

"I'm going to put you in the tent."

She nodded, and at the same time found her feet being swept off the ground, as her body was pulled up against his, his arms cradling her, surprisingly gentle for a man with his strength.

He carried her to the tent and set her down on a blanket inside. Then he left her, returning a moment later with a skin filled with water.

"Drink."

She obeyed the command. And discovered she was so thirsty she didn't think she could ever be satisfied.

She pulled the skin away from her lips and a drop ran down her chin. She mourned that drop.

"I hope you weren't saving that," she said.

"I have more. And we'll stop midmorning at an oasis between here and the city."

"Why didn't we stop at the oasis tonight?"

"I'm tired. You're tired."

"I'm fine," she said. His tenderness was threatening to undo her, if you could call the way he was speaking to her now *tenderness*.

"You must be realistic about your own limitations out here," he said. "That is the first and most valuable lesson you can learn. The desert can make you feel strong and free, but it also makes you very conscious of the fact that you are mortal."

She lay down on the blanket and curled her knees into her chest, her back to Zafar. She heard the blanket shift, felt it pull beneath her as he lay down, too.

"The wilderness is endless, and it makes you realize that you are small," he said, his voice deep, accented, melting over her like butter. She felt like the ground was sinking beneath her, like she was falling. "But it also makes you realize how powerful you are. Because if you respect it, if you learn your limitations and work with them, rather than against them, you can live here. You will never master the desert…no man or woman can. But if you learn to respect her, she will allow you to live. And living here, surviving, thriving, that is true power."

Her eyes fluttered closed, and the world upended. "I'm cold," she said, a shiver racking her.

A strong arm came around her waist, and she was pulled into heat, warmth that pushed through to her soul. It was a strange comfort. It shouldn't even be a comfort, and yet it was. Being held by him felt good. Human touch, his touch, soothed parts of her she hadn't known had been burned raw by her nights in the desert.

His fingertip drifted briefly along the line of her bare arm. A soothing gesture. One that stopped the chill. One that made her feel like a small flame had been ignited beneath her skin.

Her last thought before losing consciousness was that she'd never slept with a man's arm around her like this. And the vague sense that she should be saving this for the man she was marrying.

Except that didn't make sense. This was just sleeping.

And she badly needed sleep.

So she moved more tightly into his body and gave in to the need she'd been fighting against ever since she'd been kidnapped.

And slept.

CHAPTER THREE

"You need to wake up now."

Zafar looked down at the sleeping woman, curled up on the floor of the tent like an infant.

The sun was starting to rise over the mountains, and in a moment, the air became heated. Enough that if you breathed too deeply it would scorch your lungs. And he didn't relish riding through the heat of the day. He wanted to get to the oasis, wait it out, then continue on to the city.

He didn't want to spend another night out here with this fragile, shivering creature. He needed to be able to sleep, and he could not sleep beside anyone.

Plus, she was far too delicate. Far too pale. Her skin an impractical shade of pink, her hair so blond it was nearly white, her eyes the same blue as the bleached sky.

She would burn out here in the desert.

She stirred and blinked, looking up at him. "I…" She pushed into a sitting position. "Oh, no. It wasn't a dream."

"No. Sorry. And are you referring to me or the kidnapping? Because I should think I am preferable to a band of thieves."

"The kidnapping in general. This entire experience. Ugh. My whole body hurts. This ground is hard."

"I'm sorry. Perhaps you should talk to the Creator about softening it for you."

"Oh, I see, you think I'm silly. And wimpy and whatever." She pushed a hand through her hair, and he noticed her fingers got hung up in it. He wondered how long it had been since she'd been able to brush her hair. He imagined she hadn't been given the opportunity to bathe or take care of any necessities really.

And he wondered if they had gone with her when she'd had to take care of certain biological needs. If they had stood guard. If they had made her feel humiliated. It heated the blood in his veins. Made him feel hungry for revenge. But he couldn't follow the feeling. Emotion didn't reign in his life. Not now. Emotion lied. Purpose did not.

And it was purpose he had to follow now, no matter the cost.

"I think very little about you, actually. At least, about you as a person. Right now, you are an obstacle. And one that is making me late." He'd been contacted by one of his men. There was an ambassador Rycroft, a crony of his uncle's who was anxious for a meeting. Zafar was about as anxious for it as he was for a snakebite, but he supposed that was his life now.

Meetings. Politics.

"Excuse me?" She stood now, her legs shaky, awkward like a newborn fawn's. "I'm making you late? I didn't ask to be kidnapped. I didn't ask for you to buy me."

"Ransomed. I ransomed you."

"Whatever, I didn't ask you to."

"Be that as it may, here we are. Now get out, I need to take the tent down."

She shot him a deadly glare and walked out of the tent, her chin held high, her expression haughty. She looked like a little sheikha. A pale little sheikha who would likely wither out here in the heat.

"I have jerky in my saddlebags," he said.

"Mmm. Yay for dry salted meat in the heat," she said,

clearly not satisfied to look at him with venom in her eyes. She had to spit it, too.

For all her attitude, she went digging through the bags, and as soon as she found the jerky she was eating it with enthusiasm. "More water?" she asked.

"In the skin."

He continued deconstructing the tent while she drank more water and ate more food. For a woman who was so tiny, she didn't eat delicately.

"Did they feed you?"

"Some," she said, between gulps of water. "Not enough, and I was skeptical of it. So I only ate when I couldn't stop myself."

"Poisoning you, or drugging you would have served no purpose."

"Probably not, but I was feeling paranoid."

"Fair enough."

"But you won't hurt me, will you?" she asked, almost more a statement than a question, pale eyes trained on him.

"You have my word on that."

He would not harm a woman. No matter her sins. Even he had his limits. Though he might see a woman thrown in jail for the rest of her life, but that was an entirely different woman. A different matter.

"I didn't think you would. That's why I slept."

"How many days?"

She shook her head. "I don't know. I was afraid to close my eyes because who knew what might happen. But it only makes things worse. It makes you…think things that aren't real, makes it all blur together and then…it's all scary enough without the added paranoia. I thought I was going crazy."

"Understand this," he said. "I'm not holding you for fun. I am not holding you to harm you in any way. I need to get a better read on the situation. I know this isn't ideal for you, but war during your courtship would be even worse."

"War would be worse in general," she said. "But maybe I can talk to Tariq...."

"Maybe. And maybe it would matter. But there are times when a man must show his strength to protect what is his. There is a time for peace, but when your fiancée has been kidnapped, I am not sure that's the time." He paused. "And then there's how my people will react. It is the sort of thing they expect of me. I will be implicated, make no mistake. Jamal will ensure it. And you know, for many leaders, it wouldn't matter. They could crush the rumors, destroy the rebellion. Me? There is no loyalty to me here. It is not the love of my people chaining me to the throne, but law. If they could see me relieved of the position, many of them would, do not doubt it."

"But you need to rule?"

"I was born to rule. It is my rightful place, stolen from me. I was exiled, banished, and I will not live the rest of my days that way. The throne of Al Sabah is mine now, and I mean to take it."

"Even if you have to hold me to do it?"

"You will be kept in a palace, surrounded by luxury that rivals anything your darling fiancé could produce for you, so I doubt you'll feel to put upon. Consider it a spa retreat."

She looked around them. "Shall I start with sand treatment? Good for the pores, or what?"

"All right, the retreat portion of the vacation starts tonight. For now, consider yourself still on the desert tour. Only this is one-on-one. And you're now with a man who knows the desert better than most people know the layout of the city they grew up in."

"I don't know whether to ask questions about the rocks or the dirt. The beauty is so diverse out here."

"The landscape in Shakar is similar. Perhaps you should

rethink your upcoming marriage if the best you can muster for your surroundings is a bit of bored disdain."

"I'm sorry to have insulted your precious desert. I'm in a bad mood."

"Your mood is the least of my worries, *habibti*. Now—" he put the bundle of tent back onto the horse, took the skin from her hand and refixed it to the saddlebags "—get on the horse, or I shall have to assist you again."

She looked up at the horse and then back at him, genuine distress in her blue eyes. "I can't. I wish I could. But my legs feel like strained spaghetti. It's not happening."

"It's no matter to me. I held you all night. Putting my arms around you again isn't exactly a hardship." Her cheeks turned a brilliant shade of red and it had nothing to do with the sun. He didn't know why he'd felt compelled to tease her that way. He didn't know why he'd felt compelled to tease her at all. He couldn't remember the last time he'd ever felt the least desire to engage in humor or lightness of any kind.

But beneath that was something darker. Something he had to ignore. A pull that he couldn't acknowledge.

"Do what you must," she said, defeated.

He locked his fingers together and lowered his hands, creating a step for her. "Come on," he said.

She looked down and squinted. "Oh, fine." She put one hand on the horse's back and one on his shoulder, placing her foot into his hands and pushing up. He lifted her as she swung her leg over the horse and took her position.

"Front or back, *habibti*, it's no matter to me."

She looked genuinely troubled by the question. And then as though she was calculating which method would bring her into the least contact with his body.

"I…front."

He found the position a bit more taxing, but the alternative was to have her clinging to his back, thighs shaped around his, her breasts pressed to his back. The thought sent a strange tightening through his whole body. His throat down to his stomach, the muscles in his arms, his groin.

No. He had no time for such distraction. She would remain untouched. Protected. He swore it then and there. A vow made before the desert that he would not break.

Fiancée or not, a man who would take advantage of a woman in her position was the basest of creatures.

And are you not more animal than man after your time out here?

No. He knew what was right. And he would see it done.

Right was why he was returning now. Back to a palace that was, in his mind, little more than a gilded tomb. A place that held ghosts. Secrets. Pain so deep he did not like to remember it.

But this had nothing to do with want. Nothing in his life had to do with want; it was simply duty. If doing right meant riding into hell, he would. While the palace wasn't hell, it was close. But there could be no hesitation. No turning back.

And no distractions.

He got on behind her, gripping the reins tightly. "Hold on." He wrapped an arm around her waist. "If we're going to make it back to the palace today, we have to go fast."

Fast was an understatement. They made a brief stop at the oasis, a pocket in a mountain that seemed to rise from the earth, shielding greenery and water from the sun, providing shade and relief from the immeasurable heat.

Sadly, they didn't linger for very long and they were back in the sun, the horse's hoofbeats a repetitive, pounding rhythm that was starting to drive her crazy.

By the time the vague impression of the city, hazy in the distance, came into view, Ana was afraid she was going to fall off the horse. Fatigue had set in, bone deep. She felt coated in a fine layer of dust, her fingers dry and stiff with it.

She needed a bath. And a soft bed. She could worry about everything else later, as long as she had those two things as soon as humanly possible.

This was not her life. Her life was cosseted in terms of physical comforts. A plush mansion, a private all-girls school with antique, spotless furniture and women's college dorms that rivaled any five-star hotel.

Hot baths and soft beds had been taken for granted all of her life. Never again. Never, ever again. She was wretched. She felt more rodent than human at the moment. Like some ground-dwelling creature rooted out of her hole, left to dry out beneath the heat.

As they drew closer she could see skyscrapers. Gray glass and steel, just like any city in the United States. But beyond that was the wall. Tall, made of yellow brick, a testament to the city that once had been—a thousand years ago.

"Welcome to Bihar," he said, his tone grim.

"Are you just going to ride in?"

He tightened his hold on her. "Why the hell not?"

He was a funny contradiction. A man who was able to spout poetry about the desert, soliloquies of great elegance. And yet, when he had to engage in conversation, the elegance was gone. On his own, he was all raw power and certainty, but when he had to interact…well, that was a weakness for sure.

"Seems to me a horse might be out of place."

"In the inner city, yes, but not here on the outskirts. Not on the road to the palace. At least not the road I intend to take."

They forged on, through the walls that kept Bihar separate from the desert. They went past homes, pressed together, stacked four floors high, made from sun-bleached brick. Then on past an open-air market with rows of baskets filled to the brim with flour, nuts and dried fruit. People were milling about everywhere, making way for Zafar without sparing a lingering glance.

She turned and looked up at him. Only his eyes were visible. Dark and fathomless. His face was covered by his headdress. No one would recognize him. It struck her then, how funny it was.

The sheikh riding through on his black war horse, a captive in the saddle with him. And no one would ever know.

They continued on, moving up a narrow cobbled street, past the dense crowds, and through more neighborhoods, the houses starting to spread out then getting sparser. The cobbles turned to dirt, a path that followed the wall of the city, in an olive grove that seemed the stretch on for miles. Then she saw it, a glimmer on the hilltop, stretching across the entire ridge: the palace. Imposing. Massive. Beautiful.

White stone walls and a sapphire roof made it a beacon that she was sure could be seen from most points in the city. Bihar might have thoroughly modern buildings that nearly touched the sky, but the palace seemed to be a part of it. Something ethereal or supernatural. Unreal.

Zafar urged the horse into a canter and the palace rapidly drew closer. When they arrived at the gate, Zafar dismounted, tugging at the fabric that covered his face, revealing strong, handsome features. Unmistakable. No wonder he traveled the way that he did. There was no way he would go unrecognized if he didn't keep his face covered. No way in the world.

He reached into the folds of his robes and pulled out…a cell phone. Ana felt like she'd just been given whiplash. Everything about Zafar seemed part of another era. The man had ridden a freaking black stallion through the city streets, and now he was making a call on a cell phone.

It was incongruous. Her brain rejected it wholly, but it couldn't argue with what she was seeing. Her poor brain. It had tried rejecting this entire experience, but unfortunately, the past week was reality. *This* was reality.

"I'm here. Open the gates."

And the gates did open.

She was still on the horse, clinging to the saddle as Zafar led them into an opulent courtyard. Intricate stone mosaic spiraled in from the walls that partitioned the palace off from the rest of the world, a fountain in the middle, evidence of wealth. As were the green lawns and plants that went beyond the mosaic. Water for the purpose of creating beauty rather than simply survival was an example of extreme luxury in the desert. That much she knew from Tariq.

As if the entire palace wasn't example enough.

She looked at Zafar. His posture was rod straight, black eyes filled with a ferocity that frightened her. There was a rage in him. Spilling from him. And then, suddenly, the walls were back up, and his eyes were blank again.

They were met at the front by men who looked no more civilized than Zafar, a band of huge, marauder-type men. Desert pirates. That's what they made her think of. All of them. Her escort included. One of the men, the largest, even had a curved sword at his waist. Honestly, she was shocked no one had an eye patch.

Fear reverberated through her, an echo along her veins, a shadow of what she'd felt when she was taken from the camp and her friends, but powerful enough that it clung to every part of her. Wouldn't let her go.

She was in his domain. Truly, she had been from the moment she'd been hauled across the border from Shakar to Al Sabah, but here, with evidence of his power all around, it was impossible to deny. Impossible to ignore.

His power, his strength was frightening. And magnetic.

It drew her to him in a way she couldn't fathom. Made her heart beat a little faster. Fear again, that was all. It could be nothing else.

"Sheikh," one of them said, inclining his head. He didn't even spare her a glance.

"Do you need help dismounting?" Zafar asked.

"I think I've got it, thanks." She climbed down off of the horse, stumbling a little bit. So much for preserving her pride. She looked over at Zafar's sketchy crew and smiled.

"We shall need a room prepared for my guest. I assume you saw to the hiring of new servants?"

She nearly laughed. Guest? Was that what she was?

The largest man nodded. "Everything has been taken care of as requested. And Ambassador Rycroft says he will not be put off any longer. He insists you call him as soon as you are in residence."

"Which, I suppose is now," Zafar said, his voice hard, emotionless. "Take the horse."

"Yes, Sheikh."

If any of his men were perturbed by the change in status they didn't show it. But then, she imagined that Zafar had always been the one in charge. That he had always been sheikh to those who followed him.

Questioning him wasn't something anyone would do lightly. He exuded power, strength. Danger. Everything that should have repelled her. But it didn't. It scared her, no mistake, but it also fascinated her. And that scared her on a whole new level.

"Your things?" the other man asked.

"I have none. Neither has she. Remedy that. I want the woman to have a wardrobe of new clothing before the end of the day. Understood?"

The man arched one brow. "Yes, Sheikh."

Oh, good grief. They were going to think she was the starter to his harem. Or at least they would think she was his mistress. But there was no way to correct it now. This was an unprecedented point in Al Sabah's history. Zafar was taking over the throne, and the entire palace clearly had new staff. Zafar would be an completely different sort of leader to the one they'd had before, that much was true.

And it would be such a relief, not just to the people here, but to Tariq's people. She knew that things had been strained between Shakar and Al Sabah, that Tariq had feared war. He'd called her late one night and expressed those fears. She'd valued that. Valued that he cared enough to tell her what was on his mind, his heart.

It was part of why she'd fallen in love with him. Part of why she'd said yes to his engagement offer. Yes, her father had instigated it. And yes, he was a driving force behind it, but she wouldn't have said yes if she wasn't genuinely fond of Tariq.

Fond of him.

That sounded weak sauce. She was more than fond of him. *Love* was the word. No, theirs wasn't a red-hot relationship. But so much of that was to be expected. Tariq was old-fashioned and he'd courted her like an old-fashioned guy. It was respectful.

Plus, he was so handsome. Smooth, dark skin, coal eyes fringed with thick lashes, strong black brows...

She looked back at Zafar and the memory of Tariq and his good looks were knocked completely from her head.

Faced with Zafar, the sharp angles of his face, black beard covering most of his brown skin, obsidian eyes that were more like a dark flame and his lips...she really was quite fascinated by his lips...well, it was hard to think of anything else.

He wasn't smooth. His skin was marked by the sun, by wind. There was nothing refined about him. He was like a man carved straight from the rock.

She wasn't sure *handsome* was the right word for it. It seemed insipid.

"Shall we go in? It is my palace, though I have not been back here in fifteen years. I was born here. Raised here."

Which meant he'd come into the world like everyone else, rather than being carved from stone, so there went that theory.

"Must be…nice to be back?" She watched his face, saw no expression change. If she hadn't caught that moment of intense, dark emotion at the gates, she would think he felt nothing at all. "Strange? Sad?"

"It is necessary that I'm back. That is all."

"I'm sure you feel something about being back."

"I feel nothing in general, Ms. Christensen," he said, addressing her by her name, any part of it, for the first time. "I should hardly start now. I have a country to rule."

"But you're…human," she said, though it sounded more like a question than a statement. "So, I'm sure you feel something."

"Purpose. Every day since my exile there has been one thing that has enticed me to open my eyes each morning, and that has been the belief that my people need me. That it is my duty and my right to lead this country, to care for these people, as they should be led and cared for. Not in the manner my uncle did it. Purpose is what has driven me for nearly half of my life, and purpose is what drives me now. Emotion is unnecessary and weak. Emotion lies. Purpose doesn't."

In so many ways, he echoed a colder, harsher version of what she'd always told herself. That doing right was what mattered. That when people stopped doing right and started serving themselves, things fell apart. Utterly and completely.

She'd seen it in her own family. She'd never wished to bring the kind of destruction her mother had, so she'd set out to be better. To be above selfishness. To do the right thing, the thing that benefitted others before it benefitted her.

To take care, instead of destroy. To be a blessing instead of a burden.

But hearing it from his lips, it seemed…wrong. At least she acknowledged emotion; she just knew there were more important things in life than giddy happiness. Giddy happiness was fleeting, and selfish. She felt it was just her mission to make sure she didn't put her feelings above the happiness of others. There was nothing wrong with that.

"You know what else doesn't lie? My muscles. I'm so stiff I can hardly move."

"A bath then. I will have one drawn for you."

"Th-thank you."

"You sound surprised."

"You're giving me nicer things than my last kidnapper."

"Savior, Analise. I think the word you're looking for is *savior*."

She looked into his midnight eyes and felt something tug, deep and hard inside of her. Something terrifying. Something that touched the edge of the forbidden. "No, I really don't think that's the word I'm looking for."

"Come," he said, walking toward the doors of the palace.

Zafar didn't wait for the double doors to open for him. He pushed against them with both palms, flinging them wide, the sound of the heavy wood hitting the stone walls echoing in the antechamber.

He simply stood for a moment, and waited. For what he did not know. Ghosts, perhaps? There were none. None that were visible, though he could almost feel them. The pain, the anguish this place had witnessed seemed to echo from the walls and he felt it deep down in his bones. If he listened hard enough, he was certain he could still hear his mother screaming. His father crying.

The air was heavy. With memory, with a cold, stale scent that lingered. Probably had more to do with the stone walls than with the past.

He'd spent years living in a tent. Hell, it had been over a year since he'd actually been in a building that wasn't made from canvas. The walls were too heavy. Too thick. Making the air even harder to breathe.

He wanted to turn and run, but Ana was behind him. He felt like an animal being herded into a cage, but he wouldn't show that weakness. He couldn't.

So he took another step inside. Into darkness, into the place that had seen so much death and devastation. It was a step back into his past. One he wasn't prepared to take, but one that had to be taken.

"Zafar?"

He felt a small hand on his arm and he jerked away, looking down at Ana. She didn't shrink back, but he could see something in her wilt. Unsurprising. She must think him more beast than man, but then, there was truth in that.

"We shall have your bath run for you," he said, his voice tight, cold, even to his own ears.

He had no choice but to move forward. To embrace this because it was his destiny. And his penance. He gritted his teeth and walked on.

Yes, this was his penance. He was prepared to pay it now.

CHAPTER FOUR

IT WAS ZAFAR'S great misfortune that Ambassador Rycroft was near and insisted on a meeting immediately. With Zafar in his robes, filthy from traveling. He had no idea how he must appear to the immaculately dressed, clean-shaven man who was sitting in his office now. He had very little idea of how he appeared at all. He didn't make a habit of looking at mirrors.

The man was, per the paperwork he'd seen of his uncle's, important to the running of the country. At least he had been. Zafar suspected that many of the "trade agreements" ran more toward black market deals. But he lacked proof at the moment.

They'd been making tentative conversation for the past few minutes, and Zafar felt very much like a bull tiptoeing through a china shop.

"This regime change has been very upsetting to those of us at the embassy."

"I am sorry for that," Zafar said. "My uncle's death has inconvenienced you. I'm not certain why he couldn't postpone it."

Rycroft simply looked at him, offense evident in his expression. "Yes, well, we are eager to know what you intend to do with the trade agreements."

"Your trade agreements are the least of my concern." Zafar began to pace the room, another move that clearly unnerved his visitor. He supposed he was meant to sit. But he couldn't be bothered. He hated this. Hated having to talk, be diplomatic. He didn't see the point of it. Real men said what they meant; politicians never did. There was no honor in it, and yet, it was how things worked. "I have stepped into a den of corruption and I mean to sort it out. Your trade agreements can wait. Do you understand?"

Rycroft stood, his face turning red. "Sheikh Zafar, I don't think you understand. These trade agreements are essential to the ease of your ascension to rule. Your uncle and I had an understanding, and if you do not carry it out, things might go badly for you."

Anger surged through Zafar, driving his actions before he had conscious thought. All of his energy, seemingly magnified by the feeling of confinement he was experiencing in this place, broke free. He grabbed the other man by the shoulders and pushed him back against the wall, holding him firmly. "Do you mean to threaten me?"

Politicians might use diplomacy. *He* would not.

"No," the ambassador said, his eyes wide. "I would not…I would never."

"See that you do not, for I have erased men from this earth for far less, and don't forget it."

He released his hold on Rycroft and stepped back, crossing his arms over his chest.

"I will go to the press with this," the other man said, straightening his jacket. "I will tell them that they have put an animal on the throne of Al Sabah."

"Good. Tell them," he said, anger driving him now, past the point of reason. Past whatever diplomacy he might have possessed. "Perhaps I will have fewer pale men in suits to deal with if you do."

As she sank down into the recessed tub, made from dazzling precious stone, and the warm water enveloped her sore, dusty body, Ana had to rethink the savior thing.

These bubbles, the oils, the bath salts…it all felt like they, and by extension, Zafar, might very well have saved her life.

She would have liked to stay forever and just indulge, but she knew she couldn't. She didn't just relax and indulge. It wasn't in her. She had to be useful. There was always something to do. Except, right now there wasn't really anything.

Such a strange feeling. She didn't like being aimless. She didn't like feeling out of control. She needed purpose. She needed a project. Something to keep her mind and hands busy. Something to make her feel like she was contributing.

Being kidnapped wasn't engaging much, except the constant war between her fight-or-flight response. It was terrifying, all of it, and yet she didn't know the right thing to do.

She'd been working so hard for so many years. The desert trip was her last and first hurrah. Post-graduation, pre-public engagement. She'd wanted a touch of adventure, but nothing like this.

She pushed up from the bench and stepped out of the bath. There was a plush towel and a robe waiting for her. And she would be lying if she wasn't enjoying it all a little bit. Premature princess points being cashed in now.

Glamorous in theory. And yet, it would be a lot like an extension of the life she already had. Living for appearances. That was all normal to her. She felt like she was always "on." Even with her friends. The elite women's college they'd gone to had encouraged them to be strong, studious and polished. To conform to a particular image. And even when they had personal time, even when they laughed and let the formality drop a bit, that core, that bit of guardedness, still ran through the group just beneath the surface.

She'd always been afraid to show too much of herself.

Those tears in the desert had been some of the most honest emotion she'd let escape in years.

She wrapped herself in the robe and wandered back into the bedroom. "Oh, you are kidding me," she said, looking down at the long, ornate table along the nearest wall. There was a bowl filled with fruit on it. Figs, dates, grapes.

"All I need is a hottie cabana boy with palm fronds standing by to fan me," she muttered, taking a grape from the cluster and popping it into her mouth.

"I see you're finding everything to your liking."

She whipped around and saw Zafar striding through her bedroom doors. He looked…different. He had lost the headdress and heavy traveling robes, in favor of a white linen shirt and a pair of pale dress pants. His long hair was wet, clean and tied back. He had kept the beard, but it was trimmed short.

Somehow, he looked even more dangerous now, with this cloak of civility. Because at least before, he was advertising that he was a hazard. He had danger signs and flares all over him before. This great hairy beast with a full beard and flowing robes. With windburned skin and a thin coating of dirt. And the sweat smell. Not forgetting that.

But now she felt she could see more of him, and it displayed, to her detriment, just how handsome he truly was. Square jawed with a strong chin, and yet again, the lips.

Why was she so fascinated by his lips? Men's lips weren't that big a deal.

"Everything is lovely, all things considered."

"What things considered?"

"Does the phrase 'gilded cage' mean anything to you?"

He shook his head. "No. You are comfortable?"

She let out an exasperated sigh. "Yes. More or less. But I would feel more comfortable if I could let my father or Tariq know I was safe."

"I'm afraid that isn't possible." He started pacing over

the high-gloss obsidian floor. A caged tiger. That was what he reminded her of. The thought sent a little shiver of fear chasing down her spine. "I was hardly exaggerating when I said this incident could push us into war. Neither of us want that, am I right?"

"They must be frantic!" she said. "Honestly, can you... can you channel what it might be like to feel, just for a second? They probably think I'm dead. Or sold. Which I was. But...but they probably think I'm in grave peril. I could talk to Tariq. At least give me a chance."

He shook his head. "Things are far too tenuous for me at the moment. Let me tell you a story."

"I hope it has a happy ending."

"It hasn't ended yet. You may well decide how it does end, so listen carefully. There once was a boy, who grew up in an opulent palace, fully expecting one day to be king. Until the castle was invaded by an enemy army, an enemy army who clearly knew how to get direct access to the sheikh and sheikha. They were killed. Violently. Horribly. Only the boy was spared. He would be king; at sixteen, he could very well have ruled. But there was a problem. An inquiry, suggested by the boy's uncle, which indicated he was to blame for the death of his parents. And he was found guilty."

There was no emotion in Zafar's voice. There was nothing. It was more frightening than if there had been rage, malice, regret. Blank nothingness when speaking of an event like that, total detachment when she knew he was talking about himself...it was wrong. It was frightening, how divorced from it he was.

It made her wonder if she was as safe with the dynamic ruler as she'd initially imagined.

"Exiled to the desert for fifteen years under a cloud. The uncle ruled, the people fell into despair, the country to near ruin. And who was to blame? The boy, of course. A boy who somehow survived those years alone and is now a man. A man who must now assume the throne. You see what is stacked against me?"

"I understand," she said, shifting, the stone floor cold beneath her bare feet. She suddenly became very conscious that she was wearing a robe with nothing beneath it. "But let me tell you a story about a girl and…and…no, let me just say, I disappeared some six or seven days ago from a desert tour I wasn't supposed to be on. My friends are probably frantic. My fiancé is probably…concerned." Devastated might be a stretch. Tariq was a very even-tempered man. "My father…" She nearly choked then. "My father will be destroyed. I am all that he has…you have to understand."

Even as she said it, she hoped it was true. Strange that she was wishing for her father to be distressed, but…but she was always so afraid that his life was easier without her. It had been for her mother. No child to take care of. No one to break her lovely things.

"And *you* have to understand this. Inquiries are being made about you. Discreet ones, but it is happening. Kazeem received a phone call with a very clear threat. That the future Sheikha of Shakar was missing, and should she be found on Al Sabahan soil my reign will hold a record for brevity."

"Oh," she said, feeling dazed.

"I am all this country has," he said, his voice hard, echoing in the room. "If there is to be a future for my people, I must remain on the throne. There is no room for negotiation."

"So, what if I try to leave?"

"You will be detained. But I seriously doubt you will try to leave."

"Why?"

"Because you're a sensible woman. A woman who wouldn't want blood on her hands." He looked at her, his eyes taking on a strange, distant quality. "Take it from a man who knows, *habibti*. Whether you spill it with your own hand or not, blood won't come clean."

She believed him. Believed it was true. Believed that he knew what it meant to have blood on his hands. Not for one second would she doubt it.

Could she do it? Could she risk it?

The entire thing made her uneasy, but she hardly had a choice. She could try and run, she could try to find her way back on her own, try to call Tariq, who would storm the castle and…and…oh dear.

She looked at Zafar. Did she really trust this man? That he would release her? That he would do what he said?

She did. Because she'd been alone with him in the desert overnight, and he'd slept with his arm curled around her waist to keep her from shivering. Because when she'd needed touch, no matter whether he understood it or felt it or not, he had provided it. He hadn't taken advantage of her, had never once touched her inappropriately or in a way that would harm her.

In short, he treated her exactly like a man in his position should treat her, provided he was telling the truth.

"I require an exit strategy, Sheikh," she said.

"What do you mean?"

"When will you release me? Regardless of what is happening. There has to be a set end date. A sell-by."

"I'm not certain I can give you that."

"I require it," she said. "No more than thirty days."

"It shall be done." His agreement, the heavy tone in his voice, did nothing to ease her concerns. Thirty days. Thirty days in this palace, a captive of this man. But with that thought the oddest burst of lightness came through.

More of this solitude. These moments of utter indulgence that weren't for anyone but her.

"I am not holding you prisoner," he said.

"Oh really. So, I'm free to go?" The lightness faded, because the fact remained, she was, essentially, Zafar's prisoner.

"No," he said, crossing broad arms over his chest. "Under no circumstances."

"Then how am I not a prisoner?"

"Have I tossed you in the dungeon? Is that bread and water on your table there? No. I gave you a bed. Fruit."

"So, I'm a well-fed prisoner with a down pillow."

"If you like. The difference between this and *prisoner* is in many ways the same as the difference between…purchased and ransomed. Whatever makes you feel better."

"A nap, I think."

"Excellent. A nap. And then you will join me for dinner."

"What? Why?"

"Because, *habibti*, I can hardly have you staying here at the palace looking like a prisoner, now can I?"

"Why not? Goes with the fearsome desert-man thing you're rocking."

"A compliment?"

"Not really. Why not?" She reiterated her earlier question.

"Because, it simply won't do. A little investigation on your part and you could find out a lot of very terrible things about me. Most of them very true. And the last thing I need is any suspicion that I am keeping an American woman here against her will."

"Harem rumors shall abound."

He arched a dark brow. "Indeed."

"So what do you want them to think? Because, all

things considered, later, I will be recognized, so I can't be here as…well…a girlfriend."

He laughed, a strange, rusty sound. Clearly not an expression of emotion he'd used in a while. "I do not have girlfriends, Analise."

"Ana," she said. "No one calls me Analise."

"Ana," he amended, "I have lovers, if you can even call them that. Bed partners. Mistresses. Women who satisfy me physically as I satisfy them." His words, dark, rough and uncivilized, like the man himself, should have appalled her. Just as the man himself should have appalled her. But he didn't. And they didn't. Instead they brought to mind lush scenes of him, more golden-brown skin on display than was decent, his arms wrapped around a woman. A rather pale woman with blond hair. She blinked rapidly and tried to dispel the image.

Zafar continued. "I do not have girlfriends. That brings to mind flowers and chocolates. Trips to the cinema. I haven't been to a cinema in…ever. And I have not even seen a movie in at least fifteen years."

A movie theater was a much-less-challenging image. "That's…that doesn't seem possible."

Zafar was a magnified, twisted version of her in some ways. Never taking the time to do normal things because he was so burdened with purpose.

But really, never going to a movie theater? Not seeing a movie in fifteen years? He wouldn't get half of her jokes. But then, she wondered if Tariq watched movies. They'd never talked about that. They'd talked about weighty things like duty and honor and oil.

But not movies. And she actually liked movies.

"I was a bit consumed with daily survival and making sure the Bedouin tribes weren't completely marginalized, but yes, perhaps I should have made more time for taking in films."

"Oh…like you've never had any downtime. You *do* have mistresses," she said, feeling her face get hot. Because those same images were back. And the woman in the vision was a lot clearer this time. And *oh my*. There was no way she should be entertaining that thought. She was too practical to have vivid sexual fantasies.

"Yes, indeed, but I find sex much more interesting than watching television."

Her mouth dropped open, and she really wished she hadn't let it, but she hadn't known it was going to drop open until it did. She closed it slowly. "Well, all right. There's something I'd like to do in bed right about now. Have a nap. So…goodbye."

He inclined his head. "Until dinner. A dress will be sent."

"Good, I was worried. I would hate to look less than my best for you."

He laughed again, that same uneasy, clearly not oft-used sound. "That would be a tragic occurrence."

"Yeah. I know, right? Now out."

"You give an awful lot of orders for a…"

She crossed her arms. "Yes, that's a question…what am I?"

He regarded her closely, his dark eyes searching. "Well, you do have a lot of opinions on how I ought to do things. And you are certainly trained in the art of being royal… when you aren't letting your tongue run away with you."

"You can see my royalty training coming through?" she asked, only half joking.

"Yes. It is in the way you stand, the way you sit. Your composure, even in a difficult situation. And considering I have just had a meeting with an ambassador that has gone very poorly…"

"Have you?"

"I might have threatened to erase him from the earth."

"Oh, dear," she said.

"And he may have threatened to go to the press."

"Indeed."

"Yes, indeed. So it will come as no surprise to anyone that I am in need of a bit of help. Especially since I am due to make a showing in public very soon."

She eyed him critically. "Oh."

"And I gather you're starting to see the problem. And I think you can help me."

She swallowed. She didn't like the sound of this. A slow smile spread across his face, and that made her even more nervous.

"Ms. Christensen, I believe you are here to teach me to be civilized."

Ana had to wonder what the hell he was talking about while she put on her dress, and still while she wandered down the hall.

The palace was on bare-bones staff and eerily quiet. Not like the times she'd stayed at Tariq's palace in Shakar.

There, the palace was constant motion and sound—people moving everywhere, administrative staff, cleaning staff, serving staff, tours often being given in portions of the palace. There was always activity.

Things seemed dead here. Frozen in time. It reminded her of a fairy-tale castle, where all the inhabitants were sleeping. Or maybe turned into furniture and small appliances by a wicked enchantress.

Or maybe just that a new leader had been installed who had no subjects loyal to him beyond the broad expanse of the desert.

That was more likely.

She walked through the empty corridors and she had a sudden thought. A phone. What if she could find a phone?

She hurried through the hall, looking in opened rooms

and in nooks. And there, she found one. An old-fashioned, gilded, rotary phone sitting on a pedestal. Just waiting. She walked over to the table and stood in front of it, her palms sweaty.

She could call Tariq. She knew his personal number by heart. Not because she'd used it so much, but because she'd felt a woman ought to know her fiancé's phone number.

She stood there and imagined what she would say. And what his response would be. What if he mobilized the helicopters? And ground troops. And they swarmed the castle. And everything Zafar was working toward would be utterly destroyed because she'd had to take action.

And worse—a small voice inside of her had to say it—what if he did nothing? What if he waited? What if he too just sat back and did the thing that was most politically expedient?

That thought made her ill. And as much as she'd like to forget she'd ever had it, it was impossible to do. It was insidious, a small worm of doubt that had been burrowing its way into her for days and days now.

What if he didn't care? Sure, threats had been made. Contact established with Zafar on the matter, but this was all so political in nature. What if, when she was now more inconvenient than convenient, Tariq wouldn't really want her at all?

She backed away from the phone, her heart pounding hard. Later. She knew where the phone was now, and if she needed to make a call, she could do it later .

She wandered down a corridor, trying to ignore the sick feeling in her stomach, trying to stop her hands from shaking. She wandered until she heard movement. The kitchen. She could hear dishes and water. Voices. Finally things felt a little less haunted. And from there, she found the dining room. A serving girl was there, pouring a glass of something for Zafar, who was sitting on the floor on pillows in a semi-reclined position, a low table in front of him.

His shoes were off, no regard given to posture or manners. He had, in fact, started eating without her. He was using his hands, as was the custom, and yet somehow it just looked…shocking when he did it. Wholly sensual. He was eating too fast, like a man who had been without food for too long.

She thought of the jerky in his saddlebags. He had at least been without good food for too long.

He scooped a bit of rice in his hand and ate it, then licked his fingers. She felt a sharp, hard tug low in her stomach, one she couldn't pretend she hadn't felt. No matter how much she wished she could.

Dear heaven, if a fine was charged for looking completely disreputable, he would be forced to sell the castle to pay his debt. He just looked…dangerous and wicked, and for some reason none of it was unappealing. None of it at all. His poor table manners, the fact he was eating without her, should have offended and blotted out all the…the dark magnetism she was feeling.

But it wasn't. Why oh why wasn't it?

"Ana," he said, smiling, for the benefit of the serving girl she imagined, because she'd never seen him smile before. He still looked both wicked and dangerous. "Please come in and sit down."

She obliged, positioning herself across from him on a long, cream-colored cushion.

"Dalia, I will need privacy with Ms. Smith for the meal. We have terms to discuss. A business arrangement."

Dalia inclined her head and set the pitcher on the table. "I'll leave this for you, Sheikh. I wouldn't want you to be thirsty." She gave him a look that could only be described as adoring.

"Thank you." He took a long gulp of his drink and waved her away. She went quickly, her head bent down.

"Firstly," Ana said, when they were alone in the cavernous room, "Smith? Ms. Smith?"

"Ana Smith, much less damning than calling you by Analise Christensen, don't you think? No doubt your name will be appearing in the media, if it hasn't already. Though, I have heard nothing so I would venture to say your sheikh is conducting a covert search for you. Even more dangerous in many ways, because I have no way of knowing where he's looking."

"You mean he hasn't mobilized the military and the press and the...Coast Guard?"

"Not that I have seen, no."

"Oh." She knew there was probably a reason, and it wasn't that he didn't care, just that it was strategy. Like the strategy Zafar was employing. Greater good and all. She was just one girl. She wasn't worth uprooting national security over or anything. And stuff.

"You will be kept here at the palace. Public events would be too risky. Really, any showing in public would be. You will be known as Ana or Ms. Smith, as previously stated, and you are here to teach me...manners."

She looked at him, half-civilized and seemingly unconcerned with it. "Manners?"

"That is oversimplifying, perhaps, but that is one thing you will help me with. I am a man too long out of society, and now I must come in as a king people can stand with. They will not stand with a barbarian."

"But your serving girl...Dalia, she seemed to be a fan."

"Dalia is from one of the desert tribes. Her family owes me a debt of gratitude, and she came to serve in the palace until I could secure loyal staff."

"She likes you," she said.

"She's young. She'll get over it."

"You aren't interested?"

"Sweet young virgins are fine for some, but not for me. I don't have any interest in seducing women and breaking hearts. It's not how I am."

Sweet young virgins.

Well, indeed.

"Good. I feel better knowing she's safe." *And knowing I'm safe.*

Like she'd ever really had anything to be worried about. He wasn't a going to force himself on her, that much was obvious.

Yeah, but the seducing was worrisome....

No. Nope. No. She wasn't worried about him seducing her. That implied that she was seducible, and she was not. She so was not. But she was a sweet, kind of young...relatively. Virgin—yeah, she was that for sure—so he wasn't going to be interested. But even if he was it wouldn't matter.

Good grief, Ana, you have lost your fool mind.

He was holding her against her will, kind of, and making her play the part of Miss Manners. She had no reason to feel fluttery about him, and yet she did. Because it was easy to remember what it had felt like to fall asleep with his arm around her. How the weight of it had been warm, his body solid and comforting behind her.

How she hadn't disliked it at all, but had actually wanted to stay there in his embrace. And when she'd woken and he was standing above her, rather than lying with her, she'd been confused. She'd missed his presence.

Because she'd been half-asleep and confused, but still. It was inexcusable.

Feelings like that were a betrayal. A betrayal of the man who had...probably mobilized special forces...quietly...to find her.

In the cold light of day, she feared Zafar. His power over

her, the fact that she didn't have the control. She didn't miss having him sleep next to her. So there.

"What is it you expect me to do? Aside from telling you not to threaten dignitaries with bodily harm" she said. "Teach you which fork you eat your salad with?"

"Maybe," he said, and for the first time she developed a hint of something genuine beneath his hard tone. "Maybe you could teach me how to have meaningful diplomatic interaction. Or at least teach me how to avoid scaring people. Something I failed at today, although, I think he very likely deserved it."

"Wait…are you…serious? You mean you really want me to give you royal lessons?"

"You've passed yours so proficiently. And it would be a way to while away the time. I am officially being crowned in less than a month, and look at me," he said, sweeping a hand over his reclining figure. A fine figure it was, too. And she did look. For a little longer than she probably should have. "I am not the man that these people would want to have lead them."

"Why not? You're…strong and you are able to ransom damsels in distress when the situation calls for it, so… leadership qualities in my opinion."

"And yet, I lack charm, you must admit."

"Yeah, okay, you lack charm a little bit."

"And that cannot be."

"Just…be friendlier."

"I don't know how," he said, the words scraping his throat on the way out. "I spent…countless days in the desert alone. Speaking to no one. Sometimes I traveled with men, but then I had to be a leader, and out there…out there manners don't get things done. Diplomacy is not gutting someone when they make a mistake. I have spent the majority of the past fifteen years alone. And while my horse makes for decent company he does not talk back, which means my skills are limited."

"What is your horse's name? You never said."

Zafar's dark brows locked together. "He doesn't have one."

"How can he not have one?"

"He is the only horse. And besides that, it isn't as though he's likely to get mixed up with other horses, or that it would be unclear as to who his rider is. I travel mostly alone, remember?"

"It's just…I name my pets."

"My horse," he bit out, "is not a pet. Do you name your cars?"

"No. But I mean…people do. Some men even name their…" She trailed off, her cheeks lighting on fire. Why had she said that? What had possessed her? She didn't say things like that in front of men, or in front of trustees for charities she worked with. She knew when to keep quiet. Yeah, she got giggly with her friends, specifically the girls she'd gone on the desert tour with. They would talk about their boyfriends and their various and sundry names for their manparts, in a kind of superior way that always made Ana feel gauche. But she would laugh and blush, and generally play the part of group virgin, since that's what she was.

But she didn't just bust out the innuendo at random.

"I do not," he said, no hint of humor in his face.

"I figured as much. Unnamed horses aside—" in that moment she decided she would name the poor thing "—you really do want my help?"

"I more than want it, I need it. I need to be seen as a man and not an animal. I need to be…a king in the eyes of my people, and if I go on like I did today, it will not happen. All things considered, you might find it in you to ransom me?" he asked.

She breathed the words before she had a chance to think them through. It was a job. A project. A purpose. And she always said yes to a project. "Of course."

CHAPTER FIVE

ZAFAR WASN'T CERTAIN what had possessed him to be so honest. Except, why not? She would not be staying here; in fact, she would never speak of her being here at all. He would forbid it, and she would doubtless see the reasoning. It was all to protect his people, and her future people, after all.

Ana Christensen did not need to see him as an infallible leader, or as a fearsome warrior. Ana Christensen only needed to see him as a man, and see how she might help that man assume the throne with more ease. And preferably without being deposed by the neighboring country.

His gut kicked in at the thought of her seeing him as a man. He gritted his teeth. He did not mean it that way. He tightened the tape around his fists and repositioned himself in front of the bag he'd been pounding on only a moment earlier.

Being in the palace like this, being indoors, made him feel restless. Like he had too much energy and nowhere to channel it. That meant a lot of hours spent swimming laps in the pool, lifting weights or hitting a punching bag.

Anything that kept him from feeling like he had during his meeting with Rycroft. Like violence was a living beast just beneath the surface of his skin, waiting to tear its way out.

Anything to keep him from feeling like he was suffocating behind the walls. Or buried alive in a tomb. A tomb that held the spirits of those lives taken here.

He had spent the years since his exile in the desert. In the open. And he had not been back to the palace since he'd been driven out.

Those two made for a poor combination and created a sensation of claustrophobia he didn't like.

Fortunately, he had little time to worry about it. In a few short weeks he would become the face of the nation, and that meant he had to figure out just what face he would show the world.

Not his real one, naturally. No one wanted to engage in diplomatic discussion with a hollow, emotionless stone. A man who had left weakness and feeling behind him so many years ago he couldn't remember what it had felt like to have them inhabit his body.

Neither did he want to.

He just needed an appropriate mask. And Ana would help him fashion it.

"Kazeem told me that you were... Oh!"

He turned and saw Ana standing in the door to his workout room, her jaw slack, her blue eyes wide. Her eyes, he realized, were most definitely not on his face, but on his sweat-slicked torso. And he would be lying if he denied getting any pleasure from it.

But he would not touch her. Ever. It was impossible. A little lust was hardly worth the security of an entire nation.

And you've followed your cock down that path before, haven't you?

He banished that insidious voice. The one that would see him curled up on the floor crying like a child rather than taking action. He had no room for regret. He could only move forward.

He could not erase his past mistakes. They would always stain. The ghosts would always haunt these halls.

The best he could do was attempt to make the future better. For his people. People who had suffered for far too long at the hands of his uncle. Indirectly, his own hands.

Or perhaps not so indirectly.

"That I was what?" he asked.

"Here. But he didn't mention you were busy."

"You thought I was in here reclining, perhaps?"

"No. But…maybe fencing or something. Not…boxing…with yourself."

"This is how I keep fit. I hang the bag inside my tent when I travel."

"That tiny thing?"

"The bag or the tent?"

"The tent. The bag isn't tiny."

"The tent I had the night I acquired you is not the one I normally travel with." He turned and wiped the sweat from his forehead, then started unwinding the tape that was around his fists.

"Well, to what did I owe the pleasure of the mini-tent experience?" Her perfect, pale cheeks darkened, a pink stain spreading over them. And that blush, the acknowledgment that there was something in that night that might make her blush, threw his mind right back there.

To what it had felt like to have her in his arms. Soft. Petite.

Sweet.

So not for him. Not under any circumstances. Not even if she were just a woman he met on a city street. Even then, she wouldn't be for him. All he could ever do with a flower was bruise the petals.

A flower would wither and die out in the desert. And he wasn't just from the desert; the desert was in him. And his touch would only burn her.

A good thing, then, that she was not just a woman on the street. A fortunate thing that she was off-limits for a million reasons, because if the only reason were her well-being… Well, he simply wasn't that good a man.

But with the fate of a nation resting on whether or not he kept it in his pants? He could keep them zipped.

"I saw no point in carrying the extra weight. I traded with a man I met on the road. A smaller tent, food. And it's fortunate for you I was able to trade or I might not have had the money to buy you."

"Ransom."

"If you like."

She frowned. "I thought we agreed it was a lot less demeaning."

"It makes no difference to me."

"One makes you the hero…the other makes you a bastard."

"You say that like you think I might have a preference between the two."

"I…don't you?"

He lifted a shoulder. "Not particularly. I don't have to be good, Ana, I just have to win. In the end, Al Sabah has to win. The rest…the rest doesn't matter."

"And you'll do anything to win?"

"Anything," he said.

Ana believed him. There was no doubt. The way he said it, so dark and sure and certain, sent a shiver through her body, down into her bones. And yet it didn't repel her. It didn't make her want to run. Perversely, it almost made her want to get closer.

The shock of fear that ran through her body was electric. It sent ripples of warning through her body, showers of sparks that sent crackling heat along her veins.

She felt like a child standing before a fire. Fascinated and awed by the warmth, knowing there was something that might make it all dangerous, but not having any real concept of the damage it could do.

Even having that moment of clarity, she didn't draw back. She did take a step toward him, though. Zafar, in all his shirtless glory.

She'd thought him arresting in his robes. Handsome in the linen tunic, moisture clinging to him from his shower. Without a shirt, his long hair escaping the bonds of the leather strap that normally kept it bound, his body glistening with sweat, a bead of it rolling down his chest, down his abs, sliding along the contours of his hardened muscles…well, just now he defied reality.

He was unlike any man she'd ever seen. All hard, harsh, assaulting masculinity. There was nothing soft about him, nothing to put her at ease or make her feel safe. He bound her breath up in her body, kept it from escaping. Made a rush of feeling whisper over her skin that she couldn't identify or deny.

She knew attraction. She was attracted to Tariq. He was handsome; he gave her butterflies in her stomach. He was a great kisser, though, admittedly at his own insistence their kisses had been brief.

He was everything she could have asked for.

And yet suddenly it seemed like her eyes had just opened and she'd realized there was something more. Something more to men. To the way looking at a man could make her feel. And she wasn't sure what the feeling was exactly. Attraction or something else, because it wasn't attraction like she would have named it last week. Or even two days ago.

But it was something. Something deep and visceral and completely disturbing. And it was holding hands, tightly, perversely, with fear. Perhaps that was why it seemed so intense? Adrenaline combined with attraction, the kind any woman would feel toward a man with such…testosterone-laden qualities. It was like a biological imperative. Strong man, producer of much sperm and good offspring. It was basic high school science, was what it was.

She shook off that line of thinking and tried to focus on the conversation.

"The end justifies the means?" she asked.

"Yes. But the thing you have to understand is that I have a country to run and I must look acceptable while restoring order."

"Please tell me you aren't a crazy dictator, because I don't want to help install a man who's going to turn this country into a military state."

"I won't be any kind of ruler if I can't get my people to accept me. A head is of no use without the body behind it. In two weeks time there is a reception planned, a party celebrating the new sheikh, a show of power for the rest of the world. All brought about by my adviser."

"One of the big dusty, sand-pirate-looking guys?"

She thought he nearly smiled. "Yes."

"And what do they know about that sort of thing?"

"A lot. Before he lost his family Rahm was the leader of the largest tribe in Al Sabah. But after…he couldn't continue on. Needless to say, he is a man who understands power and how to obtain and maintain it."

"He lost his family?"

Zafar swallowed hard. "Yes. Do you know what my uncle did in his time as ruler?"

She looked away from him. "My Al Sabahan history is rusty."

"He raised taxes, most especially on the Bedouins. And trust me when I say it was collected. Even if it had to be taken from their herds. From their tents. Skins and other wares. He took it. He cut services. Mobile medical units, schools. People lost their lives because of the neglect, the poverty."

"Rahm…"

"He suffered, as well. And unlike me…Farooq did have a harem. And when possible…he stole their daughters and brought them here. Unlike me…my uncle did like sweet innocent virgins." His voice was rough, his manner filled with disgust. The rage radiating from him spoke volumes about what manner of man he really was. That at his core, no matter what he said, no matter what he claimed about the end justifying the means, he was a good man. A man who despised hurting the weak. A man who sought justice, no matter the cost.

"Did you save Dalia from that fate?" she asked, her voice choked. She was starting to understand. Zafar had a collection of the broken in his country, surrounding him tightly, acting as his helpers, his staff. And in doing that, he was holding them together.

"Yes," he said. "Thankfully. She is one I was able to help before he managed to take her too far."

"How?"

His expression turned cold. "The men who captured her did not walk away. Let us leave it at that."

She nodded slowly. "Okay."

"I told you, *habibti*," he said, "I have blood on my hands. I will fight for my people. To the death. To the end. But in order to do that…they have to trust me, and while I am confident in my ability to frighten enemies, to seek out justice and destruction for those who would seek to hurt us…I am not confident in my ability as a speaker. Or a diplomat. The guest at a nice dinner."

"If we play things right, maybe I can help you, and you can repair relations between Al Sabah and Shakar. We could have dinner together after Tariq and I marry."

"There. Vision for the future."

"Yes." Except it would be awkward. And terrible, really. Could she ever tell Tariq about this? Would they have to start their marriage out with a lie?

She just didn't like any of it.

There was always the phone. She could always call.

She looked up at Zafar, at his eyes, and she knew she couldn't yet. Not just yet.

She couldn't just leave him. She couldn't just leave him and his people the way things were. He had ransomed her. He could have left her. He could have used her. But he wasn't that man. He was the man who saved girls from being kidnapped. The man who had blood on his hands from saving those who couldn't save themselves.

And that was when she knew she would do it. She could do this. And she wouldn't feel so useless. So at loose ends. If she was going to stay here, then she would accomplish something.

And civilizing Zafar would be no small accomplishment.

"So, do you have a…plan for how you want this to go?"

"I had thought that you might…give me tips?"

"Well, you can't go to a royal dinner wearing only pants."

He laughed, and she felt it all through her body. "Probably true."

"How long has it been since you had a Western-style dinner? At a tall table? And really with a salad fork?"

"A long time."

"Of course, when you entertain here, then it will be up to those visiting you to observe your customs."

"You truly are royally trained." He leaned back against the wall, his shoulders flexing, abs shifting. The man didn't have an ounce of spare flesh on his body.

"It didn't start with Tariq. My mother left when I was really small. And it was just me and my father. My father is a very important businessman. Oil tycoon, actually."

"Ah, and your connection to Tariq and Shakar begins to make sense."

Her face heated. She didn't like the implication. That it was all oil. She knew it was mostly oil, but there were feelings. There were. The fact that she was important on more than one level strengthened things, but it was more than that.

"Anyway, as I got older I used to help him coordinate dinners. Parties. I was hostess a lot of the time. It was hard for him to be a single dad, and he was as involved as he could be with me, and it was…it was nice to be able to help him that way. So you could say that hostessing is one of my talents. As is diplomacy. I went to the kinds of schools people think of as 'finishing schools,' but it's so much more than that. It's a very real education along with intense training for dealing with social situations. I'm versed in handling all kinds of scenarios. Any time you mix a lot of people, some of them competing for jobs or oil rights or money of any kind, things can be tense."

"I assume you have tricks for defusing those situations."

"The art of conversation. Or, more to the point, the art of bland inoffensive conversation. In your case, you'll be dealing with politicians of all different world views, and that will be…"

"A nest of vipers."

"Something like that."

She was starting to feel a little energized now. Starting to feel a renewed sense of purpose. This was giving her something to focus on. A plan, a goal. She liked feeling like she was being useful. Like she was accomplishing things.

This suddenly felt bigger than she was. Fixing a country, changing the shape of things for people. Making a positive impact. Zafar was going to make things better. Zafar wouldn't let the Bedouin people's daughters be taken from their homes to serve some sadistic ruler's fantasies.

And she could be a part of that new beginning. But not if she called Tariq. Not if she let fear push her into running.

No, she wasn't going to run.

She could do this. She might not ever claim credit, but she could start her role as Sheikha of Shakar by doing something valuable.

She trusted Zafar. The realization was a slightly shocking one, but it was the truth. She might not like it an overabundant amount, but she trusted the core of his character. And that was what counted.

"Breakfast in the courtyard tomorrow," she said, because she was sure someone could arrange it. "We'll talk silverware."

"I haven't had very much in the way of real conversation in the past fifteen years, and you want to talk silverware?"

"I told you, the art to getting along with people is bland conversation. How much more bland could it get?"

It turned out that nothing with Zafar could feel bland. Especially not since she was sitting with him in a garden that rivaled anything she'd ever seen. Lush green plants and shocking orange blossoms punctuated by dots of pink covered every inch of the wall that protected the palace from the rest of the world.

The combination of the thick stone wall, the fountains and the shade made the little alcove comfortable, even at midmorning. She had a feeling that by afternoon it would be nearly as unbearable as most other places in Al Sabah, but for now, it was downright pleasant.

"I ordered you an American breakfast," she said, putting her napkin in her lap and folding her hands over it. "Bacon and eggs."

"Do you think that many politicians will be eating bacon and eggs?"

"Fact of life, Zafar, everyone likes bacon. Turkey bacon, by the way, in case you have any dietary restrictions."

"I am not so devout," he said.

It didn't really surprise her. Zafar seemed to depend only on himself. Though, there were people here in the palace. People who had loyalty to him. People he seemed to care for in a strange way.

"It has made the paper," he said.

"What?"

"That I threatened Ambassador Rycroft. He said he saw me in person, and that I am clearly a wild man. That when you look in my eyes you see something barely more advanced than a beast. Of course the press was giddy with his description as they would so love to crucify me."

"I'm sorry."

"This means that my presentation is more important. That this project we are conducting is all the more important."

She nodded slowly. "I understand."

"I have spent too many years alone," he said, his voice rough.

"The men that are here," she said, picking up her fork, "how often did you travel with them?"

"Once a month we might patrol together, but many of them had home bases, while I felt the need to keep moving. To keep an eye on things."

"You said you didn't make a lot of conversation?"

"We didn't. We traveled together, did our best to right the wrongs my uncle was visiting on the desert people. Some of them were men, and the children of men cast out of the palace when my uncle took control. Others, Bedouins who suffered at the hand of the new regime. We didn't get involved in deep talks."

"Why is that?"

"Someone had to keep watch. And I was always happy

to let my men rest. Though we did spend time telling stories."

"Stories?"

"Morality tales, of one sort or another. A tradition in our culture. A truth wrapped in a tale."

She'd heard him do that. Weave reality into a story. Blanketing it so it was more comfortable to hear.

"So you were an army unto yourselves? Out there in the desert?"

"Nothing half so romantic. We were burdened with the need to protect because our people were under siege. It was all born of necessity. Of loss."

"If your people had any idea of what you'd done for them…they would embrace you as their ruler. I know they would."

"Perhaps. Or perhaps what happened in a desert out beyond the borders of the city will make no difference. Perhaps they will only remember what happened here."

"What happened here?"

Zafar gritted his teeth. He hated to speak of it. Of the day his parents died. The day he and his people lost everything.

He hated even more to speak of his role in it, but he didn't have a lot of other options. She had to understand.

She had to know why he was so despised.

"Things had been tense. There were rumors that the royal family might be the target of an attack. And routines were changed, security measures were taken. The sheikh and his wife were preparing to go into hiding until the threat had passed. But there was a breach in the security. And the time that the royal family was to leave the palace was given to their enemies. They never had a chance at escaping. What was meant to be a wholly secure operation, moving them until the threat was over, became the end."

"And how did you get the blame for this, Zafar? I don't understand."

"It was my fault," he said. "And I have spent every year, every day since then, fighting to atone for the destruction I brought on my own people. This is why the papers, why the people, are so anticipating my downfall. My exile was very much deserved. I was responsible for the death of my mother and father, the sheikh and sheikha. And the people of Al Sabah have long memories. They won't forget who they would rather have on the throne. And they won't forget why their most beloved rulers aren't with us any longer. And it's because of me."

CHAPTER SIX

ZAFAR COULD SEE the dawning horror in her eyes, and he was almost glad of it. Because they needed something to break this strange band of tension that was stretching between them, pulling them closer to each other, even as they tried to resist.

Even as he tried to resist. With everything he had in him.

But there was something so very fascinating about her. Something so tempting. But he knew what would happen if he touched her. War aside.

It would be like pouring water on the cracked desert earth. He would take everything she had, soak it in for himself, and at the end of the day, the ground on his soul would still be dry.

"You couldn't have done anything on purpose, Zafar."

"No," he said, his voice harsher than he intended. "I didn't do it on purpose, and in many ways that makes it much worse. I was a fool, manipulated into giving the truth because of trust. Because of love."

She blinked slowly a few times, a look of confusion on her face, as if the idea of him being in love, the whole concept, seemed foreign and unbelievable to her.

Reassuring. That he didn't in any way resemble the soft, stupid boy he'd been. Years in the desert had hardened him, and he was damned grateful for it.

"But if it was an accident…" she started.

"No. There is no excusing it." He didn't want to tell the story. Didn't want to speak of Fatin or the hold she'd had on him. About how, during a time of extreme turmoil for his country and his family, he'd only been able to think of one woman. Of how he'd wanted her.

He'd been able to spare no thought for anything else. For anyone else.

Thank God he'd cut that out of himself, that weak, sorry emotion. He'd sliced out his heart and left it to burn beneath the desert sun. Until he was impervious, until he was too hard and too weathered by the heat and wind to care about a damn thing.

Nothing but the cause. Nothing but the purpose.

And she had to realize that. She had to know. What manner of boy he'd been, what manner of man he'd become.

Why he'd had to bury that boy, deep, and destroy everything tender inside of him so that he would emerge better. So that he would never again cause such unthinking destruction.

"As with most tales, this one starts with a woman."

Ana's breath caught. She was instantly consumed with curiosity. About the woman. The one who had created emotion in Zafar. Emotion he seemed to be lacking now.

She noticed he liked to tell her things this way. As though they were nothing more than tales, and he was nothing more than the storyteller. Not a player in the piece.

"She was a servant in the palace. She had been for a long time. Beautiful, and smart. Ambitious. She didn't want to be a serving girl all of her life. She wanted more. And she was willing to do whatever needed to be done to get it. Including seducing the young prince of the royal family she served."

He looked detached, cold. Once again, this wasn't an

interaction, nor a heartfelt confession, it was a performance piece. A bit of the oral tradition the Al Sabahan people were famous for.

And yet the fact that it was personal, the fact that, though he was making the woman the star of the story, he was at the center of it, and he refused to tell it in that way, made it chilling. As cold as his eyes.

"She was his first woman. And that made him incredibly vulnerable to her. So when she asked what the new schedule was, when the sheikh and sheikha would be moved for their safety…he told her. Everything. Because in that moment, with his body sated from making love, and his heart full of hope for the future, their future, he would have given her anything she asked. And what she asked was such a small thing. Just little questions. With answers that had the power to shift the landscape of an entire country."

It was hard to latch on to the words. Hard to make sense of them. He was giving facts, honestly, but wrapped in a story, though she knew it was true. But he was holding back his emotion. Keeping it from his voice. Keeping it from her.

"Zafar…how did you…how did you survive that?"

"I wasn't the target. It was easy to get rid of me in a different way."

"I didn't mean physically."

"It was simple enough. I identified the problem, and I cut it out. Metaphorically. Were this a real tale, I would have cut my wicked heart out quite literally and left it to dry in the desert and gone on without it in my chest deceiving me. As it is, I put away feeling, emotion, and I focused on purpose. On reclaiming Al Sabah, not for me, but for my people."

"And the boy who gave it all for love?" she asked, looking at the hardened man in front of her and wondering, for just a moment, if it was even possible that the Zafar of the story and the Zafar standing in front of her had ever been one and the same.

"I left him out in the desert," Zafar said.

He'd been destroyed and remade out there. She could see that.

"Don't romanticize it," he said, his tone hard.

"What do you mean?"

"Don't lie to yourself. Don't try to make it seem like a misguided romantic gesture. It was nothing more than a sixteen-year-old boy using his balls as his brain. There is nothing romantic in that. A man in love is weak after an orgasm and she knew it. She exploited it. But there is no excusing it. She would have had no power had I been stronger. And though it's far too late to make it better, it could never happen again. Not to me. There is no allegiance I hold stronger than the allegiance I have to the people of Al Sabah. And there is nothing I would ever do to compromise it." His dark eyes glittered dangerously. "Nothing."

And she knew he meant that she would be caught up in that lack of compromise, too. That no matter what she wanted, no matter how long she was held at the palace, if it would compromise his vision for what constituted safety and success for his people, he would use her to that end.

It made her shiver inside. In that deep, endless place that Zafar's presence had created. Or perhaps, he hadn't created it; he'd just helped her discover its existence. Either way, it was disturbing, and taking up more of her than she wanted it to.

It was also far too strong for her liking.

If she wasn't careful, it might get bigger, take up more room inside. Obliterate her control. And she couldn't have that.

She had a mission. And it had nothing to do with heat and shaking and tightening stomachs.

She was going to help civilize the Sheikh of Al Sabah, and hopefully secure the future of two nations.

It really was nice to have a project. To be necessary. She knew what it was like to keep atoning.

She felt like she was still sweeping up the broken glass from something she'd destroyed years ago. And she would keep on going until she got every last shard.

CHAPTER SEVEN

ZAFAR HAD NEVER seen so much paperwork in his life. Laws, regulations, pages of tax code, various things to look at, read, sign and start over. Every time he put a dent in a stack of papers, the pile was refreshed with more.

The air was stale. Damned stale. He wasn't used to being indoors like this. Enclosed in stone, feet thick. It was like being buried above ground. Doomed to sign his name over and over for all eternity.

In short, he was in hell.

He stood and inhaled deeply. A rush of that stale, paper-laden air hit him hard, and his stomach pitched. He wasn't used to this. He craved heat and space. He closed his eyes, but rather than the vision of the desert he expected, he saw a pale blonde with full pink lips.

He opened his eyes and scooped up his pen, and the stack of papers he was currently working on, and walked out the door of his office, storming down the corridor. Perhaps he wouldn't use an office. Perhaps he would do all of his work outside.

As if you need to make yourself appear more unconventional. Or unhinged.

He continued down the corridor and found himself heading, not toward the courtyard, or toward the front entrance, but toward Ana's room.

Flames roared through his blood, and he couldn't credit

it. He'd gone for very long stretches at a time without female companionship. In truth, his sex life had been largely dormant. He had lovers he typically managed to see once or twice a year. But there had also been times when he'd gone more than a year without making a visit.

He was past the one-year mark now since the last time he'd had sex, if he wasn't mistaken. Which could explain why that pale little temptress had burrowed her way into his mind like she had.

Just a dry spell. Dryer than the damned desert.

Emotion he'd eliminated the need for. But not sex. Still, it was rare to crave it like this.

He pushed open the doors to her chamber, like they were the flaps on a tent, without knocking. He wasn't in the habit of observing those sorts of conventions.

"Talk to me," he said, walking across the room and sitting in one of the cream upholstered chairs, setting his paperwork on his knee.

Ana was standing there, frozen, pale eyes owlish, her curves hinted at by a thin gray T-shirt and low-riding shorts that revealed the full length of her ivory legs. He wondered who had thought to provide her with such clearly Western attire. But then, there was no reason for her not to dress in the way she found most comfortable. She was in hiding from the public, after all.

"What are you doing in here?" she asked.

"I cannot abide that office. It's far too small. Talk to me while I finish this."

"What do you want to talk about?"

"I don't know. Salad forks. I don't give a damn. Let's have a conversation. I will be expected to do that in my position, I imagine?"

"Why don't we talk about why you knock on a woman's bedroom door before you enter?"

"Boring. I don't want to talk about that."

"Well, I do, I only just put my top on. I was changing."

He looked up and their gazes clashed, heat arcing between them. His blood rushed south, racing to his member, hardening him, making him ready. In case. Just in case the heat wasn't one-sided.

It didn't matter. It couldn't happen.

Somehow, it only made her seem more tempting. Only made his blood run hotter.

"But I didn't see anything I shouldn't have, so it's moot. Now talk to me."

"It's nice weather we're having. Oh, wait, except it's not, because the weather is never nice here. It's hotter than the depths of hell, and it's so dry when I went to scratch an itch on my arm I bled. *I bled*, Zafar."

"Do you require lotion? I can have some sent."

"Yes. I do require lotion," she said, sniffing. "And some nail polish. And some makeup. I received a whole new wardrobe, but not that. A flatiron wouldn't go amiss, either. My hair is rebelling against the dry."

He lifted one shoulder. "If you wish."

"I'm not usually this precious. I promise. But I'm bored. I don't want to walk around outside because it's oppressive and I don't know Arabic well enough to read the books. I suppose internet access is out of the question?"

"You suppose correctly." He looked down at the papers on his lap. "If you're so bored, use this as a chance to begin your project. Teach me civilized conversation. Tell me about yourself. I told you about me."

She sighed and shook her head, shimmering golden hair falling over her shoulders. She truly was beautiful. He could see why the Sheikh of Shakar had been so eager to acquire her, and potential oil transactions were not the only reason. Clearly.

Tariq probably thought himself to be the luckiest man

on earth. A marriage that would strengthen his country and wealth…and a wife who possessed such poise and beauty.

Truly, Al Sabah would suffer by comparison. He would never be able to find her match.

"Me? Boring. I'm from West Texas, though for most of my life I've only spent school holidays there. My father is an oil tycoon. He has a knack for finding black gold. He's mainly made his finds on private land and made both him and the landowners very wealthy—"

"I didn't ask about your father. I asked about you."

She blinked a couple of times, as though she'd been hit over the head. "Oh. I guess…people are usually very interested in what he does."

"And you spend a lot of time organizing his events and so on."

She nodded. "Yes."

"Well, let's assume for a moment that I don't give a rat's ass about oil or money. Because I don't. And let's also assume that I feel the same about power and status."

"Okay," she said, trying to suppress a smile now, the corners of her lips tugging upward slightly. She was amused and a little shocked. And he found that he liked it. Liked that he'd made her feel something almost positive.

"Now, *habibti*, tell me about you."

Because he found he wanted to know. Suddenly he was hungry for information, for every detail about her. About this woman who was so contained under pressure, who appeared soft and vulnerable, but who possessed a core that was a pillar of stone, holding her up unfailingly no matter how the sands shifted beneath her.

"Um…I went to a girl's school in Connecticut. It was very strict, but I enjoyed it. All of our focus was on education, not on boys. I came home in the summer and around holidays—"

"To help with your father's events, I would imagine."

She bristled a bit at that. "Yes."

"And where was your mother?"

She looked up, out the window. "She left. When I was thirteen."

"Where did she go?"

"I don't know. I mean…she was in Manhattan for a while. And then she was in Spain. But I don't really know where she is now. And I don't really care."

"You are angry at her."

She bit her lip, as though she was trying to hold back more words. Words she didn't think she should speak, for some reason or another. "Yeah. Of course I am. She just left."

"And without her…he had you."

"Yes. When did you get insightful?"

"I have had too much time alone with my thoughts in the past decade or so. Too much thinking isn't always good. But it does produce some insight, whether you want it or not."

"I see. And did you have any great epiphanies about yourself?" She crossed her arms beneath her breasts, and his eyes were drawn down to them. Just perfect, enough to fill his palm. He could imagine it easily, her plump, soft flesh in his hands, her nipples hard against his skin.

"Just the one," he said, his voice rough.

"And it was?"

"That I was weak." His current train of thought mocked the implication that his weakness was in the past. "And that it could not be allowed to continue."

"Is that really it?"

"That I would be better dead than as I was," he said. "Because then I could do no more damage at least. But if I lived, I could perhaps fix what I had broken. So I lived."

"I can't say I ever thought I would be better off dead, but I know what it feels like to need to fix the broken things."

"Ah, *habibti*, I know you do. But at least you weren't behind the destruction."

She blinked and shook her head. "Does it matter in the end, Zafar, who caused it? Or how big of a thing it was? Broken is broken. Someone gets the blame. Someone has to try and hold life together after."

"So, that is what you are," he said. "The glue."

"I guess so. I hope so."

"And now?"

"I'll help you hold this together, too. Whatever you need."

"Why are you so willing to help now? You sound almost happy to be a part of my civilization."

"I am. It's my…project now, and I can tell you this with total honesty—if I say I'm going to do something, I'm going to do it, and I'll do it right."

"Being right is important to you."

"The most important."

Ana was a little embarrassed by her honesty, but really, why not? He'd told her everything. Had confessed to a youthful indiscretion that had caused the deaths of his parents, for heaven's sake. Why not tell him this. She'd never told anyone, not in so many words. How she had to be good. How she had to make the right choice. How everything felt like it was resting on her all the time. How she had to make herself needed so that the last remaining people in her life didn't decide she was too much trouble.

Didn't walk away because of her mistakes.

"See, I don't think being right or good is the most important thing," he said. Zafar looked down at the paper in his lap, taking a pen in hand and holding it poised above the signature line. He signed it, then moved it to the floor, holding his pen above the bottom line of the sheet that had been below it.

"You don't?"

"No. The important thing is how it all ends. It doesn't matter how you got there."

"This from the man who rescued women from ending up in his uncle's harem?"

"This from a man who bought a kidnapped woman from a band of thieves in the middle of the desert and is holding her captive in his palace until he is certain his country is stabilized," he said, looking up at her, his dark eyes intent on hers.

Her cheeks heated. Her heart pounded hard. Anger. She was angry. That was all, because she really didn't like remembering that she was at such a big disadvantage here. She wasn't used to it. She was used to being in charge. To making things happen.

She didn't like acknowledging that Zafar held the power here. That he held the keys to her very pretty prison cell. And that he walked into it whenever he liked.

"You need to shave," she said. Because she was going to start making some rules. Because she was going to take control of her project. And if she was going to stay here, she didn't need to make it easy or fun for him.

"I need to shave?"

"Yes. You look like you just crawled out from under a sand dune, which you did." He didn't really. He looked dangerous. Wicked and sexy and a whole lot of things she didn't want to admit. "You need some polish, which is what you want me to give you, right? A polish?"

He arched one dark brow. "That is a bit more suggestive than you might have meant."

Her face warmed. She wasn't entirely sure what he was getting at. What could she possibly polish that would… Her cheeks lit on fire. "I didn't mean it that way. Stop being such a man. Must you make everything…sexual?"

"It is something men have a tendency to do."

"Yeah, well, don't."

"Why does it bother you? Because you fear I might make an advance on you?"

She shook her head. "No. I know you wouldn't." It would undermine all of his other actions. And he had a young woman right here in the palace who clearly had a crush on him. Outside of that…she imagined there were a lot of women willing to submit to the desires of the sheikh.

Oh…wow. That sentence made her feel warm all over.

"Ah," he said, his voice deep, knowing. "You fear it because you enjoy it. Either because you find it entertaining, and know you shouldn't, or because you are…fascinated by the way it makes you feel, and you really know that should not be allowed."

"Not fascinated, as you put it. Not even amused."

"I don't believe you."

"And so what if you don't? What if I was? Would it make a difference?"

She held her breath during the ensuing silence, unwilling, unable to do anything to shatter the tension that was filling the space between them.

"None at all," he said, his voice hard.

"I didn't think so. Not to me, either. We're both bound by the same thing, Zafar. The need to do right. The need to fix. Now…how about the shaving?"

He rubbed his hand over his chin, the whiskers whispering beneath his touch. "I shall order a razor."

"You're going to do it here?"

"Yes. I had thought I might seeing as you are a large part of my civilization."

"All right. Order the supplies."

Ana leaned against the sink in the bathroom as Zafar looked down at the bowl of hot lather, the brush and the straight razor that had been provided by one of his serving girls.

A tremor ran through her body when she thought of the blade touching his skin. His hands, so large and masculine, didn't look geared toward fine work like drawing a blade over his skin without causing serious damage.

"Hold this," he said, handing her the end of a leather strap. She complied and he gripped the other end, bracing the back of the blade on the surface and dragging it down the length of the belt. Then he turned it and did the same, drawing it back up. He repeated the motion, again and again, her stomach tightening with each motion.

Then he handed the razor to her. "I think it's best if you oversee the project."

"Me?"

"Yes. I am yours to civilize, and this was your idea. Complete your project."

She felt like he was challenging her. Probably because he was. And she wasn't about to back down. Not now.

"Pretty gutsy of you. Handing me a blade and asking me to put it against your skin."

"You say that as though I think you could ever take advantage of me physically."

"I have a weapon."

He wrapped his hand around her arm, pressing his thumb to the pulse in her wrist. She knew he felt it quicken, knew he could feel just how delicate her bones were beneath his hand. He was very strong, and in that moment, she was very conscious of the fact that, if he had a mind to, he could break her using only that one hand.

She might be holding a weapon, but he was one.

"Indeed you do," he said, smiling, a wicked gleam in his eye. "Frightening." It was obvious he didn't mean it.

He released her and stepped back, gripping the bottom of his shirt and tugging it over his head, pulling the breath from her lungs right along with it. He cast the linen tunic to the floor and braced himself on the sink, his hands gripping the edge tightly. She couldn't help but look at him, at the movement of his abs with each breath he took, at the dark hair that did nothing to conceal his muscles but screamed at her, aggressively, insistently, that he was a man.

Much more man than she was used to.

She swallowed hard. "Right. Great."

"I suggest you gather your courage. The last thing I need is an unsteady blade."

"I don't use a straight razor but I shave my legs every day." She crossed her arms, deciding today, in this moment, she would lay diplomacy aside and go for bold. She'd been bold once. A child who ran instead of walked. Who laughed loud and often. Who spoke her mind. Until all of that brashness, all of that activity, had driven her mother away.

Until she feared it would drive her father away, too. Or the friends she'd made in school. Or Tariq.

But none of them were here now. She and Zafar were stuck with each other. She was going for broke. "I shave my bikini line. That's delicate work. I think I can handle this."

Something dark flared in his eyes, something hot and intense that she'd never, ever seen directed at her before. Not by anyone. Not by Tariq.

And she craved it. She had craved it for a long, long time, and she hadn't known it until this moment. Until the excitement and heat of it washed over her skin, sinking down through her, into her veins, pooling in her stomach.

Her breasts felt heavy, her nipples sensitive. She was suddenly aware that she could feel her nipples. So aware of parts of herself that she'd never been aware of before. He was magic. Except that sounded too light or impossible. He was something else altogether. Something dark and rich and indulgent, creating a desire in her that she'd never felt before.

"That is all very interesting," he said finally, his tone explicit, even though his words were benign.

"Yes. Well." And after she'd just scolded him for innuendo, here she was talking about her bikini line and pondering her nipples. "Is this hot?" she asked, pointing to the small marble bowl that was full of white foam.

"It doesn't matter to me."

"It does to me," she said. "Open pores would be nice. I don't really want to scrape your skin off."

He shrugged. "You can't hurt me, *habibti.*"

"Because you're immortal?" she asked, picking up a black-handled brush with soft bristles.

"Because I have felt all the types of pain there are. There is no novelty there, nothing new. It all just slides off now."

"You're way too tall. I need you to sit."

And he did, on the tiny, feminine vanity stool that was there for her benefit. It was his own fault for insisting they use her bathroom.

It was made for a woman. This entire chamber was clearly made for a woman. Though, oddly, being in the middle of all this softness only made Zafar sexier. Yes, he was sexy, she would just admit it.

Because here he seemed rougher. Even more of a man, if that were possible.

And it appealed to her. To this new, wild piece of her that was moving into prominence.

She took a white cloth that was in a bowl of warm water and pressed it over his neck, his face, letting it sit for a moment while she took the brush and dipped it in the shaving cream, swirling in the thick foam.

"Tilt your head back." And he did. A little thrill raced through her at the sight of Zafar obeying her command.

She removed the towel, brushing it over his skin before setting it back on the edge of the sink. Then she bent in front of him, picking up the brush and applying the cream to his skin with circular motions. She could feel the roughness of the hair catching beneath the brush, could hear nothing but the sound of their breathing and the lather being worked over his face.

Her own breathing was getting heavier. Raspier. It was certainly a lot harder to accomplish the closer she got to him.

"Okay," she said. "Hold still because I don't want to be responsible for the assassination of a world leader."

He obeyed again, his dark eyes trained on her as she started to work the razor over his skin. She had a knot in her throat, in her stomach. Because it was tense work. Because she was so close to him.

She took her other hand and gripped his chin, holding him firmly and angling his head to the right so that she could get a better look at his face, so that she could skim the razor over the square line of his jaw with ease.

She dictated his movements, and he obeyed. It was an interesting thing, holding a blade against her captor's skin. And yet, that wasn't her dominant thought. It was about how near he was. How good he smelled. Like spices today. Like soap and, now, shaving cream.

"Hold really still," she said, when she got to the line between his nose and upper lip.

He put his hand on her lower back, just before the metal touched his skin. "Be careful," she said. "Don't surprise me."

"I'm bracing myself," he said, his eyes locked with hers.

She should tell him to remove his hand. But she didn't. It was warm and heavy on her body, and it reminded her of that first night in the tent. When she'd let go of all her tension and slept, rather than standing vigil. Rather than fearing for her life. When, for the first time in…maybe ever, she'd released every worry and simply drifted into deep, heavy sleep, his protective hold on her, making her feel safe.

But this wasn't a protective hold. And it didn't feel safe. Not in the least.

But she didn't stop him.

She touched the steel to his flesh and breathed out as she moved, leaving his skin smooth. Taking away years with each stroke. It was like uncovering something he left buried, pieces of him revealed before her.

She couldn't fully focus on it, or enjoy it, because his touch was sending waves of sensation through her that were impossible to ignore and that took up far more of her brain power than she cared to admit.

When she ran the blade over his neck, his Adam's apple, a shiver of that same disquiet she'd felt when he'd first pulled out the razor went through her.

"This seems very dangerous," she whispered, her face so close to him that her lips nearly brushed his neck.

"Perhaps a bit," he said, his hand sliding to her hip, his fingers digging into her, and she wondered if they were meaning the same sort of danger.

Then she had to wonder which kind of danger she'd really been referring to.

"Quite a show of trust," she said. "For a man who, I imagine, doesn't trust very many people."

She looked up at his eyes and was surprised to see confusion there. "It is true," he said.

"You trust me, don't you?"

"I have no real choice," he said. "You have the power to upend my rule. To start a war between two nations. And at the moment—" he angled his head, tilting it back so that the edge of the blade pressed harder into his skin, so very near his throat "—you have the power to end me if you choose." For a brief, heart-stopping moment she almost thought he was requesting it. As though he wanted her to do it.

Instead, she just continued her work, trying to steady the tremble in her hand, more determined than when she'd started that she wouldn't so much as graze his skin. Wouldn't spill a drop of blood.

"There," she said, her voice a whisper. She wasn't capable of more. "Finished."

She stepped back, away from him, moving away from his touch. Then she took the towel and wiped off the excess shaving cream, leaving him sitting before her, an entirely different man.

She could see him now. See that he was a man in his early thirties, handsome beyond reason. She'd known he was arresting, that he had a mouth made for sins she could scarcely imagine, but she'd had no idea he was this...beautiful.

Because this was beauty. His jaw was square, his chin strong, lips incredibly formed. The loss of dark hair on his face made his brows more prominent, made his eyes that much more magnetic.

With shorter hair, he would look even better. With nothing to distract from that perfect face.

"You are staring," he said, standing, forcing her to look back down at his bare chest. She needed to look somewhere more innocuous. Somewhere that wouldn't make her feel tense and fluttery and...sweaty.

But there was no safe place to look, except at the wall behind him. Because everywhere, absolutely everywhere, he was a woman's deepest, darkest fantasy. The kind that came out in the middle of the night when she lay in bed, restless, aching and unsatisfied. The kind that she knew she shouldn't have, shouldn't give in to.

But did. Because she didn't possess enough strength to do anything else.

"I'm just surprised at what I uncovered," she said. Best to be honest, because she didn't have the brainpower to come up with a lie.

He laughed. "Expecting hideous scars, were you? Those are just in here." He pounded on his bare chest.

"I didn't know what to expect." She swallowed. "I do think you should cut your hair, and you should definitely enlist someone other than me to do it."

"Why is that?"

"I'll answer why to both possible questions. Because you don't need to hide behind all the hair. You'll shock people more if you step out completely clean, I think. Defy expectations and exceed them—that's what you want, isn't it? And secondly, because the only way I could cut your hair is if we took the fruit bowl in my bedroom and emptied it, then turned it upside down on your head. I don't think that's the look we want."

He laughed and it made her warm up inside. "I suppose not. And I see your point about…out-polishing their expectations."

"It would be good for you," she said. "Think about it… you show up at the party in a dark suit, tailored to fit, and your hair cut short, clean shaven. You won't look like a man who's just stepped out of exile, but a man who was born to his position. Which, you are."

He shook his head slowly. "I am glad I didn't walk a straight line from the cradle to the throne. I strongly regret what happened. The loss of my parents. But without it…I would have been a weak, spoiled and selfish ruler. I fear I would have been no better than my uncle. At least out in the desert I learned self-denial. At least I learned about what mattered. It is the one good thing to result from it all. I will be better for Al Sabah because of it. Sadly, Al Sabah is starting from a place of weakness. Because of my own weakness."

"You've transcended that weakness," she said. "You've spent the past fifteen years doing it. So show them, Zafar, show them your strength. Give them a reason to stand behind you."

CHAPTER EIGHT

ZAFAR LOOKED IN the mirror, which was something he didn't particularly like to do. It was a difficult task over the past few years, as he, in many ways, hated the man he saw. Plus, it wasn't like he carried a compact in his pocket. He saw no point in owning a mirror out in the desert.

But he was looking now. He'd had a haircut, and he had shaved himself in the few days since the shave Ana had given him.

He looked very different than he'd thought he did. He'd seen himself as a boy. Since then he'd always had a beard and long hair, and he'd looked at himself infrequently.

Seeing himself without anything covering his face, his hair short, was more shocking than he'd thought it might be. He was a stranger to himself, this, admittedly, more civilized version of the man he was looking back at him from the mirror.

His appearance had never mattered to him. Every day he rode through the desert, the safety and well-being of the people there his job. His duty. If he had word his uncle's men were around then he was there with his men, preventing any injustice that might happen, by any means necessary, and then melting back into the desert as though they had never been there.

As far as Zafar knew, his uncle had never known it was him. His uncle hadn't known of his continued existence.

He was sure Farooq imagined that he'd gone back to the dust, another victim of the unforgiving desert. And that had suited him well. The Bedouins were loyal to him, above all else. And the few times he'd tangled with soldiers from the palace...

They had left no men to return with a tale.

He looked at his reflection again, caught sight of the ruthless glint in his eye. The pride. The lack of remorse. Ah, there he was. This was the man he knew.

He pushed off from the sink and turned to walk out of his chamber and into the hall. He would find Ana. He needed to see if his new appearance met with her approval.

His gut tightened at the thought of her. He'd avoided her over the past few days, and it had been easy to do so. There was a lot of work to be done, more papers to sign, people to start meeting with, scheduling to sort out. Media to speak to.

For a moment, his hand burned as he thought of how he'd touched her while she'd shaved his face. She had curves, soft and womanly. The epitome of feminine appeal. Her face had been so close to his and it had taken every bit of his self-control not to lean in and claim her mouth.

But then, he very well might have found himself with a blade pressed to his throat in earnest.

He went to her room, but she wasn't there.

For some reason, the discovery made his chest feel tight. He walked quickly through the corridor and to the double doors that led to the courtyard.

And there she was, a shimmer of gold in the sunlight, sitting on the edge of a fountain.

"Ana."

She turned and her eyes widened, her lips rounding and parting. She'd looked at him like that after he'd shaved. A look of shocked wonder. Like someone who had been knocked over the head.

It was quite endearing in its way.

For his part, were he not well-practiced in hiding his responses, he was sure he would be wearing a similar expression. Seeing her out in the sun, in a white dress that left her legs and shoulders bare, pale hair shimmering in the light, was like a punch in the gut.

Heat pooled down low, desire grabbing him by the throat and shaking him hard. In that moment, he suddenly wanted so badly to touch her skin, to see if it was as soft as he imagined, that he would have gladly sold his soul, traversed the path into hell and delivered it to the devil by hand, just for a touch. A taste.

And it would cost his damned soul, no mistaking that.

But then, as it was damned already, did it really matter?

Yes. It did. Because Al Sabah mattered. His people mattered. He was beyond the point of redemption. He wasn't seeking absolution, because there was none to be had. But he would see his people served well. That was what he intended. To lead. To lead as a servant.

Anything else was beneath him. Any chance for more gone years ago.

It didn't matter how beautiful she looked with the sun shining on her, with her hair spilling over her shoulders like a river of liquid gold. It didn't matter that her breasts were made to fit in his hands, and he was certain they were.

A man only had so much emotional currency, and his had been spent the day of his parents' deaths. He'd forfeited it. To better serve. To better make amends.

And now he simply had nothing. So he would have to look, only. Look and burn.

"You look…"

"Civilized?"

"Um…I don't know if that's the right word. You are…" She bit her lip, and he envied her that freedom. He would love to bite that lip. "Look, this whole experience is all a bit, out of time for me. I'm used to having to be appropriate and well-behaved, to…contribute and be useful. But right now I'm just going to be honest. You're a very handsome man." Her cheeks turned pink.

"I'm not sure anyone has ever said that to me," he said.

"That surprises me."

"It has been a very long time since I was in a relationship where words like that were used. It has been…it's been longer than I can remember since I told a woman she was beautiful. You are beautiful," he said.

"Me?"

"Yes, you." It was a mistake to tell her that. A mistake to speak the words, and yet, he found he couldn't hold them back.

"Now, there's something I don't hear very often."

"Now I have to question the sanity of every male you've had contact with in the past five years."

"Thank you," she said. "But I've been engaged to Tariq for four years and as a result I haven't dated. And we've mostly dated remotely so…"

"And he has not told you how beautiful you are when he's holding you in bed?" he asked, knowing he shouldn't ask, because images of her in bed, naked and rumpled, made him crave violence against the man who had just had her. And even more, it made him crave her touch.

"I…we haven't…it's been a very traditional courtship. And by traditional, I mean the tradition of a hundred years ago, not the tradition of now." Her cheeks were even darker now, embarrassment obvious.

"What a fool," he said.

"What?"

"Tariq is a fool. If you were mine I would have staked a claim on you the moment I had you within reach."

She blinked rapidly. "I…our relationship isn't like that."

"And yet he loves you?"

"He cares for me."

"And you love him?"

"Waiting doesn't mean I don't love him. Or that he doesn't love me. In fact, I think it shows a great deal of respect."

"Perhaps. But if you were mine, I would rather show you passion."

"But I'm not."

It took him a moment to realize how close they had gotten to each other, that he was now standing near enough to her that if he reached his hand out, he could cup her cheek, feel all that soft skin beneath his rough, calloused palm. A gift far too fine for his damaged skin. For his damaged heart.

"No," he said, "and you should be grateful for that fact. Your fiancé sounds as though he's a better man than I."

"I'm sure he is," she said. She raised her eyes, and they met his. "But I…I don't feel…" She raised her hand, and it was her who rested her hand on his cheek. "What is this?"

"You're touching my face," he said, trying to sound normal. Trying not to sound out of breath.

"You know what I mean, I know you do. And I know… I know you know the answer."

He did. Chemistry. Sexual attraction. Lust. Desire. There were so many names for the feeling that made his stomach tight and his body hard. But it wasn't something he wanted to expose her to. It wasn't anything he could expose her to.

She put her other hand on his face, aquamarine eyes intent on his. "I don't even like you," she said. "I think I might respect you in a vague sort of way, but I think you're hard. And scary. And I know I don't have a hope in the world of ever relating to you. So, why do I feel like there's a magnet drawing us together?"

"Is it just since I shaved? Perhaps it's that you think I am…handsome, as you said."

She shook her head. "It started before that."

"Perhaps you should discontinue your honesty," he said, his voice rough. "It will not lead us anywhere good."

"I know," she said. "I know. But…can I try this? Please? Can I just…" She closed her eyes then, blocking her emotions from view. And then she leaned in, pressing her lips to his.

It was a soft touch. But it was like touching a live, naked wire to sensitive flesh. Quick, nothing more than brief contact, but it burned everywhere. Everything.

She drew back, her breath catching, her eyes wide-open again now. And he knew she'd felt it too, just like he had. Like an electric shock.

"Does it answer your question?" he asked.

She nodded.

"And I was right. Wasn't I? It is best not to be so honest from here on out, I think."

Ana felt like she'd been singed. Her heart was pounding in her chest and she was shaking inside. Everywhere. She had no idea why she'd just done that. Why she'd touched him. Why she'd kissed him.

Only he'd walked out of the palace, looking like a fantasy she'd never known she'd had, and for a moment the entire world had shrunk down to him, her, and the way he made her feel. The things he made her want.

And she'd needed to know. Was it all adrenaline and fear? Confused by the fact that he was an appealing, powerful man? Or was it attraction. Deep, lusting attraction that wasn't like anything she'd ever felt before.

The moment their lips had touched she'd had her answer. She didn't like her answer.

She'd kissed Tariq a few times. And before that, she'd kissed three or four boys at inter-school mixers. Light kissing, with a little tongue. Some of the boys had given more tongue than she'd liked.

But this had left them all so far in the dust it almost didn't seem like it could be considered the same activity. It was so dissimilar to every other kiss she'd had, she wondered if it was something different. Something more. Or if those first kisses had been failures. But they hadn't seemed like it at the time.

She'd liked kissing Tariq. Had thought dreamy thoughts about what it would be like to kiss him more. To do more than kiss. She'd been looking forward to being his wife in every way.

And then there was Zafar. He had walked into her life and swept her up in his whirlwind, leaving so many things devastated in his wake.

"Just tell me one thing and then we'll suspend honesty on the subject," she said, fighting the urge to reach up and touch her lips. To see if they felt hot.

"I will decide if I'll tell you after you ask the question, *habibti*."

"Okay." Normally she would be so embarrassed. Normally, she would never have kissed a man like that, and normally she would never ask the question she was about to. But normally, she lived life to keep everything around her smooth. She lived life in a calm and orderly fashion. She never ruffled feathers or made things awkward.

At least, that was what she'd trained herself to do after an act of clumsiness had resulted in her mother telling her all of her faults. All of the little ways she ruined the other woman's life. And then in her mother leaving. Because she couldn't stand to live with such a child anymore.

But in the past two weeks she'd left home to see her fiancé, the man she would marry, taking a step toward becoming sheikha of a new country, to becoming a wife. Then she'd been kidnapped. Then she'd been ransomed by Zafar and taken back to the palace and given the job of civilizing a man she was starting to think was incapable of being civilized. So she felt like she was entitled to be different.

She was starting to feel different. More in touch with the girl she'd been before pain had forced her to coat herself in a protective shell. To live her life insulated, quiet and never making waves.

Now she didn't mind if she made waves. Not here with Zafar. Here she felt bold. A little reckless. In touch with her body in a way she'd never been before.

"Is it always like that?"

"What?" he asked.

"Kissing. Does it always feel like that? And when I ask this question I'm assuming that the kiss made you feel the way it made me feel. I'm assuming it made you feel like you'd been lit on fire inside and like you wanted more. So much more it might not ever be enough. If it did...is it always like that?"

"I should not answer the question."

"Please answer."

He leaned in, resting his thumb on her bottom lip. She darted her tongue out, instinct driving her now, not thought, and tasted the salt of his skin. Heat flared in his dark eyes.

"No," he said, the word sounding like it had been pulled from him.

"No, you won't answer, or no, it's not normally like that?"

"It's never like this," he said. "I do not know how the brush of your lips against mine can make me *want* like this. Like the basest sexual act never has. But it doesn't matter."

She nodded slowly. "Yes. It matters."

"Does it change anything?"

"No."

And it didn't. But in some ways it was gratifying to know that she shared what was probably a normal level of chemistry with Tariq. That this thing with Zafar wasn't normal. That it wasn't something you were supposed to feel, that it wasn't something everyone had, that it was something she was somehow missing with the man she was going to marry.

That would have been a harder truth.

Maybe.

It wasn't actually all that comforting to know that she was experiencing some sort of intense, once-in-a-lifetime type attraction to a man she had nothing in common with. A man she could never, ever touch again.

Not if she valued her sanity. Not if she valued her engagement.

And she did. She valued both quite a bit.

"But I wanted to know because…because if it's something you feel with everyone, but I somehow don't feel it with Tariq…well, I needed to know that. But this is better."

"Is it?"

"Yes."

"I find it near the point of unendurable, and I have endured a lot. Dehydration. Starvation. All things you can forget if you go deep enough inside yourself. But this… with this, it comes from deep inside of me and I'm not certain how I'm supposed to escape it."

Ana swallowed hard, her throat suddenly dry, and she couldn't even blame the desert heat.

She looked down. "We just ignore it. There's no point to it anyway."

"None at all."

"So, in the spirit of ignoring this, you do look very civilized, but we are going to have to work on your manners."

"My manners?" he asked, his brow arched.

"Yes. What sort of dinner are you having at your big event?"

"Western-style dining."

"I thought as much, with all the ambassadors coming from Europe. How long has it been since you used a fork?"

"Certainly since I lived here at the palace. I did have some…etiquette lessons naturally, but it has been a long time since I've been expected to use any of it."

"You had to learn a whole new culture, didn't you?" she asked, realizing that royalty didn't act the same as the masses. And the Bedouin culture was different to the people in the city.

He nodded. "Yes. But I found acceptance there. And purpose. It was a place to rest and to find reprieve from the effort of existence. On your own, in the desert, survival is nothing short of a twenty-four-hour struggle. There is no end. There is no real sleep."

"I had a taste of that when I was out there. With them."

"I know you did. I wish I could have spared you that."

She shrugged. "I don't know. I wasn't hurt. Not really. Scared, but not hurt. I was lucky."

"You were unfortunate enough to get caught in the crossfire. I don't think I consider it lucky."

Except it was strange. What had happened before the kidnapping suddenly seemed the hazy and distant thing. Her whole life seemed hazy and distant. There was something so harsh and real about the light here, so revealing. It made it impossible to focus too much on the past. Or the future.

The present was far too bright.

"Well, as you said, this is pretty plush for a jail cell."

"You aren't a prisoner," he said.

"Except I can't leave."

"There is that."

Silence stretched between them.

"Dinner," she said. "Tonight."

"I shall make an effort to dress for it," he said.

"Great." She looked back at the fountain, the sunlight sparking off the water. She looked back at him and tried to breathe. It wasn't easy. "Pro-tip. The salad fork is on the left. Outside."

CHAPTER NINE

ANA FELT SELF-CONSCIOUS and a little silly. She had dressed up. Zafar had said he would dress for dinner, and because of that, she'd felt like she should, too.

So she was walking down the empty corridors of the palace in gold heels, provided by Zafar's very efficient dresser, and in a red dress that came up to her knees and draped over her shoulder like a Grecian-style gown, chiffon flowing over her curves as she walked.

She had her hair swept up into a French twist, her lips painted to match the dress. And she had to wonder why she was doing it. Why she was bothering.

Because the simple fact was, she was attracted to him. In spite of what she said about it not mattering. It was still there. And it was unnerving.

You can't do anything about it. You don't like him. And it would be wrong.

Yes. It would go against everything her father had been trying to build up. She had a flash, suddenly, of what Zafar had said when she'd told him about her father. That he wanted to know about her, not about her father.

But, her father aside, she had her commitment to Tariq. And she loved Tariq. Didn't she?

It was hard to picture him now. He was fuzzy, like there were heat waves standing in the way of her memories of him. And that was just wrong. It shouldn't be so easy to forget. Zafar's face shouldn't be so prominent in front of her mind's eye.

And she really shouldn't have put on red lipstick for the man. But since she'd complained about her lack of frills, more had been provided, and she hadn't been able to resist.

She sucked in a breath and turned the corner into the dining room. And was shocked to find it transformed. There was a formal, Western-style dining table with chairs all around it, and delicate white china place settings. It was something she would have organized for her father. Elegant and restrained, and odd in this setting because it was only for her and Zafar when it could have easily been a dinner for twenty-five.

And Zafar sat at the head of the table. He stole her breath. Her lungs contracted, the air rushing from them, and she couldn't breathe, couldn't think. She could only look.

He was sitting there in a black jacket, a black tie and a black shirt. The picture of masculine grace. The picture of civility.

Such a lie.

Because when she looked closer, at his face, the truth was plain. He was a predator, leashed and collared for the moment, by expectation, by duty. But it was only the leash keeping him from pouncing.

Were it not for the restraint of duty, he would be wholly unpredictable. Wholly frightening. A beast uncaged.

He stood, and she felt light-headed. His physique was outlined to perfection in the suit, exquisitely so. He was broad shouldered, broad chested, his waist and hips narrow. Impossibly hot.

She'd never seen such a good-looking man before. Ever. Not in the movies, not in magazines, just ever. And she knew that beneath that oh-so-sedate black jacket and shirt were muscles that would melt a lesser woman from the inside out.

Though, at the moment she herself felt a little melty, in spite of the fact that she was engaged. In spite of the fact that she knew she wanted nothing to do with him. Her fingers itched to put her hand on the knot at he base of his throat and loosen his tie.

Why would she want to ruffle him when he'd just now gotten all together? It was ridiculous.

"Good evening," he said. "I trust you found your afternoon restful?"

Restful? She'd kissed the man and spent the entire afternoon burning. "Quite," she said.

He moved away from his spot at the table and went to the chair that was positioned to the right of his own. He curled his fingers over the back of it, then pulled it out. "Have a seat."

She moved toward the chair, never taking her eyes off his face. She sat and he returned to his own seat.

"And how was your afternoon?" she asked.

"It was very good. A suit was delivered and I had it fitted to me. That was an experience I've not had for a long time."

"I imagine not."

She imagined tailored clothing was a luxury he'd been without since he'd been cast out of the palace. "Suspending with civil, bland conversation for a moment."

"You felt the need to notify me?"

"Just so you would know this isn't the kind of thing you'll talk about at your presentation."

He nodded. "All right."

"Are you ever angry?"

"Always, but about what specifically?"

"This." She indicated the suit. "This should have been yours. Always. You should have always had custom clothes and a position at the head of the table in the palace. You should have always been here, and not living out in the dirt in a tent. Doesn't it make you angry that you had it stolen from you?"

And she realized in that moment that part of the reason she was asking was because she was angry about everything she should have had.

About everything that had been taken from her because of the selfishness of others. Because of her mother. Because her mother had made her hate the girl she'd been. Had made her fold inward, smooth every rough edge. So that she would never again be in the way. Never be impulsive. Never truly be herself.

Why was she thinking about that? She'd never thought of it that way before, and now here she was having some kind of epiphany in front of an empty dinner plate with her captor to her right, looking at her like she'd lost her mind.

"I deserved to lose it," he said. "I've never been angry on my own behalf."

Neither had she. Until now.

"I'm just saying…you expect something from life. You're born into it, and it seems like you have some guarantee based on those beginning circumstances. Like… you're born into a certain family and you think…and you think you're going to have a certain future and then… you don't."

"Are we still talking about me?" he asked.

"Maybe. I don't know." She took a deep breath. "What's on the menu for the evening?" *Something bland, I hope.*

Any more excited and she was going to start saying and doing even dumber things. As if that were possible. What was it about this man? This place? It changed her. Made her say things, want things, feel things.

Maybe it was being kidnapped. She'd been freaking kidnapped, by a band of desert marauders, and she'd survived it. It made her feel stronger somehow. Made her feel like she'd found a hidden well of resilience she hadn't even known about.

But along with that, was the desire for more. Because she'd found more in herself. Because she knew there was more out there.

It was a dangerous desire. One that was coming too late. And one that really shouldn't be acted on. After all, she was under duress. And stuff.

But it was hard. So hard to ignore when everything in her felt like it was broken apart and shifted around. Like gigantic tectonic plates had shifted inside of her, creating an earthquake that wreaked havoc on her soul.

Dramatic, but there it was.

"What did you expect?" Zafar asked.

"Me? From life?"

"Yes."

"I didn't expect my mother to leave, or the way it would make me feel. Or for my father to need so much. I didn't expect for…I didn't expect for Tariq to be introduced, and for that union to be so important to…to…"

"But you love him, don't you?"

"I…yes." But for some reason the answer didn't seem as true this time. Not as true as it had seemed nearly two weeks ago when she'd been snatched out of a desert encampment and taken prisoner.

It went along with her sudden epiphany about her life growing up. With the change inside of her. What would it be like to make noise again? To stop walking so softly.

"And yet you characterize him as an unwelcome surprise?"

"Unexpected. Let's leave it at that. I just…you know, I was thirteen when my mother left. I thought I would be able to talk to her about boys. I thought that I would date. I thought I could be a kid. But…but my being a kid…that was what drove her away." She still remembered that moment, her mother, holding the broken doll and screaming at her about her clumsiness. Her childishness. "And so…I had to take care of my father and…I couldn't be another burden on his life. I had to go away to school because he didn't have a lot of time for me. I had to leave my home. And at school…they expected me to…be quiet. Be invisible. Then when I was home I had to be a hostess, as good as my mother would have been, even though I was only a child."

"Your father didn't bear his loss well."

She shook her head. "No. She was always fragile, and temperamental, but beautiful, a wonderful hostess. She liked having eyes on her, liked planning parties and organizing their social life. And she made vows to him. Of course he expected her to be there. Of course he wasn't equipped to deal with her leaving."

"And it was up to you to hold it all together?"

It was more than that. Deeper than that. But she didn't want to confess it. "Someone has to do the right thing, Zafar."

Something changed in his eyes, suddenly darker, hollower. "Yes, it's true. Someone must do the right thing even when they don't want to. Even when emotion asks you to do something differently. I never managed it. For my part, I cannot resent my lot in life because I was the cause of so much of it. Not like you. Your life has been upended through no fault of your own. And here I have only served to do more."

No fault? Maybe. Maybe not.

"Guilt, Sheikh?" she asked, her stomach tightening. Because she'd seen him look blank, she'd heard him profess guilt in a matter-of-fact manner. But she'd never heard it in his voice.

She heard it now.

"A useless emotion," he said, his voice blank now. "It fixes nothing."

"But you feel it."

"Another useless emotion to add to the day," he said, adjusting the fork on the table. "Salad fork," he said, lifting it. "Do I have that right?"

"Yes," she said, looking down at her plate. "Is dinner soon?"

As if on cue, the serving staff entered with silver trays, laying them on the table before them and uncovering them. There was rice and lamb, an Arabic feast on their Western table settings.

Like a melding of cultures. Except she felt like there was a wall between them. One that she wanted to breach now, and for the life of her she couldn't figure out why. Because she should want the wall. She should want the distance.

She was here to civilize him. Not to let him effect a change in her.

She'd spent her whole life striving to do right. To contribute rather than take. To be useful rather than a burden.

More than that, she just believed in right. In good. In doing good and being right. Because it was the best thing. It was the thing that kept the world from folding in.

It was who she had to be.

"It looks wonderful."

"Salt?" he asked.

"Oh, no, I couldn't."

"Blandness must be preserved," he said.

"At all costs. That's safe conversation."

"Ever the hostess."

"Yes indeed, but then, aren't I here to teach you?"

"You are. So I will leave it up to you to decide, then. Is it considered safe conversation to tell your hostess that she is beautiful to the point of distraction?"

"A bit too much like adding salt," she said, her cheeks heating.

"Then I shall refrain from telling you that I think your skin is like alabaster, though I think it's true. And even if there was no reason for me to abstain from complimenting you, I should never use those particular words. Because I think lines like that only seem romantic to a sixteen-year-old. Though, I think in truth I haven't made any attempts at being romantic since I was sixteen." He looked at her, his dark eyes blazing. "But perhaps it is for the best I stick to compliments of that nature. Because if I complimented you as a man…well, that would, I fear, over-salt things quite a bit."

"There's a very real possibility of that." Her pulse was pounding hard at the base of her throat, and she was sure that he could see it, almost certain that, in the silence of the room he could even hear it.

"Then I will say nothing. In the interest of safe conversation."

They'd passed safe conversation a few minutes ago. Maybe a few hours ago. And she wasn't sure what she could do to get things back on the right footing. Wasn't sure what she could do to forget the way his lips had felt beneath hers. Wasn't sure she could forget the rush of pure, unadulterated heat that had burst through her, like nothing she'd ever felt before. Like nothing she'd ever known was possible.

"I think that's for the best," she said. Then something in her rebelled, pushed her, prodded her. The deep, inner part of her, the Ana that had been repressed for so many years. "And I will say nothing about how that suit is cut so that you could almost be wearing nothing. Or maybe you'd be less indecent if you were wearing nothing. As it is, it just teases me."

"Now that, I fear, is not bland conversation in the least."

"I'm sorry. I don't know what came over me." She looked down at her plate again, then back up at him. "It won't happen again."

"I find myself disappointed by that."

"Then you'll just have to be disappointed." She sniffed and picked up her salad fork. "There is no salad."

"An oversight."

"I don't believe that," she said.

"Eat your rice with it."

She laughed. "I can't. It would be wrong."

"That will be my goal," he said, unapologetically taking a bit of rice with the aforementioned fork. "To uncivilize you a bit. A favor, as you're doing one for me."

"I'm afraid violations of table manners just can't come into it," she said, sniffing and picking up her entrée fork.

"Then perhaps we will have to think of other violations?"

She nearly choked. "Um…I think, as kind as the offer is, you have to be the focus for now."

"I don't know, in terms of needing to be uncivilized… you're about as far away from it as I am to being ready to walk into a room full of dignitaries."

"Then we'll fix that. You, I mean, not me. I don't have any wild Spring Break events coming up so it doesn't seem like I'll be needing any help with the…letting loose."

He breathed out heavily, dark eyes bleak. "And how do you propose to fix me, *habibti*?"

"You don't happen to know how to dance, do you?"

"I doubt I will be dancing at this event," he said.

"But you will eventually," she said, "and it's my job to make sure that you have adequate education in all matters of civility."

Zafar eyed the petite blonde in front of him. She was wearing casual linen pants and a loose tunic top, an adaptation of what he often wore around the palace. Though he had shown up for their dancing lesson in his suit. He felt strange about that decision now.

He had imagined she might revisit the red dress from the night before, but she had not.

"You dressed up," she said.

"It does no good for me to learn to dance if I can't manage to do it in a suit."

"I suppose that's true."

"Though I still question the necessity."

"You'll take a wife one day, won't you?"

He tried to imagine it. He had lovers, he had women that shared his bed for a couple of hours in an evening. Women he shared his body with. But that wasn't a wife. It wasn't sharing his life.

And he seriously doubted he had it in him to open himself up that much. To share all of himself. And he had to wonder what sort of life it would be for a wife. Being here in this castle, wandering around alone, going to sleep alone.

He would not share a bed with a woman, not after he slept. Because that was when the darkness crept in, unfiltered. In sleep, he had no purpose but to dream. And so he had no defense against the insidious, grasping claws of memory, guilt and unending shame.

Things he shut out in the day. Things he lived forever in the dark. His own private hell. Endless blackness. Weeping, wailing, suffering. Always.

He didn't know what he did during those dreams. If all of the screaming was in his head, or if he let it out. None of his men would have ever dared say. The desert kept secrets well.

But here? Yes, here he might truly find out the depth of the damage done. And he could very well not be able to hide it from his people.

If he let it, the enormity of everything would crash in on him. Breach the walls that he'd built up so strong, and swallow him whole.

"Yes," he said. "I will have to take a wife."

"Then you should learn how to dance. So that when you see her…across the crowded ballroom, and your eyes meet, and you make your way to her…you have something better to do than talk about the weather."

"I thought I wanted bland."

"Not with someone you're trying to know."

"Who says I need to know a wife? I simply need to marry her."

"Oh…Zafar. I only have a week left to civilize you?"

"Only a week until my unveiling. You could stay after. You might very well have to. I had thirty days, if you re-call."

"I recall," she said. "Now, give me your hand."

He extended his hand to her and she wrapped her slen-der fingers around it, drawing him into her body. "Hand on my waist," she said, reaching down and grasping him with her other hand, putting his palm against her lower back. "And this one out."

"Music?" he asked.

"We'll count. A waltz is a three-count dance."

"A waltz? What the hell is this? A Jane Austen fantasy?"

"You know Jane Austen?"

"I have been out in the desert for fifteen years. I may have missed popular culture, but not classics."

"And you even consider her works to be classics?"

"I am a barbarian, but I'm not entirely without culture." He pulled her more tightly against him. "And anyway, one has to amuse themselves somehow." He paused, looking down at his feet. "Books were a luxury not often afford-able. I came upon one, a gift from a merchant I aided. *Pride and Prejudice* in English. It is the only book I owned."

"I never…I never considered that. Not having access to books."

He shrugged. "Elizabeth Bennet is nice company. She has a sharp wit. Reminds me a bit of you."

"Oh, Zafar, you should have no trouble finding a wife."

"Although, I'm not exactly Mr. Darcy."

"Not so much."

"One, two, three," she began, her voice in staccato rhythm. "Follow my lead, one, two, three."

"I thought men were meant to lead."

"Not when they don't know how to dance. You can lead when you get this down. One, two, three."

He followed her steps, but everything in him was focused on where his hand rested, just on the rounded curve of her hip, on the brush of her breasts against his chest.

"One two three," she continued, but he could hardly hear. His eyes were focused on her lips, on the movement they made when she said the words. Numbers, an endless repetition. Something that shouldn't make a man feel anything, much less a fire in his blood that might reduce him to ash on the spot.

Blazing, hotter than the desert sun. He'd thought he'd withstood the most destructive heat in existence. In the wilderness. In his nightmares.

But this was a different kind of heat altogether. One that burned but didn't consume. Endlessly going on and on. Just when he thought the peak had been reached, it only went up higher.

Hotter.

What magic did this woman possess? Living out as he did, he could not discount the presence of the supernatural, and part of him wondered if she had some sort of power. Something to snare him.

Like a Jinn, made of smokeless, scorching fire. Whispering to his soul and telling him to commit sins he knew well he could not.

And when he looked in her eyes, he saw nothing but clear blue. It made him wonder if the desire for sin came, not from her, but from the depths of his own soul. It shouldn't be able to speak to him. It should have been choked out, dried and left to rot on the sand, along with his heart.

Both his heart and soul were so deceitfully wicked. That was why he tried to shut them down. To keep them from having a say in his actions.

When a man didn't have a trustworthy conscience he had to learn his purpose in his head and stick to it.

No matter how soft a woman felt beneath his hand. No matter how enticing the brush of her breasts, the promise of pleasure on her lips.

"Tell me something bland," he whispered, trying to ignore the burn beneath his skin. Trying to ignore the rush of blood to his groin. The ache that was building there.

"I'm counting. Isn't that bland?"

He looked at her pale pink lips. "It is not."

"I don't know how I could be more boring." She kept moving him to soundless music that must be playing in her mind, never losing the beat.

"It is your mouth," he said. "I find it distracting."

"That isn't my intent."

"Intent doesn't matter. It's the result. And the result is that I find myself unable to look away. And when I look at your lips, all I can think of is how it felt for them to touch mine."

"I'm engaged," she said, her tone firm. "Engaged and in love and…"

He pressed his lips against hers and the dancing stopped. She froze beneath his mouth, her body rigid for a second, and then it softened. Her fingers went to the lapels of his suit jacket, curling in tightly as she rose up on her tiptoes, deepening the kiss.

If there had been fire before, this was the introduction of oil. A burst of flame that threatened to destroy everything in its wake.

Her tongue slid against his, and he was pulled into the darkness. There was nothing else, nothing but the slick friction, nothing but her soft, perfect lips.

Until her, it had been a long time since he'd been kissed. Longer still since a kiss had been simply a kiss. And that simplicity gave it the power to be so much more.

He wrapped his arms more tightly around her and pulled her flush against his body, bringing those full, gorgeous breasts against his chest as he'd fantasized about doing for…had there ever been a time when he hadn't? Had there truly been a moment when he hadn't wanted her?

When he'd seen her as nothing more than a pale, fragile creature diminishing beneath the Al Sabahan sun? How had he ever seen her that way? In this woman lay the power to bring kingdoms crashing down. To bring a sheikh to his knees.

He wrenched his mouth from hers and kissed the curve of her neck, his teeth grazing the delicate skin at her throat. He pressed his thumb to the hollow there, felt her pulse pounding wildly. Felt each raw catch of breath.

He growled, his response feral, beyond thought or reason. Quite beyond civility.

She moved her hands to his shoulders, her fingers digging into his skin through the layers of his coat and dress shirt. Not enough. It would never be enough. He pulled away for a moment, shrugging his coat off and letting it fall to the floor.

Her fingers were fumbling with the knot of his tie. Of all the times, why the hell had he chosen to wear a suit now? A linen tunic was easily cast aside, robes quickly dispensed with. This Western style of dress gave no concession to lust-tinged urgency.

He struggled with the tie, and the collar of his shirt, tearing something, the tie or his collar, he wasn't sure. He didn't care. He was a sheikh. More clothes could be bought. Passion like this…it could only be taken in the moment.

"Oh…Zafar."

That, his name, seemed to suddenly knock her back to reality and she pulled away from him, struggling in his embrace. "Stop," she said, "stop."

He released his hold on her immediately, his hands at his side, his heart thundering so hard he feared it would simply stop before the next beat.

"What?" he asked, knowing he sounded angry, shocked. But he had felt, for a blissful moment in her arms, as if the blistered, hardened shell that covered him had been rolled back and he'd been exposed, new and tender, but feeling. And it had been incredible.

It had been beyond anything he'd ever before experienced, even with Fatin, who he'd believed he loved, who— damn his foolish, romantic soul—he *had* loved.

Ana's kiss made him feel like a new man.

Ana's kiss was more than he deserved.

And then the horror of it dawned on him, as the blood receded, as it went back to his brain, he realized what he had done.

Once is carelessness, twice is the measure of a man.

Or rather the foolishness of a man's measure. His body betraying him yet again. His cock controlling him.

He straightened. "Of course we have to stop."

"I'm engaged to Tariq."

An animal in him raged, wounded and seeking to lash out. "I don't give a damn about your engagement!" he roared. "The fate of a nation rests on me. Whether or not you're faithful to your fiancé is none of my concern. But war is. And I would never compromise the lives of my people, the future of my country to spread your legs. You are not so valuable as that."

His head pounding, heart threatening to burst through his chest, he turned and walked away, leaving her standing there, staring after him.

He had hurt her. He didn't care.

It was better he hurt her now. Better he hurt her this way.

Images flashed before his mind, images that were curled and burned around the edges, tinged in red. Blood soaked and inserted so deep into his mind it could never be removed.

It was this palace. These walls. That woman.

He wanted to vomit. He stopped walking and pressed his head to the wall, the cold stone cooling his blood. He stood for a moment, breathing through the nausea, through the pain that seemed to be everywhere. His mind, his treacherous member and his heart, as events from the past wove their way into the present and tangled themselves into an indecipherable mass in his mind's eye.

Violence was the only thing that stood out clearly. The reminder of why he must resist her. Of what he must spare her and all of his people from.

He pulled himself away from the wall and headed toward the gym. Simply walking away wouldn't be enough. There had to be a consequence. His body had betrayed him. And he would have to mete out punishment.

That was how she found him, two hours later. In the gym, soaked in sweat, knuckles raw, split and bleeding from punching the bag repeatedly.

"What are you doing?" she asked, standing there, feeling numb.

She was still dizzy and hot and ashamed from that kiss,

and after sulking in her room for a while she'd decided she had to go and find him and…something. Explain herself. Scream at him. Tell him he didn't know her life and he couldn't judge her.

And then she'd walked into his gym and seen him like this. Like a man possessed.

"Zafar," she said, "what are you doing?"

He looked at her this time, eyes black, soulless. He turned away, rolled his shoulders forward, sweat rolling down his back, running over sharp, defined muscles, down to the dip at his spine, just before the curve of his butt, barely covered by his descending suit pants.

He punched the bag again, a spray of pink sweat spreading through the air on contact.

"Stop!" she said, the shout torn from deep inside of her. She didn't care if she was loud. She didn't care if she was a nuisance. She didn't care if she made him angry or made herself seem less useful, or more of a burden.

She shouted it, let it fill the silence of the space.

It seemed to jolt him out of whatever world he was lost in. "What do you want?"

"Maybe you should tape your knuckles before you do that."

He looked down at his hands and lifted one shoulder. "Why?"

"So you don't turn your fists into hamburger."

"Doesn't matter."

"What do you mean it doesn't matter? What's wrong with you?"

"I deserve it," he spat.

"Why? For kissing me?"

"For endangering my entire country, yet again, because I can't seem to think with my brain." The implication was crude, and to Ana, it felt like a slap in the face.

"It only endangers things if I tell. I won't."

"It doesn't change my actions, you telling or not. It doesn't change the fact that *I* haven't."

"Were you kissing me because you love me?"

Those dark eyes swept her up and down. "No."

She nodded slowly. "I think you've changed. Granted, I didn't know the boy you used to be, but the man standing in front of me would never sacrifice anything for love. I doubt he could even feel it."

"I thank you."

"It wasn't a compliment."

"It can be nothing else to me. I have a country to defend, to take into the modern era, and I can't waste surplus energy on abstract emotions that don't matter."

"How can love not matter?"

"Why would it?"

"Because what drives you if not love? Don't you love your people?"

"I am loyal to them. I can hardly love them."

"Love is the fuel that keeps loyalty burning," she said, not sure where she'd found the strength to argue with the man standing in front of her. Because this wasn't her civilized dinner companion, or her dance partner. This was a wholly different beast. A man with scars on his skin and his soul, both cracked and bleeding. A man who radiated barely contained rage and violence.

"Is that right? Is that what keeps your engagement to your precious Tariq so strong? Loyalty fueled by love."

"No," she said, the realization creeping over her slowly. "That's not it. It's…my dad. I…I have to do this, Zafar, because *he* loves me. Because when everything in his life crumbled, when everything in my life crumbled, we were all each other had, and I feel like if I don't do this, I run the risk of losing the one person who was always there for me. The person who gave so much for my happiness."

"What did he give you, Ana? What did your precious

father ever give to you? You said yourself, you were the one who organized his life. You were the one who held it together. He sent you to school, used you as a party planner when you were home."

"He didn't leave me!" she shouted. "And you wouldn't think that would be too spectacular for a parent, but my mother *did*. So something must be difficult about me. Something must make people want to be away from me. But he stuck it out. He stayed. He gave me a home, and a place to come back to. I owe him for that."

"And you don't want to lose him."

"No. I don't. Does that make me sad and pathetic? If so then fine. But I've proven that I'm easy to walk away from, so I think I have just cause to feel paranoid."

"You are not easy to walk away from. Even a man with ice in his chest can see that."

"You walked away, too. So I think basically it's all a bunch of crap."

"I saved you. I ransomed you."

"So now you want a medal for not leaving me out in the desert with a bunch of criminals?"

"I spent the last cent I had on you. I thought it might mean something. That's all. Of course I wouldn't have left you there. I have many faults, and I am heartless, make no mistake, but I also know what is right. And *right* is not leaving an innocent out there like that."

She shook her head. "And when there's no emotion behind that kind of sentiment, it means very little. Hard to have my heart warmed when I know that moment was as fraught for you as the moment you have to choose what color underwear to put on in the morning."

He advanced on her, and she fought the urge to shrink back. She never considered herself brave. She'd never considered herself outspoken, or a fighter, but Zafar made her feel just strong enough to take on the world, somehow. Even when he was the main part of the world she was taking on.

He made her feel loud.

"Intent is irrelevant, as is emotion. Action is all that matters. Result, is all that matters. I poured my heart out to the woman I loved, because of love, and that love didn't stop her from relaying that information to the enemies of my family. It didn't stop them from brutally killing my mother and father. In front of me."

That stopped her short, cold dread making her fingers tingle. "Zafar..."

"Intentions mean nothing," he ground out. "Not when everyone is dead and you're sent out to the desert to rot. Tell me then, what did love mean? What did it fuel?"

"Zafar..."

"You can think what you want, what you *need*. But love is a trap, Ana. A lie. It is being used, in this case, to keep you in line. To manipulate you as it was used to manipulate me. That's the purpose of love."

"No. I can't believe that."

"Why? Because if you did then you would have no reason to do what you're told?"

"Because I would have nothing!" she exploded, her hands trembling, her stomach pitching. "You are the most horrible, horrible man. Stay here and pound the skin off your hands. I don't give a damn."

He advanced on her then, reaching around her waist and tugging her hard up against his body. He lowered his head, his nose nearly touching hers. "No, you couldn't. Because if you believed me...there would be nothing to hold you back, and then you might have to do something out of the box, something that takes you beyond your safe little world."

He dipped his head and took her mouth, hard and swift, his lips nearly bruising hers.

When he pulled away, she simply stared at him. She wouldn't back down. She wouldn't look away. "I have been kidnapped, then bought, dragged through this godforsaken desert back to your godforsaken castle. I have been held here against my will. I have overseen your personal hygiene and attempted to teach you to waltz. You have no right to call my world little. You have no right to imply that I am not brave. No right to imply that your words could crumble my life. I'm stronger than that. I'm better than that."

She tugged herself free from his grasp and spun on her heel, turning to walk out of the room.

"A big speech, *habibti*. And yet, you are still doing everything you're supposed to be doing. You are so well-trained."

She gritted her teeth and kept walking, trying to ignore the echo of truth in the words that settled in her bones.

CHAPTER TEN

THEY SPENT THE next several days avoiding each other. Zafar knew she was avoiding him because every so often he would be walking down a corridor and he could hear footsteps, or see a brief flash of gold as she disappeared quickly back around a corner.

It was his own fault. He had failed thoroughly in the assignment of acting civilized. Kissing her, yelling at her and then kissing her again.

But she made him feel that way. Wild, reckless and a bit unpredictable. He didn't like any of it.

But the event was tonight. His debut, for lack of a better word, and he wasn't feeling confident. Put him on the back of the horse, in the middle of the desert. Let him fight with his bare hands, to the death, any man who dared threaten his people, and he had no fear.

A ballroom and cocktail shrimp were another matter entirely.

And thanks to that article in the paper, everyone here was watching. Waiting to see if he was a madman. Or a man at all.

He supposed he had no choice but to show them.

He rolled his shoulders forward, already bound up in his tailored suit shirt and jacket. And there were ghosts here. Everywhere. He couldn't sleep at all or their icy fingers invaded his dreams.

He was starting to feel a little crazy, which was what he'd feared would become of him from spending so much time alone in the desert.

Ironic that it was more pronounced now that he was back here. Surrounded by an ever-growing staff, by civilization, by modern life, which should make things easier. Instead he saw shadows everywhere. Claws pulling him down into the abyss every time he closed his eyes. Forcing him to fight against sleep.

But he had no time to deal with it. And no interest in taking pills. They would only drag him under further. God knew if he would ever come back out of something like that.

He laughed, the sound flat and bitter in the empty corridor. He was grim today. Or perhaps he was every day.

Damn, but he was coming apart. He craved space and dry air. Not these obsidian walls that felt more like a tomb than a castle.

And then he saw her, out the window, in the courtyard, her hair like a golden flame, and he could breathe again.

He walked through the hall to the doors as quickly as possible, his heart pounding hard. He needed air. He needed to see her.

"Ana," he said, striding out into the heat. She turned, the sun catching the side of her face, illuminating clear blue eyes, and he could swear his heart started over. As though every day since he was born it had been going, steadily, enduring the beatings life had thrown his way. Now suddenly, it was back at one. New. Untarnished.

The feeling only lasted a moment. Still, the exhilaration of it lingered.

"Ana," he said again. "If you could stop being angry with me for a moment, I would appreciate it. I have a big event for myself personally and my country tonight, and I have no time for you to persist in your tantrum."

Her eyes widened. "In my tantrum? I know you didn't just say that."

"I did," he said. "And I meant it. The fate of a nation is at stake. I doubt a snit is worth the fate of a nation."

"A snit? You undermined my entire belief system and told me I was stupid and imprisoned by my notion of love."

"I didn't say you were stupid."

"Only that my worldview was."

"I didn't come here to fight."

"Oh no? Why are you here?"

"Because this damned thing starts in a little over three hours, I have additional staff infesting my castle and I have to put in an appearance that is both polished and civil and I thought you might…be available to speak to me for a moment."

"About?"

"Tell me that I can do this," he said. He hated displaying this level of weakness. This level of need. That he had to use her as an anchor for his sanity. To remind him he was a man, and that somewhere in his past he had been a man who understood these types of things. A man who could walk into a room full of people and command it, command them.

He didn't know why he thought he could get all of that from her. Except he wasn't getting it from the palace. The palace was splintering him, his mind, his thoughts. And the nights were getting so bad.

She somehow made it all seem better. She made it all seem clear. Her grace and poise made him feel like he could absorb some of it himself. Like it existed in the world and all he had to do was reach out and take it.

When he was left to himself, to his own devices, he couldn't find it.

"You need a pep talk?" she asked.

"I didn't say that."

"You sort of did."

"So, what if I do?"

"I didn't think you needed anyone. Fierce sand pirate that you are."

He frowned. "Are you joking?"

"Yes. Humor. I've even made time for it in my unexciting life. You should try it sometime."

"I've never had much time for joking. I've been too busy…"

"Surviving. Making amends. Wreaking havoc on your horrible uncle's men. I know. But now you're here. And you're going to have to play the part of suave, capable ruler. Check in your pockets for loose charisma if you need to."

He felt a laugh rise in his throat, escape his lips. "This is why I needed to see you," he said.

"Why?" she asked.

"Because you make things feel…not as heavy. You make my chest feel lighter. Breathing is a bit easier."

"You've been having trouble breathing?" she asked, the look in her eyes intensely sad.

"It's this place."

"Can you tell me? Everything?"

"I wouldn't," he said.

"Why?"

"I would hate to make your chest heavy, too."

Ana blinked, her eyes stinging. And she couldn't blame it on the sun. Something in her felt like it was being twisted, tied up in knots. Like he was holding on to vital pieces of her and manipulating them somehow.

She swallowed, then nodded. "I know. It's okay. I'm just glad I made you able to breathe. Zafar, you can do this."

"And you can't be there."

"I know."

"But I will remember this."

"Our conversation?"

"How it made me feel."

She took a deep breath. "Why are you being so nice to me? A few days ago you kissed me and then you freaked out at me and…and I don't get where we stand."

"Something about being near you…your civilization tactics have worked, clearly, and I feel more connected with that, with the more polished side of myself when I'm with you," he said, his voice rough, dark eyes compelling. "And beyond that…I want you. But there is nothing that can be done about that. I can do nothing to compromise the relations Al Sabah has with Shakar. And I can offer you nothing but an isolated life here in this glorified graveyard. I would never ask it of you. Which means the only thing that can come from my wanting you is sex. And that isn't sufficient, either."

"I know," she said. But it didn't stop her from feeling the same way. From wanting him. Even while she was still mad at him for the crap that he'd pulled the other day.

But the truth was, he was right. She'd been thinking about it, and nothing else, ever since their confrontation in the gym. And he was right.

She was afraid. Afraid of losing her father's love. His approval. And she did so much to make sure she never did. To make herself important to him so that he couldn't just leave her, too. To be quiet, to be good so that at the very least, if she wasn't important, she wasn't in the way.

And the reason things had felt so different since she'd come to Al Sabah was simple. There were no shackles here. There was no one looking at her with disapproval or expectation. She had to make her own decisions to survive, to keep sane, and there was no one to guide those decisions.

It made her see things a little bit differently. It made her see herself differently.

It made her see herself. Not as other people saw her,

but just through her own eyes. And it was different than she'd imagined. She looked at herself and saw the Stepford Daughter. Someone who was doing just as she was told so that she wouldn't make waves.

Someone who was earning favor with good deeds. And she wasn't even certain her father had ever asked for those things from her. But she'd been so afraid. After her mother left she'd wondered what she'd done to make it happen. Had been consumed with ensuring she never had to endure another abandonment like that.

And it had all made sense. Doing right kept things together, doing wrong, like her mother, made it fall apart.

She hadn't even realized how much of that reasoning was borne of fear. The fear that saying no to one of her father's requests would make him leave her. That she would be left with no one.

It made her think of Tariq. It made her question her feelings for him. Made her wonder if she was just agreeing to marry him, if she only thought she loved him, because it was the course that would make the least waves.

Because what she felt for Zafar was like nothing else ever. And no, she was sure she didn't love Tariq. Under the circumstances, that was impossible. But shouldn't a bit of the lust and need spill over to a future spouse? Shouldn't some of the heat and flame she felt for Zafar be there for the man she loved? Instead, all she felt for Tariq was a drive to cement their union. Almost like he was the finish line of her good deeds.

The thought made her feel…it made her feel frightened. And more uncertain than she'd ever felt in her life.

Like a butterfly breaking out of a cocoon. But her wings felt wrinkled and wet, and she just wanted to climb back inside and curl up. Go back to sleep. Back to feeling like security was all she needed, rather than feeling curiosity about the size of the world. About how high she could fly.

Except now it was too late to stuff herself back in the cocoon. But she wasn't ready for more yet, either.

"You'll do fine tonight, Zafar," she said. "And I really hope people realize how lucky they are to have you. I hope they feel everything you've given for them."

"What if they only remember what I took?"

And she realized she didn't have an answer for him. She was just a scared girl who had no idea what she was doing with her life, no idea what she wanted. And she was trying to tell a man who had witnessed unspeakable tragedy, who had lived his life in exile, who now had to rule a country, what to do. Trying to offer reassurance in a situation that very few people on the entire planet would ever have to face. If there was even anyone else dealing with it.

Zafar was alone. In his duty. And she couldn't walk with him. Couldn't hold his hand. Couldn't lead him in the waltz or remind him to smile.

She ached to do those things. To be there to help him. Not because it was the right thing, but because for some reason she wanted to stand beside this man while he tried to fix the broken things in his country.

"Just..." She cleared her throat. "Just make sure you use the right fork. All sins can be forgiven in light of good table manners."

"Then it is a good thing I had an excellent teacher."

If the palace empty made Zafar feel like he was enclosed in a crypt, full of people it felt like a crowded crypt, and that was even worse.

Leaders from around the world were in attendance. And some of Al Sabah's wealthiest citizens.

Tariq was not in attendance thanks to the damaged relationship between Al Sabah and Shakar. But in truth, Zafar wasn't in any way sad about it. If Ana's fiancé were present, he would feel obligated to send her back with him and damn appearances.

But he wasn't. Which meant Zafar could keep her, if only for a little while longer. Just until he had a chance to think of a solution.

Yes, because you've been working on that so diligently since you brought her here.

In truth, he knew he had not. Because he liked having her around. And if the sins of his past didn't prove what a bastard he was, then surely that did.

He affected a false smile and directed it at the very lovely ambassador from Sweden, who was currently giving him a winning smile of her own, trying to entice him to come and talk to her, he was certain.

She was lovely. Pale, with the same kind of Nordic beauty that Ana possessed. And yet, on her it was a bit too stark, unwelcoming. Looking at Ana was like stepping into winter. Crisp and clear and bright.

The ambassador started to move toward him, and he started looking for exits. Everyone wanted to talk to him. For hours now, he had been making conversation. Likely more conversation than he'd ever made in his life, and it had all occurred on one night.

He looked around the glittering ballroom, scanning the surrounding for an excuse to sidestep the woman making her way to him. He looked up, into the shadowy balconies that were set into the wall of the ballroom, and he saw a flash of red that sent his pulse into overdrive.

Ana wouldn't show up, would she? She had no reason to. She had every reason to hate him, considering the way he'd treated her a few days earlier. So then, perhaps that would be incentive for her to come, to see him make a fool of himself in front of dignitaries and kings.

He looked harder into the shadows, but didn't see any more movement. No more red.

He started moving toward the back door of the room, not caring how it looked. Not caring that he was surely ignoring people who wanted his attention. He was a sheikh now, after all, and it would stand to reason that he would have important business to do.

A brief flash of memory filtered through his mind.

When you see her...across the crowded ballroom...and you make your way to her...you have something better to do than talk about the weather.

It certainly wasn't the weather on his mind. He looked around him, took a sharp breath and continued on.

No one needed to know he was chasing after a woman. No one needed to know that he was following his weakness yet again.

There would be hell to pay for this, later. In nightmares. In physical pain, probably meted out in the gym. But right at the moment it seemed worth it. It seemed necessary.

He walked through the double doors and into the corridor, passing the security he hired for the event without making eye contact, as he went to the curved staircase that led up to the recessed balconies.

He put his hand on the railing, his fingers sliding over smooth, white stone as he made his way upstairs. He listened as intently as he could, keeping his footsteps silent. Wondering if he might hear the whisper of her gown's fabric. Hear her breathe.

He heard footsteps, and then, a soft, warm body collided with his with a muffled "Mmph."

He reflexively grabbed the person by the arms and held them out, steady, so he could get a look. "Ana," he said.

"Guilty."

"You aren't supposed to be here," he said.

"I know, but I had to make sure you were doing okay."

"And what did you observe?"

She lifted her chin. "You're the best looking man in the room."

"That, my dear, could be construed as non-bland conversation."

"I know. I don't…I don't think I care."

"Ana, you don't know what you're inviting."

"I probably do. I think…Zafar…I've been thinking. But I don't want to talk just now." And then she was leaning into him, soft lips pressing against his. His body was on fire in an instant, all caution, all common sense gone as her tongue traced the seam of his mouth gently.

He opened to her, and let her explore, let her take.

Because he was powerless to do anything else.

"Do you have any idea what you're doing?" he whispered.

"No," she said.

Ana had to admit it, because it was the truth. She didn't know what she was doing. She'd never kissed a man quite so passionately. She'd never wanted a man with quite so much ferocity.

She'd known she couldn't show her face at the party. She wasn't supposed to be here. No one could ever know she was here.

But she hadn't been able to resist. She'd put on the red dress she'd worn to dinner. And eventually she'd gotten up the courage to slip up to the balcony to catch a glimpse of him.

No one would recognize her, even if they saw her. Not from that distance. At least, that had been her reasoning.

Now there was no reasoning at all. She hadn't planned this. She hadn't expected it. She had no idea what it would mean for her future, or why she was taking such a chance. She only knew that she couldn't seem to stop herself.

That she didn't want to stop.

That for the first time in longer than she could remem-

ber she wasn't getting tripped up pondering the whys and
why nots of every action she performed. That she wasn't
worrying about what other people would think. Or what
they might wish she would do differently.

How could she worry about it when nothing had ever
felt so right? When the press of his mouth against hers
seemed essential?

And then she found herself backed against the hard
stone wall, the cool rock at her back, the heat and hardness of Zafar in front of her. She wrapped her arms around
his neck, clung to him, poured everything she had into
the kiss.

Desperation. Passion. Confusion. Anger.

She felt all of it, swirling inside of her, creating a perfect
storm of emotion that seemed to push her harder, faster.

She was so consumed with it, with him, that she hardly
realized her fingers had gone to the knot of his tie. That she
was loosening it, tugging it from around his neck. That she
was working the buttons on his shirt as quickly as possible.

She didn't realize it until her hand came up against hot,
bare skin, rough chest hair that tickled her fingertips as
she swept them beneath his collar so that she could get
closer to him.

He kissed her hard, pressing his body to hers. And she
could feel the hard ridge of his arousal against her thigh,
evidence of how much he wanted her. That she wasn't
feeling this alone.

And she wanted to weep with the triumph.

Because someone felt passion for her. Because even if
Zafar only wanted sex, and her body, she was certain it
was more need than anyone else had truly felt for her in
years, if ever.

Her father wanted her to help him maintain the status
quo. To help him shore up his profits. Tariq wanted her
for a revenue increase to his country.

No one wanted *her*. And no one was honest about it.

Except that wasn't true now. Zafar wanted her. And if there was one thing she knew, even with her near nonexistent experience with men, it was that erections didn't lie. It was blunt, brutal honesty at its most basic and she reveled in it.

She arched against him, pressing her aching breasts to his chest, her heart thundering so loud and hard she was certain he could hear it, certain he could feel it.

He abandoned her mouth and kissed the side of her neck, her collarbone. The curve of her breast revealed by her dress.

"This is a beautiful dress," he said. "But it doesn't give me enough of you."

He reached behind her and tugged at the zipper tab, pulling it down and loosening the dress so that it hung off her curves. Then he pushed against the single strap that held it up and it fell to the floor, leaving her standing there in a darkened stairwell in nothing but a black strapless bra and matching panties.

If she'd been thinking clearly, she probably would have protested, or expressed some form of outrage. But she wasn't. So she didn't.

He put his hands on her waist, ran his fingertips over the line of her spine. The action, so simple, so seemingly sedate, sent a riot of need through her that made her breasts ache, made her slick between her thighs.

She'd never known what it was to want a man. Not like this.

He pressed a kiss to the valley between her breasts, then traced a line there with the tip of his tongue. And she shivered.

She laced her fingers in his hair, wanting to hold him there forever, wanting to tighten her hold and tug him back up to her lips so she could kiss him again.

She just wanted. With everything in her, with her entire being. And damn anyone else's opinion. Damn the consequences. Damn quietness.

He raised his head and kissed her again, and she made quick work of the rest of the buttons on his shirt. She pressed her palms flat against his hard, muscular chest, sliding her hands downward, to his stomach.

She'd never seen a man who looked like him. He'd completely shocked her the first time she'd seen him without a shirt. Bronzed and chiseled and so sexy it nearly hurt.

She'd never noticed how sexy men were because she'd never let herself see. Because she'd been so committed to an ideal she'd shut that part of herself off and channeled controlled bits of it to the "appropriate" place.

This was like a dam burst, and there was nothing appropriate about where her desire was being channeled. And she didn't care. Not in the least.

All that mattered was how amazing he felt. How right it felt to have his lips against hers. How she felt like she would die if she didn't have more of him.

All of him.

"I want you," she said, the words torn from deep inside of her, from a place she hadn't known existed. One filled with passion, with desire that stood apart from expectation and judgment. A place that was all hers.

And, in this moment, Zafar's.

He put his hands on her lower back, pushed his finger down beneath the waistband of her sheer black panties, the reached in farther, cupping her.

The intimate contact shocked her a little bit, but not enough to make her stop. And then he dipped between her thighs, his fingers skimming her slick folds and she jumped, arching into him.

"Shh," he said, kissing her, cutting off the strangled cry she hadn't realized had been on her lips. "It's okay. Do you like it?" He stroked her slowly and her whole body shook, internal muscles she'd been unaware of until that moment contracting tight.

"Yes," she whispered, letting her head fall back. He kissed her jaw, her neck, and pushed a finger into her, slowly. Her breath caught and she held on to his shoulders.

"Still good?" he asked, pressing deeper, moving one finger farther forward to her clitoris as he stroked in and out of her gently with another.

"Yes." She closed her eyes and leaned into him, widening her stance so he had easier access to her body.

She shuddered as he continued to subject her to sensual torture with his hands, his lips hot on her neck, his tongue sliding over her tender skin.

Everything in her went tight, so tight she could scarcely breathe. She thought she would break. And just when she thought she couldn't endure anymore, his final stroke over the sensitized bundle of nerves made everything in her release.

It was like chains that had been holding her, for months, years, all of her life, had suddenly let go. And she was falling, weightless, pleasure coursing through her body. And there was nothing, no thought, no worry, no fear of judgment, or anything else.

Nothing but the white-hot pleasure that burned on and on, leaving her scorched, but unharmed. Leaving her new.

Like a phoenix from the ashes.

And for one whole minute, as she rested against his chest, her breathing returning to normal, she felt stronger, more sure, than she ever had before.

But the minute passed too soon.

And then she realized she was in a stairwell in nothing but her underwear, and she'd just let the man who was holding her captive, the man who was not her fiancé, bring her to orgasm with his hands.

There weren't enough swearwords. There really weren't. So she went through them all in her head. Twice.

And then she said one of them, the worst one she could think of, out loud because why not? Only Zafar was here. And he had just seen the most shameful, embarrassing moment of her life. She didn't have to worry too much about manners in this case. Especially not when he was holding her half-naked body against his.

But he was the one who drew away suddenly, his dark eyes haunted, his hands shaking as he pushed them through his hair. He was pale, a sheen of sweat on his gray-tinged forehead.

"I…I am sorry. Forgive me." And she was pretty sure he wasn't talking to her. "Forgive me," he said again, buttoning up his shirt as he walked down the stairs, away from her, leaving her standing there staring after him, her body buzzing, her head pounding. Her heart aching.

What had she done?

She dropped down to her knees, her legs too weak to hold her up.

"What did you do?" she said out loud.

She shifted so that she was sitting, her back to the wall, and she picked up her dress from the ground, sliding it onto her lap, holding it up over her breasts. A tear slid down her cheek. She hadn't even felt tears building, but they were here, and they were falling, faster than she could wipe them away.

If her father knew, if Tariq knew, they would hate her.

And everything would be for nothing. Her whole life, all that quiet, would be for nothing.

She scrunched her face up, lights filtering in from the ballroom below splintering and turning into glittering stars, fractured by her tears.

What had just happened with Zafar had been the single most beautiful moment in her life. In his arms she'd felt alive. She'd felt more like Ana. The Ana who was waking up from hibernation. The Ana she might have been if life really did come with a guarantee.

If she'd been free to grow up without all the baggage. Without all the fear and anxiety that one wrong move would see her abandoned by both parents.

But the beauty of the moment withered and died quickly. And it left behind the reality. She had betrayed the man she'd promised to marry. She'd done what she wanted to do, instead of doing what was right.

And she feared that, just like her mother's priceless porcelain doll, everything was too broken to be put back together.

That she had, once again, cut the tether that held the people she loved in her life.

It couldn't happen again. She could never speak of it. She couldn't even remember it. She would weather the rest of her captivity, and then she would go back to Shakar. Back to Tariq and her father.

They would never see how badly broken she was inside. And everything could go on as it was supposed to.

There was no other option.

CHAPTER ELEVEN

"WE HAVE TO LEAVE."

Zafar's voice pierced her sleep-fogged brain. She looked out the window and saw that it was still gray out. Ana rolled over in bed, put her hands over her face. "Right now?"

"Yes," he bit out. "Now."

"What about liaising and being diplomatic?" Cold dread washed over her and she sat upright. "Unless you talked to Tariq."

"No," he bit out, "I didn't. But I have been awake all night and I have decided that you failed in your task."

"I…failed." The words sent a cold stone of dread sinking down into the bottom of her stomach. So strange, because it shouldn't matter if Zafar thought she'd failed at something. But failing, being wrong, being worthless, was such an ingrained fear that no matter who spoke, the words had the power to wound her. "Why? What did they say about you? What did they say about the ball?"

"Oh," he bit out, "they loved me. They've called Rycroft a flaming idiot and said that he was slandering me in his article. Suave, they said, and handsome. But, Ana, I am not civilized, no matter what they say. And that was your job. To civilize me. And you did not. Why else would I be keeping a woman locked in my palace, keeping her from her father, her fiancé, giving no notice that she wasn't dead, rather than sending her straight back to her home, regardless of the fallout? There is no honor in that. No civility."

"Zafar…you did what you had to do."

"Stop it," he growled. "Stop trying to placate me. Stop trying to smooth things over. Some things cannot be fixed. Some things are not in your power to repair." He paced at the foot of her bed, frightening and mystifying in his anger. "Do not absolve me. It is a heresy. You don't know the sins you're trying to forgive."

"Fine. Stay in your self-imposed hell then, Zafar Nejem. I don't care. But make good on your word and take me back home. You can castigate yourself for all your wrongdoing on the way."

She flung off the covers and got out of bed, realizing she had nothing to pack. That nothing here was hers. That she would leave everything, including Zafar, behind and there would be no evidence that she was ever here. No evidence he had ever been part of her life.

That he'd been the first man to kiss her passionately. The first man to touch her intimately. The first man to give her an orgasm.

The first man to make her wonder if there was more to life than she was allowing herself to live. The first man to make her want to stand out in the open and scream at the sky so people would know she was there. So she would stop just blending in.

And she would just leave it. Leave him. It would be nothing more than a blip on the radar of her life. A couple weeks out of time, with nothing more than the life she'd led at home with her father coming before, and nothing but her marriage to Tariq after.

All the anger drained out of her, leaving her lips feeling cold. Leaving her feeling dizzy.

"That is the question. Commercial flights to Shakar

were barred during my uncle's rule. If I fly you there, we may create more of a spectacle than we would like."

"Take me back the way we came in," she said. She pictured it then, the journey to the palace on the back of his horse, the wind, harsh and arid and clean in her face.

"On a horse?"

She nodded. "Yes. No one will have to know. Leave me where I was taken. I'll lie about what happened."

"It's not so simple, and you know that. Were it that simple we could have done that from the beginning."

"I know. But…I'll lie to buy you time. Or I'll tell Tariq how you saved my life, but I'll make sure that I express nothing but deep gratitude to you and to the people of Al Sabah. I won't let there be a war."

She didn't know where the strength was coming from. She'd always liked to fix things. Had always tried to take a chance at reclaiming her life. At fixing what she'd broken.

So odd how, in all ways, she saw Zafar in herself. Guilt, blame and shame, a constant companion, and the need to try and remake everything, make it new again, fix the damage caused by their actions, an ever-present drive and burden.

But this was different. This was true conviction. A vow she was making to him that she would keep no matter what.

"Trust me," she said. "I'll fix it."

"Why do you want to do it this way?"

"Because…because I need to finish my adventure before I stop having them. Especially sad since this was my first one."

"Is that what this has been for you, *habibti*?" he asked. "An adventure?"

She shook her head, her throat tightening. "No. It's been more than that, but I'm not sure what to say. I don't even know what I feel."

He let out a heavy breath, then straightened, every inch the commanding king. "Dress yourself. Pack adequate clothing for three to days of travel. The desert is unpredictable and often there are obstacles that prevent things from going as quickly as we might like."

"Sandstorms."

"Yes. But you will be with me. I will not let any harm come to you." She felt like he was talking about more than just the desert. Like more than just physical harm. "I promise you that."

"I believe you."

"I will gather tents and food. It will not be as rough of a journey as it was coming here."

"And will you bring servants?"

Their eyes locked, tension crackling between them, and the despair she'd felt last night in the stairwell was burned away by the heat that ignited in her veins. "No," he said. "It is best not to involve any more people than necessary."

She nodded, feeling like a hand was tightening around her throat. "No, that wouldn't do."

"Not at all."

"I'll get ready, then."

"I will wait out in the courtyard. No one can see us leave. There is still extra staff here. People who are not mine."

"I understand."

He nodded once and turned and walked out of the room, leaving her standing there, feeling like, yet again, her life had been turned completely upside down.

Strange how she was coming to expect it. How it seemed to jar something loose in her. How she sort of enjoyed it.

Well, it was coming to an end now. Because she was going back to Shakar. Back to Tariq.

She sucked in a shaking breath and started looking for a bag to pack her clothes in.

* * *

"Ready?" Zafar looked down from his position on his horse, his face mostly covered by his headdress.

She nodded her pale head. She looked…different. There was a quiet strength to her posture, her hair drawn back into a tight bun. He had always seen her as extremely self-possessed, the exception being the brief emotional meltdown she'd had when he'd first rescued her from her kidnappers.

But now she was somewhere beyond self-possessed. She had a core of steel, and he could see it. Could see that she wouldn't be bending. But he didn't know what she'd set her will to. And that was the part that concerned him most.

Aside from what being alone with her might do. Aside from what his own intentions might actually be. God have mercy on his tattered soul.

Last night he had been inexcusable with her. And no mater the outcome, he had to return her to her fiancé. To her father.

He had been wrong to keep her.

And he had been more than wrong to touch her. In that moment, when he'd pressed her against the wall and kissed her, when he'd put his hand between her thighs and felt all of her heat about his fingertips…he'd been conscious of the gates of hell opening up behind him, the flames licking his back, demons threatening to pull him in.

But not before they'd spurred him to commit the deadliest sin possible. A fitting end to his life. Except it wouldn't really be the end. He couldn't even count on being dragged into the comparable bliss of hell.

He would have to stay in this life and deal with consequences. Yet again.

Consequences he'd earned with his libido, with his disgusting lack of control. Control he'd thought he'd found out in the desert, deprived of every good thing. But back here, back where he'd started, he seemed to lose all the strength the desert had infused in him.

This, then, would be the test.

He reached down. "Need help?"

She shook her head and approached the horse, putting her small bag of clothes into the saddlebag with his other supplies before pulling herself up behind him onto the horse, wrapping one arm around his waist, her thighs bracketing his, her tempting heat against his back.

Soon the desert sun would block that. Would make it impossible to distinguish her body from the arid air.

He took the head scarf from his lap and handed it back to her. "Take this, *habibti*. You need protection from the sun."

She said nothing, but she took it from him, and the movements behind him seemed to indicate that she was following orders.

She wrapped her arm back around his waist, leaning forward, her chin digging into his back. The contact, and the pain, soothed him.

"Let's go," she said.

His agreement came in the form of spurring his horse on and heading toward the back gate of the palace. Out into the desert.

Here, he would find his salvation or his damnation.

And he wasn't entirely sure which one he was hoping for.

He didn't push his horse the way he had that first day they'd met. Instead, they rode at a more decent pace, and they arrived at the oasis just as the sun was becoming too punishing for her to endure.

"We'll stop here," he said, indicating the outcrop of rocks. "There is water just behind the rocks. I'll set up the tent there. Under the trees."

He got off the horse, and she dismounted too, pausing to stroke the beast's nose. "He needs a name, Zafar."

Zafar turned and looked at her, brow raised. "Why?"

"Calling him *horse* is stupid. I don't call you Grumpy Man, do I?" Approaching the subject of the horse's name was easier than confronting what had passed between them last night.

Thinking about the horse's name was easier, too. Which was why she'd spent the silent ride to the oasis pondering that instead of how being in his arms had felt. Of how hard and muscular he was, and about just how much she'd enjoyed contact with that hard muscular body last night.

Yes, thinking of a name for the Horse was much safer.

"I was thinking Apollo," she said, following Zafar to the oasis, where he was headed, bundled-up tent in hand.

"Why?"

"It's transcendent. Godlike."

"He is neither."

"Excuse me. Are you maligning the noble steed carrying us through the desert on its back?"

"I'm hardly maligning him. I just don't think it's a good name for him."

"You've had him for how long?"

He tossed her a quick glance before setting the tent down by the water and continuing on in his labor. "Nine years."

She shook her head. "And you haven't named him. Any name is better than Horse."

"Not Apollo."

"Achilles. Archimedes. Aristotle?"

"Why Greek and why all with *A?*"

"He seems Greek. And also I'm moving alphabetically."

"He is an Arabian horse. He should have an Arabic name."

"All right, name away."

"Sawdaa. Means black."

She crossed her arms beneath her breasts and didn't bother to keep herself from looking at his backside while he worked on the tent. "Original."

"Better then *Horse,* yes?" he asked, finishing with the tent's frame.

"Barely."

"All right then, what would you call him? Not the name of a Greek god, demigod or philosopher, please."

"Since you said *please.* How about Sadiqi. Friend."

"I know what it means."

"Well, he's your friend."

"He's my horse."

"You love nothing, Zafar? Nothing at all? Are you so determined to keep it that way that you can't even name your horse?"

He straightened and shot her a dark glare. "You know nothing about what I've been through. Telling you…it doesn't make it real for you. You don't know what I had to do to survive. To move forward. To make myself a valuable person."

"I admit," she said, walking down to where he stood and taking a position beneath the shade of a palm, "my life story has less blood spilled than yours. But I know what it's like to try to change yourself so you can have some value. I know what it is to break everything."

She closed her eyes and leaned her head back against the tree as she let her least favorite memory wash over her. "I ran through my mother's sitting room. She had her own sitting room, a parlor for entertaining her friends. And she kept her collection of antique dolls in there. She loved them." She swallowed. "I was always loud. Brash. And I moved too quickly. So one day I ran through her sitting room and I knocked against the doll cabinet."

She could still remember the little sandy-haired doll

tipping off the shelf, landing wedged between the locked cabinet door and the shelf. And she'd prayed so hard that it wasn't broken.

Her mother had come running in and opened the cabinet, and pulled out the now-hollow-faced doll, the porcelain reduced to dust on the bottom on the ground.

"I broke it," she said, trying so hard not to picture the look on her mother's face. Trying and failing. "My mother said…she said I was making her crazy. That I was always ruining things. That I'd ruined everything. Ruined things she'd loved." She swallowed the lump that was building in her throat. "I don't think I was one of the things she loved anymore."

Ana breathed in deep. "She left the next day. I'm twenty-two years old, and I know my mother didn't leave me because of a broken doll. I know there were other things. I know she probably had some problems. But then…then all I could think was…if I were more careful. If I had taken more care to listen to her, to move slower. Maybe be quieter and more poised. More helpful.…if I had been those things she wouldn't have left. And if I wasn't careful…maybe my father would leave, too. After all, I ruin everything."

Her voice choked off. She hated this. Hated that she was doing this now, with him. But this was the truth of it. The truth of her life, that she hid behind fake smiles and feeling polished and pulled together.

She'd pulled her hair into a bun and learned how to say yes to everything, to be efficient, to do what was expected of her.

"You do not ruin everything," he said, his voice rough. Then he swore, vilely, harshly. On her behalf. It made her stomach tighten.

"Zafar…"

He crossed to where she was standing, every inch the desert marauder he'd been when she'd first met him, only a small wedge of his face visible, the rest concealed by his headdress.

He tugged the bottom of it down. And she saw the difference from the first day she'd met him. His clean-shaven jaw. She'd done that. She'd changed him, at least on the outside.

It made her feel strange. Powerful.

"You did not make her leave," he said. "My mother was taken from me by death. No force in heaven or hell could have removed her from me, no matter my behavior, had she been given a choice. And it is not because I was a better son than you were daughter. I was dissolute. Lazy. Obsessed with women, sex. And yet she loved me, because of *her* heart, not because of mine. Your mother's rejection… it was not because of you. It was her heart, *habibti*. It was her heart that was damaged, not yours."

"You say that but…you claim you don't even have a heart. How do you know all this?"

"Because," he said, his voice hoarse, "these past years my emotions have been dried out, unused. Dead. If anything on earth would make me wish to have them back… Ana, it's you."

A tear rolled down her cheek and she didn't bother to wipe it away. She had always tried to be who she thought she had to be. Had always tried so hard to be perfect.

But with Zafar, something in her was unleashed. The wild child she'd been born as, maybe. The girl who'd run through the halls of her family home, who'd liked to laugh and be silly. Who hadn't trembled at the thought of having a grade point average that dipped below perfect. Who hadn't been consumed with making sure she improved every situation, rather than being a bother.

She'd constructed a shield for herself. So perfect and shiny. And she wanted it gone now. She didn't want to be the person she'd built herself to be. She wanted to be the person she was born to be.

She remembered her despair last night after their near-lovemaking session in the stairwell. It hadn't been because she was sorry. It had been because she was afraid. Afraid of wanting something for her, something that her father wouldn't want for her.

And Tariq…clearly she had to examine her options there. She did not love him. She'd never been more certain of that. She'd wanted to marry him just to please her father; she'd just been too stubborn to acknowledge it.

Right now, she knew what she wanted.

"Zafar," she said, her voice a near whisper. She cleared her throat. She wasn't going to ask for this with any shame, any embarrassment. "I want you to unmake me. Out here. Just like it happened for you. I don't want to be who I was. I don't want to be weak. I don't want to be quiet. I don't want to live for anyone else. I just want…Zafar, I want. For me. Please…"

"You want to be…unmade?" he asked, his voice rough.

"That's what you told me the desert did for you. That it took the boy you were and made you the man you were. That you had to unmake yourself so you could reemerge the man you needed to be. I need that."

She pushed away from the tree and closed the distance between them. "I have spent so much of my life walking on tiptoes. Trying to be the person I thought I needed to be in order to be bearable. But it's not bearable to me anymore. I don't like me. I am trained to do as I'm told, and that day in the gym…you were right about me, Zafar—I dare not step out of line because I'm afraid if I do my father, or my friends, or the teachers I had who were more like mentors, that they would decide I wasn't worth the trouble. So I made myself indispensable to them. Want to plan a party? I'll help. Need me to marry a sheikh so you can secure easy access to oil? I can do that, too. I'll even do my best to love him. So…no one could get rid of me because I made everything easy for them."

"Except me," he said. "You don't make my life easier. You make it a damn sight harder."

"I'm glad," she said. "I'm…I'm so glad. And I know you want to get rid of me, but honestly, I can't blame you."

"Circumstances being what they are," he said, his voice rough.

"Yes. Naturally."

"How would I go about unmaking you, *habibti*?" he asked, his tone lowering, dark eyes intense on hers. She looked away, her breath coming in short, uneven bursts. "Ana," he said, his voice surprisingly soft. She looked back at him.

Then she turned away, running to the edge of the water. And tilted her head back, the sun scorching her face. She opened her mouth and took a breath, air burning all the way down.

And then she screamed. Her voice echoing all around them. Her. Ana. She was here. She wanted to be heard. She wanted to make a sound. Make an impact that was bigger than the dreams of other people. Have a life that meant more than serving the desires of other people.

Then she turned, shaking, her throat raw, and walked back toward Zafar, his expression looking as though it was carved out of stone.

"I don't want to be quiet," she said.

"And so you are not."

She shook her head. "No. I'm not. And I want…I want more than that even." She met his eyes, dark and intense. "Make love with me."

"Ana…I can offer you nothing. Nothing beyond a physical encounter. Is that really what you want?"

"Yes."

She debated whether or not to tell him she was a virgin. And decided against it. Because, given her very obviously inexperienced kissing technique, he'd probably guessed. And she didn't want to bring it up and make things any more awkward than they were.

"Why would you want me?" he asked. "I am a great sinner. Responsible for the near fall of a nation. Plus, I have not treated you admirably."

On that, she would give him total honesty. He was giving her honesty, the look in his dark eyes haunted. He needed to know why she would choose him, and she had so many reasons.

"Because, before you…I can't remember the last time I felt this way. Not just the desire, the sense of wildness. That's what it is, Zafar. I've felt from the moment I first met you that you'd opened up this part of me I'd tried to choke out. A part I'd thought just didn't exist anymore. But I was wrong. It's the part of myself I closed off. Because I was afraid of being rejected. But I wasn't afraid with you. Mainly because I wanted you to let me go." She laughed. "I didn't have to please you and I just pleased myself and I found this part of me I'd buried. A part of myself I'm so glad to have back."

She put her hand on his cheek. "And as for the desire… I've never known anything like this. I don't want to go my whole life without exploring it."

"Attraction is easy enough to come by. You will find it, maybe with Tariq."

"Not like this," she said. "Tell me honestly, and then I'll leave it alone. Has another woman made you feel the way that I do? You told me this wasn't normal. That this was stronger than most lust. It must be, because I spent most of high school being a paragon, focusing on school and things that made me…useful. And then even more in college because of Tariq, because of that alliance. Even my major, International Studies…it was all for the future with him. To be useful in that future and that meant forsaking anything else. But I can't ignore this, and that right there, that says something. But if it's not the same for you, then tell me. And maybe I can let it go."

He looked away. "I have never felt this before."

"Then take me," she said. "Have me. Give us both this gift."

"I cannot," he said, the denial dragged from him. "Whether you like the idea of it or not, according to custom, you belong to the Sheikh of Shakar, and my taking you is grounds for war. I have caused a war because I couldn't resist a woman. I caused death and destruction because of my lust."

"But I don't want to manipulate you. I just want you," she said. "I have belonged to other people for a long time. Tonight…I don't want to be Tariq's property. And I don't want to be yours. I want to be mine. And I know what I want."

He growled and dipped his head, kissing her hard and deep, swiftly, pulling away from her abruptly. "Be sure," he said. "Be very sure, because I can't stop myself. I am shaking, down to my bones, Ana. For you. Because of you."

Her heart tightened, ached. "I'm sure," she whispered, kissing him. "I'm sure."

"I am so glad I don't have to make conversation about salad forks now. Because all of those times, what I wanted to say was that you were beautiful. That I wanted you to the point of distraction. That your body is enough to make grown men drop to their knees and give thanks to God that they were born men. I wanted to tell you that your red dress should be illegal. That taking it off you was one of the single greatest privileges I'd ever been given. But of course I could not, because I was relegated to the bland. But not now."

"No. Not now. Now I just want you. All of you."

"You don't know what you're asking for," he said, tracing a line over her cheekbone with his fingertip, down to her lips.

"Then show me."

"Ana…"

"Zafar, what do you see when you look at me?"

"Beauty," he said, without hesitating.

"Anything more?"

She looked in his eyes, and she realized she didn't need more. He was here, putting everything on the line for her, betraying himself for the passion that had ignited between them.

There was heat and sand and Zafar.

Everything else burned away.

"There is so much more," he said, his lips on her neck, her collarbone, his hands tugging at the hem of her shirt, drawing it up over her head. "So much," he said, pressing a kiss to the curve of her beast, just above the line of her bra.

"Show me," she said, lacing her fingers in his hair, fighting the release of the sob that was building in her chest, pressure so intense she was afraid she might burst.

He stepped away from her and turned, his back to her, his eyes on the water in front of them. And then he reached in front of his body and started working the tie on his robes, divesting himself of the layers, placing them on the sandy ground, until he was completely naked.

Her breath caught, choked her. She'd never seen a more beautiful sight than the view of him, lit by the sun, his shoulders broad and powerful, the muscles in his back sharply defined, his waist trim, dimples just above his truly glorious butt, round and muscular and just everything she thought a man's backside should be.

And when he turned, she was certain her heart stopped. He was really, well and truly beyond her experience. She'd never seen a naked man in person. She'd seen limited pictures of the male member. But hadn't seen much in the way of erect men. Unwanted spam emails, the contents of which she always closed her eyes against and deleted as quickly as possible, hardly counted.

A textbook drawing outlining the different parts of male anatomy also didn't count.

He was much larger than she'd imagined he might be, but she wasn't worried. She knew that generous size was supposed to be a good thing. So she was fairly certain that, first time, mandatory pain notwithstanding, his proportions were an asset to her.

He made his way back to her and took her hand, leading her to where he'd left his robes laid out on the sand.

He pulled her down to the soft ground with him and pulled her into his strong arms, stroking her hair as he kissed her, as he held her up against the hard, bare length of his body.

She wrapped her arms around his neck, tangled her legs, still clad in jeans, with his. He put his hand on her back, spread his fingers wide over her skin before grasping the clasp of her bra and releasing it, pulling the undergarment off and tossing it aside.

He continued to kiss her, not giving her a moment to be concerned about her nudity as his hands skimmed over her curves, sending delicious sensation all through her body. She already knew how good Zafar could make her feel, with just ten minutes and one hand he'd rocked her world completely. Now, with him pressed to her, his hands roaming her entire body, no scratchy lace between her chest and his, no chance of anyone discovering him, she had a feeling he might truly demolish her world and build a whole new one.

And she didn't mind.

He gripped her hips and pushed her onto her back, settling between her legs, his erection pressed hard and firm into the cradle of her body, still covered by her jeans.

He kissed her deep, his hands bracketing her face then roaming down to cup her breasts, tease her nipples, drawing a hoarse cry from deep within her.

He moved his hand down between her thighs then, stroking her through the denim. She arched against him, needing more. Needing everything.

He undid the snap on her jeans and reached inside, his fingers brushing over the thin fabric of her panties, the touch enticing, the lace's sheer veil adding something to the feeling, making her more sensitive somehow.

Then he reached beneath the web of lace, his fingers touching her damp heat. "Oh, yes," she breathed, resting her head on his shoulder, her fingers curling into his skin, her nails likely digging into his flesh, but she didn't care.

She had to hold on to him, had to keep herself anchored to the ground somehow.

He pushed her pants and underwear down her hips, and she helped, pushing the bundle of fabric off to the side with her foot, then returned to the very important task of kissing him. Everywhere. His lips, his neck, his chest and back to his gorgeous, perfect mouth. She thought of all the years he'd gone without being touched.

Oh, yeah, she knew he'd had lovers. Mistresses. Bed partners. But they hadn't touched him like this. They hadn't wanted to just have his skin against theirs to feel close. Hadn't wanted to touch him because not touching him was as unthinkable as not breathing.

She knew it. She just did.

She could feel herself getting close to the edge again, his hands in between her thighs, stroking and teasing as he'd done that night at the palace.

"Not like that," she said, kissing his neck. "You. Inside me."

"Not yet," he said. "Not yet."

He lowered his head and kissed her between her breasts, before shifting and taking one nipple deep into his mouth, sucking, sliding his tongue over the tightened bud.

Then he worked his way down her body, his lips and tongue creating an erotic path that she was so glad he'd decided to forge.

Then his broad shoulders were spreading her thighs, his breath hot against her sex. And he leaned in, his tongue stroking long and wet over her clitoris. She arched against him, her hands going to his head reflexively. To pull him away, to hold him there, she wasn't sure. But instead of doing anything, she just laced her fingers through his hair and let the dark pull of pleasure drag her under.

Her orgasm swept over her like a wave, crashing through her, robbing her of breath, leaving her spent and shaking in the aftermath. Gasping for air.

And then he was claiming her mouth again, hard and deep, while the head of his penis met the entrance to her body, her slickness easing the way for him as he pushed inside of her.

It was tight, and painful at first. No sharp horrible pain, which some of her friends had professed to experience. But it was still more something to be endured than something she was enjoying. It was so foreign, being filled by another person, being so close to him.

She looked up into his eyes, just as he thrust fully into her, and a sharp cry escaped her lips.

"Are you okay?" he asked, concern written on his face.

"Yes," she said, feeling so full she might burst. "Yes. I'm so much more than okay."

"I didn't know," he said, his voice choked.

"I know. I'm sorry."

"I'm not." He put his hand on her thigh, lifted it so that

her leg was draped over his hip, seating him deeper inside of her. "I'm not."

Then he lowered his head and started moving inside of her, his thrusts steady, measured, and the more he moved, the less it hurt, the more pain gave way to pleasure, discomfort to dissolving and making way for a deep, soul-rending sensation that was building low in her body, in her chest, spreading through her, taking her over.

She wrapped her arms tightly around his neck, beginning to find her own rhythm, moving her hips back against his, bringing her clitoris into contact with his body, like striking a match every time he pushed back inside of her, sending a streak of heat through her veins.

"Zafar," she said, her climax rising inside of her, everything in her tightening to an unbearable degree, preparing for the release she knew would come. A release she wasn't sure she could withstand.

"I'm here," he said, his words labored. "I'm here for you, Ana."

Her name. Not an endearment. *Her* name.

His pace increased, his movements becoming erratic, hard and intense. She cried out her pleasure, ripples of it working its way through her body endlessly.

Then, too soon, far too soon, he withdrew from her, still over her, his hand on his shaft, stroking himself twice until he found his own release, spilling himself before lowering himself to kiss her lips again.

"Ana," he said, breathing hard. "I…"

"Later," she said. "There will time for yelling at me later. I'm so tired now."

"We need to get in the tent." He stroked her cheek with his thumb. "You'll burn out here."

"I can't move."

He hauled himself into a sitting position and scooped her up against his chest, standing, and walking her into the small structure, bigger by quite a bit than the one they'd traveled in at first. "Wait here," he said.

She stood in the center of the bare, clean tent, feeling dizzy. Shocked. Wonderful.

He returned a second later with a large bedroll under his arm. He spread it out on the floor of the tent. "Sleep now," he said. "We'll talk later."

"Will you sleep, too?" she asked.

He shook his head, his dark eyes unreadable. "I don't sleep with anyone."

CHAPTER TWELVE

ANA FELT LIKE she'd been wounded. "Not even with me? Not even…after that?"

"I can't," he said, turned and walked out of the tent, closing the flap behind him.

She lay down on the mattress, her knees curled up to her chest. She had just given everything for this man. Her virginity. Her future.

Because she loved him, she realized that now.

That was why she just wanted to touch him. It was why she wanted him to hold her.

Of all the stupid things.

Loving Zafar wouldn't make her father happy. It would make Tariq very unhappy. Hell, Zafar would probably be pissed, too.

A slow smile spread over her face. She didn't care. She just loved him. It didn't matter if it would make anyone else's life easier. It didn't matter if it made other people unhappy.

She wasn't sacrificing her life to make other people happy. She wasn't marrying a man who didn't inspire her passions. She wasn't marrying a man she didn't love just to make her father love her more. Just to find a piece of security.

She was Analise Christensen. And there had been a

time when she'd had fun. When she'd run instead of walking. When she'd lived loudly.

But she'd let life blow out her spark.

And Zafar had helped her find it again. So this was all his fault, really, and if he didn't like it, he was going to have to deal with it.

Her smile broadened. Two or three weeks ago, she would never have done this. Wouldn't ever have stepped so far off the path she'd been assigned to.

But now she was off that path. Pushing her way through the forest, through the trees and bushes, finding her own way. Terrifying. Liberating.

She rolled into a sitting position and pushed up off the mattress, suddenly not so tired anymore. She was completely naked, but she didn't much care.

She pushed open the tent flap and saw Zafar leading the newly named Sadiqi down to the water.

He was dressed now, but not in his robes. In thin pants and a tunic top, his hair ruffled, standing on end. Because of her.

"You can't just walk away."

Zafar looked up from where he stood at the edge of the lake, his heart lodging in his throat, all of his blood rushing back to his groin as he looked at Ana, standing in the sun, pale and pink and completely naked.

Her blond hair tumbled over her shoulders, her breasts highlighted by the late-afternoon light. So round and soft. Utter perfection in his hands. In his mouth. Against his chest while he was inside of her, chasing ecstasy.

But she'd been a virgin, and he'd made a very grave error. Even without that little revelation, it had been a grave error. But now he knew there would be no hiding their affair.

"I think it's pretty rude to do all that to a woman and then walk away," she said.

"Ruder still would have been staying and doing it again," he said, his throat tight.

"I don't think I'd mind that."

"Perhaps not."

"But you don't want to come back in there with me?"

"This cannot be… Ana, you were a virgin and you are not now. I imagine Tariq will notice."

"First of all, you can't undo what's been done. Second… I'm not going to marry Tariq."

He felt like he'd been punched in the chest. "Why?"

"Because I don't want to. Because I was only doing it to appease my father. I thought it was love, but honestly, if you put your mind to it I think you can manufacture love quite simply. That's all it was. I was told marrying him would be good for our family, and so I set my mind to loving him so that I could please my father. And…and I thought, if I had a husband who was a sheikh, who was bound by this kind of duty…no matter what happened he would never cast me out. A royal couple stays together, if for no other reason than the media. And that's pathetic, and sad, but I didn't know how else to keep someone with me, Zafar. But now…now I don't care. I just don't. I'm the one that has to live my life. I think…I think I started feeling this way when my friends and I went on the desert tour. I wanted to experience a taste of freedom, of something a bit wild. Something not strictly sanctioned, and so I arranged that. But it was more than that. I just think I wanted something more. Then I was kidnapped, and then there was you. And now here we are. And I feel different. I feel like this was the journey I had to take."

"I'm glad that my personal hell was a step along the way of your journey," he bit out.

"That's not what I meant."

"It's what you said."

"You…Zafar, you were unexpected. Unwanted." A

tear slid down her cheek, her face crumpling. And he just
wanted to pull her into his arms and tell her everything
would be okay. But he couldn't promise that. He could
promise her nothing. "But you are absolutely the most
important thing…I could never have found this, I could
never have found me, without you. I would have made
vows to a man that I had no business making them to. I
would have…I would have ruined my life and never fully
realized it. Like suddenly the fog cleared and now I see
everything, where before I could barely see past my nose.
And I didn't even know how far life went, how broad the
scope. I would never have known."

Zafar left Sadiqi standing at the river's edge. The horse
wouldn't wander off. He never had. He truly was a faithful friend, regardless of what he'd said earlier.

He was glad she'd talked him into giving him a name.
What was she doing to him?

"I must take you back still. You know that, right?"

"I do."

"I need to see you returned safely, and from there whatever you choose to tell your father and Tariq, whatever decisions you make, are yours."

"It's hot."

"I know. That's why we stopped."

"Will you come into the tent and lie down with me?"

Such a sweet, open request and he felt unable to refuse
it. The truth was, he wanted nothing more than to pull
her into his arms, her sweet softness against him, his face
buried in her hair, inhaling her scent, a hand cupping her
breast. He wanted it so much it made him ache.

But it wasn't her status as another man's fiancé, which
she claimed she no longer was, that made it an impossibility.

It was him.

He couldn't sleep with her. For fear the darkness would

swallow them both. That he would lash out against her in the night. He couldn't ask her to stay with him because he would use her as a dying man used an oasis. He would quench his thirst with her body, her soul, and give nothing back.

He would be able to give her nothing. He would be worth nothing.

He had to keep his eyes on his people. He had to focus on his kingdom. Wishing he could love a woman, aching over a woman, was that same old weakness, and he simply couldn't allow it.

Yet he wanted to. So much it was a physical need that tore through him, leaving emotions he'd thought long dead in tatters.

"For now," he said. "While we travel...I will have you in my bed."

She nodded. "Yes."

He would endure days of not sleeping just for that privilege, for this little moment out of time where he would be Zafar as he was meant to be. So that he too could be unmade, here with her, and simply be the man he might have been.

A man whose past wasn't stained with blood. Whose future wasn't filled with endless, rigid responsibility.

Just a man who wanted a woman. He looked into Ana's clear blue eyes. Yes, just for these few days. It would be enough.

It would have to be.

He watched her walk around the tent from his position on the mattress. She'd never dressed after the first time they'd made love. She reminded him of Eve, walking around naked and unashamed. As though she was comfortable just as she was made. As though she had sprung from creation, formed...not just for him.

For herself.

She was so fierce. Glorious in her nakedness.

He was undone.

"Come here," he said.

She smiled at him and it hit him hard. There was such warmth in her expression, such desire. She looked at him and saw the man he might have been, and that was a gift he treasured. Something he wanted never to destroy. But if he stayed with her, he would.

She would see.

"Zafar?" She got down on her knees in front of him and bent to kiss him, her hair sliding forward, creating a glossy curtain around them. "You look too serious," she said, kissing him again.

He put his hand on her back, lowered it, cupping her backside. "It is nothing," he said, looking at her clear blue eyes, like the sun-washed Al Sabahan sky. Only there was caring there. Forgiveness. And he deserved none of it. She was too much beauty, too much strength.

"Let me help you forget."

He wrapped his arms around her and kissed her deeper, pulling her down so that he was on his back and she was over him. He wanted her, no matter what it meant for him. No matter if it meant all the honor and purpose he purported to have wasn't nearly as strong as the weakness of his body. No matter if it reached in and undid the years of exile.

Almost especially because it reached in and undid the years of exile.

He was parched, so thirsty for touch, for connection, for her, that there was no way he could deny it. A man who would drink poisoned water in the middle of the desert just for that moment of satisfaction.

Though Ana wasn't the poison. It was all in him.

He shut that thought out, turned his focus away from

the flames of hell, still licking at his ankles, as they had been for the past fifteen years, and focused on the heat of her lips, of her bare body against his.

He pushed all thoughts and recriminations away so he could listen to the sound of her palms sliding over his chest, her breathing increasingly labored as she became more aroused, the breathy sounds of pleasure that came from pale lush lips.

He kissed her neck and she moaned, low and long. "Ever so much more enticing than a one, two, three count," he said, remembering the day she'd tried to teach him to waltz. "Though I found that quite distracting, as well."

"Did you?" she asked, her voice choked.

"Yes." He pushed into a sitting position, her legs wrapped around his back, her breasts at just the right height for him to taste her. And he did. He traced the tightened, sugar-pink buds with his tongue, relishing her sweetness. Sucking her deep into his mouth. She arched against him, her hands in his hair, tugging, the slight pain the only thing keeping him anchored to earth.

He lifted his head and looked up at her face, flushed with desire, her eyes focused on him. "I liked you giving me instruction."

"Really?"

"Yes, I think you should do it now."

"What?"

"Count, *habibti.*"

She huffed out a laugh, then lifted a trembling hand to trace the line of his lips. "My pleasure, I suppose."

"Ours," he said. "Are you ready for me?"

"Always."

She drew up slightly, onto her knees, and he positioned himself at the slick entrance of her body, gritting his teeth as she lowered herself onto him, as he sank deep within her body. He could drown in this, in the pleasure, white-hot, so much so it was nearly painful.

She raised herself up, hands gripping his shoulders, fingernails digging into his skin. "One," she said, "two," back down, "three."

He held tightly to her, his hands on her hips, letting her lead, for the moment, holding her steady.

"One, two, three." She repeated the numbers with the motions, her voice a bit more strangled each time, her nails biting harder into his skin. "One, two… Ohhh."

He chuckled. "Do you think I'm qualified enough to lead this dance?" He kissed the top of her shoulder.

"You were right," she said, panting. "I need to be uncivilized. And right now, I don't need you to act polished. I just need you."

It was all the permission he needed. He growled and gripped her waist hard, reversing positions so she was on her back and he was over her. She arched, pressing her breasts to his chest. "Yes, Zafar. Please."

She didn't have to ask twice.

He put his hand beneath her, on her butt, lifting her up into his thrusts as he pushed them both toward pleasure. There was nothing quiet or civil about their joining. His skin burned where her nails met his flesh, his heart pounding so hard he thought it might bruise his body inside, leaving a dark stain over his chest.

She draped her legs over his calves, locking him to her, holding him. He increased the pace, and she went with him, matching his every thrust, his every groan of pleasure.

And when he felt himself being tugged downward, his orgasm gripping him and taking him down beneath the waves, he felt her go with him. And they clung together, riding out the storm in each other's arms.

The desert was still there, dry and harsh around them,

and they were insulated from it, refreshed, renewed. Lost in another world, another space and time, where there was nothing but this.

Nothing but Zafar. Nothing but Ana.

He held her afterward, his arms locked tight around her, breathing an impossibility. He was still lost to the world, to reality, floating underwater with Ana. He rested his head on her chest, between her breasts, listening to her heart-beat. So alive. So soft and warm and perfect.

If only this was all there was. If only he had been created this second, born from the sand. If only he didn't have all those years, all those sins, all that blood in his past.

But in this moment, it didn't matter. Nothing mattered but this.

Nothing mattered but Ana.

Zafar smelled sulfur. As he always did when hell found him on earth. Fire and gun smoke. And screaming. And pain. So much pain.

And his mother's face. Her eyes. So scared. Wounded.

Then they met his. And he wanted to scream that he was sorry. That it was his fault. He wanted to fall down on his knees and take the beatings. But his enemies seemed to have no interest in hurting him. Not physically.

They just wanted him to watch. Wanted him to see what his confessions to Fatin had enabled them, empow-ered them to do. How the foolish prince of Al Sabah had given power over to another nation.

His hands were chained, his legs chained, his mouth gagged. The confession pushed at his throat, made him feel like his chest would explode. He wanted to scream and he couldn't.

Instead, tears streamed down his face, the only release his enemies had allowed him.

As he watched his mother die. In pain. In fear. As his

father watched, part of the older man's torture. And then met the same fate.

Zafar was back there, his cheeks wet, waiting to be killed.

Praying he would be killed.

And then he woke up.

He was gasping for breath in the dark, a feral shout leaving his throat scraped raw, his skin slick with sweat, his face damp with tears.

He was poised, ready to fight, ready to kill. To destroy those who had hurt his family, who had killed them. And he realized he held his enemy in his hand, fingers curled tightly around his neck.

Zafar reached for his knife, which he always kept near his bed, and discovered it wasn't there. And he was naked, no weapon in the folds of his robes. Nothing to use against the people who had killed his parents.

Who had left him here to deal with the pain by himself.

But his thumb was pressed against his enemy's throat, and one push would end it all.

"I will kill you with my bare hands, then," he growled, looking down for the first time, trying to focus on his enemy's face. All he saw was a pale shadow, glistening eyes in the darkness.

Slowly everything cleared, and he realized where he was. Who it was in his tent.

Damn him to hell. He had fallen asleep. With Ana.

"Ana." He released his hold on her immediately and she fell back. He wanted to go to her, to comfort her, to touch her. But he had no right to touch her. Not after he'd put his hands on her like that.

He was still breathing hard, each breath a near sob, sweat coating his skin. He shivered as the heat in him died out, gave way to a chill that permeated his entire being. "Ana, I'm sorry. I'm sorry. I would not hurt you. I would not."

She stood, slowly, her whole frame trembling. And he looked away.

He didn't want to see her eyes. He didn't want to see her now that she'd truly seen him. Now that she'd seen everything ugly and destroyed inside of him.

Now that she'd nearly been cut on the jagged edges of his soul.

"I know," she said, her voice shaking.

He collected himself enough to find his bag, and pulled out a battery-powered lantern, lighting it so that he could see.

And then he wished he hadn't. There was a tear glittering on her cheek, sliding down to her chin. And she didn't wipe it away.

"Ana," he said, the pain wrenching his soul so deep he thought he would break. "This is why I don't sleep with anyone. This is why…"

"What do you see?" she asked.

He shook his head. "No…Ana…do not ask for that. Do not try and help me when I have…"

"How can you live with it inside of you?" She approached him and extended her hand, as though she meant to touch him.

He jerked back, unable to take the balm of her touch. Undeserving of it.

"I have to," he said. "It was my fault. It was my…it is my burden, one I earned."

"Tell me."

"No." He shook his head. "No. I have done enough damage to you." He raised the light and saw a slash of red on her neck. "Oh, Ana, I have done enough damage to you," he said again, his voice rough.

"Zafar, let me have this. Let me help you."

He shook his head, turning away and forking his fingers through his hair. "You know it already. I told Fatin where my parents would be that day. When they were moving to an alternate location for safety. Because she asked and I thought nothing of it. It was all very Samson and Delilah. If only I had been betraying myself alone. But it was them, too. We were all captured. Held in the throne room of the palace." He started shaking while he spoke of it, but now that he'd started, he couldn't stop, he had to finish. "We were bound. I was in chains. They were not just content to kill my parents. They had to torture them. My mother first, so my father and I could see. Then my father, for me to watch. To watch the strongest man I had ever known be reduced to nothing. A demonstration of power and evil I had never before fathomed."

He drew in a breath. "My hands were bound. My feet. My mouth gagged. I wanted to tell them it was my fault. I wanted to beg them to kill me. I could say nothing. I could only…I could only cry like an infant, desperate for his mother to hold him. Knowing it would never happen again. And that it was my own fault. You see, Ana, I thought I was a man, but I realized in that moment I was nothing more than a foolish child whose stupidity had torn away everything important in his life."

He swallowed. "And they didn't kill me. They left me and I prayed for death, lying on the floor of the throne room with my parents' bodies. I prayed for death." He closed his eyes. "I didn't receive it. My uncle found me in the morning. Our army defeated theirs in the end. But it was too late to save my parents."

He looked down at his hands. "And he asked me how it had happened, so I confessed. And he sent me away. I am under no illusions here. It suited my uncle to tell me those things. He was not the one who had led the rebellion that killed my parents, but he was just the sort of man to seize the chance to have power if there was an easy way to grasp it. He told me there were bound to be rumors and I would be better off if I wasn't in the city. That I had to leave the palace. That I would never make a king of Al Sabah. And I believed him. So I ran. Out into the desert until my lungs burned. Until I lay in the sand and waited to die there. But again, I was denied."

"The Bedouins found you."

"Yes, it was the beginning of my allegiance to them. Because I realized that while death was certainly the kinder option for me, it would do no good for anyone else. Especially when it became clear the manner of man my uncle was. Power hungry, with much more love for himself than for the people of my country. But I was a disgraced boy, and he was a man with an army, so my battles had to be waged another way."

Ana couldn't breathe. Zafar had woken her from her sleep with a guttural scream and then his hand had wrapped around her throat. It had been terrifying. Confusing. She'd frozen, searching his face in the dark. And she'd realized that he wasn't there, tears on his cheeks, his eyes unseeing.

She'd been afraid to move. Afraid to make a sound. She knew what sort of man he was, how strong, how able to end her with the press of his thumb.

Now, hearing his story, she understood what demons tormented him. What haunted him in his sleep.

She pushed her fear aside. Pushed everything aside and focused on him. On his pain. His need. She crossed to him and wrapped her arms around his neck. He stood stiff, but she didn't care. She stroked the back of his neck. Held him like he was a child, because it had been too long since someone had soothed him that way.

"Zafar, it's not your fault."

"It is," he said, his voice tortured.

"No. It's not. Zafar, I would tell you anything now because I trust you, and if you betrayed that trust and went and caused harm with it, whose fault would it be?"

"Ana…"

"No. Zafar, if a child breaks a doll and their mother leaves, whose fault is it?"

"Ana, please don't do this."

"Whose fault is it?"

"Never yours, Ana. Never yours."

"And yet it was yours?"

"I didn't break a doll. I broke the whole country. I broke my life. My parents' lives. I might as well have landed the killing blow myself."

"No." Her heart broke for him, his pain living in her, roaring in her chest. "Zafar, you can't think that. You have to…you have to stop blaming yourself or you'll never be free of it."

"You're wrong, Ana. I have to realize my own fault so that it never happens again…even knowing it… Have I not made the same mistake? I was too weak to resist you."

"This is different."

"Is it?"

"I love you," she said.

"She said she loved me."

Anger, passion, desperation, mixed together in her chest, combusted, exploded. "I'm *not her*," she screamed, so easy for her to do now. To make a sound. To demand she be heard. "I gave you my body, my soul. I gave you who I am, and there is no one else on earth who has that. I love you."

He shook his head. "No. You don't love me. You love who you think I could be, maybe, but you're wrong."

"About loving you?"

"About who I could be. I am broken, Ana, so deep it won't ever be fixed."

"Love goes deep, Zafar. Let it in. Let it heal you."

"That's not how it works."

"Enough water can quench even the most cracked earth. An oasis like this can be here, even in the middle of the desert. You don't know how much love I have to pour out. Don't tell me what it can and can't do."

"It is a drop of water in an entire desert, *habibti*," he said. "It will never be enough."

A tear slid down her cheek. "You think so? I thought you knew me, but now I doubt it."

"It is you who doesn't know me."

"And you think my feelings don't matter? You think me naive? Zafar, I just saw your worst." She took a step toward him, wrapped her hand around his and placed it at the base of her neck. "I know what manner of man you are, Sheikh Zafar Nejem, and I'm standing here offering you everything."

He lowered his hand, his fingers trembling. "Then you are naive and a fool."

"And you…do you feel anything for me?"

"I am the desert. I have nothing to give. I'll only take."

"Don't give me your mystic storytelling metaphors. Give me words. Tell me you don't love me," she said, her lips cold.

"I do not love you. I love nothing, *habibti,* not even myself. I just want to ensure my people get returned to them what I stole. That is all I am. I will never be a husband to you. Never a father for your children."

"But you said you would marry."

"Someone else. Not you."

She felt it like a blow. "Then what was this? This compromising everything so we could sleep together? So you could get off? That's just…stupid."

"Lust and heat. Both addle a man's brain."

"What if I'm pregnant? You weren't…careful last time."

He nodded once. "I will offer whatever support you need. But it would be better if I wasn't involved in any way beyond the monetary. Let us pray that there is no child."

He was gone, her Zafar, the man she had made love to for hours today. The man who had made her reach down deep and find her own strength. The warrior had returned—the fierce, frightening man he'd been the first moment she'd met him and he'd paid for her with a bag of silver.

Strange how he had purchased her with the last of his coins, and yet, in the end, she felt she'd paid the highest price.

"Take me back," she said.

"Now?"

She nodded. "Yes. I've had enough sleep."

"As have I," he said. "Dress. We will be ready to leave in a few moments."

Zafar left the tent, his clothes still outside by the water. And Ana stood there, her heart falling to pieces inside of her. It wasn't fair. She should have known better than to believe there was a future with him. Going into it, she hadn't even wanted one, and yet her feelings had grown.

And in that moment when he'd been his darkest, she'd realized the truth. That seeing him as he was, seeing all of the brokenness, she only loved him more. Knowing what he'd been through, knowing the man he was in spite of it, because of it, she wanted to be with him.

He was strong. He was brave. He was hurting.

But he didn't want her love. He didn't want her.

She dressed quickly, putting on new clothes, not the clothes she'd been wearing before they'd made love the first time. Her hands were shaking, her stomach sick.

She would leave Al Sabah. And she couldn't bring Zafar, the man, with her. But she would bring Al Sabah and Zafar with her. He was in her, his effect on her blended in with the marrow of her bones, strengthening her, reminding her of who she could be.

He couldn't ever take that from her. In spite of all the pain she was in now, at least he couldn't take her newfound strength, her resolve to find her own place in life, her own happiness.

She would leave here stronger for having known him. And with a broken heart for having lost him.

She was fatigued and windburned by the time they reached the border that stretched between Shakar and Al Sabah. They had ridden for hours without stopping, time melting into a continuous stretch that she could only measure in painful, tearing heartbeats.

"I will have you call your father now," he said. "And I will wait with you until he is here."

"But you…"

"I won't be seen.".

This man who thought he had no heart.

"Good. I don't want you to be injured." It was too late for her heart, but even so, she didn't want him to get hurt.

She dialed her father's number with shaking fingers.

When he answered, it was like a dam inside of her burst. "Dad," she said, her throat tightening, a flood of tears pouring from her eyes.

"Ana?" her father sounded desperate.

"Yes."

"We were searching," he said. "Please know that we were. But we didn't want the media in on it. We couldn't risk making your captors nervous. Where are you? Do they still have you?"

"No," she said, looking at Zafar, his eyes blank. "No. I'm free." The word held so many layers, so much meaning. And all because of the man standing before her.

"How?"

She knew she couldn't say. Knew she could never say. "I was ransomed by a stranger. I'm near the encampment where I was taken. Can you please come and get me?"

Zafar handed her a paper with the GPS coordinates on it, silent, watchful. Ana read them off for her father.

"I need to go," she said.

"Ana...wait."

She hung up. She knew Zafar wouldn't speak to her while she waited. But she wasn't going to spend her last moments with Zafar talking to someone else, no matter how much she missed her father.

She would miss Zafar so much more.

They were in a vast area, only an outcropping of jagged rocks there to provide shade. And it was almost like seeking shelter in a clay oven, the rocks absorbing the heat and radiating it outward.

Still, Zafar stood by them, watching, and she stood with him, a small space between them, both of them looking in the direction her father and Tariq would be coming from. They didn't speak; they didn't touch.

But she drank him in. She would have to fill herself now, because after this she wouldn't see him again. Her life an endless, vast desert without him.

"Only a minute now," he said, finally.

She turned to him. "Look at me."

He obeyed, and she let the image of his face burn into her. The hard planes and angles, his golden skin and dark eyes. Those eyes, which held so much pain, so much passion.

"I need to memorize you," she said.

"I have already done so," he said.

Her heart squeezed tight. "I wish you the best," she said. "I'll be back in America. If you're ever curious."

He closed his eyes for a moment, as though blocking out an onslaught of pain. "I will forget that information. I can't know. Then I might search for you. And it would be a disservice to you."

She heard the sound of helicopter rotors in the distance. "Go," she said, feeling panicked. They couldn't find him. They could never know.

He nodded once and went back to Sadiqi, covering his face and head again, and riding off toward another rock formation. And then she didn't see him anymore, as though he'd melted into the sand.

Ana saw the helicopter now, drawing closer. Her salvation. Her family.

And yet, for the first time she felt undeniably homesick. And when she thought of home, it wasn't the old mansion in Texas, it wasn't the boarding school in Connecticut where she'd spent much of her teenage years. It wasn't even the palace in Al Sabah.

It was in Zafar's arms.

And it hit her then that she would never be home again.

Ana dropped to her knees as the helicopter descended to earth, and wept.

Zafar rode until his lungs burned, until his eyes were blinded by sharp, stinging sand. He suspected the sand wasn't entirely responsible for the stinging in his eyes.

Leaving Ana was like leaving behind part of himself.

Parts of the heart he'd imagined he'd cut out. But no, it was there. It was beating. Beating for her. And it was why he had to leave.

How could he consign her to a life with him? A life with a man so filled with darkness? A man who might wrap his hands around her throat in the night, thinking her an imaginary enemy?

He couldn't do that to her. He couldn't love her right.

He did love her. In a broken, selfish way. He would bring her back to his palace and keep her for himself. Keep her in his bed. Watch her stomach grow round when she was pregnant with his child.

She could even be pregnant with his child now. But he thought of his hands, covered in innocent blood and the blood of the guilty, cradling a child, and he ached inside. How could he be a father? How could he ever be a man worthy of Ana?

He looked into the distance, into the sun.

He would be a man worthy of his people. And he would hope that someday she would read about him, about Al Sabah, and she would have something to be proud of him for.

If that was all he could ever have, then he would take it.

He didn't deserve for her to love him, but he would try to earn it. He would try to be a man worthy of Ana's love.

It was the very best he could have. Somehow it still left him feeling cold inside.

That night, he lay down without a tent, his eyes fixed on the inky black sky. His thoughts on Ana. His heart beating with love for her.

And when he slept, there were no nightmares.

CHAPTER THIRTEEN

ANA SAT ON the edge of the bed. The room was large, light and airy. A room fit for a princess. Kind of Tariq, since last week she'd told him, officially, that she wouldn't become his sheikha.

He'd insisted that she stay until she'd had a full recovery. Whatever that meant.

There would never be a full recovery. Not from this.

Heartbreak wasn't fatal. It was worse. It hurt all the time. And she had a feeling it wouldn't just heal. Not when she was so changed from her time with Zafar. Not when her strength had been unveiled by him.

She would be marrying Tariq in the next year if not for Zafar. And it would be the wrong decision. She would be making choices to please everyone else still. And now... now she couldn't. She knew her father wasn't happy about the dissolution of her engagement to Tariq, and how could he be? It was costing him millions in profits.

But he was staying here in Shakar with her. And he'd never expressed his disappointment to her. She just knew it was there. But he hadn't left. He hadn't disowned her. He'd even told her he loved her several times.

She looked out the window, at the gardens. At the beauty. She didn't regret that this wouldn't be her home. She felt nothing for Tariq now. Nothing except for a kind of…affection. Because she did know him, and she did like him. But she didn't love him.

That had been underlined by the fact that when she'd seen him, her thoughts had stayed firmly occupied with Zafar. That she'd never once wavered on her decision to break off the engagement. Not even when she was afraid of how her father would react.

A clear head, time and distance had also made her sure of two other things: She wasn't pregnant with Zafar's baby. And she wanted to be with him more than anything.

She let out a long slow breath and closed her eyes, picturing his face. So precious. So perfect. She missed him, and every second of missing him was a slow and painful hit on her heart. Each beat another punch against the bruise.

There was a knock on her door and she stood, taking a deep breath. "Yes?"

Tariq walked in, tall, broad and handsome as ever. And her heart did nothing. "Good afternoon, *habibti*."

"Please don't call me that," she said.

He frowned. "I know things aren't that way between us now. But I confess I keep hoping you might change your mind."

"Do you love me?"

"No." His answer was instant, void of venom or emotion.

"Then I won't."

"And I won't lie to change your mind, on that you have my word."

"Thank you." She looked away from Tariq, out the window and past the gardens this time, toward Al Sabah. "Tariq, you've been good to my family."

"There is no honor in forcing a woman to marry you," he said. "And no honor in treating you poorly for making the decision."

"You are a good man."

"It has been said, though I'm not certain I have reaped any particular reward for it."

"You could still make deals with my father."

He nodded slowly. "I intend to. It is wise, whether or not you're my wife."

"Have you spoken to him yet?" For a moment she was afraid her father already knew. That he was already aware of the fact that he would have no bad consequences for her breaking the engagement, and that was why he'd been so quick to forgive her for it.

"No," Tariq said. "I will, over dinner today."

She let out a breath. "I'm so pleased to hear it." And then she had a thought, one that might fix things. It might not fix them either, because in the end, Zafar was still the one who had to make the final decision. But she could take care of everything on her end.

"Tariq, our marriage was supposed to ensure loyalty and fair treatment. And I would like for us to strike a deal together, separate from the deal you're making with him."

"What would that be?"

"Swear to me that you will be loyal to my family. That we have your protection. Always."

He regarded her closely, his dark eyes unreadable. "I swear it."

"No matter what. If, of course, we don't mount an attack against Shakar."

He arched a brow. "If you do not mount an attack against Shakar?"

"Covering the bases."

He looked at the wall behind her. "Especially for the indignity you suffered, I shall swear it. On my life, your family, however large it becomes in the future, has my protection. You have my word, and I am a man of my word. But if you would like it in writing...you may have that, too."

"I would," she said, her heart lifting, tears stinging her eyes. "I would like that very much. And the use of a helicopter. For my indignity."

"For your indignity," he said slowly.

Her throat tightened, her hands shaking. "Appreciated."

Zafar woke every night, but not to visions of death and violence.

To the illusion of soft skin, soft sighs of pleasure. To the impression of Ana in his arms and in his bed.

But she was never there.

He closed his eyes against a wave of pain. It was a particularly bad one. Waves like that crashed over him a few times a day, in contrast to the low-level ache that hummed in the background constantly.

He moved to the window of the throne room, the damned mausoleum. The scene of the most horrendous moment of his life. But fifteen years on, and that pain was finally fading. Because of the emotions he'd let in.

There was no longer room for anguish, anger and pain to be the star of his heart. Not when he'd started loving Ana.

Except he'd sent her away. But what other choice did he have?

"Sheikh." One of his men strode into the throne room, his expression fierce. "There is someone here to see you."

"May I ask who?"

"Of course. It is the woman. The woman who came here with you the first day."

He shook his head. "No. It cannot be."

"But it is. I would not mistake her. Ever. I have never seen a woman so pale."

"It cannot be a hallucination, because you wouldn't hallucinate on my behalf, would you?" he asked, feeling stunned.

"Sheikh, do I send her away?"

"No. No, send her to me." Zafar's heart was pounding, and as his man left the room, he thought of every possible scenario that might bring her here. To warn him of war, to share her engagement. To throw herself into his arms.

Considering his treatment of her, the last was the least likely.

It was only a moment, one that felt like an eternity, and she walked into the throne room, blond hair in a bun, her curves showcased by a knee-length dress that was sophisticated and sexy as hell.

"Zafar," she said, her expression neutral. "I came to deliver something to you."

"What is it?"

"An agreement. From the Sheikh of Shakar."

"I see." He wondered if that meant her engagement to Tariq remained intact. For all that he imagined she would be better off with the other man, the thought made him see red. Made him feel like his world was falling down around him.

She held out a sheet of paper, folded in half. "Read it."

He took it from her and unfolded it. "This is...a pledge from the Sheikh of Shakar. To protect your family, as it is now and as it grows. Always. Why show this to me?"

"Because I think I found a solution to your problem. But you have to hear me out. I'm not offering you this to fix your problems. I'm offering it to fix mine. This isn't to make you love me."

"What do you mean, *habibti*?"

She smiled. "I like it when you call me that."

"Explain," he said, his heart pounding.

"Become my family. Marry me. You will not have to worry about war breaking out over it. This—" she pointed to the paper "—protects you. It protects me. It protects Al Sabah. But only if you marry me."

"Are you proposing to me, Ana?"

"Yes," she said, her voice choked. "Yes. And do you know why?"

"Why?" he asked, his voice rough.

"Because. More than a week away from you, and you're all I can think about. Because, in spite of everything you said to me, I still love you. Because you helped me find my strength. Because you are a horrible dancer. Because you don't respect the salad fork, and God knows there has been far too much respecting of salad forks in my life. You made me want more, Zafar. You make me want to do more, feel more, be more."

"Ana," he said. "I…I want so badly to accept, not just the treaty offer, but your hand. Your love. But I'm so scarred inside. Why would you want me? You are everything beautiful and life giving. You talk about what I've done for you, but do you have any idea of what you've done for me?"

"No," she whispered.

"I have felt, for so many years, that death would have been the sweeter option for me. That I should have died that day. That the gates of hell were open and ready to pull me in. But you closed them. *You* did. When I sleep at night…I see your face and not that day. For years I didn't sleep right, Ana, and it was worse when I came here. But today I stood in this room and I saw your face instead of the images of that day."

"What changed?" she asked. "Because that last night… it wasn't me you were dreaming about."

"I let myself love you. And when I let that in, I couldn't be filled with anger and hopelessness anymore. I could no longer wish for death with even the smallest part of myself. You filled too much of me. You filled this place with new memories. And you've made me want again. I've been so afraid of wanting, because I was so sure I was as weak as I had ever been and that if I wanted…I would crumble. I would destroy everything again. But I can't call loving you a weakness, because I have never felt stronger. My heart, my soul…I no longer feel I've left them in the desert. I feel like they're in me, where they belong."

"Zafar…if I ever had a doubt that you were the man for me, I don't now. Because we healed each other. You were the man I needed. It was your brokenness that helped me see my own, that helped me find my strength."

"And it was your strength that lifted me out of the pit."

"Then stop talking crazy about why we can't be together."

"You could have a better man than I am."

"I don't want a better man. I want you."

He laughed. "Thank you."

"You know what I mean. I want to stand by you and help you fulfill your purpose here. I want Al Sabah to be my purpose, too. Your home is my home. Because it's where you are."

"And my heart is yours," he said, his voice rough. "It is damaged. I foolishly gave it to someone once before and saw my whole world crash down. I removed it from myself so I would never make the mistake again. Left it neglected and dying. And you revived it. Revived me. If you would take it, knowing all of that, then I would be the most blessed man in all the world."

"I will," she said. "Gladly."

"Know this, Ana, my love, you will never have to be anyone but yourself with me. You will never have to quiet yourself. Whether we decide to be civilized for a ball or uncivilized in our bedroom, it will be fine, because I only want you. I don't want you to simply please me or make me comfortable. I don't want you to slot meekly into my life. I want you to challenge me, tell me when I'm wrong. Butt heads with me. I want you to be fire and strength. To be who you are."

She closed her eyes and tilted her head back, a smile curving her lips. "Those are the most wonderful words I've ever heard. And you are the first person to ever say them."

"I will never stop telling you," he said. "Every day I'll tell you how much I appreciate you."

"I love you," she said. "I love you. I love you. One. Two. Three."

"Perfect." He pulled her into his arms and kissed her, pouring all of his love into the kiss, all of his passion. "Oh, Ana," he said, kissing her brow, her cheek, the corner of her mouth. "Do you remember that day I took you from the kidnappers?"

"No," she said, smiling. "Forgot. Not a big deal. Of course I do."

He swung her up into his arms and pulled her against his chest, taking them down the corridor that led to his bedchamber.

"I told you," he said, pushing open the door. "I was your salvation."

"You did."

He crossed the room and laid her on the bed, pulling his shirt over his head and joining her. "I was wrong, Ana."

She cupped his cheek with her hand, blue eyes looking into his. "Were you?"

"Yes, my love." He bent and kissed her, a kiss full of promises he would keep for the rest of their lives. "You were mine."

* * * * *

THE TRUE KING
OF DAHAAR

TARA PAMMI

For my sister and my friend
You're an inspiration to me, always.

Tara Pammi can't remember a moment when she wasn't lost in a book – especially a romance – which was much more exciting than a mathematics textbook at school. Years later, Tara's wild imagination and love for the written word revealed what she really wanted to do. Now she pairs alpha males who think they know everything with strong women who knock that theory and them off their feet!

CHAPTER ONE

Dr. Nikhat Zakhari followed the uniformed guard through the carpeted corridor of the Dahaaran palace, assaulted from every side by bittersweet memories. Eight years ago she had known every inch of these corridors and halls, every wall and arch. This palace, the royal family, they had all been part of a dream she had weaved as a naive girl of twenty-two.

Before it had come crumbling down upon her and shattered her.

She stepped over the threshold into the office and the guard closed the door behind her. The formal pumps she had chosen instead of her usual Crocs sank into the lush carpet with a sigh.

She had been in this office one night when the Crown Prince had been the man she had loved, the two of them slipping in like thieves in the night.

All because she had voiced a juvenile wish to see it. Her long-sleeved thick silk jacket couldn't dispel the chill that settled on her skin at the memory.

Drawn to the huge portrait of the royal family behind the dark sandalwood desk, she gave in to nostalgia.

King Malik and Queen Fatima, Ayaan and Amira, each member of the royal family was smiling in the picture except Azeez. Because of what Nikhat had told him that day eight years ago.

A cavern of longing opened up inside of her. Even thousands of miles away, she had felt as if she had lost her own family when she heard of the attack. Her throat ached, her vision felt dizzy. She ran trembling fingers over Azeez's face in the photo.

She leaned her head against the wall. Seeing this familiar place without him was shaking the very foundations of the life she had resolutely built for herself.

And she couldn't—she wouldn't—give that much power to a memory. Couldn't let it undo everything she had accomplished.

"How have you been, Nikhat?"

She turned around and stared at the new Crown Prince, Ayaan bin Riyaaz Al-Sharif, the boy she had once tutored in chemistry. His copper-gold gaze shone with warmth. The cut of his features, so similar to Azeez's, knocked the breath out of her.

She had gone into shock the day she had heard of the terrorist attack. To see Ayaan again, so many years later filled her with a joy she couldn't contain. Nikhat reached him, and hugged him.

Something she wouldn't have dared do eight years earlier.

A soft chuckle shook his lean frame. Stepping back, Nikhat fought the urge to apologize for her impulsive gesture. Her composure was shaken by being back here but not torn. A woman, and one not connected to the royal family in any way, would never have hugged the Crown Prince. But she was not the average Dahaaran woman anymore, bound by its traditions and customs. "It's good to see you, Ayaan."

He nodded, his gaze studying her with unhidden thoroughness. "You, too, Nikhat."

He led her to the sitting area, where a silver tea service waited. Settling down opposite him, Nikhat shook her head when he inquired if she wanted something.

The Ayaan that she had known had always had a twinkle in his eyes, a core made of pure joy. The Crown Prince that looked at her now had the mantle of Dahaar weighing him down. There was grief in those eyes of his, a hardness that had found a permanent place in his features.

She had been back in the capital city of Dahaara hardly a day before she had been summoned to a private meeting by the Crown Prince. Not something she could have actually refused, even if she had wanted to. "How did you know I was back in Dahaara?" she said, getting straight to the point.

He shrugged and crossed his legs. Hesitation danced in his eyes before he said, "I have an offer for you."

Nikhat frowned. After eight years with no word from her father, she had been beyond thrilled to hear his voice. But now..."You ordered my father to call me home," she said, the unease she had felt the minute she had received his request solidifying. "You knew how eager I would be to see my family. That's a low blow, Your Highness."

Ayaan rubbed his brow, no hint of guilt in his steady gaze. "It's the price I have to pay for that title, Nikhat."

His words were simple, yet the weight of responsibility behind them struck Nikhat. Clamping down her anger, she remained seated. "Fine, you have me here now. I should warn you though. I'm not a genie to automatically grant your wish."

A sudden smile split his mouth, warmth spilling into his eyes. And the flash of another face, smiling like that, similar yet different, rose in front of her eyes.

Her chest felt incredibly tight and she forced herself to breathe through it. There were going to be reminders of

Azeez everywhere in Dahaar. And she refused to spiral into an emotional mess every time she came across one.

She had done that long enough when she had left eight years ago.

"I see that you have not changed at all. Which is good for me."

"No riddles, Ayaan," she said, forcing herself to address him as the young man she once knew.

"How would you like to spearhead a top-notch women's clinic here in Dahaara? You'll have complete authority on its administration. I'll even get the Ministry to sign off on a health-care-worker training program, specifically for women. It is something I have had in mind and you are without a doubt the best candidate for it."

Shock spiraling through her, Nikhat had no words.

All the longing she had held at bay for eight years, the loneliness that had churned through her, rose to the surface. It was what she had wanted when she had begged her father to let her study medicine, her one goal that had become her focus and anchor when everything else had fallen apart, the impossible dream that had pulled her back to Dahaar from a prestigious position in New York.

She had readied herself for an uphill battle against prejudices masquerading as traditions, and so much more. The sound of disbelief ringing through her must have escaped, because Ayaan clasped her hand.

"You can make a home here in Dahaara, Nikhat. Be near your family again," Ayaan continued.

Nikhat nodded, eternally grateful for his understanding. Ayaan had always been the kinder of the two brothers. Whereas Azeez…there had never been any middle ground with him.

She returned his clasp, clinging to the high of his announcement. "It's all I've ever wanted, Ayaan."

A flicker of unease entered his gaze. "There's something I require from you in exchange, however. A personal favor for the royal family."

Nikhat shook her head. "I owe my profession to your father. Without King Malik's aid and support, my father would've never let me finish high school, much less study medicine. I don't need to be manipulated or offered incentives if you need something from me. All you have to do is ask."

Ayaan nodded, but the wariness in his gaze didn't recede. "This position, this is something I want you to have. It's what my father wanted for you when he supported your education. But what I'm about to ask stretches the boundaries of gratitude."

Nikhat nodded, trying to keep the anxiety his words caused from her face.

He sucked in a deep breath. "Azeez is alive, Nikhat."

For a few seconds, the meaning of his words didn't sink in.

It felt as if the world around her had slowed down, waiting for the buzzing in her ears to pass. The tightness in her chest morphed into a fist in her throat as she saw the truth in his eyes. A stormlike shiver swept through Nikhat and she fought to hold herself together, to fight the urge to flee the palace and never look back.

How many times was she going to flee?

She had worked so hard to realize her dream, had waited all these years to see her family again and she couldn't let anyone stop her now. Not even the man she had once loved with every breath in her body.

Letting herself breathe through the panic in her head, she forced calm into her voice. "I haven't heard a word about this."

"Because no one other than a few trusted servants and

my parents know. Until I can be sure that revealing that he's alive doesn't have a negative effect on Dahaar, I have to contain it." His voice shook and Nikhat reached for his hand this time, even as she fought her own alarm.

How could he be alive after all these years? How was he now?

"I found him four months ago in the desert and I still have no idea how he survived or what he did these past six years. He refuses to see our parents, he barely tolerates my visits. The true prince of Dahaar is now my prisoner." Utter desolation spewed into his words. "I have managed to keep it a secret until now. It would crush the people of Dahaar to see him like this. They…"

"They worshipped him, I know." He'd been their golden prince, arrogant but charming, courageous, born to rule his country. And he had loved Dahaar with a passion that had colored everything he had done.

His love, his passion…they were like a desert storm, consuming you, changing you if you came out alive.

"I'd hoped that he would get better, that sooner or later, he would decide to rejoin the living." Powerlessness colored his gaze, his words raw and jittery. "But with each passing day, he…"

Azeez is alive.

The words rang round and round in her head. But with the dizzying of her emotions also came the control she had developed in order to flourish in her career. "Ayaan? What's wrong with him?" she demanded, forgetting propriety.

"He is little more than a breathing corpse. He refuses to talk, he refuses to see a doctor. He's refusing to live… Nikhat, and I can't lose him all over again."

A knot of fear unraveled in her stomach now. "What exactly is this favor that you want to ask me?"

"Spend some time with him."

No. The word rang through her. Shaking her head, she stepped away from Ayaan. "I'm an obstetrician, Ayaan. Not a psychiatrist. There's nothing I can do for him that all your specialists can't."

"He won't let anyone see him. You...you he won't refuse."

She felt brittle now, as if her calm was nothing but a facade, as if she would fracture under it. But she couldn't fall apart, she refused to let pain and powerlessness wreak havoc on her again. "You don't know what your brother will do if he sees me."

"Anything is better than what he is now."

"And what about the price I'll have to pay?" The question escaped her before she knew she had said it.

His head jerking up, he studied her. Nikhat looked away. The air between with them reverberated with questions he didn't ask and she didn't answer.

Ayaan reached her, his jaw tight with determination. There was no grief or comforting familiarity in his face now. He was the man who had come back to life against all odds, the man who fought his demons every day to do his duty by Dahaar.

"Would it be such a high price? All I'm asking for is a few months. I'm running out of options. I have to find something that will pull him from this spiral. Spend some time with him alone in the palace. Talk to him, try anything that might—"

"If word of this gets out, I'll be damned for the rest of my life in Dahaara," she said, only realizing after she spoke that she was even considering the proposition. "That clinic you are baiting me with will be nothing but a sand castle."

"The Crown Princess Zohra is pregnant. She needs someone who will stay in the palace, a dedicated ob-gyn.

And as to any time you spend with Azeez, no one will know you are with him. I give you my word, Nikhat. I will protect your reputation with everything I have. My coronation is in two months. At that time, whatever state he is in, you can walk away from him. No one will stop you."

Two months with a man who would once again plunge her into her darkest fear. Two months revisiting everything she couldn't have, couldn't be. *Ya Allah, no.* "You've no idea what you're asking me to do."

"I was hoping that you would accept my proposition, but I cannot give you a choice, Nikhat. Desperation never leaves you with one. As of this moment, you're either the Crown Prince's guest or prisoner. If I have to lock you with him, I'll…" His words reverberated with a pain she herself was very familiar with. "He's my brother. He was once your friend. We owe it to him."

Her friend? Hysterical laughter bubbled up inside her.

Azeez bin Rashid Al Sharif had never been *just* her friend. He had been her champion, he had been her prince, and he had been the man who had promised to make her every dream come true.

And he had kept each and every one of his promises.

Nikhat sprang to her feet and straightened her shoulders. She met Ayaan's gaze and nodded before she could refuse, before ghosts of the past crippled her courage, before her bitterest fear trampled her sense of duty.

She would do it because she owed it to King Malik for turning a middle-class girl's fantastic dream to be a doctor into reality; she would do it for a childhood friend who had been through hell and survived; but more than anything, she would do it for the man who had once loved her more than anything in the world.

It was not his fault that she wasn't the woman he had

thought her. "I will do it," she whispered, the true consequences of what she had accepted weighing her down.

Strong arms embraced her tightly. "I have to warn you, Nikhat. He's not the man you or I knew. I'm not even sure that man exists anymore."

There she was again, tall, beautiful, graceful.

Like a mirage in the desert, she appeared every day during this time to taunt him, to remind him of everything he was not.

The darkest time of the day when dawn was a mere hour away, when he found himself staring at the rise of another day with nothing but self-loathing to greet it with.

However drunk he got, it was the time the reality of everything he had become, everything he had done, pressed upon Azeez.

He had been the Crown Prince once. Now he was the Crown Prince's prisoner, a fitting punishment for the man responsible for his sister's death, his brother's suffering and so much more.

Just the passing thought was enough to feel the palace walls close around him.

A cold breeze flew in through the wide-open doors to his right. The cold nipped at his bare chest, slowly but silently insinuating itself into his muscles. He would feel the effect of it tomorrow morning. His right hip would be stiff enough to seize up.

But his imagination was stubborn tonight, the moment passed, and he saw her again.

Tonight, she wore a dark brown, long-sleeved kaftan made of simple cotton with leggings of the same color underneath. She had always been simple in real life, too, never allowing him to splurge on her, never allowing him anything he had wanted to do with her, for that matter.

Like kiss her, or touch her or possess her.

And yet, he had been her slave.

Her hair, a silky mass of dark brown, was tied back into a high ponytail in the no-nonsense way she had liked. Leaving her golden skin pulled tightly over her features.

A high forehead that had always bothered her—a symbol of her intelligence—almond-shaped copper-hued eyes, which were her best feature, her too-long nose—a bit on the strong side—and a wide pink-lipped mouth. If one studied those features objectively and separately, as he had done for innumerable hours, there was nothing outstanding about any of them.

And yet all together, she had the most beautiful face he had ever seen. It was full of character, full of laughter and full of love.

Or being a naive, arrogant young fool, so he had thought. Until his love for her had destroyed him, shattered him to pathetic pieces.

Leaning over the side of the lounger he was sitting on, Azeez extended his right hand. The movement pressed his hip into the chair and a sharp lance of pain shot up through it. Reaching the bottle of scotch, he took a quick sip.

The fiery liquid burned his throat and chest, making his vision another notch blurrier.

But the image in front of his eyes didn't waver. In fact, it became much more focused, as if it had been amplified and brought much closer for his very pleasure.

Because now he could see her long neck, the neck he had caressed with his fingers so long ago. The cheap, well-worn cotton draped loosely over her breasts, losing the fight to cover up their lushness. The fabric dipped neatly at the curve of her hip.

Wiping the back of his mouth with his hand, he grabbed the bottle with his other hand and stood up abruptly.

White-hot pain exploded in his right side, radiating from his hip, traveling up and down. He had been sitting for way too long today and had barely exercised since his brother had locked him up here in the palace.

Gritting his teeth, he breathed through the throbbing pain. He leaned against the pillar and looked up.

The sight that met his eyes stole his breath. The intense throbbing in his hip was nothing compared to the dark chasm opening up in his gut.

Because, now the mirage was torturing him.

The woman had tears in those beautiful eyes. Her lips whispered his name. Again and again, as though she couldn't help it, as though her very breath depended on saying his name.

In the mirage, the woman he had once loved more than anything else in life, the woman who had eventually destroyed him, was standing within touching distance. And for a man who had almost died happily, only to discover that he was alive, and a cripple at that, it was still the cruelest punishment to see her standing there, teasing him, tormenting him.

With a cry that never left his throat, he threw the bottle at the mirage, needing it to dissolve, needing the torturous cycle of self-loathing to abate.

Except, unlike all the other times he had done it, the woman flinched. Even as the bottle missed her, shattering as it hit the floor with a sound that fractured the silence.

Her soft gasp hit him hard in the gut, slicing through the drunken haze in his head. Shock waves pulsing through him, he moved as fast as his damaged hip would allow.

His fingers trembled as he extended his hand and touched her cheek. Her skin was as silky soft as he remembered. Bile filled his mouth and he had to suck in a harsh breath to keep it at bay. "Nikhat?"

Fear and self-loathing tangled inside him, his heart slamming hard against his rib cage.

The sheen of liquid in her beautiful dark brown eyes was real. The tremble in those rose-hued lips was real.

Azeez cursed, every muscle in his body freezing into ice. And before he could blink again, she was touching him, devouring him with her steady copper gaze.

She caught his roughened palm between hers, sending a jolt of sensation rioting through his body. It was as though a haze was lifted from his every sense, as though every nerve ending in him had been electrocuted into alertness. "Hello, Azeez."

He pushed her away from him and jerked back. Leaning against the pillar, he caught his breath, kept his eyes closed, waiting for the dancing spots in front of him to abate. He heard her soft exhale, heard the step she took toward him.

Suddenly, utter fury washed through him, ferociously hot in contrast to the cold that had frozen his very blood just a few minutes ago. "Who dared to let you in here? I might be a cripple but I'm still Prince Azeez bin Rashid Al Sharif of Dahaar. Get out before I throw you out myself."

Nikhat flinched, the walls she had built around herself denting at his words. But she couldn't let the bitterness of them seep in and become a part of her. This was not about her. "I have every right to be here, not that I think you're lucid enough to understand that."

He didn't snarl back at her as she expected.

He just stood there, staring at her, and she stared back, eight years of hunger ripping through all her stupid defenses.

Jet-black eyes set deep in his face, and even more now with the dark shadows beneath, gazed at her, a maelstrom of emotions blazing within. His aristocratic nose had a bump to it that hadn't been there before. It looked as if it had been broken and had never healed right.

And then came the most sensuous, cruelest mouth she had ever seen. Even before the terrorist attack, even before she had left him without looking back, he had had a fierce, dark smile that stole into her very skin and lodged there.

Being at the receiving end of that smile had been like being in the desert at night. When the Prince of Dahaar had looked at you, he demanded every inch of your focus and you gave it to him, willingly.

Right now, the same mouth was flattened into a rigid line.

The white, long-sleeved shirt he wore was open half-way through, showing his thin frame. His long hair curled over his collar.

"Leave, Nikhat. Now," he said, drawing her attention back to him. His gaze didn't linger on her face. He didn't meet her eyes, either. "Or I won't be responsible for what I do next."

"Apologize to me. That bottle could have done serious damage," she said, giving up the fight against herself.

The moment she had stepped out of her suite into the dimly lighted corridor, unable to sleep a wink, and wandered through this wing of the palace, wondering if he was nearby, exposing herself to the guard outside, she had given up any sense she'd ever had.

Only, she had thought she would take a quick look and slink away in the dark of the night. Self-delusion had never been her weakness and she couldn't let it take root now.

"No," Azeez said without compunction. "Didn't my brother warn you? You took the risk of visiting a savage animal in the middle of the night."

"I'm not afraid of you, Azeez. I never will be."

She took another step, bracing herself for the changes

in him. He had lost weight and it showed in his face. The sharp bridge of his nose, and those hollowed-out cheekbones, they stood out, giving him a gaunt, hard look.

"Ayaan told me about you last night," she said, opting for truth. One gut-wrenching lie was enough for this lifetime. "I couldn't wait. I...couldn't wait till morning."

He fisted his hands at his sides, his fury stamped into his features. "And?" he said in a low growl that gave her instant goose bumps. He clasped her cheek with his fingers, moving fast for a man in obvious pain. His grip was infuriatingly gentle yet she knew he was holding back a storm of fury.

His gaze collided with hers and what she saw there twisted her stomach; it was the one thing that did scare her. His eyes were empty, as though the spark that had been him, the very force of life that he had been, had died out.

"Have you seen enough, *latifa?* Is your curiosity satisfied?"

She clutched his wrists with her fingers, refusing to let him push her away.

And it wasn't for him. It was for her.

She hadn't cried when she had learned the news of the terrorist attack and of his death. Her heart had solidified into hard rock long before then. And she wouldn't cry now. But she allowed herself to touch him. She needed to know he was standing there. She touched his face, his shoulders, his chest, ignoring his sucked-in breath. "I'm so sorry. About Amira, about Ayaan, about you."

With a gentle grip, he pushed her back. There was nothing in his gaze when he looked at her. Not fury, not contempt, not even resentment. His initial shock had faded fast and he looked as if nothing she said would ever touch him. "Are you, truly?" he whispered.

"Yes."

"Why, Nikhat?"

She wasn't responsible for the terrorist attack, she knew that. And yet, nothing she had said to herself had prepared her for the tumult of seeing him like this.

"You're not responsible for what I've become. But if you want, you can do me a favor."

The force of his request didn't scare her. If she could do something to help him, she would. Ayaan had been right. She owed it to Azeez. "Anything, Azeez."

"Leave Dahaar before the sun is up. Leave and never come back. If you have ever felt anything true for me, Nikhat, do not show me your face ever again."

Nikhat stood rooted to the spot as he walked away from her. It seemed she was always going to disappoint him.

She couldn't leave now, just as she hadn't been able to stay when he had asked her eight years ago.

CHAPTER TWO

AYAAN PUT HIS coffee cup down on the breakfast table when he heard the sound that hammered at him with relentless guilt. The sound of his brother's approach.

Catching his wife's gaze, he saw the same shock coursing through him reflected in her eyes.

In the four months since he had practically dragged his brother to the palace, Azeez hadn't stepped foot into the breakfast hall once. Despite Ayaan's innumerable pleas. And today...

Ayaan signaled for the waiting staff to leave just as the sound of Azeez's harsh breathing neared the vast table. He pushed his chair back and looked up. Suddenly, the morning seemed brighter. "Would you like some cof—"

He never saw the punch coming. Shooting pain danced up and down his jaw as it landed, his vision blanking out for a few seconds.

Her loud, abrasive curse word ringing around them, his wife reached him instantly. Ayaan rubbed his jaw and looked up just in time to see Zohra march around his chair and push his brother in the chest.

Azeez's mouth was curved into a fiendish smile, and Ayaan was about to interfere, when Azeez stepped back from Zohra. He mocked a curtsy, his mouth curled into a sneer. "Good morning, Your Highness, you look...lovely."

"You are acting like an uncivilized thug," Zohra said, her gaze furious.

"*I am* an uncivilized thug, Princess Zohra," his brother replied with a hollow laugh. "And it is your husband who is keeping me here."

Flexing his jaw, Ayaan turned to his brother and froze.

Ferocious anger blazed out of that jet-black gaze he knew so well. The same gaze that had been filled with emptiness, indifference, for four months. The constant, hard knot in his gut relented just a little. "What was that for?"

"You are the future king of Dahaar, Ayaan, not of me. Keep your arrogant head out of my affairs."

Settling back down into his chair, Ayaan took a sip of his coffee. "I have no idea what you refer to, Azeez."

"I want her out of here."

The vehemence in his brother's words doubled his doubts. "Why are you so concerned about Nikhat's presence?"

Leaning his hip on the solid wood, Azeez bent. "I think all this power is going to your head. Don't manipulate me, little brother. Or I will—"

"What, Azeez?" Ayaan refused to back down. His cup clanged on the saucer in the ensuing silence, hot liquid spilling onto his fingers.

"You'll shoot yourself? I fell for that until now, but not anymore. If you were going to kill yourself, you had numerous chances to do it over the past six years. You would have been killed by that bullet. And yet here you are, stubborn as ever and intent on destroying yourself the hard way." Silence snarled between them. "Nikhat is not going anywhere. Not for at least six more months."

Emotion flashed in his brother's gaze but Ayaan had no idea which one.

"If your plan is to bring back memories that will suddenly fill me with a love for life, how about some good ones, Ayaan? Why don't you invite one of the numerous women I slept with six years ago to the palace?" He slanted a wicked glance at Zohra before looking at Ayaan again. "There used to be a particularly sexy stripper in that night-club in Monaco who could do the wildest things with her tongue. If you want to see me rejoin the living, send the starchy doctor away, build a pole in my wing and have that stripper on a…"

His words tapering off, his brother looked as if he was the one dealt a punch.

Nikhat stood at the entrance to the hall. Against the colorful, blood-red rug on the wall behind her, she looked deathly pale. Their gazes locked on each other, Azeez and Nikhat stood unmoving, as if they were bound to each other.

Tension coiled tighter and tighter in the air around them.

His brother recovered first. And watching him closely, seeing a dark light come to life in his eyes, Ayaan realized that he'd made a terrible mistake.

"I'm regaling my brother and his wife with stories about Monaco. Was it the year right after you left?"

Beneath the humor, something else reverberated in Azeez's words, filling the vast hall with it.

"Does it matter *when* it was that you went around seducing the entire female population in Monaco, shaming Dahaar and your father with your wild exploits?" Nikhat delivered with equally lethal smoothness, even as her skin failed to recover its color.

Walking around Ayaan to Zohra's side, Nikhat whispered something to her. And walked out of the hall without another glance at his brother.

"Enough games, Ayaan. Why is she here?" Azeez roared the moment she left.

"Zohra is pregnant and is having complications. Nikhat is one of the best obstetricians in the country today. I need her to take care of my wife."

Azeez turned toward Zohra, his gaze assessing. "Congratulations to both of you. If she has to be here, keep her out of my way. Tell her she's forbidden from seeing me."

"I won't tell her any such thing. Nikhat is practically a member of this family. And she's doing me a favor. So unless you want to be my personal prisoner for the rest of your life, you better behave yourself."

"You've become a damn bastard, brother."

Ayaan laughed, the first in a long time he had truly done that. "I had to become one for Dahaar, Azeez. See, I wasn't born one like you are. It's the reason why you were so good at being the Crown Prince too. The minute you want it back, the crown's yours."

"That was a lifetime ago." Tight lines fanning around his mouth, Azeez stepped back. As if Ayaan had asked him to jump into the fiery pit of hell. "It's all yours now."

Azeez left the room, leaving a dark silence in his wake.

Once, his brother would have given his life to Dahaar. Once, a fire had shone in his eyes at the mere mention of it.

"Something's changed in him," Zohra said, a hint of warning in her voice. "And…Nikhat looked like she would break apart with one word from him."

Reaching for her outstretched hand on the table, Ayaan nodded. In four months of banging his head against the intractable wall that his brother had become, this was the first time there was a faint crack. He felt tremulous hope and excruciating guilt.

"Did you know if they were more than friends?"

Ayaan shook his head. He hadn't known before, but something his servant Khaleef had said in a throwaway comment had stuck with him. So he had taken a gamble and commanded Nikhat's father to summon her.

Being right had never left such an ugly taste in his mouth.

After a couple of wrong turns, Nikhat reached the courtyard behind the wing she had been shown to three days ago. High walls surrounded the courtyard, shielding it from any curious gazes.

It was only ten in the morning but the sun was already bright and hot. Wiping the beads of sweat on her forehead, she sat down on the bench near a magnificent fountain. The rhythmic swish of the water, the scent of roses coating the air…it was a feast for the senses, but she couldn't get her stretched nerves to relax.

For three days, she had been busy with Princess Zohra and yet going out of her mind, intensely curious to see Azeez again.

She had dreamed of him so many times when she had thought him dead, had imagined all the things she would say if she had one more chance to see him, to touch him, to hold him…

Reality, however, didn't afford her the same recklessness.

Closing her eyes, she leaned back and felt the sun caress her face. She couldn't let him unsettle her any more than she could weave silly dreams again just because he was back from the dead.

She would be of no use to Ayaan either way.

Taking her Crocs off, she dipped her toes in the water. It was forbidden to do so, but the cold water tickled her feet. Drops splashed onto her leggings. Her jet lag was gone, but she still wasn't used to the quiet that surrounded her after the mad rush back in the hospital in New York. Nor was she happy with the way things were run here, even though she had known to expect it.

Even with Ayaan's command that she was solely in charge of Zohra's care, her instructions had been met with resistance from the numerous medical advisers and staff that surrounded the Princess. Which only made her realize how much she would need the royal family's backing to succeed in Dahaar and even more resolute to make a difference.

It couldn't have been more than two minutes when her skin prickled in alarm. The hairs on the back of her neck stood up. The relentless heat of the day receded for a minute. A shadow. Her heart stuttering in her chest, she realized who stood over here, stealing the warmth from around her.

Keeping her eyes closed, she took a moment to pull herself together. She opened her eyes slowly and sat up straighter on the bench.

His gait uneven, Azeez walked to the bench on her left. His face tightened, his right hand flexing into a fist as he slowly slid into the seat.

He hadn't shaved and the beard coming in made him look even more dangerous. His eyes still had that haggard, bruised look, the planes of his cheekbones prominent.

The pristine white shirt hung loose on his frame while his cotton trousers hung low and loose on his hips. They made him look darker than usual, but not enough to hide the tiredness from his face.

His will was a force of nature and offense was her best course if she wanted to get through. She made no effort to curb the stinging comment that rose to her lips. "That hip will be permanently useless if you continue like this. Even in the state you're in, I believe…"

Those thickly lashed eyes trapped hers, a puzzle in it. She couldn't have looked away for anything in the world.

Everything else she could control, curb, but not the greediness with which she wanted to look at him. "I believe you still have enough sense to know that."

"*Ya Allah*, stop looking at me like that." His low growl rumbled over the silent courtyard.

"How am I looking at you?" she said, tucking her feet beneath her legs.

He leaned his head back, giving her a perfect view of the strong column of his neck. Even dressed in the most casual clothes, he epitomized supreme male arrogance and confidence that had always messed with her usually practical personality. And continued to do so, if she was ready to admit the truth. "Like you cannot stop, like you want to eat me up alive."

The heat rising through her cheeks had nothing to do with the sun. "That's not true."

He leaned forward, his gaze thoughtful. "Yes, it is. There's a temerity in your gaze now. You always knew your own mind, but now, it's like your body has caught up."

She shrugged, holding herself tight and still under his scrutiny. The look he cast in her direction was thorough. "I'm not a shy twenty-two-year-old anymore."

"I can see that." A lick of something came alive in his gaze. "I can almost see you staring down your patients into good health."

She laughed, half to hide the little tremble that went through her. "I do have a reputation as the scary doctor. If only things could be fixed so simply. And you're right. I can't stop looking at you. I can't stop wondering what in Allah's name you think you're doing to yourself."

His jaw tightened, his nostrils flared.

For anyone looking from afar, they would seem like two old friends chatting up each other. And yet the courtyard felt like a minefield. She had to take every step carefully with him. And not because she was scared of him, but of herself.

Her stupid midnight jaunt had already proved her brain wasn't functioning at its normal, rational level.

He ran his palm over his jaw, his gaze never moving from her. "Is it true?"

"Is what true?"

"The palace has been ringing with it. And apparently, it is the first time in three days that you have a minute to yourself."

"So you're not completely oblivious to the world around you? That's always a good sign."

"Don't show off your credentials with me, Nikhat. Is Princess Zohra having complications with the pregnancy?"

There was no nuance to his words. She had no idea if he was worried for the Princess, no way to gauge how deep the emptiness in him was. And more than anything, the very thought she might not be of any use to him scared her. "Yes."

"How serious is it?"

"I have ordered some more tests for her. Her blood pressure is at dangerous levels. She needs rest and she needs to take it easy. Stress is adding to her complications. From what I've seen in the last two days, you're at the root of it."

"Just because I punched her husband?"

"You punched Ayaan? Why?"

Because Ayaan had brought her here, the answer came to her in the taut silence.

Do you hate me so much?

The pathetic, self-indulgent question lingered on her lips. But there was no point in asking it. There was no point in giving the past even a passing thought.

"You have really changed," she said, hoping to find a hole in that indifference he wore like armor, hoping to land a blow. "The Azeez I knew would have never lifted his hand against his brother, would have never thrown a bottle at an innocent, harmless woman."

He chuckled, and the unexpected sound of it shocked her. Sharp grooves appeared in his cheeks. "You are neither innocent nor harmless. I was drunk. It was your own fault for walking into a man's wing in the middle of the night where you're forbidden."

"And you throw bottles at imaginary figures when you are drunk?"

"Only at you."

The barb cut through her, knocking her air from her lungs. She drew in a jagged breath, swiping her gaze away from him. This was the future she had wanted to avoid eight years ago—his resentment, his bitterness. Because Azeez had never hidden from what he felt, neither had he let her. And yet, after everything she had done, she was right where she didn't want to be—the cause of that resentment.

She looked up and found him studying her with a curious intensity. "I'm serious, Azeez. Princess Zohra needs to rest and relax. Unless you do something that allays her concerns for Ayaan, she's only going to get worse.

"She…loves Ayaan very much. And the fact that he's worried about you is directly transferring to her."

"She's the future of Dahaar. I don't want anything to happen to her."

Did he realize he had betrayed himself? From everything Ayaan had said, Azeez had claimed he didn't care about anything. "Is it only the future of Dahaar that concerns you? Not what you are doing to Ayaan, to your parents? To yourself?"

He shot to his feet so quickly that Nikhat jerked her head up. Just in to time to see the flash of pain in his face. "This is where this session ends. You're not my friend. You're definitely not my doctor.

"You're a servant to the royal family. Do your job. Look after Princess Zohra. Believe me, there's nothing you can do to help me. Except disappear, maybe."

"I'm not leaving, Azeez. Not until I accomplish my job. And as to Ayaan's belief in me, I've never let down the royal family's trust in me until now and I never will."

"Never, Nikhat?"

Her breath trapped in her throat, Nikhat hugged herself. "Never."

Nodding, he came to a stop at the wide arched entrance, the sun shining behind him casting shadows on his features. She had no idea what he saw in the mirror when he looked at himself, what tormented him from the past. But the fact that he was here, concerned for the Princess, gave her hope like nothing else could.

"I never thought of you as naive."

Uncoiling her legs from under her, she took a moment to compose herself. The last thing she wanted was him talking about her. "I used to be. But not anymore. I'm not the girl you once knew, Azeez."

"Why obstetrics of all the specializations? Why not cardiology?"

She stayed painfully still, amazed at how easily, even after all these years, he could drill down to the heart of the matter. How well he knew her.

"Your mother's been dead for eighteen years, Nikhat. You cannot save her or the child she died giving birth to."

It took everything in her for Nikhat to stay standing.

"Do I need to have your case history checked?"

"What do you mean?"

"Princess Zohra is valuable to Ayaan and Dahaar." This time, Dahaar was the afterthought to his brother. "Will you be able to keep your objectivity when the time comes? Or are you fighting a never-ending battle with yourself and trying to save your mother again and again?"

She flinched, his words finding their mark. She could feel the blood leaving her face, but in this, she would not keep quiet. In this, she would not let him find fault.

"Hate me all you want, Azeez, but don't you dare insult my ability as a doctor or my reasons for it. I chose obstetrics because, with all the progress your family has made for Dahaar, there are so many things in women's health that are still backward, so many antiquated notions that dictate a woman's life.

"My profession has nothing to do with the past. It's my life, my future."

"As long as you are remember that, Dr. Zakhari. Because you paid a high price for that, didn't you?"

Nikhat sank back to the seat, her own lie coming back to haunt her.

He still thought she had left him because her love for her dream had been more than her love for him. And crushed under the weight of the truth, she had let him believe the lie.

She *had* paid a high price. She had paid with her heart, with her love. She had paid for something she couldn't change. And she had meticulously built her life from all the broken pieces to let even the Prince of Dahaar shatter it.

CHAPTER THREE

AZEEZ LEANED AGAINST the wall outside Ayaan's office and sucked in a harsh breath. Sweat trickled down his shoulder blades after the long walk from his wing to this side of the palace. Closing his eyes, he rubbed his palm over the right hip, willing the shooting pain to relent.

But of course it didn't. He'd spent the past four months drinking himself into oblivion, uncaring of if he ate or moved. His negligence was coming back to him in the form of excruciating pain. His hip was sore from months of inactivity, from lack of exercise. Breathing in and out through the dots dancing in front of him, he slowly sank to the floor.

His brother had been right. There had been more than one occasion when he had wished himself dead. But he hadn't actually indulged the thought of killing himself.

His list of sins was already long enough without committing one against God, too. So he had carried on, uncaring of anything, uncaring of what a wasteland his life had become.

But his self-loathing, his lack of interest in his life, his lack of respect for his own body—as long as it had been only him who faced the consequences, he had been fine with it. But now…

Now it was beginning to fester into his brother and his wife.

After everything he had gone through, after recovering from the blood loss because of the bullet wound he had taken during the terrorist attack, waking up amidst strangers with a useless leg, realizing what he had become, after the excruciating pain of keeping himself away from his family, he could not allow this.

Whatever rot was in him couldn't be allowed to spread, couldn't be allowed to contaminate the good that was finally happening in his family. He couldn't be allowed to take more from them, from Dahaar.

And if the price was that he give up the last ounce of his self-respect, if the price was that he stop hiding and face his demons, face the reality of everything he had ruined with his reckless actions, then so be it. He couldn't have escaped the consequences of his actions forever anyway.

"Azeez?" Ayaan's question reached his ears, unspoken, guarded, with a wealth of pain in it.

Azeez licked his lips and cleared his throat. The words stuck to his tongue. He forced himself to speak them. "Help me up, Ayaan."

For a few seconds, his brother didn't move. His shock pinged against the corridor walls in the deafening silence. Gritting his teeth, Azeez strove to keep his bitterness out of his words. "Do you want to exact revenge for that punch I threw three days ago?" he mocked. "Will you help me if I beg, Your Highness?"

A curse flying from his mouth, Ayaan spurred into action. Shaking his head, he tucked his hands under Azeez's shoulders. "On three."

Azeez nodded, and took a deep breath. He gripped Ayaan's wrists and pulled himself up.

Ayaan leaned against the opposite wall and folded his arms. "Is it always like this?" There was anger in his brother's words and beneath it, a sliver of pain.

Curbing the stinging response that rose to his lips, Azeez shook his head. "It's my own fault. The less mobile I'm, the worse the hip gets."

"Why didn't you just summon me then?"

"I never did that. You are the one forever coming into my suite for one of your bonding sessions."

Frowning, Ayaan opened the door behind him and held it for Azeez. Azeez stepped inside and froze.

Smells and sensations, echoes of laughter and joy, they assaulted him from all sides, poking holes in his deceptively thin armor.

A chill broke out over his skin as his gaze fell on the majestic desk at the far corner. A wooden, handmade box that had been in the Al Sharif dynasty for more than two centuries. The gold-embossed fountain pen that had passed on through generations, from father to son, from king to king. And the sword on display in a glass case to the right.

The sword he had been presented in the ceremony when his father had announced him the Crown Prince and future King, the sword that had represented everything he had been. Now, it was his brother's, and Azeez didn't doubt for a minute that it was where it belonged.

A portrait of their family hung behind the leather chair.

The smiling face of his sister, Amira, punched him in the gut. He had killed her as simply as if he had done it with both his hands.

Enough.

He hadn't come here to revisit his mistakes. He'd come to stop more from happening.

Shying his gaze away from the portrait, he walked toward the sitting area on the right and slid into a chaise longue. Ayaan followed him and took the opposite seat.

"Nikhat says it's because of me," he said without preamble. He needed to say his piece and get out. He needed to be out of this room, needed to be back in the cavern of self-loathing that his suite had become. Before the very breath was stifled out of him by broken expectations, by excruciating guilt.

Ayaan frowned. "What is because of you?"

"Zohra's complications with the pregnancy."

His mouth tight, a mask fell over his brother's usually expressive face. Cursing himself for how self-absorbed he had been, Azeez studied him, noticing for the first time the stress on Ayaan's face.

Dark blue shadows hung under his brother's eyes. His skin was drawn tight over his gaunt features.

"I wouldn't put it quite like that," Ayaan spoke finally, with a sigh. "For reasons the doctors say they can't speculate over, it's been a high-risk pregnancy from the beginning."

"Then what did Nikhat mean by saying it was because of me? I know she didn't say that to manipulate me."

"I thought you didn't want to see her or hear a word from her mouth. Now you trust her opinion?"

"Nikhat wanted to be a doctor since she was ten years old. If there's one thing that she would never betray, it's her profession. So if she says I'm the reason for Zohra's stress, then I am. What I don't understand is why. I might be a cripple but I have a working mind."

"Do you? Because, so far, I haven't seen evidence of it."

Azeez continued as though his usually even-tempered brother hadn't just snarled at him. "I have watched your wife growl at me like a lioness, as if she needs to shield you from me. I don't think she would crumble because her husband is dealing with his difficult brother. So what is it, Ayaan?"

A flash of utter desolation came alive in his brother's gaze. Azeez stared, shock waves shivering through him.

Ever since he had learned that Ayaan had returned after six years, Azeez had known that his brother would do his duty, no matter what. And Ayaan *had* risen to every challenge.

Only now did Azeez realize what he had overlooked. His brother had fought his own demons for so long and Azeez had not given a passing thought to it until this moment.

"She's worried about what this—" he moved his hand between Azeez and him "—is doing to me."

A chilly finger raked its nail over Azeez's spine. "What do you mean?"

"I have nightmares, vicious ones. I have had them every night ever since I… since I became lucid. Sometimes, they are minimal. Sometimes, I get violent. And…"

Azeez held his head in his hands, feeling his breath leave him. Guilt infused his blood, turning him cold from inside out. Looking up, he forced himself to speak the words. "They have become worse since you found me."

Ayaan shrugged.

There was no shame or hesitation in his brother's gaze. Only resigned acceptance. And in that minute, Azeez realized what he had been too blind to see until now.

His brother had lived through his own version of hell and had come out of it alive and honorable. And Dahaar was blessed to have him.

Unless he, Azeez, ruined it all again.

"I keep reliving that night and every time I see all that blood in the stable, your blood, I wake up screaming. And Zohra is right there with me, suffering through them, right by me."

"Why didn't you tell me?"

"When would I have told you? In between the punches you threw at Khaleef and me? When you refused point-blank to see Mother even though you could hear her heart-breaking cries on the other side of the door and informed

Father to assume that his firstborn is still dead? Or in the few hours that you have been sober in the last four months?"

Azeez shifted in the seat restlessly. He wanted to run away from here. "Be rid of me," he growled, his power-lessness eating through his insides. "All this will be solved in a minute."

Ayaan rocked forward onto his knees, a fierce scowl on his face. "You think I can just wish away your existence as you have been doing?"

"Then send your wife away. Protect her."

"I can't," Ayaan said, a sarcastic chuckle accompany-ing his words. "I am to be crowned king in two months, but I can't dictate my wife's behavior. I have ordered her to sleep in a separate wing, to go back to Siyaad for a few days. But, like you cleverly noticed, my wife has a will of her own. She won't leave my side."

From the moment he had met her steady gaze, Azeez had realized how much Princess Zohra loved his brother. Something he had wanted once, something he had thought he had once.

He swallowed back the surge of envy that gripped him. He would not envy the little happiness that Ayaan had. This had to stop today, now. "Fine. What is it you want from me?"

"What?"

"Tell me what you want me to do. Tell me what I can do to make this…make you better and take this stress off Zohra."

"Why now, when you have all but thrown back my re-quests in my face?"

"Because there's already too much blood on my hands and I don't want more."

Ayaan's face tightened, his gaze filled with pity that Azeez didn't want. "Azeez, that's not—"

"This is your chance to protect your wife, Ayaan. Don't waste it on useless matters."

"Fine," his brother said, standing up. "I want you to take care of yourself. I want you to have physiotherapy, I want you to see a psychiatrist, and I want you to see Mother and I want you at my coronation in a—"

"Don't push it," Azeez said, feeling the shackles of his brother's demands binding him to Dahaar. Just the word *coronation* was like sticking a steel spike into his heart.

With his hand on the armrest, he pushed himself off the chaise. There was only one choice left to him, only one solution to stop the ruin he had begun again. And everything within him revolted at it. "I will do this, but I will do it my own way."

"What do you mean?"

"I won't see a team of doctors. Nikhat can attend to me in between attending to Zohra."

"Azeez," his brother's voice rang with warning as Azeez walked toward the exit, keeping his gaze away from everything in the room. "Whatever you are planning to do, don't. She is here by my request."

"Exactly. *You* brought her into this, Ayaan. Now that I'm following your orders, don't complain about it."

Stepping outside his brother's office, Azeez slowly made his way back to his own quarters. He still planned to leave Dahaar. For his own sanity, he had to.

But he would postpone it until things were right with Princess Zohra. And he couldn't live the rest of his life the way he had been doing, either.

He would do what his brother asked him to do because nothing else would be enough for Ayaan. However, there was no point in a team of doctors poking through his head. There was nothing anyone could do to fix him.

But Dr. Zakhari, he had been mistaken to dismiss her

so quickly. She owed him. And she would become his route to freedom from this palace, from a life that would slowly but surely do what a bullet hadn't been able to do— kill him.

Nikhat finished her dinner and dismissed the maid from her quarters. Ten seconds later, she couldn't remember what it was that had been served to her in the glittering silverware.

She only remembered looking at her reflection in the plate, rushing to the long, oval mirror in her bedroom and redoing her unruly hair.

She stood before it again now, going over herself with a critical eye. Her long-sleeved, high-collared caftan in unrelenting black was made of a stiff silk that instead of clinging to her breasts sat on her shoulders like a tent. Small diamond studs, a gift she had given herself for her thirtieth birthday, were her only jewelry.

Sighing loudly, she grabbed another pin and slapped it over one strand of hair that refused to sit back in her braid. Satisfied with how she looked, she pressed her temples with her fingers and massaged.

She was used to braiding her hair back tight for the operating room. But this time, she had done it so tight that her head ached.

She checked the pile of gifts she had spent hours wrapping, unable to sit still. Had she known that Princess Zohra would allow her father to come straight into Nikhat's suite in the far-off wing of the palace that housed her, she would have straightened a little more. As it was, she had made the maid nervous with her own twitching and needed to dismiss her.

Pulling her sleeve back, she checked her watch again. Her father was due any minute.

She was pacing the floor, wearing out the ancient, priceless rug when a knock sounded. Her feet flying on the floor, she opened the door.

And froze.

Azeez stood on the other side of the threshold. His jaw was clean-shaven, his gaze steady, a glimpse of the old him peeking out of it. She had forgotten the compelling effect his very presence held.

Her already strung-out nerves stretched a little more.

The fact that he was a few doors away in the same wing as her, night and day, rang like an unrelenting bell in the back of her head however busy she was. Seeing him outside her suite, in the palace of all the places, was a shock that needed its own category.

"I need to speak with you."

He didn't wait for her answer. In true arrogant-prince fashion, he pushed his way past her into the suite. Flustered at his sudden appearance, Nikhat turned around.

"Close your mouth, Nikhat. And the door."

She shut her mouth, not the door. Hopefully she looked defiant, because inside she was trembling. "Why?"

The curve of his mouth turned up in a smirk, his gaze shining with an unholy light. That spark, that smile, had once played havoc with her senses, and apparently it still could. Because her legs were barely holding her up.

"Are you afraid to be alone with me?"

She closed the door shut behind her with a thud that should have silenced the resounding yes in her head.

Her luxurious and vast suite, which had mocked all her New York sophistication, suddenly seemed impossibly small with him standing in the middle of it. He was like the sun, reducing everything around him to colorless insignificance.

Standing close, his gaze moved over her like a caress.

"Why are you dressed in that awful thing? And what happened to your hair?"

Nikhat stared back at him, all her worldliness, her sophistication, sliding away like sand between her fingers.

She had prepared herself to bear the brunt of his contempt, even hatred, in the coming months. But his attention, especially of a personal nature? No amount of preparation could help her deal with it.

"If this is how you dress usually, no wonder they were so happy to be rid of you in New York."

"I left of my own volition. I left a good position in a cutting-edge hospital to come back." Too late, she realized he was playing with her. His whole demeanor today was different. It was as if he had a strategy, as if all the fire of his emotions was neatly packed away for now. And even as he cut through her with his acerbic words, she still preferred him like that. The real him. "To build something that's very much needed here in Dahaara."

"Ah....I heard about all your plans for the clinic. Princess's Zohra's pregnancy, Ayaan's desperation to fix me, your history with me, everything's falling into place for you, isn't it? Like always."

Anger burst through her. "You think it's easy for to me to be back here? To leave behind the freedom, the position, the respect I had in New York? To constantly fight against invisible prejudices just because I'm a woman? Even being the Princess's personal physician is still apparently not recommendation enough."

"If you expected anything different, then you're a fool, Nikhat."

"Because I want to change some things for the better in Dahaar? You had a dream like that once, Azeez. Or have you completely wiped out everything from the past?"

He remained unflappable, even as her temper soared.

"You chose a difficult path for yourself and an even harder one by coming back. Why stay if it's so hard?"

"Because I know that I can make a difference. I want all the hard work I put in to amount to something for Dahaar. And I refuse to let any prejudice masquerading as tradition stop me."

His silence this time didn't grate on her. Because being back in Dahaar was harder not only on a professional level but a personal one. She had tasted freedom in New York. She could go wherever she wanted, she could talk to whomever she wanted to, without written permission, without seeing questions lingering in gazes wherever she turned.

"No, you never stray from your path once you decide, do you?" A grudging respect filled his words. "Just don't expect any changes overnight, Nikhat."

She nodded, fiercely glad for this discussion. Because even if he said his words in a mocking tone, Azeez gave her a sense of being understood that she needed so much.

"So, dressing like you're going to your own execution is the first step to convince everyone here to take you seriously?"

She raised a brow and smiled, smoothing a hand over the stiff silk. "Your mask of indifference in slipping, Azeez. You sound rather interested in how I'm dressed."

Something playful entered his gaze as he shrugged. "You look like a black hole, Nikhat. Unless you tell me why, I will assume it's to dissuade my interest. Then I'll have to inform you that I would rather take another bullet in the hip than touch you."

Heat flaring under her skin, Nikhat glared at him. "My father is coming to see me any minute. And my sisters. If you need me to be your punching bag, I would like to schedule the session for some other time that suits me better."

She checked her watch again, unable to contain her anxiety.

"You have to look like this to see your father? Is this some new law that Ayaan passed?"

She looked down at herself, knowing he was right. But she didn't want to give her father any more reason to be angry with her, or to find fault with her in any way. Loneliness she had battled for eight years solidified in her throat. "I...I have not seen him in eight years, Azeez. My sisters... can you imagine what Noor would look like now?" she said, thinking of her youngest sister. "Please, just leave, for now. I don't have the luxury to turn my back on my family like you have done."

The humor faded from his face. "Why didn't you see them all these years?"

"My father's condition for when I left Dahaar to study was that I not return. What you don't know, and I didn't realize, is how intractable he is. He forbade me from seeing him or my sisters."

Before he could reply, a knock sounded on the door. Panic tying her stomach in knots, she grasped his hands and jerked back as the contact sent a jolt of sensation through her. "Please, Azeez," she whispered, turning toward the door.

With a hard look at her, he walked around the sitting area and into her bedroom.

Only after she heard the click behind her did Nikhat's heart settle back into place. Wiping her forehead with the back of her hand, she opened the wide, double doors.

The smile froze on her mouth when she saw her father, alone. "Hello, Father," she said, unable to pull her gaze away from the eerily silent corridor.

His hands folded behind him, her father stepped into the suite. He stood there stiffly, casting a glance around the room, not a hint of warmth in his gaze or welcome in his stance.

Swallowing back her disappointment, Nikhat gestured toward the seating area. "Would you like something to drink?"

"I cannot stay long, Nikhat. There's an urgent security issue that I have to address with Prince Ayaan."

Nikhat nodded. "I understand how busy you are. I just… I thought the girls were coming with you."

His gaze remained steady on her, nothing betrayed in his set face. "I wished to make sure it was suitable for them to visit you here."

"It's the palace, Father. It's the most secure place in Dahaar. Ayaan said—" She caught herself at the spark of displeasure in his tight mouth. "Prince Ayaan informed me himself that I have permission to have guests. I'm the personal physician to the Crown Princess, not a prisoner of state," she said, bitterness spewing into her words.

"I did not think you were a prisoner." Even more hardness settled into his features, making his expression intractable. "I have heard rumors, however. Nothing I would repeat. In fact, it is what I need to address with the Crown Prince. But between the rumors and his sudden command to call you back to Dahaar, I do not like the conclusions I had to draw."

Anger filled her, replacing the powerlessness that had been clawing at her. All she wanted was to see her sisters. One small thing. And it seemed as if the whole universe was conspiring to deny her that. "What are these conclusions, Father?"

"I will not repeat them. And certainly not in front of you."

Hot fury filled every inch of her. "Yes, you will. I am your daughter and I'm thirty years old. I have lived outside

Dahaar, in a foreign land among strangers for eight years. Without any man's protection, I have seen the world. I have not only taken care of myself but I have also flourished in my career. If I'm being denied the chance to see my own sisters—" she knew she was shouting at him now, that her voice was breaking, but she didn't care anymore "—you will damn well tell me why not."

"Swearing when you speak to your father? Is this what you have become?"

She gritted her teeth. For so many years, she had kept quiet. Even before she left Dahaar, she had always tried to be a model daughter, tried to be the son he had always wanted. "What have I become? What have I done that is so wrong that you're still punishing me for it?"

He shook his head and Nikhat felt the one thing she had wanted slipping away from her hands. Everything she had achieved amounted to nothing if she still couldn't see her sisters. "You owe me the truth at least."

"Who are you serving, Nikhat? The Crown Princess Zohra or Prince Azeez?"

Nikhat could feel the blood fading from her face. "You cannot mention your suspicions to anyone. You cannot betray them."

Her father flinched. "I would never betray the royal family. It's all the small things I've been hearing. And no one else can come to the conclusion as I have. You and Prince Azeez…" He looked away from her as though his very thoughts were shameful. "I knew there was something between you all those years ago. Time and again I reminded you to keep your distance from them, to remember the disparity between our life and theirs. You never paid any attention to my warnings. You never do once you settle on something."

Nikhat tried to wrap her mind around what he was saying. The truth of it shone in his unforgiving eyes.

He had known she had been in love with Azeez and he had assumed she had left Dahaar because her relationship with the prince had fallen apart. She didn't know whether to laugh or cry at how perceptive her father was. "I have never done anything to bring shame upon you." Even when she had known that she had to walk away, she had still refused herself what she wanted more than anything in the world.

"It does not matter. But if the Crown Prince has summoned you back to the palace, if he's keeping you here because he thinks it will...*help* Prince Azeez...then I can't risk bringing your sisters here. Your life, your reputation, it's out of my hands. You took the right to protect you away from me when you left Dahaar. When you finish this...assignment, you will leave again. Leave whatever scandal you might create behind you. Your sisters have to live here, marry and make their lives. And I am still their father. I have to protect them."

"What would you have me do, Father? Deny the Crown Prince's request after everything King Malik has done for this family?"

"No, do your duty, whatever it...entails." Tight lines fanned his mouth, and Nikhat knew what it cost him to say those words. And yet, it didn't shock or surprise her. Her father had served King Malik for forty years. His loyalty was what had brought Nikhat to the palace to be educated at Princess Amira's side. "But do not ask me to involve your sisters in this. Not until whatever you are doing for the Crown Prince is finished, not until I know this will not affect their reputation."

Without another word, he walked out, shattering her hopes.

Nikhat slid to the seat behind her, too shaken to even shed tears.

She had thought that she had molded life to suit her will, that she had survived through her biggest pain, that she could tackle anything life threw at her, and yet, back in Dahaar, when it came to the one thing that truly mattered to her, she was truly powerless.

Useless rage boiled over inside her, the urge to pack up and leave without looking back pounding through her blood.

She heard Azeez's slow gait coming toward her. And for once, she couldn't care to hide her desolation.

He came to a standstill on her right, leaning against the dark chaise her father had just vacated. "And here I thought Ayaan had convinced you to whore yourself out to me in return for your big clinic? A reunion with your family is the prize you're going for?"

Anger burst through her, liberating and consuming, fraying the last rope of hope that had been holding her together. His words cheapened everything they had once shared, minimized everything she had become.

She shot to her feet, and reached him, adrenaline pumping through her blood. The force of her fury shaking through her, she slapped him hard.

The sharp sound reverberated around them, the impact of it jarring her arm, shaking her very breath.

He ran a hand over his jaw, an unholy light shining in his eyes. "Feel better?"

Her stomach folding on itself, she fisted her hand to stop the tremors. He hadn't even tried to stop her.

She had played directly into his hands. His gaze burned with a fire that she knew not to go near. But she couldn't step back, couldn't break eye contact with him. "You provoked me on purpose."

Pity and something indefinable danced in his gaze. "You looked like you would perish from the grief running through you, like you would never hope again. It was either I slap you or you slap me."

She didn't want to owe him more than she already did. "Now you know what we all see when we look at you."

She thought he would laugh at her. Instead, a thoughtful look dawned on his face. "Is that why you are here, Nikhat? Because you pity me?"

Folding her arms, she faced him. "That's the one thing I can truthfully say I have never felt for you, Azeez. You make it hard to pity you."

Relief dawned in his gaze. With his hands gripping the armrest, he sank into the chaise. "Ayaan will order your father to let you see them. He will have no choice but to follow his orders. Having to choose between your family and your profession, or anything else, is not something anyone should have to face."

Their gazes held, a wealth of memories fighting for breath in the air around them. He had spoken those words to her before too. He had made promises and he had kept every single one of them.

She…she had made one promise. And she hadn't been able to keep it.

Shaking her head, she pushed those memories back to where they belonged. "My father's right. I don't know where I'm going to be in six months' time. With a future so uncertain, it is better I stay away from my sisters."

"Or you could simply leave. I will help you get out of the palace. Ayaan will not force you to return."

"Are you so eager to be rid of me, Azeez?" She regretted the words the instant they were out.

"Yes, I would like nothing more than for you to leave,"

he said with crippling honesty that had always been a part of him.

Taking the option he was giving her, going back to New York where she had unfettered freedom, where her every movement, small and big, wasn't dictated by someone else, away from the man looking up at her with a dark fire that drew her nearer every day, it was the easiest thing to do.

She could save both of them from the misery of reliving a painful past because, try as she might, it kept rearing up its head.

And she wouldn't feel this desolation at being so close to her sisters and still not seeing them. But the same loyalty that was in her father's blood filled hers too.

"I made a promise to Ayaan. Whatever happens in the next few months, I want to live in Dahaara. I want to head that clinic. There's a lot of good I can do here."

He rubbed his forehead with long fingers. "Of course. You have goals, and plans to accomplish those goals. And if something fails, you dust yourself off and move on."

"Why did you come here, Azeez?"

"I want you to help me convince Ayaan that everything is wonderfully perfect up here," he said, poking himself in the head.

"So that you can leave the palace and get yourself killed?"

"I don't have to leave the palace to accomplish that." He said the words softly, slowly, as if he was crushed by a weight he couldn't shake. He stood up from the chaise and walked toward the door, his frame tight with tension. When he met her gaze, the depth of pain in it shook her. And they all thought he didn't care, that he had become a shell of his former self. "I cannot bear to be here, Nikhat. I have to convince Ayaan that leaving Dahaar is the best thing for me, for him, for our parents. I have to leave Dahaar. And it has to be done in such a way that Ayaan feels no guilt."

Nikhat shook her head. "That's a tall order. I'll never be able to convince him, because I don't think it is the best thing for you."

"But you will do it."

The arrogance in his tone stole her breath away. "Why will I do it?"

He leaned against the wall, his hand gripping his hip. "Do you want me to die a slow, painful death?"

A shiver went through her at the desolation in his eyes. She reached him, desperate to relieve his pain, desperate to do something. "Azeez, you can't—"

He threw an arm out as if to halt her from coming near him. When he spoke, it was through gritted teeth. "This palace is eating me up alive. Everywhere I turn, I see the destruction I have wrought on Ayaan, on my parents, on Dahaar itself. If I have to live, it has to be outside these palace walls."

Dahaar had once been an integral part of him, his life, his blood, his passion. To hear him say it was stifling the life out of him was the most painful thing she had ever heard.

For whatever reason, Azeez held himself responsible for everything that happened, and as long as he did, he couldn't breathe in here. Broken dreams, and ghosts of a glorious past, the palace was full of it—it was a pain she felt, an agony that she understood.

Which meant she had no choice but to agree.

What he was asking of her, it was a betrayal of her promise to Ayaan, a betrayal of the promise she had made to herself. But, as it always had been, when it came to Azeez, nothing else mattered to her. Not even her own happiness.

She wanted him to live, and if she could help him do that the way he wanted, then so be it. "I will help you, Azeez," she heard herself say.

And was rewarded by a puzzled nod from him.

CHAPTER FOUR

NIKHAT FOLLOWED THE palace maid down a maze of intricate marble-lined corridors, her heart slowly climbing up her throat with every step she took.

Agreeing to Azeez's proposal was one thing. Venturing into his suite with an action plan in hand, another. At least, Ayaan had been pleasantly surprised when she had informed him what she had in mind, during Princess Zohra's morning checkup.

With a nod, the maid pointed her to intricately designed double doors and left. Clutching her iPad with shaking fingers, she stepped over the threshold and stilled at the utter magnificence of the suite. She had thought her suite was the lap of luxury. Compared to this one, hers was more like a storage room, in sheer size and the magnificence of it.

She had been here that first night, but in her anxiety to see Azeez, she had paid no attention to her surroundings. She had spent innumerable hours in the palace, roamed most of the corridors and wings with Amira, everywhere but here. Because it was the Prince's wing and had been forbidden to all of them.

Azeez's suite, she discovered, looking past the main area, backed onto private gardens and was a cavernous bedchamber rather than a mere suite. She walked past the vast foyer into the main area and stilled. Her breath hitched in her throat. Cream-colored walls flowed seamlessly against the similarly colored marble floors, inlaid here and there with gold piping. She knew it was gold because she had once asked Amira, her mouth falling open to her chest.

Dark red velvet curtains brocaded with gold threads hung heavily beside the floor-length windows. A sitting area was on her left containing gilt-edged sofas and chaise lounges with claw-feet made in intricate detail. Lush Persian rugs in colorful designs lay here and there. A silver tea service, along with a variety of mouthwatering dishes on the table, all lay untouched.

A crystal decanter, which looked as old and priceless as the rest of the trappings of the room, stood next to the tray, the gold liquid swirling at the bottom telling its own story.

Against the opposite wall sat a vast bed, almost waist high, with a wide, intricately designed metal headboard, and sheets again of the darkest red. A velvet-covered stool stood off to the side.

Cushions and pillows of every possible size lay haphazardly atop the sheets. A white cotton shirt was at the foot of the bed that looked half crumpled.

Her feet carried her to the bed—because really she had no idea she had decided to walk toward it. A hint of sandalwood, underlaid with a scent that was *his,* reached her nose, invading her skin with a lick of heat.

She sucked in greedy bursts, drawing it deep into her lungs before she realized that she was doing it. The sheets were soft and warm against her shaking fingers, and her mind conjured an image of him tangled in them.

A low, thrilling pulse rang all over her body like a bell. She had imagined being in his bedroom, countless times and in a countless number of ways all those years ago. And her body still reacted to it in the same way, even with a gulf of pain and dreams separating them more than ever.

She was in the Prince of Dahaar's bedroom—an intimacy that was strictly limited to his immediate family and the woman he would marry, the woman who would irrevocably belong to him.

The very thought sent a stab of pain through her middle, cooling the illicit thrill.

She clasped her nape, and rubbed it, fighting the wave of melancholy. *Ya Allah*, what madness had led her to agree to this?

A slow burn of awareness inched under her skin. She turned slowly, bracing herself for a caustic remark from those cruel lips.

Azeez stood at the doorway of the bathroom, clad only in loose white trousers that tied with fragile strings.

Sinuous heat drenched Nikhat inside out, zigzagging across a million spots, places she shouldn't be thinking of in front of him but was painfully aware of.

His shoulder blades were outlined by his lean frame. The golden olive of his skin gleamed dark against the white fabric, stretched tight over his abdomen, delineating every bone and muscle. Sparse chest hair covered dark nipples, arrowing down in a line that disappeared into those trousers. Her gaze instinctively sought the evidence of the bullet wound. Only a small length of a scar, puckered and stitched up roughly, was visible above the band of the trousers.

He didn't have a whole lot of muscle on him, and yet there was no softness to his abdomen either.

Suddenly, all she wanted was to trace the angular jut of his collarbone, rake her fingernail over his nipple, see if he felt the arc of electricity between them as strongly as she did.

She met his gaze, and something flared into life between them, contracting the space and world around them, as though shoving them both into a world of their own. His breath left him in a soft exhale and she watched as the lean chest rose and fell with it.

Liquid desire, she realized what it was, flowed through every nerve in her body, a thrill coiling her muscles. She wanted to move forward and touch him, feel the heat of his skin slide against hers, smell that intoxicating masculinity that had made her realize her own femininity for the first time.

Eight years ago, she had been naive, green, too overwhelmed by what and who he was to understand the raw awareness between them, too caught up in society's rules and her own insecurities to comprehend the power and beauty of this thing. The dark heat of his glances, the fire of his checked desire, the power with which he had leashed it so that he didn't scare her, she had never fully comprehended it. Until now.

It was not her body that had caught up, as he had mocked. It was her mind. And it reveled in the raw charge between them, reveled in the fact that she could put that feral look in his eyes.

The slight rise of his brows, the almost undetectable hint of widening of his jet-black irises—he was amused and yet it was not the eviscerating kind. He was as surprised as she was at her daring.

Coloring, she fought the instinct to look away, to hide from what he made her body feel. She had denied herself so many things. But the simple thrill of watching the Prince of Dahaar, of holding that intractable gaze without shying away, she couldn't deny herself this. It made her dizzily alive. In that moment, she could believe herself his equal.

His mouth didn't turn into a sneer, his gaze didn't mock her for her unwise audacity. He just stood there and stared at her, as though waiting to see how long she could hold it.

She could drink him in for the rest of her life. But of course, she had a job to do.

Searching for that brisk efficiency that she had become well known for among her colleagues, she waved the iPad toward him. "Since you refuse to see an actual physiotherapist, I contacted a friend of mine and downloaded some videos he recommended. Most of them are pretty easy to follow, but I have requested that Khaleef be present in case you need physical—"

He shook his head.

She instantly knew what he was saying no to. "But Khaleef can—"

"I want you."

She swallowed at the searing heat that blanketed her as he pushed off the wall and moved closer. He had said those words deliberately, she reminded herself. He was testing how far her recklessness of a few moments ago would carry her. And yet they had no less effect on her. "Fine. For this week, our goal is to get you moving again, and for you to attend a dinner with Ayaan and Princess Zohra at the end of the week. And figuring out where it is that you want to go when this is…over, and what you will be doing there."

Every muscle in his face stilled. "Where I want to go?"

"Yes. I thought about your…leaving Dahaar a little more." It was all she had done, she felt consumed by it really. This time, she was going to be here and he was going to leave.

She had long ago resigned herself to a life without him and she had accomplished far more than her wildest dreams.

Still, the thought of living in a Dahaar that didn't have him in it was a reality she had never imagined. "Ayaan won't just let you wander back into the desert. It seems more feasible that Ayaan, King Malik and Queen Fatima will—" he grimaced at the mention of his mother, and she willed herself to continue "—will let you leave if you show an interest in one of the worldwide business ventures that Dahaar invests in.

"You cannot cut them out of your life completely, Azeez. Nor are you capable of wiling away your life doing nothing. That, of all the things in the world, will kill you."

He didn't question her assumption. "I can try."

She didn't qualify that with a response. "I asked Ayaan a few questions, pretty much lied and said it would give me something to talk about with you."

"I've forgotten how meticulous you are when you set your mind to something."

"Your options are the investment house in New York, the race course in Abu Dhabi and, of course, your all-time favorite, Monaco." The last words stuck in her throat like thorns, refusing to come out.

She had developed the most violent and irrational hatred toward that place every time she had looked at the paper and read about his exploits in the year before the terrorist attack. His words that first morning had only intensified it.

A challenge glimmered in his eyes. "Is there something you would like to say, Nikhat?"

The question simmered in the air between them, like an explosive in the middle of a peaceful desert. And the slightest hint of demand from her could detonate it and crumble her carefully constructed life.

She shook her head, clinging to ignorant sanity.

Walking by his side, she adjusted her stride to match his slow one.

"I saw that—" she breathed in a deep gulp as his forearm grazed hers "—I noticed that you're not completely out of shape, but you're also obviously in pain."

He laughed, but there was no real joy in the sound. "Don't tell Ayaan. When he captured me in the desert, he knocked me off my feet and I landed on my bad hip violently. Fighting him cost me—"

"And yet you did it."

He continued as though she hadn't interrupted him. "Also, the longer—"

"The longer you sit around, drinking and throwing bottles at imaginary figures, the worse the pain gets."

"Yes. But it was too much fun, Nikhat."

She shook her head, even as a smile rose to her lips. That roguishness—it was incredible to see that still inside him. "I figure the logical step is to get you to move as much as possible every day. I inquired about a hydro-pool, but the *hammam* should do quite well for our purposes. The steam will loosen the hip joint before we do a little exercise every day. Do you know who I can contact about requesting some medical records about your bullet wound?"

"There are none."

Her mental gears checked through the list of things she had to do so rapidly that it took her a few seconds to understand. "But then who—"

"Once they realized I would be of no more use to them, the terrorist group left me in the desert to die and moved on with Ayaan, as far as I can figure. He was still valuable to them." His voice was so low, so weighed down with whatever he felt, that it raised goose bumps on her skin. "I had already lost a lot of blood. The Mijab found me, and patched up my hip the best they could. Luckily for me, I was unconscious for most of it."

Shock removed the filter from her words. "But the Mijab are not even the most advanced tribe. It's a miracle you're still standing."

Instant regret raked through her.

Because it wasn't a miracle. She had never believed in them.

Even having gone through everything he had, even weighed down by the bitterest self-loathing he seemed to be under, Azeez Al Sharif was too much a force of life to just wither away and die. The fact that he was still standing was a testament to the man's sheer willpower and nothing else.

"I like to think of it as my penance, rather."

"Penance?"

"Death would have been—it still is—too easy a punishment." His tone was matter-of-fact, as if there was no doubt about what he said. "Living my life is the harder one."

Her throat felt raw, her entire body felt raw at the quiet resignation of his words, at the emptiness in them. "Why should you have to serve penance at all? Why didn't you come back when you recovered a little?"

This was the thing that hurt and confused Ayaan the most. And her, too. The very fact that Azeez Al Sharif had chosen to stay away from Dahaar, his family, it shook the very foundations of every truth she knew.

He turned away from her, signaling an end to this conversation. "You'll have to accompany me to the *hammam*."

Whatever she had been about to say misted away. Enjoying a minute of uncensored, unwise desire she felt for him without guilt and shame was one thing, accompanying Azeez Al Sharif to what was essentially a steam room was another.

She had delivered babies, she had no false modesty or squeamishness left in her. But this was…*him*.

He halted at the door. "Unless you think what I ask is beyond the bounds of propriety and want to call the whole thing off, Dr. Zakhari?"

She fisted her hands, wanting to wipe the mockery off his face. He was constantly going to try to push her to leave. "There are servants to help you there, Azeez."

"Do you know that Ayaan had all the old servants, like

Khaleef, people who have seen me as a baby, reassigned to work in this wing?"

She frowned, remembering what her father had said. "Yes. I thought it a good security measure since you insist on not letting the people of Dahaar learn that you're alive."

His mouth set into a bitter line. "These are the same people who carried me on their shoulders in the palace, taught me how to ride a bike, celebrated with me when my father announced me Crown Prince. These are people who have known me my entire life, Nikhat. And now, when they look at me, all I see is their pity. That pity...*Ya Allah*..." He sounded tortured, his shoulders shaking with the enormity of it. She wasn't the only one who had loved him—the entire palace, all of Dahaar had worshipped their magnificent prince. "It haunts me day and night, jeers me for the mockery I have become. I hide from my parents and yet...there they are, silent witnesses to my inadequacy, to my guilt."

He turned away from her. Ayaan had truly no idea how much his brother was suffering inside these walls. "If it scares you to be around me, helping me, then say the word, *latifa*. But I will not accept help from anyone else."

That resentment would have frayed her at one time, but not anymore. Each little facet of his pain that she saw only strengthened her resolve.

Somehow, or especially because he wanted to punish her by keeping her close, he had decided she would be the one he leaned on. And even though every word from him, every moment spent with him, poked holes through her will, she still wanted to do this.

She met his gaze, striving for a casualness that she was far from feeling. "I used to feel overwhelmed and afraid and thrilled and God knows what else by you, all those years ago. I don't anymore."

His gaze swept over her cotton tunic top and leggings. "I can see that. Living away from Dahaar apparently suits you very well. You will have to change out of those clothes."

"I'm your servant, remember, not your spa buddy." That teased a smile from his mouth. "And I have already showered."

He stiffened next to her, and slowly pulled his arm away. "I know. I can smell the scent of your jasmine soap. You smell exactly like you did eight years ago." He said it as if it was a curse he was enduring. And for her, it was as if someone had sucked out the oxygen from the room. "But I'm going to need help and you will melt if you enter the *hammam* in those clothes."

CHAPTER FIVE

IN THE END, Nikhat didn't give in to his demands. At least, not completely.

The first room, which was a heat room, was an architectural marvel—a huge cavernous room with sweeping archways, its interiors made of gold marble that glittered in the billowing steam. Candles threw dim light around, just enough to spot the seats and pillars. The smell of eucalyptus filled the air, while crystal decanters in a variety of intricate shapes lay around.

Azeez lay on the marble platform in the middle, the pride of the room, his face down, his lower body covered by a thick, white towel. A concession for her.

Tendrils of her hair stuck to her forehead, her skin tingling and heating everywhere. Except to lend a hand as he settled over the marble bed, she hadn't really helped him. But suddenly, she felt the most rampant curiosity to see his wound.

Seeing it wouldn't particularly serve a purpose. And yet, she couldn't talk herself out of it. From what Ayaan had said, Azeez spoke of his wound with no one, not even a doctor. But he had spoken of it with her, in a matter-of-fact voice that glossed over the horror of it, but still he had.

She was it—his doctor, his psychiatrist, his nurse and his

friend. Had he realized what he had asked her to do? How had fate once again brought them to this point?

The timer she had set outside for thirty minutes pinged. Wiping her face on her sleeve, she made her way to him.

Bending at her waist, she placed her hands on his shoulders. His skin was like raw velvet under her hands. "Azeez, it's time to leave."

He leaned his chin on his hands, his coal-black eyes glittering with a thousand emotions in the flickering candlelight. The razor-sharp angles of his cheekbones, the strong jawline—he was a visual feast. "You have to help me up."

There was no smile on his face, but there was no bitterness, either. She wondered if he came to the same conclusion as she did.

Nodding, she pushed her sleeves back and tucked her hands under his shoulders. His muscled arms anchored around her waist, he rose up, leaning on his left side. The scent of him enveloped her, the sweat from his body mingling with hers, and he slowly slid off the marble.

She averted her gaze as he pulled on another fresh pair of loose cotton trousers. She flicked the light on and walked back to him before her courage deserted her.

"I want to see it, Azeez," she spoke in a rushed whisper. The cavernous room amplified their voices, enveloping them together.

"Not the best time to see it, *latifa*. Steam tends to do things to it," he said with a sinful curve of his mouth.

"What?" Heat scorched her cheeks as his meaning sunk in. "I'm not talking about your…your…"

"Yes, Dr. Zakhari? What precisely are you *not* talking about?" Challenge glinted in his words, his mouth tugged up at the corners.

That glimpse of his old roguish humor—it sent a blast of longing through her.

She had graduated with honors in her class. She was an ob-gyn, yes, but she had seen naked men before. And she wasn't going to let the Prince of Dahaar reduce her into a blushing twit. "Your penis, okay? That's not what I want to see. And you know what? I can also say sex, vagina, erection and—"

He threw his head back and laughed. A rich, powerful, hearty sound that brought prickling tears to her eyes, and the most painful tightness to her chest. She wanted to hear it again and again, see the flash of his teeth, feel the warmth of it steal into her. To forever be the one who made him laugh like that.

The corners of her own mouth tugged up.

"It is like you are a different woman, Nikhat. More fun, daring…" His gaze gleamed with an inferno of emotion. "*Whatever* it is that you…did in New York really agrees with you."

The unspoken question sizzled in the silence. But she didn't take his bait this time.

"I want to see your wound."

His laughter died. "There's nothing you can do for it."

Her bare feet almost slipped on the floor and she grabbed him for support. She grasped his forearms tight, refusing to let him move. "I prefer to be the person making the judgment. And as arrogant and all-knowing as you are, I'm the one with a medical degree here."

His fingers tightened on her arms, the thin cotton of her caftan no barrier to his touch. His eyes ate her up. "But I'm the Prince. I'm the one with all the power. I make the rules between us, Nikhat. I decide what I will use you for and what I won't. You seem to be under a fantastic delusion that you're as important to me as you were eight years ago. You are not. It is only your history with my family, your usefulness to me, that has you standing here. Don't mistake it as anything else."

The breath-stealing arrogance in his words bounced off her. But the fact that he belittled her presence here…she couldn't tolerate it.

In a perverse little twist, she wanted him to acknowledge that she was here because she *was* the girl he had known once, the girl he had loved once. The need for that acknowledgment burned through her even as she realized that it was dangerous.

She was standing on a precipice, and all she wanted to do was jump. "You will not steal the little I have. You've no idea what I have faced, what I still face, to be standing here in front of you without shattering into a million pieces."

His mouth, enticingly close to hers, hardened, the intensity of his focus a fierce little thing. "Why are you pushing me, *Nikhat*? Why does it matter what I think after all these years? And whatever you have faced, it was all your own doing. You chose this path, don't ask for understanding now."

"You think me heartless, you think it is easy for me being near you, seeing you in pain." She blinked at how easily the wound she closed could open again. "It is not. Every minute I spend in this palace hurts me just as much as it hurts you."

A dark smile curved his mouth and she held her breath at the stark beauty of it. He pushed a tendril of her hair behind her ear, then clasped her jaw, the rough ridges of his fingers and palm chafing against her skin. She shivered, every inch of her body focused on the minute contact. "After everything I have done, everything I have brought on myself—" his gaze caressed her eyes, her nose, her mouth, a dark fire in it "—you would think that wouldn't have given me the satisfaction it does. But I've never been magnanimous or kind or—"

"Or anything but your true self. Since you're satisfied that I'm suffering as much as you are, let me see your wound, Azeez."

"Why are you hell-bent on plunging us both into misery again? How much more do you want me to suffer?"

And just like that, he gave her back all the power he stole from her. He hated the servants seeing him like this, his brother seeing him like this, but above all, it was her presence that tortured him the most.

Why? Did he think she would be revolted? Did he not see the very strength inside him that still kept him standing there?

Suddenly, it became irrationally imperative that she learn everything he had suffered, if only to share his pain.

She would have done that much for even a friend. So she stayed silent, refusing to back away.

With a curse that punctured the air, he undid the string of his trousers and Nikhat wondered if he could hear the *thump-thump* of her heart. Breathing hard, she moved to the side to let the blazing lights overhead illuminate the small sliver of flesh he uncovered.

She breathed hard at the first sign of a violent scar— stitched up roughly, almost the width of her wrist. Closing her eyes, she laid her hand on his hip. His skin was blazing hot under her palm, the muscle clenching into rock hardness as she moved her fingers.

He stiffened but she couldn't stop herself.

A picture emerged in her mind as she moved her hand, traced the ravaged tissue, learning the breadth and length of it. She clutched her eyes closed, locking the searing heat back.

She couldn't help imagining the kind of pain he must have suffered. And following that, hope flooded through her.

She had been right. He had survived because he was Azeez Al Sharif. And if he could survive that wound, he could survive anything.

There was no smooth flesh left on the side of his hip. It was a jagged mass of muscle, the patched-up scars abrasive against her soft palm, running down his thigh. The moment her fingers fluttered lower and she felt the coarse hair of his thighs against her fingers again, it was her turn to shudder all over.

His skin here was hot and different against her palm, but the muscles rock hard.

A pulse of something else clamored between them—a heated awareness at how intimately she was touching him. He was half turned away from her, his hard body pressing into her front, his arm brushed up between her breasts, his long, rough fingers anchored around her nape.

Every inch of her came alive at the delicious pressure in all the right places. His breathing sounded harsh, too, every hard muscle that pressed into her tight with tension.

She righted his trousers, her fingers deceptively steady, as if she did this every day, as if she hadn't pulled them through an emotional firestorm goaded by a fiercely selfish desire. "Did the bullet shatter the bone?"

He sighed, as though accepting that she wasn't going to back off, and she wrapped her arms around his waist. "No. It hit the bone and dropped momentum somehow. From what I gathered from them, the Mijab were able to quickly extricate it. They took me to a hospital at the border of Zuran. A small metal joint was inserted to hold the bone together until it could grow back."

"They left it inside," she said, finally understanding the

source of his pain. "That's why it gets so stiff, why it hurts so much."

He nodded and his hands pulled her hands away from his hip. "Are we through?"

Nikhat straightened and looked away. "Here, yes. We will start stretching immediately."

She halted at the exit, her skin gleaming with vitality, her eyes blazing with piercing honesty. The fabric of her caftan stuck to her body and with her hair curling around her face, she was the most striking woman he had ever seen, and a sharp hunger, unbidden and unwelcome, yet one that made him feel fiercely alive, clawed at Azeez.

All he would have to do was close his eyes to feel the feathering touch of her fingers over his flesh, hear the sinuous whisper of her breath over his skin.

"You can't imagine what Khaleef and the others see," Nikhat said. "They see the prince who always had a kind word for them, they see the prince who remembers their name without hesitation, they see the prince whom they mourned with tears and their hearts—they do not see your limp or your scars or your guilt. And what you see is not their pity, Azeez, but their love.

"I would give anything to see my mother one more time. Think about what you're doing to yours."

His hip muscles sore, but also surprisingly limber, Azeez slid himself onto the bench in his private garden.

He had expected Nikhat to decline his invitation.

Was she as curious about him as he was about her?

The silverware tinkled as she poured him mint tea. Sitting here, as the sun streaked the sky gold and red, surrounded by lush roses, the scent of Nikhat, jasmine and something undeniably her, shouldn't have registered at all on him. Yet, as she handed him the tea and took a sweet date cake for herself, the scent of her wafted over him, teasing arousal from his beaten body.

The sensation was fierce, sharp, after so many years of feeling nothing.

He took a sip of tea and grimaced. His hip was throbbing, the muscles in his thighs and arms shaking from the strenuous stretching after four months of inactivity. "I need something stronger than this."

"No alcohol, Azeez. Not as long as you want my help."

He frowned, and yet was unable to stop smiling at the relish with which she said it. "You're enjoying this, aren't you?"

"Yes. How many women can claim Azeez Al Sharif bows to her every command?"

"None."

The cake shook in her fingers. Coloring, she put it in her mouth.

She licked a crumb from the corner of her mouth, and another kind of ache shivered in his muscles. He felt incredibly hungry for a taste of her mouth, for a taste he had been denied for so long. And the fact that he hadn't touched a woman since the attack, the six years of celibacy, had little bearing on his desire for her.

The delicious tightening of his muscles, the coils of heat spreading like wildfire through him, they were all because of the woman who had boldly traced his scars with her hand even as her breath had hitched in her throat.

She was such a mixture of strength and vulnerability, of caring and indifference, every word from her a contradiction to her actions, he felt as if he would never understand her.

For as long as he could remember, she had been the one woman who hadn't cowed in front of him, who hadn't thrown herself at him, the one woman who had always spoken her mind, pushed him into broadening his.

Whether it was philosophy they had discussed, or the state of education for women in Dahaara, he had never been the Prince of Dahaar with her. Her answers, her arguments, they had held a piercing honesty that had been as compelling as her artlessness. For all his impulsive and passionate nature, he hadn't fallen in love with her overnight.

He had fallen in love over a period of ten years, or even more, maybe—slowly, unknowingly, tempered into it like water chipping away the surface of a rock, molding it to its will. One morning, he had woken up in his hotel suite after a night of raucous partying and suddenly wondered what she would say if she saw him then, what words she would use to skewer him, and with a fire in his blood, he had realized he had fallen in love with her, that he had found his future queen, that nothing in the world would stop him from making her his.

Except he hadn't realized the iron will of the woman herself.

And when she left, she had not just broken his heart or dented his ego, though it had been that, too. She had ripped away a piece of him that had belonged only to her and taken it with her, had left a terrifying emptiness that he'd had no idea how to fill.

Bitter jealousy vented through his veins as he studied her. Because now, now she was even better than before, now she was magnificent, everything he had imagined she would grow into and more.

Age had only refined her beauty, and from the little he remembered of when she had held on to him in the *hammam*, she was in incredibly good shape. But even better than physical beauty, she had seen the world, she had held her own in a foreign country and she had achieved everything she had set her mind to. And he…he was barely a man.

His curiosity wasn't going to simmer down quietly. He didn't even pretend he could control his emotions, or himself, when it came to her. All he could do was limit the damage to himself and her.

This…might have begun with the debilitating need to hurt her, but it wasn't anymore. In a cruel twist of fate, which didn't even surprise him, she had become the only way out for him.

"Why didn't you marry?"

She stilled, her hand midway to her mouth. He saw her fingers shake as she put the last piece of the date cake on the small silver plate. She made a show of wiping her fingers. Buying herself time, he realized. *Why?* "Are you expecting an honest answer?"

He frowned, trying to make sense of her, of everything he knew about her, of everything she had done eight years ago. Because as much as he wanted to consign it to the back of his mind, the fact that she was here in Dahaar, seeing him through this, it had to mean something.

Whether he wanted to face it when his life was already in such turmoil, he didn't know. "When have I ever asked you for anything but the truth? You're successful, you're beautiful, and as your father mentioned, you're not bound by Dahaaran traditions or customs. So why are you still single?"

She wrapped her arms around herself, her shoulders unsteady.

His heart slammed hard against his rib cage. "Or do you have a boyfriend tucked away somewhere, Dr. Zakhari, just waiting for your signal to show up?"

Something moved across her face—defiance, a challenge. Her spine locked, her mouth settling into a stubborn line that he detested. "And if I did?"

He gripped the armrests of the chaise, perverse fury filling his veins. "I have no wish to see you and your lover parade through my palace."

She leaped from her seat as though propelled toward him by a desert storm. She bent toward him, bringing her face close to his, her gaze blazing with resolve. An expression he had never seen on her before—a reckless willfulness, danced in it. And he felt the strangest little thrill gripping his insides. "I thought I didn't have to choose between my career and personal life."

She was taunting him, she was relearning what effect she had on him and testing it. And yet, he rose to meet it.

He clasped her cheek. "Do not pretend to misunderstand me or be so reckless as to challenge me, Nikhat.

"You are the woman I loved once, the woman I chose for my future queen, the woman I wanted to give birth to the future heir of Dahaar. Everything's changed in eight years, hasn't it? But the thought of you with another man, the image of any man possessing your body, staking his claim on you, it will always reduce me into a savage that would make my marauding ancestors proud.

"What I consider mine once, I would not share it, even in thought. So unless you want to add to my long list of sins, Nikhat, tuck your lover away until I leave."

He pushed himself to his knees with a savage force that sent a shock wave through his leg. He could not bear to look at her, he could not bear to look inside himself. He had thought after all these years, after everything that had happened, there was nothing left in him that would react to her, and yet, there still was.

He had wrought destruction on himself, on his family, he was directly responsible for the death of his sister and for the atrocities his brother had suffered, because of how broken, how reckless he had become when Nikhat had left him.

"I was engaged three years ago, to a colleague," she said behind him, and he halted. The very thought crept into his head and taunted him.

That she was telling him this was not to assuage his pride or to balance the scales between them. That she was offering a piece of truth was something else. Something that stole into him with an insidious inevitability that filled ice in his veins. But he would not accept it, he could not go down that path ever again, and certainly not with her. "But it didn't work out."

"Why not?" he said, the question falling from his lips before he could stop it.

She shrugged, and he instinctively knew whatever she was going to say was not the truth. "He broke it off a week before the wedding, changed his mind about what he wanted in life." Pain streaked across her gaze. "I am not... made for relationships."

Without waiting for a response, she left him in the garden, his mind roiling with every little word she had spoken.

You have no idea what I have faced, what I still face, to be standing in front of you without shattering into a million pieces.

Maybe he didn't and, for once, Azeez was thankful for his ignorance. Because the rate at which they were going, it wouldn't be long before they ripped each other to pieces.

With a self-preservation instinct that had kept him alive until now, he realized he didn't want to face any more truths.

CHAPTER SIX

SHE HAD NOT come for two days.

Two long days that Azeez had spent wondering why he cared and then eviscerating himself for the fact that he did. First he had had to check if Princess Zohra was in good health.

She was fine, the Princess had informed him with a ferocious glint in her eyes, obviously surprised that he had cared enough to check for himself.

But there was something about riling the fierce princess that loosened the chain of guilt around his neck. She had not only glared at him but had also had the temerity to warn him that Nikhat was under her protection.

Before informing him finally that Nikhat hadn't seemed well yesterday morning. And the thought of Nikhat all alone in the palace, because he was sure she wouldn't have asked anyone for help, had finally dragged him out of his suite.

He stood outside her suite now, staring at the dark wooden door with its intricate designs. They had finally settled down into a sort of routine.

He visited the *hammam* in the morning, followed by a strenuous bout of physiotherapy—in which the madwoman drove him like the very devil intent on punishing him for all his sins. Sometimes she would stay and have lunch with him. They ate in silence—not completely awkward. But not pleasant, either, as though they were still reeling from the words they had thrown at each other two days before.

He had caught her casting puzzled looks at him, seen the way she caught herself when she was irked by his politeness, astonished that he was even capable of it with her.

Now, standing outside her door, he questioned his sanity again. He needed to treat her like any other employee, any other servant that his brother had. Let her come find him whenever she was well and offer him an excuse.

But he couldn't stop wondering about what would cause the ruthlessly efficient woman to be absent.

He pushed the doors and stepped in. It was early evening, but the French doors to her suite were still open, and brought a chill inside.

Frowning, he closed them. The suite bore her stamp clearly. The subtle scent of jasmine and her skin, wafted over him, knuckling him in the gut, unlocking a million memories inside his head.

There were medical journals, an iPad and a scarf dangling on the table in the lounge. An old framed picture of her with her three younger sisters sat next to the scarf.

A low, keening moan came from the bedroom. He turned instantly, a slow chill racing up his spine. He pushed the bedroom door open.

She lay in the middle of the bed, dressed in loose white pajamas that hung low on her hips and a loose cotton tunic in faded yellow. Her thick, wavy hair fanned out against the white sheets shone like copper-gold silk. Lying on her side, her arms clasped her belly so tight that her knuckles showed white. She moaned again and this time, the pain in the sound made the hair on his arms stand.

He got onto the bed slowly, making sure not to put too much weight on his right hip. She looked so pale, the golden hue of her usual color all but gone. Her eyes were red and swollen. That she had shed tears was a fact he couldn't believe even when presented with evidence.

Nikhat never cried. He remembered the day when her mother had died. She had been twelve. And yet Azeez only remembered her resolve to be strong for her younger sisters. Shifting closer to her, he pushed the sweat-slicked hair back from her forehead. His breath left him in a long exhale, thankful that her skin wasn't burning up.

She stiffened suddenly, as if a hot poker was lancing her next to him, and then shivered uncontrollably as another wave of pain hit, he realized. He clasped her fingers with his tightly, willing her to draw strength from him. He felt the tremble slowly fade from her body, heard her breath leave in a jagged exhale. The whimper of relief that accompanied it caught the breath in his throat. "Nikhat, *ya habeebiti*, look at me," he said. Watching her like this, he felt powerless and, at the same time, gripped with a fierce determination to see her through it.

She jerked her head back, her gaze flying to him. He thought she would stiffen and move away, demand to be released, tell him she didn't need his comfort.

"Azeez?"

"Yes, Nikhat."

Fresh tears welled up in her beautiful eyes, and he felt as if someone had kicked him in the gut. She scooted closer to him on the bed, and her arms went tight around his waist. "It hurts, Azeez. So much. Every time that wave comes, it feels like I will die." Her tears leaked out of her eyes, drawing wet tracks onto her cheeks.

He wiped them with a shaking hand, his heart jammed in his throat. "Why, in God's name, haven't you summoned help? I'll have them fly a specialist in, anything you need. Is it some kind of fever, an infection?"

She shook her head and hid her face in his abdomen. But

not before he caught a shadow of something in her eyes. He sunk his fingers into her thick hair, rubbing her scalp in a soothing manner. "I'm going to get my period soon," she said with no hesitation that belied the way she hid her face.

And suddenly he remembered how she used to disappear every month for a few days, and shy away when he asked her about it. Knowing that it would only make her retreat from her, he had never pressed her about it. "Have they always been so painful?" he asked now. It galled him to imagine her suffering like this every month for so many years.

And he thought he knew everything there was about pain.

She nodded, and her nose tickled his abdomen. He tightened his muscles, willing his body not to betray its automatic reaction to her nearness. "As far as I can remember."

"So what do we do?"

"I have learned to manage it with medication and exercise, and breathing techniques. It's so stupid, but I...forgot to renew my medication on time before I left. It's on its way from New York. Should be delivered tomorrow morning."

"And until then?" he said, his throat dry.

"Until then, I just bear it the best I can. It's really bad only for a few hours," she whispered in a small voice. He pulled himself up until he was sitting a little straighter. Her palm moved from his abdomen to his chest, and his heart thundered like a wild animal under her tentative fingers. The thin cotton of his tunic was no barrier to the feel of her touch.

"Azeez?"

Her breath feathered over his neck, the scent of her drugging arousal into his blood. He felt engulfed by her, as if he was standing on shifting sands that could pull him under any minute.

"Yes, *habeebi?*" he finally said through a throat as dry as the desert.

"Will you stay with me tonight?"

He froze. She had never asked him for anything when he would have given her the world. No matter, she didn't have the right now, the saner part of him argued back.

"Please, Azeez."

"You will hate me tomorrow for seeing you like this, *Nikhat.* You have never liked sharing your pain or grief," he said, remembering what a stoic little girl she had always been. It was that very strength that he had found endlessly fascinating.

But circumstances had forced her to become like that and she had never complained. He had watched her learn to cook and manage her sisters at a young age, ecstatically happy that she was being allowed to do the one thing she most wanted—to study by Amira's side. It had taken very little for her to be happy.

She sighed and hugged him tighter. Her chest grazed his, the soft push of her breasts against his muscles was more torture than he could take. His blood sang at the pleasure, but it was seeing her like this—pain-ridden and vulnerable—that tightened his gut.

"I won't, Azeez." He heard her sniffle. "The strange thing is, I could never hate you whatever you do or say. You…have this power over me. I've always considered myself a strong woman, I *am* a strong woman. But when it comes to you, I…" She exhaled, and burrowed closer to him.

Eviscerated by her admission, he chanced a look at her. She looked drowsy, her eyelids swollen. "Did you take any painkillers, Nikhat?"

"Hmm…" she whispered, blinking. "Yes. These just take longer to kick in. Will you stay with me?" Her lush mouth curved into a smile. "Can we also pretend that you don't hate me for a few hours?"

He closed his eyes and wrapped his arms around her. She was so soft all over, her fragility a complete contrast to the steely core of the woman.

He had never held a woman close like this, never offered comfort. Except with Nikhat, he had only ever wanted and taken only physical release from women.

"You make the most outrageous demands of your Prince, Dr. Zakhari," he said, holding her that way costing him. "But I will try."

She melted into him with a sigh. And the satisfaction in that sound, coupled with the way she held him, hard and unrelenting, sent ripples of powerful hunger through him. "I like it when you call me that, even as you shred me to pieces doing it."

He moved his fingers over her arm in a slow ripple. "I'm the one who paid the price for that degree, *ya habeebiti*. Of course it sounds special when I say it."

He felt her smile just before she gripped him hard again.

Her body writhed against his, her hand bunching over her lower belly, as though to fight that pain. She made a long, gasping sound with her throat and stiffened against him.

Ya Allah, what he wouldn't give to take that pain away from her. Clutching her tightly against him, Azeez held her hard. He couldn't tear his gaze away from her, couldn't uncouple himself from her pain, from her strength.

Just as he heard her breath even out, something inside him, something that he had no control over asked the question. "Nikhat, this condition you have, does it have a name?"

"Stage four endometriosis."

His mind latched onto the word, and Azeez knew it would never leave him alone.

Your Prince.

He had referred to himself as her prince. It had a very nice ring to it, Nikhat decided, snuggling languorously into the solid warmth of his body.

He was hers, the man who had promised to make every silly little dream of hers come true.

Against all odds, Azeez bin Rashid Al Sharif, the magnificent and breathtaking Crown Prince of Dahaar had somehow fallen in love with her. He had laughed all her doubts away when she had said she was not suited to be queen, he had forsaken all other women, the prince who had women throughout the world falling over him, for her, had promised her that he would always love her and keep her happy.

She would have to be the queen, of course. But with him by her side, Nikhat felt she could rule the whole universe, if that's what was required.

An echo of a dull ache spread through her lower belly, and suddenly all her dreams shattered into a million pieces around her. It was the bitterest kind of reality to wake up to, but it was her reality, her life.

Her happiness, she had realized, hadn't been in his power *or* hers.

Opening her eyes, she saw that she was coiled around Azeez like a vine. Delicious warmth spread under her skin. Licking her dry lips, she glanced at the bedside digital alarm clock. It was half past two. The bed lamp was still on.

She was lying on her left side, her legs tangled with Azeez's, her arm tight around his hips. She gasped as she realized how hard she was holding him, pressing her left hand into his damaged hip. She was about to jerk it back when he grasped her wrist and held it there. "That pressure feels good, *habeebi*."

She stilled, a thousand different voices clamoring to be heard inside her head. And yet, not a single one of them was even a token protest. She only felt exhilaration, only the utmost lethargy. Not shame, or disbelief or any such thing.

Azeez Al Sharif, even when he considered himself a cripple, was a perfect specimen of masculinity that would induce knee-jerking reaction in any woman. And the intimacy of waking up next to him like this was like a drug that filled her with inexplicable longing.

What she felt, coiled against him, was healthy, thrilling, one of the few things that validated her femininity. After the last day of pain that was a reminder of everything she was not, the warm languor in her muscles, the slow burn of desire, she welcomed it wholeheartedly.

He was hard against her and warm. He smelled the way he always did—of sandalwood and exquisite heat and dark, sinful promises. She sucked in a deep breath, savoring the scent of him. Against the onslaught of those sensations, the dull ache in her lower belly was almost negligible.

Feeling his gaze on her, she glanced up. His features looked strained, dark shadows under his eyes. Had he slept with his torso leaning against the headboard? She made to move, but his arm around her didn't budge. "I'm sorry. You must have been very uncomfortable."

He shrugged, his gaze devouring her with a quiet intensity that should have alarmed her. Instead, it swathed her with an electrifying thrill. "I don't remember the last time I slept through the night anyway. It was only a few hours. And every time, I tried to make myself more comfortable, you held on so tight that I was afraid to hurt you, or even worse, wake you up when it looked like you finally had some relief."

She felt color swamp her cheeks. "Thank you for staying with me. I have forgotten how awful it gets."

"And when you take these medications that you are waiting for?"

"It's quite different because they are pure hormones, they make my body..." She blinked, trying to backtrack slowly. "The pain is quite manageable coupled with regular exercise and deep breathing."

"All those trips you made in Dahaara and then overseas?"

She winced, remembering those trips with her father's sister. The despair that she would never find relief, it was the thing she remembered most. "I had already seen every doctor I could in Dahaar. None of them ever gave me a conclusive diagnosis. Just kept telling me it was normal, that I had to just cope with it.

"That pain...it would cripple me every month.

"My father—" she cleared her throat "—I used to get so angry with him. My mother was already gone when the pains started and he..." She felt the force of Azeez's anger and released hers. "He...couldn't talk about it with me, wouldn't even come near me. He was too traditional for that. But he didn't give up on me, either. He sent me to New York with a family friend. Someone recommended a...specialist there. She ran a lot of tests. And within a week, she recommended these drugs and other measures."

"This is why you became an ob-gyn?"

She nodded, glad to be able to share at least half the truth. "No one should have to go through this kind of pain for so many years. I want to bring more awareness to the condition. It's already a hard subject for a young girl to talk about. Then when someone does have the courage to speak up, she is told again and again to just live with it, that it is natural. Nothing about this pain is bearable."

His fingers tightened over her arms and she clasped them with hers. When he spoke, his voice was low, gravelly and full of pride. Her heart sang at it. "You will succeed, Nikhat. I have no doubt. Draw up a proposal. Vet out some experts in the field that would like to work in Dahaar. Think of every resource that you might need and put it on that proposal. You have my complete backing and my personal fortune at your disposal."

Tears prickled at the back of her eyes, and this time, she didn't stem them. They were not borne of pain or grief. Those first couple of years after she had left, being amongst strangers, thinking he was forever gone, she had lost her faith, doubted her ability to do what she had wanted.

The pride shining in his eyes felt like her true prize. He thought she was strong, but hadn't she always measured her words, her actions, through his eyes, his honor?

"And here I assumed you were an impoverished, deadbeat prince," she said, laughing through her tears. "I have to remember to be nice to you."

His mouth curved into a smile, the long sweep of his lashes mesmerizingly beautiful as his gaze widened. "Charming the prince for money? Very disappointing of you, Dr. Zakhari," he said with mock insult, and she laughed some more.

Giving in to the urge that beat at her relentlessly, she clasped his cheek. Traced his jawline with her thumb, the stubble on it rasping against her skin. She heard his breath hitch as she moved her finger to his mouth, saw the warning flash in his eyes, but she couldn't stop.

His upper lip had a perfect bow shape to it, while the lower one had an indulgent lushness.

She had wanted to touch him for so long, without shyness, without being consumed by her insecurities. Just for how good it made her feel, just for how right he felt. He clasped her wrist, halting her. "Nikhat? Do not—"

She jerked herself up to a sitting position, traced the seam of his lower lip. His breath hissed out, the cushion of his lip soft and warm against her finger.

Her own breath rushing out of her, she slanted her head and touched her mouth to his.

He became incredibly still. If not for the rough rumbling sound he made in his throat, she would have thought him a block of marble, a hot one. Anchoring her hands on his shoulders, she pressed little kisses along the seam of his lower lip, along every inch of his perfect, bow-shaped upper lip. His lips were soft and rough at the same time, sending sparks of heat careening to every tip of her body.

Impatient for more, she licked his lower lip when he exhaled a jagged breath, and then tugged it with her teeth.

And he exploded like a volcano that had finally reached its erupting point. His hands found her hips and pulled her toward him so hard that her breasts slammed against his chest, and she fell onto him sideways. His fingers crept into her hair, held her tightly as he devoured her mouth with his.

He had kissed her once all those years ago. She had been avoiding him, going out of her way to minimize seeing the dark and blindingly beautiful prince she had foolishly fallen in love with.

And one afternoon, he had cornered her in the library where Amira and she usually studied, locked the door behind him and kissed her.

It had lasted maybe be a few seconds before she had pushed him away, shaken and overwhelmed at the maelstrom of sensations it had stirred within her. If that had been a minor tremor in an earthquake, what he did to her today with his mouth was a hurricane.

The scent of him filled her breath, his muscles digging and shifting against her body.

He nibbled her lower lip with a growl that gave her goose bumps, and a lick of heat swept through her, waking up every nerve ending. With his tongue, he laved her, pushing for entrance, and she let him in with a moan.

He licked at the interior of her mouth, tangled with her tongue with such erotic intent that her breasts felt heavy, and a different kind of ache began in her lower belly. Their teeth clanged and scraped, their tongues tangled. She was awash in such sensations, such mind-bending delirium, that it took her a moment to realize he had ripped open her tunic in the front. Her nipples tightened into needy knots as his gaze, hot and erotic, fell on her breasts clad in a lacy black bra.

Her gaze flew to his, and held, a storm of desire gleaming in his. Never wavering from her, he moved his fingers to the seam of lace. The moment his fingers touched her flesh, everything inside Nikhat shuddered, gathered behind that contact, waiting for more.

Because, God, she wanted more.

Twin bands of color streaked his cheekbones, his breath sounding swift and harsh.

Anticipation coiled in every muscle, a feverish heat broke out on her skin.

His face taut with desire, he slowly set her away from him. Nikhat felt his retreat as sharply as if he had slapped her. "So I take it this…this sexual independence is another by-product of your relationship with your colleague?"

She laughed, hiding her unease at the swift change in conversation, and pulled the mass of her hair away from her neck and tied it up with her scarf. His gaze darkened, the stamp of lust on his face flooded her with utter satisfaction. He might hate her, but he desired her still. Even acknowledging that it was an utterly useless response, Nikhat reveled in it. "I am a doctor, and I am thirty years old, Azeez. I don't find anything shameful about sexual pleasure."

His fingers tightened over her arm, he dragged her until she hit the wall of his chest. The savage snarl of his mouth, instead of frightening her, thrilled her. "That's quite a shame, isn't it? Because eight years ago, I was on my knees, begging for a single kiss. I didn't touch another woman for two years because I wanted you."

Pushing away his resisting arms, she burrowed into his warmth. So many regrets and not a single one that she could explain. "You have no idea how much I regretted it."

"What did you regret?"

She looked up at him, knowing that, once again, she was going to disappoint him. "Not making love with you. There were so many nights that I dreamed you were next to me, kissing me, touching me, so many moments when I wished…" She moved out of his reach, bitterness swiftly adding a chill to the air. "And in the morning, I would see another article about you with a new woman. The Prince of Dahaar sowing his wild oats in Monaco, leaving every single party with a new woman. What had they called you, the insatiable prince?" But still, she hadn't been able to help herself, she hadn't been able to stop herself from dreaming about him.

He frowned, his gaze drilling into her. "You walked away. I offered you everything."

"So, of course, that means you can sleep with countless women, doesn't it?" The words slipped out on a wave of bitter jealousy that scoured through her. She had no right to ask these questions. There was no need to add more bitterness to this fire between them. But she couldn't stop. "Tell me, Azeez. Was it so easy to forget me, to wipe every thought of me from your mind, from your life?"

And the moment the words spilled out, she wanted to pull them back. Shivering at the slow dawning of anger in his eyes, she clasped her hand over his mouth.

He pulled her hand from his mouth slowly. "Afraid to hear the answer, *ya habeebiti*? Would you prefer it if I lie?"

There was no point in asking him to lie. Because he would not. The Prince of Dahaar never lied, not for his sake, not for hers.

"You think it was about hurting you, about proving that you were nothing to me?" His soft words landed on her like fiery lashes, burning into her skin.

"Every woman I slept with, I was only cheapening myself. Their faces faded one after the other, the pleasure I found with them transient and shameful...I would wake up in the middle of the night, tangled in bare limbs, sick to my stomach." The set of his mouth matching the blazing disgust in his eyes, he shuddered. "In my eyes, what you didn't want was worth nothing to me. I went on a rampage, wondering how I would fill the void, becoming reckless in pursuit of relief, raining down destruction on myself and..."

The shiver in his hands as he ran them through his hair, the utter loathing in his eyes, it was like a slap to Nikhat. How selfish and destructive was she to ask that question?

He slipped out of the bed and walked away. At the door, he turned back. "Let Princess Zohra know if you continue to be unwell. She should be able to arrange anything you need."

The silence of the suite bore down upon her as Azeez closed the door behind him. Nikhat pulled the sheets toward herself and they bore the scent of him. She clutched it to herself.

What you didn't want was worth nothing to me.

Those words lanced through her, leaving invisible, permanent marks on her. She had asked for it and he had given it to her, shredding the last thread of lies she had held on to all these years.

Telling herself that he had instantly cast her out of his mind after she left Dahaar, reading about his exploits almost greedily during that first year, she had found a kind of solace in the fact that he had moved on, fooled herself that she had been nothing but a novelty at a distance.

All of them delusions she had set in place to protect herself.

Now his words left her nothing to hide behind.

He had loved her, by his own confession, he had plunged himself into a reckless lifestyle to fill the void she had left... She hugged her knees, the pain of her body paling in comparison to the pain his words had unleashed.

Guilt tightened like an iron chain around her throat, choking her.

Staying here after learning that he was alive—what had she been thinking? How had she forgotten what it had cost her last time to walk away? How had she forgotten how strong this pull between them was?

Throwing the existence of her relationship, even a failed one, in his face, challenging him with her presence every step of the way, giving in to the urge to kiss him, to touch him, playing with his emotions and her own, there was no excuse for her behavior. When had she become so reckless as to tempt fate again, so selfish as to satisfy her own twisted sense of self?

She needed to remember why she was here, and what Azeez had already been through.

Learning that she might never conceive, accepting her inability to be the woman he needed her to be had wrecked her. For months, she had thought herself less than a woman, her entire identity as a woman fracturing because she might not be able to give the man she loved the heirs he needed. And in the end, her love for him had asked for a sacrifice of her own happiness.

She had, somehow, survived through it and built a life for herself. She couldn't risk all that again.

CHAPTER SEVEN

A WEEK LATER, Nikhat arrived at the breakfast hall in the morning, and came to a halt, her heart thudding.

Azeez and Ayaan stood on either side of the table, their hands fisted, their expressions similarly battling fury and more. Princess Zohra was standing by Ayaan's side, her gaze flitting between the brothers.

A needle dropped into the room would have sounded like an explosion.

Nikhat's gaze invariably went to Azeez. And first thing that came to her mind was how good he looked even as his face was currently wreathed in tension.

He wore a snowy-white cotton tunic that was open to his chest, the startling white of the fabric contrasting against his sunburned throat and face. His jaw shaved, the unhealthy pallor that had been there when she had first arrived was gone.

And his jet-black eyes had the biggest difference.

With each passing day, the arrogance, the confidence that had made him, came back.

Heat swamped her, but she couldn't look away before stealing a look at that sensuous mouth. It had been just a kiss.

But it had started a fire in her that couldn't be quenched, whatever she did. Not that there had been a hint of interest from him again.

His withdrawal was so absolute that there was no need for her to worry that she would weaken again. Not when he looked at her as if she was the plague he was determined to avoid. There were no more cutting remarks, no allusions to past or present, nothing but a polite, entirely painful, coldness.

Taking a deep breath, she looked around the room, the tension in it sinking heavily into her shoulders. "Is something wrong?"

Nerves at breaking point, Azeez turned toward Nikhat and was instantly assaulted by the taste of her mouth, her soft curves that had fit so perfectly against his. Desire slumbered in his blood, a constant companion that mocked him.

This seesaw of emotions every time he looked at her was the last thing he needed in his life right now. He had to get away from the palace, from her, from his brother. He had to do something useful or go crazy.

"I proposed a trip to the desert and my brother is threatening to lock me up and throw away the key."

She paled, her angular features even more stark. Dark circles hung under her bright eyes. For once, he didn't feel the sadistic pleasure that she wasn't handling this any better than him. "Why?"

"Because, as you are well aware, I'm going mad sitting here doing nothing."

"I have to run this country, Azeez. I don't have time to come looking for you nor an answer for Mother if you disappear again. You can't do this to her again."

Azeez flinched, even as he deserved his words. How did he explain to his brother how useless he felt here, even as every single palace matter around him seeped into his blood? His mind, not drenched by alcohol, and his body making slow progress toward less pain, he needed to get out.

He chose his words carefully, the very idea that had come to him this morning filling him with renewed energy. But he didn't want his brother to latch onto it and use it as weapon to bind Azeez to Dahaar permanently.

"Khaleef said there have been problems with communications to the Sheikh of Zuran."

Just as he expected, a light came on in Ayaan's eyes. "I think Khaleef needs a lesson in protocol, and a reminder about who the Crown Prince of Dahaar is now."

"I'm still the bloody Prince of—" Azeez gripped the back of his chair, fighting the urge to knock off that knowing smile from his brother's lips. A lifetime of duty and privilege in his blood was hard to get rid of. "Is it true or not?"

"Yes," Ayaan said, moving to the window. "I persuaded the Sheikh Asad to sign a treaty four months ago, along with Zohra's father, about better protection along the borders for all three nations. Now he's not responding, nor is the High Council of Zuran." Ayaan ran a hand along his nape. "I don't like the silence on their side."

"That's why it's imperative that I go."

"I don't understand."

His brother had truly become everything he needed to be king. Azeez knew Ayaan was only acting ignorant to force him to put the proposal into words. But anything was better than being stuck here, visiting the past in a relentless loop. "I have contacts, Ayaan. How do you think I gathered the information that I fed you before you brought me here? I can have them dig out information on what's going on in Zuran for you. Sheikh Asad was always a thorn in father's side, too."

The silence that met his statement was more deafening than an explosion. And it pulled his already stretched patience thin.

The restlessness inside him grated at him. He had never in his life been without purpose like this. And he had to find one, first a temporary one and then a permanent one.

"I don't know that you're physically up to—"

"Of course I am. I survived without you or your doctors for six years. I came back from a wound that tore my hip apart. I remained sane as blood left my body remembering Amira's face and yours." Azeez held his brother's gaze, hating him in that moment.

"This is the one thing where I can do something to help, instead of being trapped here in this palace," he said through gritted teeth, willing his brother to understand him. "I'll never be anything but a prisoner inside these walls, Ayaan. When will you see that?"

A tightness inched into his face as Ayaan studied him. "Fine," he finally said, his mouth compressed into a thin line. "Nikhat will accompany you then."

"No."

The denial, spat out at the same time by Nikhat and he, reverberated around the vast hall.

Both Ayaan and Zohra cast them looks, confusion and concern ringing in their gazes. "No choice for either of you," Ayaan announced.

Azeez clicked his jaw shut, fighting for control over his temper. "Fine." He turned toward Nikhat. "We leave at dawn tomorrow morning."

Nikhat shivered as Azeez moved past her, and the heat from his body beckoned her. But she couldn't let him pass without doing her duty, without asking the question that she needed to. She clasped his wrist just as he turned. "You missed your sessions two days in a row."

His fingers landed on hers before she could blink, his mouth bared in a snarl. But whatever he had thought never came out. "No. I didn't. I just took Khaleef with me," he whispered in a low voice that pinged over her bare nape.

But his unguarded expression told her everything he didn't say. He had been getting increasingly short-tempered and restless these past few days, as though struggling against invisible chains.

And just like that the pieces clicked into place. She loosened her grip on him, and he left.

She had heard the quiet whispers among the older servants about the charity function tomorrow, the annual presentation for the educational trust that was set up in her name...

How had she forgotten?

She had looked at her calendar as she always did, this morning, too, without a second's thought.

"Would you like to explain, Nikhat?"

Nikhat braced herself and turned to face Ayaan. "There's nothing to exp—" It was the first time she saw real fury in his copper-colored gaze.

"What in God's name did my brother mean about always being a prisoner?"

She could just tell him it was nothing or she could tell him the truth and hope he would begin to understand. Because it was never going to be easy to accept. Thinking Azeez had been dead was one thing. Knowing he was alive somewhere in the world, but away from Dahaar, would be a special kind of torture. On every one of them. "He needs a breather, Ayaan. From you, from the palace, from everything that's been going on."

Princess Zohra bristled next to Ayaan. "He's the one who's—"

Nikhat met the princess's gaze full on. "You do not know what he suffers, Princess. Believe me, none of us do." Only after the words were out did she realize how defiant she sounded.

Ayaan leveled a thoughtful look at her. "Say what's on your mind, Nikhat. Without hesitation."

"It's Amira's birthday tomorrow."

Ayaan looked as if she had struck him. Zohra's hand found his and tightened. That's what Azeez needed too. And despite her resolve to keep everything utterly professional between them, Nikhat realized she couldn't leave Azeez alone. Not tomorrow, of all days.

"He..." She ran a shaking hand over her face, struggling to find the words. "He's suffering, Ayaan, in the palace. He's trying, for your sake, but—"

Ayaan shook his head, refusing to let her finish. "You promised me, Nikhat. You gave me your word—"

"Yes, to help *him*," she burst out.

She held his gaze, saw the threat that rose to his lips.

Fear rattled inside her. She was antagonizing the future King, the man who could crash her dreams in Dahaar with one word. And for all his kindness, she had no doubt Ayaan would do *anything* to keep his brother close.

But even with her future hanging in the balance, she couldn't back down from her promise to Azeez. She took a deep breath, wondering why she even put up a fight with herself. Nothing was ever simple, ever free of emotions when it came to Azeez Al Sharif. "I'm sorry I didn't make this clear sooner. But Azeez will always have my loyalty first."

"Then you seal your fate along with his."

"It would seem so." Nikhat nodded at him and Princess Zohra and left the hall with her head held high.

He was creeping through his own palace like a thief of the night, but he had left himself no choice. Behind him, the deserted corridor was bathed in yellow light from the lamps. He chanced a look at the courtyard, and the utter silence in there, in this whole wing, jeered him.

Azeez leaned his head against the closed door and struggled to get air into his lungs. He couldn't hide forever from this. He nodded at Khaleef to open the door, and another figure appeared in the corridor and joined him.

Instead of recoiling, as everything inside him was wont to do, he let Nikhat lace her fingers with his. He didn't question how she knew that he was standing outside Amira's door at the first light of dawn, or how terrified he was of facing this day.

The palace was not the same without his sister's laughter. But he had to apologize to her and he wanted to do it here, in her suite where she had laughed and cried, where she had lived such a vibrant life before his recklessness had shortened it.

He pushed the door and stepped in. The scent of Amira as he remembered—roses and something sweet—hit him in the gut. His knees buckled and tears clogged his throat, and he let them fall.

As Nikhat turned on the light, he walked around the huge chamber where everything had been left as it was before her death. Her jewelry lay haphazardly on the dark dresser, her nightstand overflowing with novels.

How he wished he could change his reckless behavior all those years ago, how he wished he had realized sooner that Amira and Ayaan had stayed back to confront him that night in the desert, how he wished he had taken the bullet that had claimed her life...

Her arm clamped around his middle, Nikhat hugged him tightly. And for once, he couldn't find it in him to push her or the comfort she offered away. They stood like that for several minutes, drowning in memories but anchoring each other.

"Do you remember the time you complained that your prized bottle of single-malt whiskey had disappeared?"

Frowning, he nodded.

"You raised hell about it, turned the palace upside down. For so many days, I remember seeing the palace staff whispering, scared to tell you that they hadn't found it. It was like martial law had been declared in the palace."

He turned toward her. "What are you talking about, Nikhat?"

"Amira paid one of the maids to steal it." She made a choking noise with her throat and stepped back as he advanced on her. Her hands up in front of her, her head shaking, her mouth wreathed in smiles.

It made her face light up, reminding him of a carefree time. "I saved it for so long, I..."

"I begged her not to, Azeez. It was the vilest thing I ever tasted in my life. I mean, after the first few sips, I couldn't even stomach it. I told her we should return it, but by that time you had guards outside your wing like the crown jewels were lost. We had to pour the stuff down the toilet and I smuggled the bottle out of the—"

His mouth fell open. "That was eighteenth-century whiskey that my father gave me." He suddenly remembered something else. "She was sick that next day. Did she—?"

Nikhat was openly laughing now. "She had a whole glass of it, and she called me a coward."

That sounded very much like his sister, always getting into trouble, always trying to find new ways to defy their mother's rules.

"She was so drunk, Azeez. You should have seen her. She used to mimic you...you know, the way you walked and talked, the way you would blush every time you saw Queen Fatima's friend's daughter. She was hilarious that night. I always wished I had been more like her. So full of life, treating every day as if it was an adventure.

"Her life might have been short, but she lived it to the full. Amira had been so happy that she was going to marry the man she loved, she couldn't stop smiling. And you, you had made it all possible, Azeez."

And then he had led her to her death before it had come true.

She put her arm around his. "She was so angry with me when I left that she refused to see me when I came to say goodbye. I miss her so much, Azeez."

Nodding, Azeez pulled Nikhat close, the grief inside him tempering in that moment. "Thank you for bringing back fond memories for me."

Her hand moved over his back, her breasts pressed into his side and suddenly, an uncontrollable hunger swamped his insides. With measured movements, he pulled her out of Amira's suite and closed the door behind him.

Her hand still in his, Nikhat looked up at him. And he studied her greedily.

Her long lashes cast shadows on her cheekbones. The little light from the wall lamps bathed her mouth in golden light. And sinking under the quagmire of grief, he took the only way out.

He pushed her against the wall and took her mouth. She tasted like honey, and it went straight to all the broken places inside him, all the places that hurt for what he had done, all the places he was killing to survive another day.

He pushed his tongue into her mouth, pressed his lower body into hers until she felt his arousal, until the imprint of her soft body was all over his.

Her hands stole under his T-shirt. Her palms were against his body and, breathing hard, he pulled back. Need pinged inside him, a sharp slice of awareness running through his blood, jolting him awake as nothing had for six years.

Her eyes were hazy with desire, her mouth swollen with his kisses. He wanted to take her right there, he wanted to forget. For one blessed moment, he wanted escape. And he would find it in her body, he knew it in his bones.

The attraction between them had only intensified with time, because now she was truly magnificent, both in mind and body.

He took a step back. "Leave, Nikhat, before I—"

She slapped her hand on his mouth, shaking her head. Her eyes were bright, the pulse at her neck throbbing, as if calling for his touch. A smile danced on her lips, of understanding, of comfort. "Please don't say another word."

With shadows covering half her face and revealing the other half, she was temptation and retribution come together. This woman and his desire for her, it seemed, were very much still an uncontrollable aspect of his life. And it robbed the sweet taste of her from his mouth.

She would save him and she would damn him.

"How far will you go to alleviate the guilt?"

She flinched. And yet he couldn't stop. He didn't want to hurt her. He just wanted her to stop acting as if she cared.

"I have not been just to you. Everything I did, everything I caused, they were my actions, *Nikhat*. I could fall lower and hold you responsible, but the fact is that I did it all. I don't want your guilt or your reparation."

"Wait," she said, halting him with her fingers on his wrist. There was a resolve to her mouth that he remembered so well. "Maybe some of it is guilt, maybe some of it is a misplaced sense of responsibility.

"But whatever the past, Azeez, we're in this together

now. Whether you believe it or not, whether you want it or not, you have my loyalty above everyone else, and you have my friendship."

Nikhat rubbed her eyes, jolting awake as the helicopter landed. From her seat, all she could see was a specter of light behind her, illuminating the vast dunes of sand in front of her. In the twilight, the dunes looked like a sea of glistening reddish-gold, stark and yet beautiful.

She turned in place, taking in the beautiful landscape, and stilled. A resort stood about half a mile ahead of them, a fluorescent white glow lighting it up like a mythical fortress against the darkening sky. She thought she knew everything about the royal family. But she hadn't even heard a whisper that this place existed, and she wondered if the outside world had, either.

Thankful to Azeez for reminding her to wear a jacket, she extracted a scarf from her handbag. She stood to the side as he had a word with the pilot and then the chopper left.

Only then did she make out the dark shape of a four-by-four with the old bodyguard that she remembered, Khaleef, at the wheel.

She wrapped the scarf snug around her face just as Azeez motioned for them to walk toward the resort. A gasp fell from her lips as lights came on in front of them, illuminating a wooden bridge that resembled an old drawbridge from ancient times.

Laughing, she ran a couple of steps and stepped onto the bridge. Small lights placed along either side turned on, causing tall shadows to fall from the date trees. With turreted domes and shadowed arches in front of her, she felt as if she had stepped into the pages of a book she had read when she was a child.

And the prince…

She turned around to find Azeez standing still at the first step, his coal-black gaze resting on her. She let the magical quality of the dusky evening seep into her.

Deciding that she wanted to help Azeez, not because her own future was dependent on it, not because her guilt demanded it, but because it would give her satisfaction, but because she cared what happened to him, was a relief. She felt as if a weight had lifted from her heart.

She was not going to weave impossible dreams, neither was she going to lie that they didn't mean anything to each other.

"A bridge, really?" she said, holding on to the humor she had found in it just seconds ago.

She glanced at the fortlike structure, the exquisitely maintained lawn in front of it with a fountain and the strategically placed lights.

"No one knows this place exists, do they?"

Resuming his slow tread, he shook her head. "Only us and a handful of servants."

"And I'm not allowed to tell anyone that I have seen it."

He reached her, and again she felt his gaze like a physical caress on her features. "No one will believe you." Said with a simple smile.

She extended her arm and he looped it around his without comment. Drawing in a deep breath, they walked ahead. Every now and then, she felt him studying her. She slowed her stride to match his, the tang of sandalwood and his skin combined, brushing up against her senses every time their bodies grazed ever so lightly.

"Going away on a trip with me to an unknown destination without Ayaan's protection or the buffer that the palace offers doesn't bother you?"

"No."

"And if I leave you here and disappear, as my brother fears?"

"I know you're hurting, and you can't see past your grief and guilt, but I know you, Azeez, probably better than anyone else. You won't leave until Ayaan himself permits you to go."

He didn't jeer, or call it misplaced confidence. His fingers tightened over her arm and Nikhat returned the pressure.

Had they finally achieved some kind of peace with each other?

She was more than reluctant to go inside as they reached the walkway that led to the foyer of the palace, when an echo of laughter and conversation reached her.

The high voices sounded familiar and yet...

Tensing, she clasped Azeez's hand and moved to stand behind him. "I thought we were supposed to be the only ones here."

Tugging at the hand that she had laid around him, Azeez met her gaze. "Go in." He ran a finger over her cheek. He inclined his head toward the palace. "Everything you require should be inside."

Suddenly, she didn't want to bid him goodbye just yet. "I would like to come with you. Wherever you're going, I'm sure I can be of help."

He shook his head, a small smile digging grooves in his cheeks. She locked her hands at her sides when all she wanted was to trace those grooves.

Was it so wrong if she did? The attraction between them was as strong as it had ever been. Why deny them both what they wanted?

"Nikhat?"

Heat suffusing her skin, she met his gaze.

"I need to be stealthy. And you, with your big eyes and

your modern attitudes, you will be hard to blend in. I will
return in two days. In the meantime, enjoy your stay."

Nikhat nodded as he left. Before she could utter another
word, she heard her name behind her. Stunned, she turned
and saw a woman of around twenty run down the stairs.
Her heart crawled into her throat, her chest felt hollow,
her head dizzy as the woman's long legs ate up the stairs.

Before she could draw another breath, Nikhat was enveloped in two pairs of arms, laughter and surprise rolling around her. Grabbing Noor and Noozat, her youngest
sisters, she looked up and saw Naima, who was four years
younger than her and closest to her in temperament.

Joy and excitement and shock and gratitude—everything
barreled through her, robbing her of speech.

Tears fell onto her cheeks and Naima's gaze met hers,
shining with her own. Nodding and sometimes replying
with a yes or no, Nikhat hugged her sisters, her heart incredibly tight in her chest.

Between Noor's questions about her return, and Naima's silent speculation, Nikhat turned around, hungry for
a glance of Azeez. But he was already gone from the bridge
and then she heard the squeal of tires. Wiping at her cheeks,
Nikhat followed her sisters inside, her heart bursting to
full with gratitude and something more that terrified the
life out of her.

She wanted to crumple to the floor and howl. Because
she was being tested again.

A rush of self-pity drenched her and for once she had
no strength to fight it with. She didn't want any reminders
of his kindness, she didn't want to remember how mag-
nificently glorious it felt when his gaze was on her, of how
effortlessly he could reduce her whole world to himself.

She had already begun to see flashes of the man he had

once been and she couldn't fight her attraction anymore. He was magnificent, he was kind and he was honorable.

How many times was she supposed to walk away without taking anything she wanted? How many times would she have to break her own heart into tiny little pieces?

She had trained herself to find satisfaction in her work and she did. She pushed herself every day to strive harder and to set new goals. She had made a life for herself. And yet, being in Dahaar brought out a loneliness she was too exhausted to see in New York. It settled deep into her bones.

And it was because of him.

She knew that. Despite every assurance she threw at herself that this time she was prepared, that she had walked away once, she still felt herself wavering, weakening and wishing for things that never could be.

CHAPTER EIGHT

REFUSING THE INVITATION to stay another night, Azeez turned just as one of his contacts stepped into the perimeter of the encampment and nodded at him.

He had visited two different camps in the last twenty-four hours across a hundred miles, trying to locate him. Glad that Nikhat wouldn't be lonely and wondering about him, because she would had her sisters not been there, he took his leave from the chief of the Mijab.

The older man clasped both his hands, his gaze dancing with a million questions.

"You'll always have a place with us," he said in an older dialect of Arabic that the bedouins had used and that his father had insisted he learn. The chief had recognized Azeez within a week of finding him in the desert, and he would always be grateful to the older man for keeping his secret.

Azeez shook his head, knowing that now he couldn't bear to live in the desert anymore. He thanked the chief for his hospitality for the past day and joined his contact.

His heart thumped loudly in his chest as he walked a mile off the beaten path where another man, a native of Zuran was waiting for him. Fierce satisfaction fueled him. The network of contacts he had built over the years was still intact, and something almost like a thrill chased his blood.

But this time it wasn't just the fiercely alive feeling that had kept him going for six years. This time it was coupled with the fact that he could go back to Ayaan and give him some much-needed information.

Signaling his contact to stay behind, Azeez slowly made his way to the small group gathered outside a tent. One man stood up from the group and walked inside as soon as he spied him. Checking that the pistol he had strapped to his left leg was still intact, Azeez stepped inside the tent.

Shock waves pulsed through him as the man turned around, and the feeble light from the two hanging lanterns illuminated his features in a garish yellow glow.

His own features wreathed in mirroring shock, Zayed Al Salaam, his oldest friend, stared back at him. "*Inshallah*, it *is* you."

Dressed in combat uniform, his face half covered in sand and mud, his dark golden eyes gleaming in the half light, Zayed covered the distance between them in two steps and embraced Azeez hard. "Of all the things to crawl out from under the desert sand...*Azeez Al Sharif...*" Zayed said, his voice harsh and yet unable to hide the tremor within. A spark of anger colored his gaze as Zayed studied Azeez with undisguised intensity. "I would have given anything to have the aid of an old friend these past years, Azeez."

Azeez closed his eyes as a cold sweat seized his insides. His breath fisted in his throat, cutting off his words.

Would there be no end to the faces that greeted him from the past? Would he never be rid of the unrelenting guilt?

He had done everything he could to bring Zayed and his sister, Amira, together, and done it so covertly that even his parents and Ayaan hadn't known. He had made it look like a treaty agreement to Zayed's uncle, Sheikh Asad, who had used Zuran and its people as pawns in his pursuit of power. Azeez had convinced his parents that marrying Zayed, the army commander of Zuran, was better for Amira than marrying Sheikh Asad's spoiled, degenerate son.

Just because Amira had begged him to help, just because, flouting every convention, his rebellious sister had fallen in love with Zayed. And Zayed with her.

And yet, he had killed her two months before her wedding to Zayed.

Had he, in a way, killed Zayed too?

"There was nothing I could do for anyone, Zayed. I was—"

Zayed shook his head. "I do not believe that. I do not believe that Azeez Al Sharif could become so heartless that he didn't even have a word for his oldest friend who had lost the woman he loved, that he had to hide himself from the world.

"I heard rumors about a man who collected information for Dahaar," Zayed spoke again, more than a hint of distrust creeping into his words now, "about a man who appeared with the Mijab suddenly six years ago...but then I thought why would a man born to rule his country hide like a coward in the shadows? Why would he forsake his parents, his friends and everyone else who needed him?"

"Zayed, you have no idea—"

"I do not, Azeez. But that is the way you wanted it, isn't it?"

The hardness in Zayed's eyes, the savagery in the tightness of his mouth, the undiluted arrogance in his words pierced through Azeez. And suddenly, he realized how much Zayed must have suffered losing Amira in such a way; Zayed, who had been captivated by her boldness and laughter; Zayed, who had never known any love or kindness.

Hardening his heart, Azeez infused steel into his voice. He was not here to reminisce with an old friend. "This from a man who pretends ignorance while his uncle wreaks havoc on the nation that he's pledged to protect, the man who should have been the rightful ruler of Zuran?"

"Not anymore, Azeez. How fortunate that I won't let an old friend return empty-handed." A dark smile crept into Zayed's eyes, any hint of the kindhearted man Azeez had known gone long ago. "Tell your Crown Prince or whoever you serve that Zuran is done being Dahaar's puppet.

"You're speaking to the new high sheikh of Zuran."

Renewed shock pulsed through Azeez. "Your uncle…"

"Has been killed by my men." A chill climbed up Azeez's spine. It was like looking at a reflection of what he had been a few months ago. And he didn't like it.

"Weren't you the one who always talked about our debt to our land, Azeez? Personal loss might have dimmed your sense of duty, whereas I have found mine only after it."

Without waiting for Azeez's response, Zayed walked out of the tent.

After waiting for a few minutes, Azeez walked out, too. Whatever the politics between Dahaar and Zuran, Zayed would never betray him.

But having seen his friend, having heard the threat in his words, Azeez was filled with renewed purpose.

There had been a coup in Zuran, which meant every small tidbit of information he could gather would be precious to Ayaan.

The chain of his guilt relenting, Azeez walked back to where his contact was waiting. He gave instructions to the man. He would need another couple of days in the desert.

He shivered as the chilly wind howled through him. The horizon stretched ahead of him in endless golden sand dunes.

He had loved the unforgiving heat, the harsh, stark landscape of the desert for as long as he could remember.

Even after he had recovered and realized he couldn't go back to Dahaar, the desert had soothed him, provided an escape from the constant guilt and shame inside him, the harsh life of traveling with the Mijab forcing him to focus on mere survival.

His mistakes, his guilt, his yearning to be close to his family, they had all been minimized. *He* had been minimized by the brutality of desert life. That's why he had clung to it for so long, that's how he had gone on living.

Could he accept never coming back here again? Could he wrench away a part of him and leave it in Dahaar when it was time to leave?

For the first time since Ayaan had captured him and dragged him to the palace against his will, the answer to his own questions wasn't absolute.

Neither could he dismiss the woman who had, just by her sheer dogged determination, breathed new will into his life.

Walking around the pool that was built in the shape of a drop of water pulled along in every direction, a gleaming blue between a maze of tall trees and walkways, Nikhat smiled, remembering every last word her sisters and she had said to each other over the past three days.

As the sun had set, small lights along the perimeter of the pool had come on, making the entire courtyard look like a jeweled necklace. The view of it from the terrace was magnificent, as if a slice of paradise had been brought to life in the middle of the desert. The contrast against the starkness of the desert dunes was lush, wondrous.

They had talked and talked until they had all been exhausted. They had laughed, cried, spent both nights, well into dawn, sitting by the pool, talking about their mother, father and so many things about the future, both near and afar.

Like Naima's upcoming wedding that Nikhat was going to miss, to Noozat's aspirations to be a midwife.

And Noor's relentless questions about the desert hideaway they had been brought to under a cloud of silence, and her awe that the royal family had done such a personal favor for Nikhat.

She had cried when it had been time to go this morning, as Noozat had railed against the situation that kept Nikhat away, while Naima had watched it all silently.

Their innocence about the world, the contentment she had seen in their eyes for their lives, fueled her own resentment in a way she had never expected, filling her with a restless energy.

She had never been like that, innocent or carefree or just plain happy.

She had always worried about her mother's health, worried about her sisters, worried about what trouble Amira would get into, worried about whether she would be allowed to pursue her dream and for how long. Despite her growing attachment to Azeez and the shock of his love for her, through it all, she had worried what the future would hold for her.

But in the end, her worrying, her cautious nature, had never helped her.

Until Richard had pursued her relentlessly for three years, she had let herself consider happiness again. She had revealed her condition, believed him when he said that he would be happy only with her. And yet, for all her worrying, his rejection had come, because suddenly he had realized he did want children, and she had been heartbroken.

Wasn't that what she had been doing since she had returned, too?

Worrying about her clinic, worrying about her sisters,

worrying about the pulse of attraction between her and Azeez...

For the first time in her life, she didn't want to think of the future, or the consequences of the decisions she made today. She didn't want to be the responsible one. She wanted to be selfish, she wanted to be carefree.

She wanted to live in the moment. She was in the most beautiful place she had ever seen with the one man who had always ensnared her senses with one look, one touch.

And still did.

Her fingers fluttering, she ran them over her mouth, remembering his kiss, remembering the pleasure she found in her own body, the power that had flown through her when he had shuddered.

The palm trees swayed stiffly in the breeze. Dusk painted the horizon orange, casting a reddish-golden glow over everything around her. And suddenly the evening was awash with possibilities, as though for this night, she could be anything she wanted.

She had wanted to be worthy of Azeez Al Sharif, the magnificent Prince of Dahaar. And she had accepted that she never would be.

But tonight, she would be everything that *she* wanted to be.

A few hours later, Nikhat waited in the moonlit courtyard, standing out among the lit-up walkways.

Lamb curry and pilaf, date cakes and sherbet made of the finest grapes—a feast fit for a prince—had been prepared at her command. She didn't care what the servants inside that bustling kitchen thought of her. Only focused on the little tidbit that she and her sisters were the only outsiders to have ever stepped foot in here.

Her heavy hair hung loose around her face, her lips

painted pink, her eyes lined with kohl. And she was dressed in a caftan made of the brightest red, made of the sheerest silk, that she had begged Naima to lend her. A cashmere shawl lay around her shoulders to shield her from the cold.

She couldn't believe her own daring in inviting the prince to dinner so boldly. But she was past caring about her reputation, past suffering through punishments without actually committing the deed.

She refused to even indulge the prospect that he was somewhere laughing that she dared summon him.

She had waited maybe ten or fifteen minutes, when her skin prickled with awareness, when it felt as if even the air around her had come to a standstill.

Leaning against a pillar at the arched entrance, Azeez was watching her. Dressed in those same loose white pants and a white tunic, he looked like a dark shadow come to life, the expression in his coal-black eyes just as inscrutable.

He scanned her slowly from her feet in cream-colored sandals, upward to where she had cinched the caftan just below her breasts with a wide, jeweled belt, to the V-shaped neckline, threaded with intricate threadwork that was just a little shy of daring, to her mouth, her nose, her eyes and then her hair. Everywhere his gaze moved, she felt touched, she felt branded, she felt possessed.

Black fire blazed into life in those eyes that didn't miss anything. He took a step toward her, to touching distance. "You look different." Another devouring, lingering glance. "You dressed up." He cast a look behind her and took in the elaborate lengths she had gone to. "Are you celebrating something?"

"Thank you for bringing my sisters here. I…"

"I understand perfectly." He smiled, a flash of raw emotion tingeing it. He looked different, as if there was simmering energy inside him. It lit a fire along her nerves, every cell in her wanting more. "Thank you for being here, Nikhat, today and three days ago and these past weeks. I don't begrudge you your success or your happiness or whatever it is that you desire."

"You mean that."

He laughed at the obvious doubt in her tone. "I do."

His smile bared his teeth, lit up his face, and the beauty of it stole her breath. His eyes, his mouth, they had been made for laughter. And seeing him like that, it was easy to believe his goodwill. "Was your little jaunt into the desert successful then?"

"Yes." A fire erupted in his eyes. With that single word, for the first time since she had come back, she believed that the true Azeez was coming back.

She covered the little distance that separated them. Their bodies grazed, their knees bumped and a tightness rendered his features stark. And she recognized the tension in his face for what it was, reveled in the spiral of hunger that ignited in her muscles.

Giving in, she touched him.

It was the lightest of contacts—the pad of her thumb rubbing against his cheek, the heat of his body a beckoning caress. The stubble scraped her palm, the scent of his skin and soap combined tugging at her senses.

His hand moved around her nape, and with sure but infinitesimal strength, he pressed. And every particle of her being gathered behind that small patch of her skin. "You're playing with fire, Nikhat." His hand moved to her hip, his fingers branding her skin through the silk. Another thread of her control unraveled.

"I can't stop, Azeez."

His palm landed square below her chest, and her heart began a race. "Do not test the breadth of my goodwill, *habeeba.* I worked very hard to achieve it. If you tempt me today, if you tease me today, I won't walk away."

She smiled and, anchoring herself against his arms, pushed herself into his touch. The sharp hiss of his breath felt like music to her ears. "Then don't. Make love to me, Azeez."

His jaw tightened like carved stone even as a dark fire glittered in his eyes. He was more than tempted and it fueled her own desire and satisfaction. "I think seeing your sisters has twisted your mind."

She clasped his jaw with her hands. "On the contrary, visiting with them only helped me see clearly. I want this. I have always wanted this. Only, eight years ago, I never understood this fire between us."

His mouth took on a bitter slant as he tugged her hands away from her. "Is this gratitude for ordering your father to send your sisters? Because I would have done the same for any loyal servant of the palace. A simple thanks is enough for that."

Hearing him put it in that stark way, it still didn't douse the fire in her. He was creating distance between them, letting her down in the only way he knew.

But he had no idea how much she had deprived herself of, how bereft her life had been of this compelling awareness she found near him. "You're the man I've always wanted beyond reason and sense. What Richard and I had—"

He cursed so colorfully that Nikhat forgot what she was saying for a minute. "Don't manipulate me, Nikhat. I don't want to hear his name."

"Our relationship was based on mutual respect and suitability. What I feel near you, I've never felt like that, ever."

"Why now, when you threw everything I offered you before at my face and went off to pursue your dreams?"

Leaning into his body, she bent her forehead to his shoulder, the truth dancing on her lips. How could she tell him that she had never stopped wanting him? That it had never been the case of not wanting him enough. "This is not me trying to revert or start something new. This is me living in the moment."

Before her courage deserted her, before she remembered the thousand reasons this was unwise, she pulled his arm around her waist and did what she had been dying to do since she saw him, did what she had dreamed of a million times and more.

She leaned into him, until her breasts were crushed against his chest, until his groin cradled hers. Until she felt the evidence of his arousal—hard against the V of her own legs.

Air left her lungs on a long whoosh, her muscles liquefying with uncontrollable shaking. The shudder that went through him goaded her beyond reason. She pressed her mouth to his jaw, the stubble on his jaw rasping her lips in the most delicious way. "Tonight, you're not the prince who's bent upon walking away from the very thing you were born for, and I...I'm not the woman who walked away from you. For one night, will you not grant us both what we want, Azeez?"

Her pulse ringing like an incessant bell in every inch of her body, Nikhat slipped away from him and left the courtyard.

CHAPTER NINE

ONE NIGHT, AZEEZ.

Azeez stood outside Nikhat's suite, her words ringing in an endless loop in his head, traveling through his blood, moving inside him with the force of a lightning bolt.

Her proposal coming on the heels of the high he had found in uncovering information, in realizing that there was still a salvageable part of him, that he could still be of some use to his brother and Dahaar, was temptation he couldn't deny.

Standing there with her kohl-rimmed eyes staring at him with the brazen need dancing in her eyes made him feel fiercely alive, made him want to ride the wave, accept the escape she offered.

For one night, she would be his.

He pushed the door and stepped in, his gaze hungrily searching for her. She lay on the bed, her face bathed in a golden light from the bed lamp. The sheets rustled as he ventured farther in, and she rose to her knees in the middle of the vast bed, her gaze glittering with a bright hunger.

Lust and something else hit him hard in the gut, little shivers sprouting everywhere, causing tremors in his muscles.

A dazzling smile, edged with anticipation, thrill and even a flash of trepidation curved her mouth. "You came."

He felt his mouth twist into a bitter curve. "Did you doubt it?"

Her eyes closed for a second, as if she wanted to shield something from him. And he realized that she was as conflicted about this as he was, just in a different way. She had asked for this night with that characteristic bluntness that he had begun to see, but it didn't mean she wasn't nervous about it.

"You're trembling, Nikhat."

"I imagined this moment for so many years and in so many ways, Azeez, that the reality of it now, it's a little frightening."

She wore a cream-colored sleeveless nightgown that almost blended with her skin, making him think she was naked for an aching instant.

Blood rushed out of his head, leaving him with a dizzying desire. But this time, that rush wasn't followed by that clawing void. This time, she didn't disappear, this time he wasn't left with cold sheets and empty arousal. This time he wouldn't feel the shame that he felt when he looked down at the wrong face.

He came to a stop at the bed. "After those months in Monaco, my father ordered me home. For the first time in my life, I was ashamed of myself, I couldn't meet his eyes.

"I haven't touched another woman since, Nikhat. And I have been given a clean bill of health by the doctors."

He touched her chin, and tilted it up, his hand shaking. He felt her tremble, but the resolve didn't falter in her eyes.

"I'm in good health, too," she said with a small smile. "And I'm protected by the drugs I take, so…"

She placed her hands on his chest and moved them restlessly, the irises of her eyes bright like flames. She unbuttoned his shirt and pushed the edges apart. Her hands found his bare skin and he hissed out a sharp breath. Her fingers explored his chest with wanton thoroughness, curled into his chest hair, pressed into his abdomen, traced the seam of his low-slung pajamas.

Back and forth, dipping into the band now and then, until every nerve in his body was tuned into the movement of her fingers. Every muscle in him curled with anticipation.

She bent and kissed his chest, and a moan rumbled out of him. His fingers sank into her heavy tresses, the hold on his control wavering at her soft, feathery kisses. Her lips moved over his neck, his pulse, trailing wet heat all over his skin, setting a fire in its wake. The second he felt the stroke of her tongue at his nipple, he tugged at her.

She looked up, a wicked smile on her mouth, her fingers clutching his waist. Her beautiful, kohl-lined, brown eyes shimmered with desire and glittered with a raw hunger. He tightened his fingers in her hair, waited for a flash of doubt or something that would puncture the spiraling need between them.

Their hoarse little breaths whispered in the room.

Still holding his gaze, her own hazy with desire, she sank her teeth over his nipple and sucked it into her mouth.

The wet rasp of her tongue, the drag of her teeth, her soft curves rubbing up against his lower belly, right above his erection…Azeez lost the battle over his already frayed control.

He pushed her back on the bed.

Settling on his good hip, he ran his fingers over her cheek, over the pulse fluttering at her neck, to the neckline of her nightgown. Her skin was like raw silk, a sheen of pink dusting all over. The soft rise and fall of her lush breasts under the satin of her gown, her breath coming in fast little whispers, goaded him. He pressed his mouth to her neck, licked her skin, and her hands sunk into his hair.

The sight of her nipples, tight and pressed against the

silk of her nightgown sent lust stabbing at him. "Take off your gown."

She raised a heated glance to him, a soft whisper falling from her lips. "Are you not going to kiss me first?"

He tugged her lower lip with his teeth, and she gasped, before grasping his shoulders with her hands and licking his lip. He pulled back, suddenly wondering if he really could be gentle with her. "Are you going to argue over every single point in this, too?"

"I just don't see why you are the one who decides what should—"

With a quick movement that surprised even himself, he sat up and ripped up the nightgown with his hands. It tore apart, leaving her magnificent breasts tipped with dark pink areolas to his gaze.

He pushed her back onto the bed with his body and sucked her nipple into his mouth.

She let out a long, deep whimper and arched into his touch, shuddering uncontrollably under him.

He rolled the tight bud with his tongue, suckled it, breathing in the scent of her skin, immersing herself in her soft curves. It was as if a fever had taken root inside him and only plunging into her, until he could forget, until he didn't think, would help. "I get to decide because I'm the Prince, Dr. Zakhari. There are certain areas where I'll never bend to your will, and a bed with both of us in it is the first one on that list."

She tasted better than the most erotic fantasy he'd ever had of her. In his darkest moments, he had wondered how she would taste, and yet not a single fantasy was close to the raw, earthy reality of her beauty.

Struggling to his knees, he rent the nightgown all the way through. The sight of her entire body, the scent of her coating the very air he breathed, the slight quake in her toned thighs, it was a moment that blurred the memory of every other woman he had ever touched to replace her.

Nikhat could feel the intensity of Azeez's gaze on every cell, every inch of her. She moved her hands instantly to cover her sex, shocked by her own audacity. Imagining him coming here, imagining his gaze on her…the fantasy had been easy.

But the reality of his heated glance stroking over her nudity, of the trembles sparking across her skin, the need knotting her nipples, her sex aching and wet even before he touched her, completely another.

He pressed a long, lingering kiss to her abdomen, and she writhed under his masterful touch, needing more, too awash in new sensations to even speak. "You thought this would be simple, didn't you, *habeebi*?" He licked a wet trail around her navel, and every muscle in her body turned liquid.

She nodded, the ease with which he read her thoughts not at all surprising her.

He pushed her wrists out of his way. One hand moved between the valley of her breasts, locking her against the bed, while the other moved over her knees, her thighs, his breath whispering right between her legs. He flicked her knees open with the slightest touch and her thighs fell apart, her breath hitching in and out.

Her spine locked, the soft nuzzle of his nose against her thighs making it hard to pull breath into her lungs.

She was a practical woman, even with her traditional, conservative background, she hadn't been shy or prudish when she had looked at a man's naked body the first time.

But now, knowing that the most intimate part of her was open to his hungry eyes, warmth filled her inside out. A heated kiss on her thighs branded her, his jagged exhale against her skin, the pads of his fingers digging hard into her flesh, told tales of his shattering control.

And then his fingers found her core.

She threw her head back on a long moan as every inch of her came alive, a searing combination of need and desperation covering her skin. His fingers brushed against the tight bundle of nerves at her core, his strokes, long, lingering, just this short of what she needed. "Please," she said, ready to beg if need be. She pressed herself into his touch, but he wouldn't let her move the way she wanted, with the speed with which she wanted.

Every time he tugged at her nipple with his fingers, she felt an answering quiver shoot down toward her lower belly. But not enough.

Then she felt his breath on her inner thighs, felt his fingers open her to him, felt a lingering stroke of his tongue against her as if she were a feast he intended to devour. Nikhat came in a splintering shaft of light and sensation, every inch of her sex contracting and releasing, pleasure waves coiling through her lower belly.

And he still didn't stop. He didn't stop until he wrenched wave after wave of pleasure from her, until every inch of her was quaking from the unbearable intensity of her climax. Sweat dampened her skin, and the tremors slowly abated.

Pushing onto her hips took more energy than she had, but she was determined not to be a passive participant.

With her arms shaking, she clutched him and pressed a swift kiss to his mouth. She undid the strings of his pajamas, pulled them down, and the hard length of his arousal sprang into her hand.

A fresh wave of desire bolted through her. He was like velvet-sheathed steel in her hands, and she wanted that hard weight inside her, possessing her, driving into her, and more than anything, finding his pleasure in her. She ran her hands over his shoulders, his skin stretched tight over his bones, and tugged him. They fell together back on the bed. Her legs parted instantly, cradling the weight of him.

The clamoring ache began in her muscles again.

With a whispered grunt, he pushed himself up and thrust into her welcoming heat.

And Nikhat heard the long drawn-out moan that fell from her own mouth, her eyes drifting shut in exquisite pleasure.

Opening them, she found his gaze boring into hers, his breath a harsh whisper in the silence, his face a stark mask of need and desire. With a hard groan, he took her mouth again, pulled her lower lip with his teeth, ravished her until the soft tug of need became a blazing inferno in her blood again.

Digging her teeth into his shoulder, she tasted his sweat and his skin, filled herself with the scent of him. "Please, Azeez. I want more."

He entered her again, her breasts dragging against his chest, his hair-roughened legs rasping against her soft ones.

She grabbed his hips to anchor herself and he instantly winced.

"Azeez, I forgot," she whispered. He touched her forehead to his and took her mouth in a tender kiss. Something glimmered in his gaze and Nikhat was a thousand times glad that she was here with him in this moment.

Pain set his mouth into a tight line. "I cannot move like I want to, Nikhat. After the last two days in the desert, my hip…it's unbearable to move, to bear my own weight."

With a frustrated sigh, he rolled off her, and Nikhat instantly felt his loss. Turning sideways, she kissed his cheek.

She continued peppering kisses on his chest, on his throat, on his jaw. Throwing caution to the winds, she straddled him, heat tightening her cheeks.

His gaze moved over her body with a thoroughness that had her sex wet again, his mouth curved into a wicked smile. "You're a stubborn, determined woman. I forgot that."

"I want my prince and I will have him, come what may," she said, more than glad to see his smile.

A bone-deep joy flickered into life within her. Another man, she knew, would have found shame in his inability in that moment, lost his confidence. But he hadn't. She couldn't help wondering if he realized it, couldn't help but hope that she had a small part in it.

The joy that swept through her had a double edge to it because it also meant that the man she had loved long ago was beginning to come back, the man who had breathed and lived Dahaar, he was still alive beneath that clawing guilt and self-recrimination.

She clasped his erection and slowly lowered herself onto him. Heat flared within the walls of her sex, a delicious friction gliding deep into her skin. She straightened her spine, and his gaze moved to her breasts, color riding those sharp cheekbones. He drew his hand over her midriff to the valley between her breasts.

Moving to his elbows, he sent her a scorching glance. "Bend down, Nikhat. I want to kiss you."

When she dutifully did, he put that sinful mouth on her breast instead.

And Nikhat arched at the sinuous heat that pooled low in her belly again.

His teeth scraped her nipple and waves began building inside again.

"Move the way your body wants you to," he said, burying his face in her neck. "I'm all yours."

Giving in to her body's instinct, Nikhat moved. Their gazes held, their breath hitched as she moved faster, finding a rhythm that sent her once again to the edge. "Come for me, Nikhat."

His words were a raw command. And to match his words, he snuck his hands to where their bodies were joined.

His dark, rough fingers on the swollen bundle of nerves, it was the most erotic sight she had ever seen. Another coil of pressure gripped her and she clamped her thighs and moved over him.

And was rewarded by his deep, hoarse grunt of pleasure.

Nikhat came in a deep, swift swamp of sensations that had her crying his name out loud. His fingers on her hips controlling her movements, Azeez pushed harder and deeper, the slap of his flesh against hers pinging around them.

The sweat beading on his forehead, the dark fire in his gaze, the very starkness of his features, the way he lingered on that last thrust, the way every muscle in his body tightened and released as he climaxed, Nikhat watched him hungrily, even as her body felt as if it would come apart at the seams.

His breath was loud and harsh in the silence, his skin sweat slicked, his chest rising and falling, every muscle and sinew hard and shuddering.

That she had done this to this powerful, beautiful man, that it was her body that sent those spasms of pleasure through him, it was the most powerful, the most magnificent, moment of her life.

She collapsed onto him, and thought she saw a flash of shock in his gaze. When he pushed her hair from her forehead and kissed her temple, she smiled, for once, in an utterly glorious place.

Sweat coated her skin, her thighs still quaking with tiny tremors and still joined with him in the most intimate of ways.

And for the first time in her life, she reveled in every sensation that pierced her body, every little quake and flutter, every little tingle and ache, for the first time in a long time, she loved her body, damaged as it was.

Smiling, she kissed his warm skin and tasted his sweat.

She had never felt more like a woman.

Adjusting their bodies so that she was on her back, Azeez slowly pulled himself from under Nikhat. Her soft snores made him smile, but his curiosity, now blazing like a wildfire, refused to be distracted. He turned on the bed lamp on his side. The feeble light threw her lush breasts into focus and for a few minutes, he was lost.

She instantly turned sideways again, seeking warmth, and he stilled her with an arm around her waist.

And there it was.

The scar he had seen just as he had found glorious climax. Not that the blinding pleasure he had found in her was in any way blunted by his sudden observation. But now, the sheets cooling off around them, now that the edge of his hunger was blunted, he couldn't stop wondering.

The scar was about a half inch wide and was right above the hair that covered her sex. It looked precise, and he realized it was the result of a surgery.

Instantly, he thought of the name she had given him for her condition, wondered at the seriousness of it.

Exhaling a harsh breath, he pushed out the concern and curiosity, too. They had both known that this was about one night.

Glorious sex after six years of abstinence was frying his brain, warping his mind. Nikhat and he were tied together by a curious twist of fate but nothing else. It had to be.

She shivered and he pulled up the duvet to cover her naked body.

He lay back down on the bed, on his side again, and gathered her close. The scent of sex and her, a delicious combination, settled deep into his skin. He pressed a kiss to her forehead, and she snuggled into him. Her eyes fluttered open, drowsy and sated, her mouth curving into a satisfied smile. "Can we do it again?"

He laughed and tasted her mouth again.

Her eyes fluttered closed. "All I need is a little rest, and I will be ready for round two." She cracked her eyes open and winked at him. "Unless it's your creaky joints that aren't up to scratch, really. If so, we will—"

He sent his fingers on a search up her thighs, until they found her buttocks and gave her a little squeeze. She yelped and hid her face in his neck.

His throat clotted, and he marveled at how easily she had made him laugh at himself. And he stilled at another realization. Even the pain in his hip, his inability to move inside her as he wanted without pain shooting down his leg, hadn't derailed him the way it usually did. And, of course, he couldn't contest the fact that it was because it was her. He swallowed the bittersweet realization. "Sleep, *habeebi*."

The next morning, Nikhat woke alone in her bed. Sunlight glinted across every surface in her room, touching everything with a golden glow. Moving to her side, she dragged the pillow next to her toward her nose and took a deep breath. That dark scent of Azeez, with undertones of sex and sandalwood, instantly evoked tingles across her skin. Smiling, she lay there for a few more minutes, reliving last night.

The same sense of lightness and contentment pervaded her as she showered and dressed in a long cotton skirt adorned with beads and tiny mirrors that fell to her ankles, and a thin silk blouse in a pale yellow. Adding large dangly earrings that she had bought in a quirky jewelry store in Brooklyn, she studied her reflection in the mirror.

Color filled her cheeks and there was a light in her eyes. She looked every inch like a woman who had been loved, very thoroughly, last night. Refusing to let her thoughts veer into negative territory, she pulled a comb through her long hair, pulled it to fall in an angled ponytail over her shoulder and set off in search of Azeez.

The vast marble corridors of the resort, the grand archways that filled every inch of it with light, the world itself, looked like a brighter place today.

She found Azeez sitting at a table filled with breakfast dishes in a veranda off the main lounge. As it was only nine in the morning, the heat was still bearable. Pausing to catch her breath, she leaned against a wall.

His head thrown back over his chair, his eyes closed, his face was covered in sunlight. Long eyelashes cast shadows onto his gaunt cheekbones, his prominent, crooked nose shading the other side of his face from view, and his mouth…

Honeyed heat gathered in her muscles at the thought of all the things that mouth had done to her. She clutched her legs together as if she could soothe the pulsing ache at the center of her sex, desperate to stave off the yearning before it turned into something else.

She had wanted one night and she had taken it. If she continued to play with fire, she would only get burned.

"You are welcome to join me, Nikhat." The hint of teasing in his tone had relief sweeping through her. She exhaled deeply, and smiled, more than glad that he was in that wicked, humorous mood. It was only a fragile cover over the deep passion underneath, the heated intensity of his emotions, but she welcomed it anyway. "I won't bite. Not now and not here."

Simple, mocking words. Yet it felt as if he had caressed her with his fingers. She sat down on the opposite chair and met his gaze.

It swept over her slowly, as if he had been waiting to do just that. "You look very—" he inclined his head, still looking, still devouring, and her heart thudded "—carefree today. Very much…"

She raised a brow, loving the wicked gleam in his eyes. "Very much like a satisfied woman? I did score—" she scrunched her face into a mock frown "—four times."

He erupted into rich laughter, and it was impossible not to join him.

Shaking his head, his mouth still curved into a wide smile that dug grooves on his stubbled cheeks, he leaned forward. "I was going to say reckless."

"Remember that time when you came back from university and wouldn't stop strutting around the palace, as though you were lord of everything you surveyed, and Ayaan and Amira bugged you incessantly—"

"I *was* the lord of everything I surveyed."

Her breath hitched in her throat. The sheer, undiluted arrogance in his words, it was so much like the old him. "Fine. Like a…." She clicked her fingers. "You were like a peacock strutting your feathers or your *mighty sword* in this case," she snorted in mock disgust. "It was so easy to see through you."

Slashes of deep color marked his cheekbones. "Your vocabulary, I see, has become just as enriched as the rest of you, *habeebi*." His eyes wide, he ran his fingers over his eyebrows, his mouth still wreathed in smiles. "Of all the things to remember, Nikhat? I never told them. At least, Ayaan, not until a couple of years later. I can't believe you…"

Now it was her turn to blush under the dawn of a slow

intensity in his gaze. "My obsession with you had already begun. I was years ahead of everyone else in biology. God, my fourteen-year-old self burned with jealousy. And I knew exactly what put that smug, self-satisfied smile on your face." She pointed her finger toward her face, unable to stop smiling.

"I believe that's what you see today."

Shaking his head, Azeez studied her, wondered at how easy she made it to laugh, how she reminded him of everything that had been good about the past.

Because there *had* been good things in the past.

He could finally see the brilliance of Ayaan's idea.

Nikhat, with her joyful stories about their family, with her infallible strength and loyalty, was the perfect medicine that his brother could have brought for Azeez.

And it was working.

Here he was, just weeks later. He had made love to a woman, the fact that it was she—he chalked it up to the curious quirk of fate—he had found invaluable information for Dahaar, he was laughing.

It would be so easy to get used to this. To having her in his bed, to laugh with her out of it. Already, she was insinuating herself into his life again, already the urge to share his shame with her, to find that relief, too, it was overwhelming.

She had him wonder if he wanted more from life, made him wonder about the future. And she made him want to forget and move ahead. And that hope, he did not deserve it.

He couldn't let her be anything more than a temporary drug on the road to recovery, couldn't let her distract him from his true purpose. He couldn't let her believe that this had been anything more than a brief interlude. He would help Ayaan and then he would leave.

Suddenly, he couldn't wait to be his brother's prisoner again.

She blinked as he stood up. A stillness emerged in her body, her laughter inching into something else as he moved closer.

He silenced the clamor of regrets inside.

It was better this way. He had nothing to offer her.

His fingers moved over her mouth as he settled on the table in front of her. Frantic for another taste of her, he took her in a devouring kiss that had their lips clinging, sucking, drawing breath from each other in seconds. She clasped his cheek as he trailed his mouth over her temple.

"Ayaan has got this whole science of managing me down very well, it seems. You were exactly what I needed. I have been thinking of myself as a cripple, have let everything about me filter down to just that one fact. I will never be able to ride a horse again, or run or, apparently, make love to a woman the way I want to...But you have also made me realize everything I *can* do. Maybe have even given me a new lease on life."

He couldn't hold back the warmth in his words. It was her due.

He pushed a tendril of her hair back. "Last night will be as memorable to me as it is to you, Nikhat.

"Now, it is time we returned. I have some time-sensitive information for Ayaan. And I am sure you can't wait to get back to being the stern doctor who has to get the dissolute, arrogant prince in shape so that he's off your plate and your life can get back on track."

CHAPTER TEN

PRINCESS ZOHRA REQUESTS your presence at dinner tonight in the Royal Hall.

The palace maid's softly spoken instruction ringing in her head, Nikhat followed her down a corridor she had never visited before. The maid, after showing her to huge double doors, partially open, left. Pushing one door ajar, Nikhat stepped in.

And her jaw met her chest at the sight that greeted her.

Every surface she saw was either golden or silver, including the edges of the huge rectangular table. Intricately wrought silver-and-gold knives and forks and plates glinted in the light thrown from the crystal chandelier overhead. The crystal had a gold tint to it, casting a bright yellow glow on everything in the room.

There were portraits of generations of Al Sharifs on the walls. Vases were overflowing with exotic flowers. Velvet-cushioned heavy chairs sat around the table, the back of each intricately carved with the Dahaaran insignia of a sword.

And on the table, an unending array of mouthwatering dishes beckoned.

Azeez stood in the darkened corner of the room, and yet she felt his gaze on her, as though he had touched her.

"Hello, Nikhat."

Running a hand over her midriff, Nikhat nodded. She couldn't speak, couldn't move, pinned to the spot by the energy instantly crackling in the air around them.

They hadn't seen each other since they had returned from the desert four days ago. She had no idea who was avoiding whom, or maybe they both were.

She had thought she would take the plunge and taste paradise for one night. What she hadn't realized was how hard it would be to have tasted it once and then having to live with the fact that it would never be hers again. A fierce need to leave a mark on him, that's what she had wanted. Instead, she felt as if she was the one who had walked away scarred, again.

She startled and turned as she heard Princess Zohra behind her. Greeting her with a nod, she walked back toward the entrance, realizing the significance of the occasion. Of course, the princess would want to celebrate.

Holding the wave of emotion threatening to pull her under, Nikhat was about to leave when the princess stopped her. "I had the servants invite you on purpose, Nikhat. My family is not with me and you have—" she flicked a knowing look toward Azeez, and Nikhat could only be thankful he didn't notice "—brought peace of mind to me in more than one way."

Her stomach twisting, Nikhat wet her lips. "I do not belong at this dinner."

Before Nikhat could leave, Ayaan entered the hall.

Unable to excuse herself, Nikhat took the seat next to Azeez. His gaze took in her shaking hands, and she clasped them rigidly in her lap, wishing herself anywhere but here.

"You're shaking. Are you in pain again?"

She shook her head. Ayaan dismissed everyone else, even the waiting servants. His hands on her chair, he leaned down and took Princess Zohra's mouth in a kiss that sent heat rushing to Nikhat's cheeks.

Next to her, Azeez leaned back into his seat, stretching his right leg. "Do you wish us to leave, Ayaan?" There was more than a hint of teasing in his voice and Nikhat instinctively turned.

He was grinning, and the joy in his face momentarily wiped everything else from her mind.

Leaning over the chair, his arm still around Princess Zohra's, Ayaan smiled at Azeez. "We are celebrating and… we would like you to be part of it. Zohra had an ultrasound scan today." He nodded at Nikhat. "We're having twin boys."

Nikhat wanted to look away and yet she devoured every expression, every nuance in Azeez's face.

He became very still in contrast to the restless energy that poured off him; even the air around him seemed to hang in suspension. Slowly, he blinked, as though coming out of a deep fog.

His gaze caught hers for an infinitesimal second and the flash of something in it left Nikhat shaken to the core. She felt unbearably frozen inside. And she fought the feeling.

She had enough to feel guilty about, enough things that she couldn't change about herself. She didn't want the burden of his disappointment, the burden of his lost dreams.

Her hands gripped the hard wood at her sides and still, she could not look away.

Finally, when he recovered, it felt like a lifetime even if it had been nothing but a few seconds. When he looked at Ayaan, there was nothing but undiluted happiness there. "It is cause for celebration." He cleared his throat. "The future king of Dahaar is going to be born," he said with such pride, such joy, that tears rose to her eyes.

Why it should hurt so much after all these years, why it

twisted her stomach in such pure agony, Nikhat couldn't say. She had delivered babies, she saw pregnant women on a daily basis and yet, this time, she couldn't stave off the pain no matter what she did.

Azeez walked to Ayaan and clapped him on the back. "You are a prayer come true, Princess Zohra." His breath hitched on the words as he pulled the princess out of her chair and enveloped her in a fierce hug that had the princess staring at him with shock filling her beautiful eyes. "For Dahaar, for my family, but most of all, my brother. Even the doctor has to agree that this calls for a drink," he said, throwing a look at Nikhat.

Nikhat nodded, her heart in her throat, her vision full of unshed tears. She forced herself to congratulate Ayaan, forced herself to smile even as her heart shattered in her breast again.

Pain sliced through her and she gasped for breath. How could this pain be as sharp as ever? How had she found herself in this moment again?

She felt Azeez's continued scrutiny, his puzzled look at her petrified silence over the next hour, but there was nothing she could do. Every moment of the royal family's happiness sent piercing pain through her and she sat through it all, wishing herself anywhere else in the world, yet bound to him, more by her own heart than any promise she had made.

Azeez finished his drink, the dark chasm of Nikhat's heavy silence next to him grating on his nerves. She had hardly touched her food, hardly spoken a word all through dinner. They had shared one beautiful night. She was not his concern, he reminded himself.

He turned his attention to his brother. The ever-present

shadow of tiredness gleamed under Ayaan's wide smile. "You were not present during the scan?"

Ayaan shook his head and clasped Zohra's fingers with his. "No. There was an official summons requiring Father's presence in Zuran last night and I went. Thanks to you, I was at least prepared."

"Zayed?"

Ayaan nodded. "He proposed changes to the economic policy Dahaar has with Zuran. He is threatening to declare war if we don't alter the terms of the peace treaty."

"That treaty was signed almost fifteen years ago. I remember Father telling me how he had to force Sheikh Asad not to gamble away all of Zuran's oil to fill his treasury."

Ayaan looked at him with increasing interest. "Then Zayed has conveniently decided to forget it. He claims Father bullied him into signing bad terms for Zuran with the threat of Dahaar's army. It's clear he views our alliance with Siyaad as a threat."

"It's just a threat to get Dahaar to—"

"I don't think you can make that claim anymore. He's not the man our sister was going to marry, Azeez. You saw him. Assure me he's not changed and I will…"

Azeez shook his head, knowing that Ayaan was right. The man he had seen had been but a shadow of his old friend. And suddenly, for the first time since he had been shot, Azeez realized what a gift he had in his family, in Nikhat.

Zayed was, and had always been, truly alone in the world.

"I will not call Father back for this. Not after everything he's shouldered alone for all these years. I need help, Azeez."

"You have experienced staff for—"

"You have a bloody doctorate in trade policy and economics. Father prepared us to complement each other, Azeez. For you to rule and for me to aid you. If you're determined to leave, at least help me while you are here."

As though Ayaan had rolled a small explosive amidst the gleaming silverware on the table, the air leached out of the room. Princess Zohra's gaze clashed with Azeez's, a defiant challenge blazing in it.

Instant denial rose to his lips. He felt Nikhat shift closer to him just as he opened his mouth. Beneath the table, she clasped her fingers with his, and he wondered if she realized what she was doing.

"Fine. Have the original treaty and the amendments he is suggesting delivered to me. I will take a look." Tugging Nikhat up along with him, he forced the fury rattling inside him to a corner.

Azeez barely kept his temper under control until Ayaan and Zohra vacated the vast hall. Planting himself in Nikhat's way, he stood leaning against the closed doors.

"What kind of game are you playing now?"

She looked wary, a haunting strain around her usually placid features. "I'm not playing any game."

"Just because we—"

She flinched and reached out a hand, as if to ward off an attack. "Please, Azeez."

The poisonous words died in his throat.

Anything he would have said would have been wrong on so many levels. He didn't want to cheapen or dirty what they had shared. His life had been enough of a wasteland for him to know that despite the past and the future what they had shared was special.

And whatever this restlessness simmering under his skin, that was gaining power inside him, that was beginning to fester as painfully as the guilt, it was not her fault. She had, as always, done what was required of her.

It was him. Suddenly, everything he had been so sure of a few weeks ago felt like shifting ground, and he didn't know how to anchor himself.

He saw Nikhat swallow, struggle to speak. "I was about to remind you that you decided to do whatever you could to take the stress off Princess Zohra. It is why I am here, Your Highness."

Her address felt like a slap in the face. "Do not call me that."

She laughed and he turned to look at her. It was a low, haunting sound, so full of despair it made the hairs on his neck stand. "No? Can you hear yourself? I finally understand the audacity of hope in Ayaan's eyes.

"How long has it been since you looked at yourself in a mirror, Azeez?

"You need a blood transfusion to be anything but the Prince of Dahaar. Not a bullet wound, not your self-loathing, not the fact that you are determined to live a half-life, nothing can change the fact that you are a prince through and through.

"Dahaar—its politics, its welfare, its economics—it's the very blood that gives you life."

"Enough, Nikhat."

Instead of heeding his warning, she moved closer to him. Her gaze blazed with some unknown anguish, her hands fisted by her sides…the tightness of her shoulders, the tension in her lithe frame coiling tighter and tighter around them. And beneath all that, the heat of her body stroked the slow burn in him to a smoldering fire.

"Admit that a part of you craves it even now, admit how much it tortures you that Ayaan is taking your place, that it is Ayaan's son who will be the next king of Dahaar.

How much it galls you that Ayaan is taking everything that should have been yours?"

He flinched, the cutting fury of her words stealing into him, hurting him.

"Yes, it does. It tortures me that Ayaan suffers every night, it tortures me that my father and mother have to grieve their daughter—a daughter who was about to get married—it tortures me that wherever I turn, there's still evidence of the destruction I wrought."

She didn't back down even then. Her lush mouth settled into a stubborn set, her chin tilting defiantly. "I know how much Amira loved you. Even if you were somehow responsible, she would have forgiven you, Azeez. She would have never wanted this...half-life for you."

"But she's not here. Because of me."

"How? How is it your fault that a terrorist group attacked all three of you and killed her?"

"They didn't attack us. I lured them there with bait. I passed on information that I would be there, set up a meet. They had been issuing threats for months.

"Without my father's permission, without letting him know my dangerous plans, I planned to stay behind with a small unit and capture them. He dismissed that unit without my knowledge, and too late I realized Ayaan and Amira stayed back.

"They stayed back to talk to me. They stayed back because they were worried about me, because I had been avoiding them. And they were caught in the crossfire."

He pushed the words out through a throat raw with ache and suddenly, it felt as if the choke hold of his own guilt and recriminations relented. Just a little. He felt her tentative touch on his shoulder, and shuddered at the thought of facing her.

But when he did, he didn't see sympathy or pity. He only saw his own pain reflected there, he only saw grief.

And then it wasn't so hard to speak anymore. It was a relief to put his agony into words, to let her see all of his sins, all of his guilt.

"I saw her take a bullet, Nikhat, one that should have been for me. I saw a bullet graze my twenty-year-old brother's head. I saw them fall one after the other, I saw those bastards drag them away and I could do nothing.

"I brought destruction to them.

"And all because I had become reckless, because I hadn't cared whether I lived or died.

"She's dead because of me. My brother has nightmares to this day because of me. I let my emotions get the better of me. Because you left, I went on a reckless rampage.

"The Golden Prince, who had never wanted for anything, who had never had anything denied him, I couldn't handle your rejection. That's how emotionally strong I was. That kind of man, who can fragment so easily, that kind of man who's at the mercy of his emotions, that man is not fit to be a king.

"But Ayaan is.

"There was a point when I thought Al Sharifs, the dynasty that ruled over these lands for two centuries, would end because of what I did. Ayaan's news today…it fills me with joy, it feels like I can draw a breath for the first time. It galls me to look at him, yes, because he is a better man than I am.

"I do not care, however, whether it is he or I on the throne, whether it is my son or his that will rule Dahaar next. I'm not guilty of that sin."

Nikhat rubbed the back of her neck with her fingers, rocking on the balls of her feet, her breath coming and going in hard bursts.

"Nikhat?" He grabbed her as she swayed. "Why do you care so much about this…about whether I leave Dahaar or not?"

"I don't want to," she said. "My life will be so much simpler if you leave. And yet, I see you and…" She had paid a high price, one he hadn't asked of her, one that she suddenly wasn't so sure about, so that he could do his duty, so that he could be the man he was destined to be, so that he could father the heir to the throne. "Leaving him to deal with all this when you can help, leaving him to deal with Dahaar, with your parents when you hold yourself responsible for all this, it sounds like the opposite of penance.

"This sounds like cowardice."

"What would you have me do, Nikhat?"

The vulnerability in his words shook her, the trust in his dark gaze, how she wished she deserved it. She clutched his hands and tugged him toward her. She kissed his cheek, loving the raspy texture, holding him as if she never wanted to let go. "I think you have punished yourself enough. Your heart is your greatest gift, Azeez. But you won't listen to me, will you?" She ran her fingers over his temple, tracing the strong lines of his cheekbones, loving him a little more in that moment.

How could she not?

"Tell Ayaan what you told me. Tell him why you want to leave, Azeez, the true reason. And if you still want to be punished, then accept whatever he decides for you as your sentence."

She didn't know if her answer angered him or affected him at all. He only stared at her for what felt like a long time before he turned around and left.

Nikhat reached for the wall behind her and crumpled against it. She felt as if she would shatter into a million pieces. Or maybe she already had and this was how it felt to fall apart.

Do you think I care whether it is he or I on the throne, whether it is my son or his son that will rule Dahaar next?

It felt as if the one decision that she had built her life around had suddenly morphed, changed shape into a question rather than a statement, and the foundations of her life were fracturing around it.

Even when she had ventured toward happiness again with Richard, she had only been hurt by his sudden change of heart that he wanted children. It had made her realize that she had been right about not wanting to give Azeez the choice between her love and the throne.

But now she was caught inside a hell of her own making, hating herself, pitying herself, questioning every decision she had ever made to arrive at this point in her life.

Because, as long as she had been confident that she had done the right thing, she had borne any amount of pain, soldiered on with her life even after losing everything that had been precious to her. But if Azeez hadn't cared whether it was he or his brother who inherited the throne, or whose child was the heir…

She sank to the floor in a boneless heap, and wrapped her arms around herself.

The only thing she understood amidst all that, the one thing she knew was that she couldn't bear to see him leave, she couldn't even breathe at the thought of not seeing him again, of not feeling his rough hands on her, of not feeling his hard body shudder in her arms, of not seeing that gaze sear through her, owning her, claiming her.

She had fought tiny little battles all her life to be able to follow her own heart, to be able to make her own destiny, to have the right to do as she willed.

Now she felt all that strength unraveling. All she wanted

was to give herself over, body and will, into his hands, and forget everything.

She would always love him, she realized with a shudder. And she was desperate enough to hold on to him for as long as she could.

The next morning, Azeez paced the length of his brother's office, shocked at the difference in his own mind since he had been here only a few weeks ago.

The room still dealt a swift kick to his gut, but at least he could breathe after those first few moments, he could bear to stand inside.

His mind, however, would not let go of Nikhat's words. *Cowardice,* that was it. Every action of his, every decision he had made in the last few years was full of his own cowardice, his ego, his dented pride. He had hidden it all under guilt, called it penance.

But she was right.

How could he walk away now knowing everything he did?

Maybe if Ayaan hadn't brought him back, maybe if he hadn't seen how much Ayaan needed him, maybe if he hadn't learned today that he was going to be an uncle... he felt divided in half, the unrelenting questions pounding through him.

Maybe he was not fit to rule Dahaar, but he could still be its servant, couldn't he? He could serve his brother, he could shoulder some of his burden.

Where was the honor in walking away from the wreckage he had created?

He walked to the portrait of his family, and let the tears prick behind his eyes. Maybe he was not completely broken. It had taken him years to realize what his father had always taught him.

His father, Azeez and Ayaan—they had all been born with a purpose—to serve Dahaar and its people. And for years, embroiled in in his own guilt and inadequacy, he had forgotten that. He had forgotten what he was capable of, he had forgotten what it felt like to be the man he was destined to be.

"Azeez?"

He turned around and faced Ayaan. His copper gaze curious, his brother stared at him warily. "Is everything all right?"

Nodding, Azeez pointed to the file he had left on the table. "I have taken a look at the amendments to the treaty. What Zayed's committee is suggesting is not completely disagreeable. If I were the new high sheikh of Zuran, my first act would be to restore all the rights his uncle signed away to their oil. My guess is that he needs this to happen so that he can thwart the High Council. Remember, in Zuran, the High Council has the final vote on everything, even electing the sheikh. If we back his victory now, we will have gained a powerful ally, we can use this to better tax treaties, even."

His shock apparent in his slow steps, Ayaan grabbed him in a sudden hug. A shudder racked his brother's body. "I forgot how much you used to rub my face in the fact that you're better than me at everything."

"Believe me, Ayaan, I'm not." For once, the memories that swamped him did not steal Azeez's breath. He cleared his throat. "I have also prepared an official statement for you. Run it by your economic adviser. We cannot—*Dahaar* cannot—look weak to Zayed. By agreeing to this, we are showing good faith, not capitulating under his threat of war. He needs to understand that."

His brother picked up the statement Azeez had written

by hand, his brow tied. "This is brilliant." Only then did he look at Azeez. "Were you up all night?"

"Yes."

Pulling the chair back, Ayaan crumpled into it with a harsh exhale. The strain on his brother's features intensified the thread of shame Azeez felt. "Because you are preparing to flee in the middle of the night?"

Azeez felt his temper flare but held it in check. He had deserved that. "My fate is in your hands, Ayaan."

"What do you mean?"

"I will tell you why I didn't come back, why I quake at the idea of meeting Father's eyes, why I can't bear to see Mother's tears. And then you decide. You decide my fate and I will accept it."

CHAPTER ELEVEN

AZEEZ CLOSED THE door to his bedchamber. He was exhausted from little sleep last night and after the eviscerating discussion he had had with Ayaan.

There had been no judgment, no anger, nothing but shared loss in his brother's eyes.

His brother and he had shed tears over their sister, he had seen what grief Ayaan hid under the strong facade, understood why the past haunted him in the form of his own nightmares, his worry for Zohra's health, his mounting concerns about Zohra's home country, Siyaad, and its administration until her brother Wasim came of age…

From every word he had said and every complaint he had left unsaid, it was clear that Ayaan was barely keeping up. They had both known and accepted that such was this life, that beneath the palaces and decadent lifestyles that the public saw, running a country was hard work, with peace treaties that fell apart at a minute's notice at a perceived insult, it was strategy cloaked as diplomacy, it was sometimes picking the least evil choice in a host of bigger ones.

His father had shouldered it all with their mother by his side, and Ayaan would with Princess Zohra by his side. And Azeez would aid him, he would do everything he could to share his brother's burden.

He would spend the rest of his life being his brother's servant.

Instantly, his thoughts turned to Nikhat. He had been avoiding her, even as her words hadn't left him alone. She had looked as if she would fall apart, as if somehow his grief had morphed her. He longed to hold her, kiss her, wanted to comfort her, and yet, he could not.

He wanted to tell her that he was going to stay in Dahaar, thank her for helping him find himself again, his sense of purpose again, thank her for sharing his shame and his pain…the list was endless.

But he wouldn't stop there. He knew what it was to kiss her, to hold her and to know every intimate sound she made, and he couldn't go back to not wanting that.

And to want her like that again, to let her tangle his emotions just as he was beginning to find a purpose to his life again, it was not acceptable.

He spied a rectangular yellow envelope on his desk marked Confidential and froze.

The reports he had requested four days ago while Nikhat had been sleeping in his bed had finally arrived.

He had no doubt it would have everything he had asked for—photocopies of every doctor's report that had been written about the woman who had skewered him with her questions, who was bent upon knowing every dark and cracked part of him. And a comprehensive write-up translating it into layman's words for him.

Walking past the desk to the dark wood cabinet behind it, he extracted a crystal decanter and poured himself a drink. He hadn't touched one in five weeks, not since he had thrown the bottle at her. He didn't have to now, the sane part of him whispered. He needn't have the drink, nor did he need to open that envelope and read what was inside.

He could trash it and walk away from this moment, forget he had ever requested it. He didn't have to know what she had been through. Not even she was worth playing this dangerous game of wills with his own emotions.

He put down the glass with a thud that resonated around him. Tearing open the envelope, he pulled out the sheaf of papers and proceeded to read.

Report after report of words he didn't understand, just as he had assumed. She had seen a lot of doctors, here and abroad. Finally he found the page that would make sense of the technical words.

Halfway through the succinct write-up, he froze, the very axis of his world tilting in front of his very eyes.

Nikhat might never be able to have children.

Suddenly, every word out of her mouth, every action of hers, made sense. She had left him not because she had loved her dream of being a doctor, her freedom more than she had loved him.

His chest felt tight, a hollow ringing in his ears.

What would he have done if she had told him the truth? He would have never thought any less of her, he would have...

His limbs felt restless, his skin too tight to contain the emotions within him.

She had never told him the entire truth. She had sacrificed her own happiness and his so that he could do his duty. She was every bit the magnificent woman he thought she was.

And with the realization brought threadbare hope and excruciating anguish. Anguish that she had never trusted him enough with her secret, trusted him enough with the truth.

After everything he had just told her yesterday, after the maelstrom of guilt and pain he had felt just recounting that horrible day to Ayaan again, he should have felt nothing. Being numb would have been a blessing in more ways than one.

But of course not. Apparently, he still hadn't killed everything inside him that felt, and hurt and was wounded. He wanted to reach inside him and pluck it out with his bare hands, he wanted to stop feeling so much.

And so he went to see her, the woman who, it seemed, would always have something to teach him, who would always guide him.

Nikhat shivered even though the water that gushed out of the gleaming silver-and-gold faucets was piping hot, and the steam from it curled her hair around her face. The subtle scent from the rose oil that she had poured into the water teased her nostrils, coating her skin with it.

If anyone had asked her what she had done today, she had no answer for them. She had wandered through the palace, wherever she was allowed, until an old guard had stopped her and inquired if she was okay.

Flushing, she had looked around herself, claimed that she was lost and walked back to her own suite.

The grandiose decor of her quarters, the view of the sky glimmering with stars, the sweeping arches and walkways in the courtyard below her balcony, nothing could hold her attention. Feeling as if the walls would close in on her, she had finally fled for some air.

And here she was now, waiting for the minimal staff to retire for the night, waiting for the minute when she could go to him. Maybe if she saw him, if she touched him, this chill she felt inside might abate.

Here in the palace there was still a fragile thread of sanity intact inside her, a small shred of propriety.

She scooped up a handful of water and threw it on her

face, to stifle the hysterical little laugh that threatened to escape her.

It was so pathetic—this tiny little nod to decorum, this bone-deep clinging to tradition when her entire world was crumbling under the weight of her very own confusion.

Pulling her wet hair back with one hand, she reached for a towel, when he suddenly appeared at the entrance to the bathroom.

His jet-black hair gleamed with wetness, his unshaved chin adding to the dangerous glint in his dark eyes. His collarbone stuck out from the opening of his white cotton shirt.

The sheer decadence of the marble-and-gold decor, the glitter of the mirror that caught the tiny little lights from the chandelier in the dome-shaped ceiling, the extravagantly soft cotton in her fingers—everything she had marveled over on her first night here in the palace—vanished in his presence.

Nothing could match the stark power of the man looking at her as though he owned her. Nothing could add or take away from the raw sensuality that was a very part of his nature.

He didn't say a word, his gaze traveling over her nakedness thoroughly, the fire in it burning higher and hotter. And she didn't shy from it, though her fingers tightened over the towel.

"Get out of the tub."

His words, spoken in low, raw tones did what the savage gleam in his eyes hadn't. It sent a prickle of apprehension across her skin, drawing goose bumps. Something felt wrong, something more than the fact that she had pushed him into reliving his worst nightmare because she had wanted to be sure she had made the right decision.

"I'm sorry about last night, Azeez. I never meant to push you—"

He leveled another look at her, and more words wouldn't come. A chill that had nothing to do with her nudity clamped her spine. Shivering, she took the chance to dry her skin.

The sound of the water whooshing out of the tub was gone, leaving them in heavy, sweltering silence. She dragged the towel against herself over one arm, then the other. His looming presence called to her like nothing she had ever known, and she looked up.

Molten fire blazed in his eyes. The fire of the desire between them, she understood. But this thing that was swelling and arcing between them, it was tempered with something else, something that she didn't understand.

She was already as fragile as a house of cards. One harsh breath of air and she felt as if she would come undone.

He had never refrained from telling her what he thought, never held back the force of his passion, or fury or anything.

Holding one edge of the towel over her breasts, she pressed it to her midriff, and suddenly realized he was within touching distance. A soft gasp fell from her mouth as he plucked the towel from her hand, threw it behind him. His long fingers clasped tight around her wrist, he pulled her forward until she landed against his chest, splashing his unbuttoned cotton shirt with drops of water.

Her fingers latched on to the soft fabric, her nipples tightening into needy little points. And then and only then did she realize the storm of fierce emotion that he was holding at bay with sheer will. It was in the way his fingers held her hips—pressing, possessing, branding instead of caressing, in the way he pushed the rigid length of his arousal into her belly, in the way he shivered, as if it cost him every ounce of control not to snap.

Her legs trembling under her, she gazed up at his face and an answering shudder went through her. He looked gloriously angry, every inch of his angular face taking on a forbidden cast.

And still, she was not afraid; still, she did not ask him to release her as every rational instinct in her was urging her to; still she did not try to pull herself from his grasp. Instead, she listened to the primitive one, the one that had roared with anger and ache that long-ago day when she had met the doctor in New York, the one who she had shut away behind a cage of practicality and duty with the chains of her will.

It made her stand her ground, it made her clasp his cheek in a brazen challenge.

He inhaled in a long-drawn breath. His thumb moved over her cheek, her jaw, before settling on her lower lip. If she had felt the anger simmering in his eyes, just before his thumb pressed against her bottom lip, she didn't know. She could only feel the little shivers spewing into life all over her, could only feel her breasts getting heavier, a rush of wetness gathering at her sex.

She dug her fingers into his shoulders as he continued to trace the shape of her lip, pushed his thumb inside her mouth. Heat bloomed low in her stomach and she sucked his finger into her mouth.

Instinct drove her and she pressed herself into him, the hard, pulsing weight of his erection leaving an imprint on her belly. Shock waves pulsed between her legs and she clutched hard with a moan.

She bent her head and licked the crook of his neck, pulled the scent of him deeper into her lungs until all she could feel was him. She wanted to say something, ask him what was wrong, comfort him if she could, and yet words would not come, as if her body was drowning under the avalanche of sensations, as if she was finally incapable of processing a thought, much less speaking it.

His hand around her waist, he suddenly moved and tugged her along with him. Anticipation and need burst into flames under her skin, heating her up as he positioned them in front of the huge marble vanity, facing the mirror.

The glitter from numerous gilded light fixtures above the mirror bathed them in golden light. She pulled another breath through her parched throat, and he shrugged his shirt off his shoulders.

She feasted her eyes on his chest, on the dark nipples, the hunger in her rising, her skin feverish with need. When he dropped his loose trousers and his erection grazed her buttocks, she gasped, as if she was drowning. Or maybe she was. But she didn't care. She didn't care about anything, couldn't think of anything except the thought of that rigid, velvet weight pushing inside her, filling all the empty places she had covered up.

Her breasts became heavy, her nipples turning into unbearable points of need at the luscious gleam in his eyes.

"Have you ever spoken the truth with me?"

His question shattered the silence and yet she couldn't digest the weight of it as his finger drew maddening circles around her nipple. The anticipation coiling inside her lower belly was too much to bear, as if the cognitive part of her brain was struggling to react under so much sensory input.

She let out a long, keen moan as his fingers finally pinched her nipple. Tremors arrowed down, drenching her sex in wetness. Her spine arched into him, she grasped his wrists to keep his fingers on the tight buds, needing more, ready to beg for more.

But he didn't comply and disappointment cut through her. With his hand at the base of her spine, he didn't let her arch into him. His fingers moved restlessly over her breasts, touching, not touching her nipples, moved over to her stomach, never still, never touching her where she wanted to be touched. An anguished sob rose through her the moment she realized.

He was punishing her. This, tonight, it was not about making love. This was about the fury that was bursting inside him seeking an outlet. And not because he was denying her what she wanted.

It was mastery over her mind that he craved. And he didn't leave a doubt. He didn't need to speak to say it. It was in everything he didn't say, in the way he wouldn't even meet her eyes.

And yet she couldn't deny him, yet she couldn't summon the single word *no*. Because if she did, he would stop. And she didn't want him to stop. And therein lay his victory, therein lay the prize he was after.

He pressed his palm at the base of her spine, willing her to yield. And she did.

Supporting herself on her hands, she leaned over until her breasts touched the marble. Her nipples tightened at the cold, but it was one snowflake compared to the burning flames of her desire.

She felt his mouth press into her shoulder blade, trail down, leaving wet heat. Sometimes he licked, sometimes he bit the flesh. And every stroke of his tongue, every drag of his teeth pushed her a little closer to the edge.

"Spread your legs." His tongue licked the seam of her ear shell, his voice like a silken caress.

Heat streaking her inside out, Nikhat did. His palm cupped her mound, the heel of it rubbing against the sensitive bundle of nerves within her core. She was panting now, moving her body to a rhythm only she knew, climbing higher and higher. Her forehead was clammy with sweat. His arm wrapped around her waist, he stopped her little movements.

Her release was so close, she could taste it on her tongue.

Her knuckles showed white where she gripped the marble, her entire body shuddering like a bow, ready to fall apart with one stroke.

But he didn't give her that.

He pressed his body into hers until his erection rubbed against her, and she turned her head and looked at him.

Desire. Anger. Fury. Everything danced in his ebony gaze.

"Azeez, please don't shut me out now." She choked on the words rushing out of her, struggling to say them, fighting to say them right.

But instead of answering her, instead of shouting at her, instead of flaying her with that wicked tongue of his, he gripped her hips and entered her in one long, deep thrust.

She clutched her eyes closed and whimpered as her nerves short-circuited and she orgasmed in a flurry of pleasure. His hoarse cry clashed against hers, drowning them in the sound of their mingled relief.

The waves piled and pooled over her lower belly, and she shivered. One arm over her spine, one around her waist, he held her tight against him until the little tremors subsided, until she could once again feel her body, until the receding waves washed away the profound sense of joy and fulfillment she had found.

Once again, leaving her empty.

She was laid out in front of him like a feast, and Azeez could see nothing past her trembling flesh, feel nothing past how she felt around him. He ran his hands all over her back, her skin like raw silk under his hands, her body molding to his will and his desire.

And still, he was not satisfied. Still, the hurt inside him would not abate.

"Azeez," she said, whispering his name like a prayer,

turning to look at him, her lithe body angling itself beneath him like a bow. He was entrenched deep inside her, willing himself to pull out, willing himself to stop before he created new hurts, willing himself to close the vein that was still bleeding out.

He looked at her then, and the anger that had pushed him to use her like this, receded. He bent and took her mouth; only desire and his cold will was left now. She returned the kiss with equal fervor, with a desperation that tugged at his heart. But the kiss could not reach it.

He was so hard and deep inside her, her pleasure, her body, her mind, and even her strong will, they were all his in the moment as he wanted, she was his the way he wanted. Absolutely, where they only existed together. He could have happily died in that moment.

Reaching under her sensuous body, he filled his hands with her breasts and tweaked her nipples.

She immediately arched into him, losing all thought of that guttural request she had made. And he pulled out and thrust back.

The sound of that low moan she made in the back of her throat, the drag of his hips against hers, the shuddering in her long legs as he set an unrelenting rhythm, he let himself drown in all the sensations she created for him. She was perfect for him in every way, as he had always assumed, and he took her, slowly, deliciously, until the walls of her sex clamped him tight.

With every slow thrust, he plundered deeper inside her wet heat, for every coil of pleasure he took, he released the anger, the hurt inside him.

He searched inside for the last ounce of his control, kissed her spine and breathed the words into her. "I would have found a way, Nikhat, I would have protected you."

She gasped, but he didn't let her recover from his assault.

He found the center of her swollen heat and tweaked it between his fingers. Her climax broke out of her, and he rode on its waves. Her sex clenched him hard, the contractions of her muscles pushing him into his own release.

His orgasm reverberated through him, shattering him and rebuilding him at the same time. Still inside her, he clutched her to him for another weak, wavering moment, breathed in her scent, tasted her skin, reveled in the cocoon of her body.

She cared about him, he knew that. And she was back here; she had helped him see through the darkness into light. But the truth she had hidden, the sacrifice she had made, it unmanned him.

She was everything he had always thought she was, and by the same token, she had set herself out of his reach.

His first instinct was to bind her to him, to shackle her with his power until there was nowhere she could go, to leave her with no avenue except him.

And he fought black the cloud of his selfish desires, the thundering darkness of his heart, welcomed the chill that pervaded him as he finally made his decision.

To shackle her to him again when it was the very thing she had walked away from with complete certainty, it would break her. And he didn't want her like that.

He would agree to Ayaan's demands, do everything his brother had asked of him and he would do it the way it needed to be done.

His passionate nature rebelled at the thought of giving her up. His heart had never been denied, he had never learned control.

And to deny his heart what it wanted while doing his duty, that was to be his penance.

He picked up Nikhat and took her to the bathtub again. He turned on the water and washed her with the jasmine

soap that she loved. He wiped her, wrapped her in a robe
and carried her back to the bed.

And then he saw the tears in her beautiful brown eyes.
She clasped his wrist and pressed her warm mouth to it as
he pulled the covers over her.

"Sleep, *habeebi*," he whispered, and walked out of her
suite without looking back.

His heart, finally, felt like a hard rock inside his chest.
Something he had been struggling to achieve for six long
years.

CHAPTER TWELVE

NIKHAT JERKED AWAKE from a fitful sleep and struggled to find her bearings. Her eyes were gritty. Sweat beaded her brow and her sheets were tangled around her hips. Unease weighed in her stomach and she turned to check the time. The little digital alarm clock said 5:00 a.m. Pushing the sheets away, she stepped down from the bed, lethargy making her slow.

Her body ached between her legs. Her abdomen was stiff, as if she had done a hundred push-ups, her arms hurt, too.

But it was more an exquisite soreness than any real pain and worth every bit.

For several seconds, she stood there, her vision dizzying, everything Azeez had said slamming back into her like pieces of a puzzle. The picture that emerged knocked the breath out of her.

I deserved the truth, Nikhat.

How did he know?

Her heart stuttered, struggling to keep up with her emotions. She changed into a caftan and leggings and grabbed a shawl to wrap around her torso.

The palace corridors were empty, eerie, and she couldn't shake off the impression that she was going to her doom.

No, she wasn't going to think like that. She shoved aside

the anxiety and hugged the relief that danced under that. Somehow, Azeez had learned the truth now. He was entitled to his anger.

But when his initial shock receded, he would surely understand why she had made the decision to leave him all those years ago. He had to. She wouldn't think about it any other way, she couldn't bear to.

Halting outside his suite's door, she sucked in a deep breath and clutched the edges of the shawl tight.

Everything inside her felt as if it hung in the balance, every minute of her life, every decision she had made falling away like sand sinking away under one's toes.

She pushed the door and struggled against the dazzling glare of light.

Approximately twenty men were inside the room, talking in small groups, some at laptops, some taking notes from Ayaan, she realized.

Had she been so lost in her own fears that she hadn't even heard a single voice?

Her heart pounded so loudly that for a few minutes all she could hear was the thundering beat of it in her ears. She felt her face heat as a sound escaped her mouth. One by one, the faces turned, the hushed whispers died down, shock and astonishment and even disapproval at her presence marring the strange faces.

For a dizzying second, Nikhat thought she would collapse under the weight of her own anxiety. Run, move, hide.

Her brain was issuing the standard flight responses, triggering fear in her, because she was standing outside the prince's wing, a wing that was forbidden to women, at the crack of dawn, her hair flowing behind her, clad in nothing but an old caftan and leggings, her eyes red-rimmed with the tears she had shed, her mouth and neck still bearing the evidence of his kisses.

And behind all of them, sitting in a gold-edged armchair covered in red velvet, his dark gaze calmly observing her, without anger, without any expression, really, was Azeez.

He looked forbidding, cold, a distant stranger, not at all the man she knew so intimately.

His gaze found hers the exact second hers found his. And still she did not turn around, she didn't fake confusion and flee as her rational mind was urging her to. She couldn't even look away from him.

She heard Ayaan's voice in a distant corner of her functioning mind, ordering them all to leave, she heard the room empty, she saw realization dawn on some faces that recognized her and curious disapproval on others that didn't. But it was all only on the periphery of her consciousness, almost as if it was happening to another poor deluded woman. Because, he, the dark Prince of Dahaar, he was at the center of her world, as he had always been.

She stepped in and closed the doors behind them. There was still no reaction in his face. He didn't blink, he didn't acknowledge her by the flicker of a muscle.

He only stared at her, an icy chill in his gaze, a remote set to his mouth, and that was when finally Nikhat began to worry.

She stopped when she neared him. Her shawl had fallen away long ago, leaving her in the thin cotton caftan separating her bare skin from his gaze.

And still, in the nothingness of his expression, in the riot of fear and worry that filled her, still, an electric charge danced between them.

There was nothing else to do but speak her mind, put her greatest fear into words. She stood in front of him, like his prisoner waiting for judgment.

"You have shown yourself to them," she said, standing awkwardly, her entire body trembling.

"As have you," he said, looking up at her, his gaze still inscrutable. "What will happen to your reputation, your dream, your clinic now?"

There was no threat in his words, implied or unsaid, but it was the utter lack of anything else that sent a shiver zigzagging across her spine. It was unbearable that he freeze her out like this, unbearable to be in front of him and see a stranger.

A fierce churning began in her stomach, but she held it off.

No, he wouldn't, he couldn't be angry with her over this, it was not acceptable to her. She had to get them through this, he would understand why, he would see how much she loved him, how much it hurt to be away from him, how much a part of her permanently froze every time she left him.

This time she didn't want to go, she didn't want to break her heart again.

"You will not let any harm come to my reputation, or my dream."

With a soft grunt, he rose to his feet. The smile that curved his mouth chilled her to the core. It was full of such resignation that she would never forget it. "You trust me now? When you didn't trust me with the biggest truth of our lives?"

She clasped his hands, her own frightfully cold. He still did not sound angry and it was the very lack of that anger that scared her. Hours ago he had been angry when he made love to her. Now it felt as if there was just an icy disdain that she couldn't reach. "I did it for you, Azeez. They said…the chances of me conceiving were next to nil. That even if I went off my medication and tried, there would be no guarantees.

"That last trip to New York, the doctor performed a surgery immediately to remove some of the lesions.

"When I came back, I was so alone, so scared. I wanted to tell you, I wanted to howl. Then…my father said your coronation was imminent. And my heart shattered.

"I barely felt like a woman and to be your wife, to be the queen…But I still came to see you. And you—" tears spilled over her cheeks "—you were so excited. You said you couldn't wait to follow in your father's footsteps, that you couldn't wait to add your own stamp to the Al Sharif history, that you couldn't wait to create a legacy your heir, and your children, would want to carry forward.

"You needed a queen, you needed a wife who would give you sons, you needed a woman whose presence by your side would add strength to your rule, to your regime."

She hiccuped and wiped her hands over her cheeks. "You were vibrant, charming, a prince of the world. I…I already was nothing compared to you. It was an uphill battle for us both. Then to find that I might never conceive, that I was broken at the one thing you did need from me…I broke my own heart."

He grabbed her then, his fingers digging into her flesh. "Don't you dare call yourself broken."

"But I am. I spent my whole life seeing my father, an average aide to the royal family, disappointed again and again that he had no son. My mother knew the risks she was taking on her health and yet she had one child after another.

"An educated man like Richard…he knew all about my condition, he said he was fine with it…except when he decided he wanted children. It hurt so much to face that reality, to be denied my chance at happiness just because…God, if that had happened with you, if it was your resentment I would have to see every day, or even worse, if you had to take another wife for an heir, it would have killed me, it—"

"How dare you compare me to another man, how dare you extrapolate my feelings like I was an object of science? You don't know what I would have said or done. I was an honorable man. I would have loved you. I would have found—"

"You think I doubted your intentions?" It was her turn to shout. Her throat was raw, her eyes stung. But beneath it all, fear fisted her chest. "I trusted your word, your love, Azeez. I just couldn't put that choice in front of you. You would have hated me later, resented me for that choice. I couldn't bear the idea of it. I couldn't—"

He pulled her to him, his arm gentle around her. She felt his breath blow over her hair, felt the shudder that went through him. "You broke my heart, Nikhat, and you didn't even tell me the truth. You only thought of yourself."

His palms on her shoulders, he pushed her until he could look into her face. And the loss she saw there, it said everything he didn't say. "I love you, Azeez. I don't remember a moment of my life when I didn't."

"Do you know the meaning of the word? Even if I could understand why you didn't tell me all those years ago, what about the last few weeks? I bared everything to you, I let you see me at my darkest. All you did was protect yourself even as you made love with me. Was it your pride or your love that led you to hide the truth even then?"

"I'm sorry, Azeez. I am here now, I will be yours in any way you want me."

Any hint of softening she had seen vanished, leaving those eyes of his empty again. He had never felt more unattainable, more out of the reach of her heart. "Because now you *think* I'm as damaged as you are?"

She flinched, as if he had slapped her, as if he had called her very soul into question. And she realized what she had done. "I have never thought that, not for a second."

"You were right. If I had married you then, we would have destroyed each other with doubts and insecurities. And now, now there's nothing but bitterness of the past, Nikhat, nothing but broken and impossible dreams between us.

Maybe we never were worthy of each other."

He turned away from her, and his retreat was final, his withdrawal leaching away every ounce of warmth from the room. "You will leave the palace tomorrow. There will be a new obstetrician for Princess Zohra.

"No one will dare to talk about seeing you here, no one will dare point a finger in your family's direction. Not after the service you have done for us. Or they will face the crown's wrath.

"You will have your clinic. You will be back with your sisters. Thank you for everything you have done for me, Nikhat. I release you from your promise."

Only a few days had passed when Azeez learned that his parents were back in Dahaara, in the palace. And yet it felt as if it had been an eternity since he had taken the decision that would dictate the rest of his life.

That was already dictating it now.

Running both hands through his hair, he drew a shuddering breath as the guard announced his arrival in their private suite.

He pushed the doors open and breathed in relief as he saw Ayaan and Zohra also waiting. He had made the right decision. But he still needed Ayaan's support in this moment.

Grief, and pain and so much more that he couldn't sift through, it all rose inside him like the wave of a tsunami as he reached his mother.

And the pain he saw in her eyes, the aching hunger as she studied him, that she quickly covered up with a quiet dignity, the piercing hesitation in her smile, it lanced through him. God, how selfish he had been to rob her of this joy in the wake of everything she had borne, how foolish to rob himself of the warmth and understanding that stole through him.

Reaching for her hands, he tugged her up, tears now running down his cheeks freely. "Will you ever forgive me?"

A cry burst free from her mouth as she hugged him hard, her tears soaking through his tunic. Wrapping his arms around her, he held her through the wracking sobs that shook her fragile frame, whispered apologies and promises, and finally felt his world finding some kind of peace.

"I knew it. And after all these years, too… Do you see this, Zohra?" Ayaan quipped.

Her mouth wreathed in smiles, Zohra turned to him. "What?"

"He's still her favorite. I don't remember her hugging me that hard when I came back," he finally explained, and laughter rippled through the room.

Meeting his brother's gaze, Azeez offered a nod of thanks. He owed his brother everything and he was determined to spend his life taking every burden away from him.

This was how it had been, his family. It had been his strength, his joy. Amira was gone, but she would always have a place in their hearts. His gaze fell on Princess Zohra and the happiness he saw there.

And he felt heartened by it.

Even with his heart cold in his chest, he still had so much in the world to live for. He placed a kiss to the top of his mother's head, the scent of her calming him.

Wiping her hands over her cheeks, his mother smiled at him. "I have my sons back." She turned toward his father, the regal dignity that had always been her strength inching back into her shoulders. "More than I ever hoped for."

Turning toward his father, Azeez clasped his hands, saw the toll the past few years had taken on him. It was time for him to shoulder that burden, time for his father to rest. No matter that he was burying his own heart in the process.

When Azeez tried to speak, his father shook his head. "Let us leave the past where it is, Azeez. You're here now and prepared to aid your brother in serving Dahaar. That's all I've ever asked of you and Ayaan."

Azeez knelt in front of his king, the man who had taught him everything he knew, the man whom he had always looked up to. And felt the rightness of what he was about to say, knew that the woman he loved, would always love, would be proud of the man he had finally become again.

"If you and Mother will allow me, and if it's acceptable to Ayaan, I will spend the rest of my life doing what I was born to do, what you have prepared me for all my life, Father. I am ready to be king, ready to be Dahaar's servant for the rest of my life."

The shocked gasp from his mother, the unconventional and totally characteristic shout of joy from Princess Zohra, the sheen of tears in his father's eyes, the glint of shining pride in Ayaan's eyes as he reached Azeez and enfolded him in a tight hug, it flew through Azeez, lending him the strength he needed.

His father's simple yes reverberated in the room, and through the congratulations that followed the rest of the day, through the very joy and celebrations that began to pervade the palace, through his brother's concerned questions about Nikhat and him, Azeez kept a smile on his face and swallowed his own heartache.

CHAPTER THIRTEEN

NIKHAT WASHED HER hands at the sink in the attached bathroom of her clinic and grabbed a hand towel. Even though the building for her new clinic was air-conditioned and she had been back in Dahaar for a few weeks now, she wasn't used to the blistering heat of the day yet.

Making sure her hair stayed in her braid, she shied away from the mirror quickly, refusing to give in to the chasm of self-pity that was just waiting to drag her down.

She walked back into her consulting rooms. After almost a month, it still caught her breath every time she looked around and realized she was living her dream.

The new clinic was more than anything she had hoped for, in scope and breadth, thanks to the Princes of Dahaar.

It had been a month since she had left the palace…or rather she had been, with the utmost respect, kicked out. She had not let herself sit down for a minute, would not let herself stop even for a second.

When night came, she fell into exhausted sleep after being on her feet nonstop for twelve to thirteen hours. There were interviews she was conducting to find more qualified personnel—nurses, even midwives, not necessarily with the highest credentials, but the ones that most of the population in Dahaara trusted.

There was inventory to be organized and sorted every

day, medical supplies to be distributed. Not that any resource that she needed had been left out.

From an administrator for the clinic to oversee bureaucratic roadblocks she came across everywhere she turned, to a finance manager who had access and control over the fund that the royal family had set up for the clinic, from a twenty-year-old woman who was pursuing her degree in health care and was putting together educational material, pamphlets, even booklets to spread word about the clinic, to an elderly woman who brought lunches and coffee for the staff...every little detail had been sorted out.

All Nikhat needed was to finalize the candidates—which was proving the hardest, because qualified female doctors, ones that families would feel comfortable about sending the women of their families to, were hard to find.

She got a thrill every time she saw her name plaque outside the building. So what if, at the same time, she felt as if there was a hole in her chest? So what if she caught a spasm of such intense longing in the middle of the day that she thought she would never smile again?

The one thing she did wish she could do was tune out the world around her. It was hard enough, every second of every day, to push back the realization that he was just a few miles away in the palace and yet he had never been farther from her.

It was a month in which every day she felt her heart breaking again, in which Dahaar and its people had exploded with the news that Prince Azeez bin Rashid Al Sharif was alive and back in Dahaara.

Clutching the cold metal surface of her desk, she swallowed back the dizzying whirl of grief that rose through her. If she gave in to one tear, she was afraid she would not stop.

"Nikhat?"

She whirled around and saw Princess Zohra standing at

the entrance to her office, security guards hovering behind her. Drawing in a deep breath, Nikhat smiled. "Princess Zohra, please come in. You could have just summoned me to the palace if you—"

She caught herself as the princess dismissed the guards and closed the door behind her. Neither Princess Zohra, nor even Ayaan, could summon Nikhat to the palace.

Nikhat's name was not to be mentioned in the palace, not even her shadow was to be near it. That was the condition Azeez had laid out in front of his brother, Ayaan had told her, his face pinched.

Azeez Al Sharif did nothing in half measures. His rejection of her was as absolute as his love for her had been.

Even though still in her second trimester, Zohra was already big, and the strain showed on her fragile features. Hurrying to the other side of the desk, Nikhat pulled out a chair for her. Drawing a loud breath, Zohra shook her head.

"I would rather stand. All I do these days seems like sitting around, waiting for people to arrange my day, and my life.

"Now that King Malik and Queen Fatima are back, even my body is not my own. Queen Fatima is driving me crazy with her advice, her rituals, hovering over me. She won't let Azeez or me out of her sight, checking on us every few hours. Ayaan said he is beginning to feel like the ignored middle child.

"How I wish you were back there, Nikhat. The new ob-gyn is terrified of the queen and agrees to everything she proposes. Queen Fatima actually forbade me from visiting Siyaad, from seeing my sister and brother, and the stupid woman just nodded.

"I finally had to threaten Ayaan that I would leave for Siyaad and have the babies there unless he lets me see you here. I will come to you every few days, Nikhat. That way, you can check my progress and I get away from the blasted palace for a few hours. Ask your administrator to call my assistant. I'm sure my being your patient can be used to spread the word about the clinic. And if there's an emergency at the palace, that woman can tend to me. Will you still handle my delivery?"

Clutching Zohra's hands in hers, Nikhat smiled. "Of course, Princess Zohra. I—"

"Really, Nikhat. Can I just be Zohra with you?"

Smiling at her assertiveness, Nikhat nodded.

"That's great." She walked around her office and Nikhat had a feeling the princess was nowhere near done. Turning around, she studied Nikhat, her sharp gaze lingering over the dark shadows under her eyes. "You have no idea how thrilled I am that I don't have to be the queen. I know that Ayaan will still be extremely busy, but at least—"

Nikhat froze. "But...the coronation, it was supposed to be in a fortnight. Is it being postponed?"

Her gaze steady, Zohra shook her head. And Nikhat realized what Zohra was saying, what she had come to tell Nikhat. Blood rushed from her head, and spots danced in front of her eyes. The truth slammed into her from every side, she swayed where she stood. "He..." *Ya Allah*, it hurt to even speak his name. "He...is to be king?"

Reaching for her, Zohra steadied Nikhat. "Yes. They are making a statement tomorrow. The aides are all running around like crazy. Can you imagine? They have just over a week to find him—"

"A wife," Nikhat said, the word burning on her lips.

A prince needed a wife to be king.

Her mind whirled, the walls of the office she had cherished so much closing in on her. She couldn't continue to live in Dahaar and see the news of him with his wife, one who would give him sons, some unknown woman taking everything Nikhat wanted.

It was unbearable.

"If you are thinking of just running away again, believe me, Nikhat, it won't help."

Nikhat turned around, astonished at how well Zohra could read her mind. "What do I do, Zohra? I broke my own heart last time. I…I can't give him what he needs."

"I don't believe the man I've come to know the last few weeks, everything I've learned about what he has been through, he…gives his heart lightly, nor will he resent you for what you can't change. You reached through to him when not even his parents and brother could, Nikhat. Doesn't that tell you something?"

"You know?"

Her hands resting on her belly, Zohra nodded. "Ayaan told me after I pestered him about you and Azeez.

"I can't imagine what you must have felt when you learned about your condition. I can't imagine feeling like I couldn't be everything Ayaan needed me to be. But how it will dictate your life, that's up to you."

There was no sympathy or comfort in Zohra's voice. Only cold hard facts. Maybe if she had had a friend like this before, maybe if she had confided in someone…Nikhat smiled through the sheen of tears gathering in her eyes, appreciating Zohra's coming all the way. "Thank you, Zohra."

"I do feel safe in your hands. But I didn't come for you. I came for him."

"For Azeez?"

"I understand now why it killed Ayaan to see Azeez like that, why he was prepared to do anything for his brother.

"Because Azeez would too.

"He agreed to everything Ayaan set in front of him, he

even agreed to bear your presence, despite his pride, so that I would feel better, didn't he? I don't like the look that has come back into his eyes. He is my brother, too, now, and my king. He has my loyalty, and my love.

"But if you go near him, make sure you know your mind, Nikhat. Because it's not his acceptance you're craving, is it?"

With that parting shot, Zohra left, leaving Nikhat reeling under the weight of her words. No one had ever spoken to her like that, ever cut through the pain she had surrounded herself with, so effectively.

For the rest of the afternoon, Nikhat went through her duties like an automaton. She visited a couple of patients in their homes, went through the inventory and finally went home.

Her sisters' laughter and conversation surrounded her with its usual warmth yet she felt as if she was removed from it all, a deep freeze surrounding her heart.

A strange sort of fever gripped her, and yet fear held her back. She went in search of her father, the only choice left to her slowly gaining power inside her head. And with that came anger, too, and the strength to speak her mind.

She found him standing on the balcony, looking out into the streets of Dahaara.

He turned as she approached, frowning. "Nikhat? Is something wrong?"

She glared at him, the haunting desperation in her finding a target. Years of pain coated her cutting words, the freedom of finally making a decision lending her the strength to lash out. "You knew he's going to be king. And yet you didn't say a word. Are you so ashamed of me? Do I mean nothing to you?"

His mouth compressed, he blanched and she thought he would walk away without a word. But she wouldn't let him.

Instead, he covered her hand with his. And tears gathered in her throat. "I have never wanted this grief for you, Nikhat."

"No, all you wanted was for me to be average and traditional, but I'm not, Father."

"You think I don't know that?" He sighed deeply, something stark in his gaze. "I never quite learned how to protect you."

Her gaze flew to him. "What are you talking about?"

"I know you blame me for your mother's death. But I never wanted a son at the cost of her life, Nikhat. She did. She was obsessed with it, weaved dreams about what I wanted."

Just as Nikhat had done. She sagged against the wall. She always thought that it had been her father who had wanted a son. And yet thinking back, he had never actually said that. "Why didn't you ever tell me?"

Her father stared ahead and she instantly realized he was not comfortable talking about this. And yet he was making the effort. "You were twelve when she died, Nikhat. You were already grieving, taking on so many duties around the house. And later, I didn't want to taint your memory of her.

"Why would I feel the need for a son when I had you, when in every way that mattered, you always helped me as much as you could?"

Shock reverberating through her, Nikhat shook her head. Lies, they had to be lies. But having lived away for so long, she had forgotten what a rigid, traditional man her father was. Had she expected him to be different just as she was now?

Clutching her hand tight between his, he met her gaze. And the pride and love she saw in those brown eyes that she had inherited, swept through her. "From the moment you were born, you were this bundle of wonder, Nikhat, unlike anything I had ever expected in a daughter.

"Like every other man in Dahaar, I thought you had very less consequence for me. I loved you as I do every one of your sisters, but you…you were a revelation.

"As you grew older, I had no idea what I would do with you, how to channel your intelligence, your thirst for more than I could provide. I was both afraid and so proud when King Malik commanded that you be educated by Princess Amira's side.

"I despaired of how I would protect you, your happiness from the world, from your own expectations…" He exhaled a long breath. "And from Prince Azeez.

"As your father, that was my foremost duty to you, Nikhat. To protect you.

"When you learned of your condition, I was terrified of what you would do."

"You knew?"

"Of course I knew. I read every report, and it broke my heart. Once again, I was afraid of what kind of future you would have in Dahaar. But you shocked me with your strength. And suddenly, I saw that you had the perfect solution. You were destined for greater things, and Dahaar and I, we would do nothing but curtail you. Prince Azeez would bring nothing but pain to you.

"So I insisted you not return. For your own good and for your sisters'."

He had given her so much thought and she…she had thought him hard-hearted, uncaring about anything but tradition. A tear rolled down her cheek. It was apparently the day she had to walk through fire. "I had a good life in New York, Father. But I needed you and my sisters, too."

"Forgive me for not realizing that, Nikhat. When you came back and when I heard the rumors, I thought history was repeating itself. And your sisters, they are not like you."

Her heart bursting, Nikhat hugged him hard, even as she felt him stiffen against her. He was not used to such blatant gestures or displays of emotion. He had never been, would never be.

And she had to accept him this way, accept that he had loved her in his own way, and had tried to protect her the only way he knew.

This was why he hadn't met her eyes since she had returned from the palace, why he had banned her sisters from voicing their incessant questions about the coronation.

And that small fact gave her a fierce strength.

She pulled back, her heart racing faster and faster. She smiled at him as he looked at her quietly. "I have to go to him, Father. I have to show him my heart. I have to hope that he will accept my love, see that I'm ready for him."

That old intractability swept into his gaze, but this time she saw it for his concern. His shoulders a tight line, he nodded. "Are you ready for the consequences, Nikhat?"

Nikhat nodded, battling the fear that knotted her stomach.

Had Azeez already made his decision that last night they had spent together? Was that why he had been so ferociously cruel with her? She hadn't realized she had presented him with a choice, that she had only wanted him if he could be anyone but himself; but the king.

Her love or his duty?

And after everything he had gone through to find himself again...

She had to believe that he still loved her. She couldn't bear to think of a future without him now. And if he did love her...if she wanted to share her life with Azeez, she would have to face the fact every day that she might never have children. Everyone would question her eligibility, a whole nation would wonder about her inability to conceive.

But he...he would never resent her. She had loved him before there had been guilt and shadows in his eyes and she loved the honorable man he was now. To imply that he didn't feel the same for her was calling into question his very honor, his very nature, the very thing that made him Azeez Al Sharif.

All along, she had thought she had accepted her condition, she had thought she had forged herself a life, went after her dreams despite it.

But she had robbed herself of her biggest happiness, run far from the one man she had loved more than life itself. Her strength had been nothing but a mirage, an illusion.

For the first time in her life, she felt as if she was ready to choose her own happiness, as if she was worthy of the man she loved.

"I've always been his, Father."

Ten more days.

There were ten more days before his coronation and he didn't know how long before he took a wife. He had met a couple of the "eligible candidates" this morning. He couldn't remember their names, much less their faces.

Nodding at his mother and her aides, he had said any one of them was acceptable to him. He knew, in the back of his mind, that he was being more than cruel to the woman in question. None of this was her fault. But seeing them was all he could manage before his gut churned with a vicious force.

None of them was the woman he wanted with every breath in him.

They knew what they were getting into, he reassured

himself, walking back into his bedchamber and dismissing his three assistants and two aides with one command.

His physiotherapist lingered, a flash of anxiety on the younger man's face. Azeez signaled for him to leave, too, even knowing that he couldn't afford to miss any sessions, not the night before the public statement was going to be made by his father.

He walked to the middle of the room and tried to move his hip joint in the way Nikhat had taught him.

But instead of that, all he could see was her face. Her lush mouth pinched, her heart in her eyes, breaking, shattering, her body gathered into a tight mass as if she braced herself against him, against his cruel words.

The chasm of yearning in his gut, it felt as wide open as ever and just as painful. He heard the door open behind him and barked an order at whoever dared to come inside after he had banished them all.

Silence met his command. And then he felt it. The way the hairs on his neck stood up, the hint of evening breeze that reached his nostrils coated with jasmine...

There was no jasmine in the courtyards of the Dahaaran palace.

He turned around just as she reached him. Her arms wound around her midriff, her face turned up toward him, she was warmth, she was light, she was the most beautiful, the most courageous woman he had ever seen in the world.

And his heart hurt to look at her and not reach for her.

He stepped back from her, ruthlessly cutting away the thread of hope that flagged within. "Who do I have to punish for letting you in here?"

She didn't answer. Only continued to stare at him—hungrily, greedily, as if she owned him. And she did, she had done for so many years.

"Nikhat?"

Blinking, she met his gaze. "Zohra."

"Ah…of course. I have never met a more stubborn woman, except perhaps you. I have no idea how Ayaan puts up with her." He turned away from her, her wind-kissed hair, the dark shadows under her eyes, challenging his very will. "Why are you here, Nikhat?"

"Will you forgive me, Azeez?"

Nikhat shivered, wondering if she'd died a thousand little deaths in the few seconds that Azeez took to respond. When he turned around, there was no softening of the hard planes of his face, no fire in his empty gaze. He looked tired, drawn, as if he was made of ice and cold rather than the heat and blaze of the desert.

And she realized, she had done this to him.

There was no power in it, only shame. She had truly not been worthy of him until now. She shoved away the clamor of fear that said she had lost him forever, that voice of despair that threatened to pull her under. If she lost him now…

Reaching into the pocket of her coat, she pulled out the box Ayaan had handed her just a few minutes ago, before he had enfolded her in a hug that sent tears to her eyes. She wished she felt half his confidence.

The long velvet case was soft in her hand. Her fingers shaking, it took her what felt like an eternity to open the jeweled clasp. He still didn't say a word.

But now, now Nikhat could feel the tension coil around them, as if someone had left a live wire around them, fizzing, crackling with expectations, and hope and love.

Her jaw fell as she saw the two rubies—one big, sitting in a stark setting, and the relatively smaller one set in twinkling diamonds. She almost lost her nerve then. She looked up to see Azeez eye the rings, saw the moment realization dawned on him.

His jaw tightened, but the fire in his eyes, she knew that fire. "Be very careful about what you're going to say, *ya habeebiti*." Instead of scaring her, however, the low warning note in his words stirred her, stroking her heart, her skin, the very core of her.

Clasping his hands, she looked up at him. "I'm sorry for running away from your love. I'm sorry for not trusting you enough. I thought my condition made me unworthy of you, but it was my fear, my doubt of your love and my own." She had to breathe to speak past the lump in her throat. "I know that you'll protect me from the world, from everyone, even my own insecurities. And I need you, Azeez, I need the joy you bring to my life. I'm ready to be your wife, Azeez, I'm finally ready to be your queen."

The fingers that tilted her chin up were shaking, and when she met his gaze, the love that glimmered in those dark depths shook her from within. "It killed me to send you away, Nikhat." A shudder racked his powerful frame and she hugged him harder, tighter, realizing it was fear. "It wrecked me to tear out my own heart like that, *habeeba*. But you, your magnificent strength, your innate duty, you left me no choice. Realizing that I was in love with you again, whilst also realizing, in that same moment, the man I *needed* to be, it tore me apart. But I couldn't ask you to bear this for me. Not when you made the choice once to walk away from this very fate."

"No. Not from you." Pressing her cheek to his chest, she curled around him, feeling the hard muscles, learning him. He was her home, her everything. "I understand now, Azeez. And I'm so sorry I took so long to realize it. I wish—"

Clasping her cheek, he pressed a fierce kiss to her mouth that shook her very soul. The scent and taste of him seeped into her, invigorating her, filling her with a dizzying joy that had her shivering.

With a hard grip, he tugged her against him, until there was nothing to look at but his beautiful, proud face. "I've never doubted your strength, Nikhat. Your strength in the face of everything you went through, your sense of purpose in everything you have accomplished, it made me realize what I needed to do.

"You showed me I couldn't walk away from my destiny. And I've only ever wanted it with you by my side, *habeeba*."

Smiling through her tears, she plucked the ring out of the case and slid it onto his finger. They had been made for each other, they had both been through fire and emerged to find each other again. "You are the most honorable, most courageous man I've ever met and you are mine."

He clasped her cheek and kissed her, and Nikhat melted into his embrace. "Always," he said, his gaze shining. He pushed the ruby ring onto her finger and kissed her hand, his heart, his love shining in his eyes. "You complete me, Nikhat. You always have. I don't need an heir, I don't need anything in the world, if you are by my side. Do you understand?"

Nikhat nodded, her heart bursting to full with joy, and fierce determination.

EPILOGUE

Seven months later...

THE SOUNDS OF infants crying, loud and wailing, as he pushed the door of his suite had the king of Dahaar doing a double take and checking he had, indeed, entered his own royal chambers.

Confirming that these were indeed his chambers, he closed the doors behind him and leaned against them. The sight that greeted him stole his breath.

His queen, Dr. Nikhat Salima Zakhari Al Sharif, was kneeling on a centuries-old rug, cooing to the little infant with jet-black hair.

The baby cooed at her in return, his toothless mouth splitting into a grin. She changed his diaper, scrunched her nose and turned to his identical twin, who instantly kicked his legs and bestowed a matching smile on her.

"You know, instead of standing there, smiling at us, you could come here and maybe help, Your Highness?"

Laughing, Azeez pushed off the door and reached her.

He slowly sank to the floor, next to her, and picked up the first one.

His nephew didn't smile at him as he did at his wife. He made a note to have his assistant block some time every week—even an hour—that he could spend with them.

Nikhat was always helping out Zohra anyway, in addition to her clinic and her royal duties. His wife, he had discovered, was a bundle of energy, always on the go. Having been so close to his sister and the palace, there wasn't a thing she didn't know. Even his mother hadn't been able to find fault with her. "Which one is this—Rafiq or Tariq?"

Shaking her head, Nikhat picked up the second infant. "How can you not tell? That's Rafiq, older by a whole three minutes, and he totally looks like Zohra. He has her stubbornness, her temper."

Azeez studied him and stole a look at the other one, seeing nothing but identical jet-black eyes like his own and not Ayaan's copper-hued ones, jet-black hair and chubby cheeks.

She cuddled Tariq, and made unintelligible noises. Azeez's breath stuck in his throat. His wife was a natural with babies, a fact Zohra seemed to be eternally grateful for, as she herself was struggling with postpartum depression.

Azeez had been so afraid for Nikhat the first few weeks after Zohra had delivered the twins almost three weeks early. She had been unable to sleep, always going over to see them, wanting to help Zohra, wanting to make sure the twins were okay. His heart had turned into a tight fist in his chest as he waited and watched, hoping and praying that Zohra, even if completely justified, didn't push Nikhat away, or get possessive about her sons. He needn't have worried.

Zohra's heart, it seemed, was as big as her smile. She had welcomed Nikhat with open arms, had leaned on her for real help, overwhelmed by her still-suffering health and her loud, premature-born sons. "Whereas Tariq here is his father's son. He's rarely, if ever, fussy, and sleeps like a dream. Your mother said Ayaan was like that as a baby."

"I guess she told you I was a terror, even as a baby."
Azeez mock frowned and rubbed his nose in Rafiq's fleshy
tummy. Little fingers instantly grabbed his hair and tugged
hard.

She laughed and they spent a few more minutes playing with his nephews. Once they began to yawn, he followed her to the matching cribs she insisted on having in
the second bedroom of their suite. An exact replica of the
ones in Ayaan and Zohra's bedchamber.

*I want to be a real aunt, Azeez, and not just one that buys
toys or plays with them for a few minutes. I want to help her.*

When he had expressed concern about Zohra, she had
smiled at him, tears shimmering in her eyes.

*Zohra said growing up, she'd always had only one par-
ent—either her mother or father—she's glad that her little
boys get two sets instead.*

Swallowing away the sudden knot in his throat, Azeez
followed her lead and laid down Rafiq. He waited as she
fussed a little more, and neatly wrapped them up until they
were snug.

Sighing, she stepped back and he instantly pulled her
tight against him. The scent of her skin both calmed and
aroused him, and he grew instantly hard.

She turned her head so that he could nuzzle into her
neck and with a groan, he grasped her hips and pulled her
into him. "I haven't seen you in a week, wife. I don't want
to share you tonight with these rogues."

"Ayaan is back from Siyaad. I thought it would be nice
if they could have some quiet. And between Zohra and me
and your mother, we don't want to leave the children overnight with nannies unless absolutely necessary."

Grabbing his hair, she angled her head and kissed him.
He sucked her tongue into his mouth, laved her lower lip,
waves of desire as intense as that first time, rolling through

him like a fierce hurricane. "The rogues won't be up for two hours, hopefully," she breathed into his mouth. She turned on the baby monitors before closing the door behind her.

"How did the interviews go in New York for new doctors?" he asked as they reached their own bedchamber. He filled his hands with her lush breasts, the graze of her hard nipples against his palms sending him into a fever. He would suckle them until she made those little noises in the back of her throat, make her climax until she was sobbing his name again.

His name on her lips when they made love, her body all wrapped up around him when they woke, the way she met his gaze across a crowded room and smiled at him, the way she had burrowed into him and sobbed after delivering the twins, *ya Allah*, he loved everything about this woman.

She mumbled some answer, shedding her top first and then peeling off her leggings, revealing long, toned thighs that sent blood rushing from his head. They were too eager, too desperate for each other to indulge in foreplay. On his next breath, she pushed him onto the bed and straddled him.

Nothing mattered but the pursuit of release, of moving inside her, of pushing her toward her own climax.

They came together in a rush of heat and pleasure. He gathered her against him and kissed her forehead, the scent of sweat and sex and her filling his nostrils.

She drew maddening circles on his chest and he caught her hands in his. He kissed each finger, her palm, the underside of her wrist, trying to soothe her, waiting for her to open up and tell him what was on her mind.

Unlike him, she never said everything that came into her head instantly, her first impulse was to worry about it herself, as she had done for so many years. But they had learned each other now. She knew he would wait, as much as he could, and he knew she would come to him, if not as soon as he wanted.

She finally met his gaze, and his breath caught again at the vulnerability in those eyes, the trust she showed him, the love she had for him. "I saw some fertility specialists when I was in New York."

His first instinct was hurt that she hadn't told him. But he fought the sensation. He pressed his mouth to her temple, ran his hand over the dip of her belly and nudged her even closer to him. That he could not take away this pain from her was the most agonizing fact of his own life. He tugged her chin up. "My mother will never again ask you about this, *ever*. Do you understand?"

You're a natural mother, Nikhat. Dahaar is waiting for its next crown prince.

A tear rolled out of the corner of her eye and his heart ached. She laced her fingers with his and kissed his hand. "It was not her fault, Azeez. We should have told her. They are all going to ask."

"I have had a discussion with my father and Ayaan. Once Zohra is a little better, we will declare Rafiq my heir, announce him the Crown Prince. If I could bear this pain for you, I would, *habeebiti*. Forgive me for wanting you, for being selfish enough to love you. That you face this question because of me—"

Her finger landed on his lips, her eyes glittering like rare gems. "It's never far from my mind, Azeez. I had resigned to spend my life alone. You're my strength, Azeez, my happiness. Tell me you believe that."

"I do."

She scrubbed her cheeks and rubbed her nose against his. "I went through a few more tests. The plan is to stop my medication and just see what—"

He sat up in such a sudden movement that his hip throbbed. "No."

His answer resonated in the silence between them. Turning around, he lay down on his side and kissed her hard. The image of her writhing in pain, he never wanted to see that again. "I don't want a child at the cost of your pain, Nikhat. This point is nonnegotiable."

"We don't know that it is even possible, Azeez. I have been on this medication for so long, it would be a good idea to just see how my body would react to other kinds." Clasping his cheek, she turned him so he was looking at her.

A shiver traveled down his spine. Even after the attack, he had never been as scared as the night she had cried after Zohra had delivered.

"I want to try this for myself."

He saw the resolve in her eyes and relented. "Six months."

She rolled her eyes and pouted. "It takes even an average couple six months to conceive."

"We are not average." He loved the gleam in her eyes when she tried hard not to laugh. "We are the king and queen of Dahaar. Normal laws of procreation don't apply to us."

Looping her arms around him, she giggled against him, her soft body rubbing against him making him hard all over again. "Yes, Your Highness. You have magical sperm that will find my mythical eggs no matter where they are hidden, and penetrate them..."

Laughing, she fell onto his lap, her mouth curved wide, tears rolling down her cheeks.

He captured her lips with his, taking her smiles and her pain. She sobered up and clung to him, her body trembling. Drawing in a deep breath, he held her hard. "You are my life, *ya habeebiti*, my pride, my power, my laughter, my joy.

"One year, Nikhat. That's all I will give you. I will not let this destroy you. I will lose the very will you brought me back if this takes you away from me. Do you understand?"

Nikhat gazed into the eyes of the most beautiful, the most honorable man she had ever seen. His embrace, his heart, his love, there wasn't a day that went by that she didn't wonder at the miracle that it was all hers. She nodded and smiled. "I'm strong enough for this, Azeez. With you by my side, I'm strong enough for anything." She lost herself in his kiss, basking in his love.

Whatever the future might bring, she had his heart and she would hold on to it.

* * * * *

MILLS & BOON®

Why shop at millsandboon.co.uk?

Each year, thousands of romance readers find their perfect read at millsandboon.co.uk. That's because we're passionate about bringing you the very best romantic fiction. Here are some of the advantages of shopping at www.millsandboon.co.uk:

* **Get new books first**—you'll be able to buy your favourite books one month before they hit the shops

* **Get exclusive discounts**—you'll also be able to buy our specially created monthly collections, with up to 50% off the RRP

* **Find your favourite authors**—latest news, interviews and new releases for all your favourite authors and series on our website, plus ideas for what to try next

* **Join in**—once you've bought your favourite books, don't forget to register with us to rate, review and join in the discussions

Visit **www.millsandboon.co.uk** for all this and more today!